ECHOES OF YESTERDAY

RACHEL WESSON

LONDONGATE PUBLISHING

Copyright © 2025 by Rachel Wesson

All rights reserved.

No part of this book may be reproduced in any form or by any electronic or mechanical means, including information storage and retrieval systems, without written permission from the author, except for the use of brief quotations in a book review.

For my amazing sister, Annie,
Who fought the most courageous battle against Sarcoma with resilience, bravery, and unwavering strength. Your fortitude was an inspiration, and the impact you had on those around you was nothing short of incredible. Your spirit lives on in the hearts of all who loved you.
Hope you are flying high, Annie. 🤍

FOREWORD

The Orphanage Chronicles is a brand-new series, beginning with *Echoes of Yesterday*. However, the characters you'll meet in this book first appeared in two of my earlier works, *The Orphans of Hope House*. You will find that series here.

CHAPTER 1

DELGANY, VIRGINIA. FEBRUARY 1936

The wind howled around Hope House, rattling its aging window frames and carrying the sharp bite of an approaching storm. Lauren Greenwood gripped her coffee cup, willing her hands to stop trembling. *It's just the cold,* she told herself, not the haunting image of Edward's bruised, ashen face gasping for air. Nor the lingering echo of Sophie's tender plea: *"Ma died from Tuberculosis. Will Daddy die, too?"*

The fragile silence shattered with the clatter of boots. Hans appeared at the top of the stairs, his face flushed, hair standing at odd angles. "Miss Lauren! Don't leave yet! Rachel has nearly finished her drawing for Uncle Edward!" The eleven-year-old barreled down the steps.

Lauren set her coffee cup in the sink, turning just as Becky called over her shoulder from the cupboards, where she was counting their dwindling supplies.

"Careful on those stairs, Hans! We definitely don't need another hospital visit."

The words struck a nerve, and Lauren glanced at the pile of letters and parcels she'd prepared for her trip to Charlottesville. Edward was recovering, but uncertainty clung to his future like the frost on the windowpanes. Each visit to the hospital brought the same questions, circling her mind like restless birds: Would he ever walk without a cane? Would he be able to hold a pen, to write again? Journalism wasn't just a job for Edward. It was his identity, his passion, his way of making sense of the world. If that was taken from him ... Lauren couldn't bear to finish the thought.

"Miss Lauren?" Sophie's small voice tugged her attention. She stood in the doorway, her pale face framed by golden hair that had lost some of its shine over the past months. What could you expect from a six-year-old who had lost her mother, had a sick father, and only a nine-year-old sibling for comfort?

Lauren kneeled beside her, smoothing the wrinkles in Sophie's dress. "He'll love it, sweetheart. And I'll make sure it gets to him today."

Sophie's quick smile didn't remove the worry from the child's eyes.

Rachel descended the stairs cautiously, clutching her drawing. Her quiet steps and gentle demeanor always made Lauren marvel at her resilience after witnessing the Nazis beat her father. His disappearance was the catalyst for Hans and Rachel, ages ten and six respectively, to be rescued from Germany by Edward and brought to Hope House.

"Please give Uncle Edward a hug from me," Rachel whispered, holding out the picture like a peace offering.

Before Lauren could answer, Becky chimed in, her tone light and teasing. "And a big, smudgy kiss, too, right, Lauren?"

Heat crept up Lauren's neck, but she couldn't suppress the smile tugging at her lips. "You're impossible," Lauren muttered, shaking her head at her nineteen-year-old co-owner of Hope House. Becky just grinned, tugging at the threadbare apron tied over her skirt. "Impossible or not, Will thinks I'm a catch. Poor man's marryin' me anyway."

Christmas, when they'd both got engaged, felt like a lifetime ago. She pictured the joy in Edward's eyes as he'd kneeled before the children and asked for her hand. That decision had cost him. His insistence on leaving the hospital to spend the holiday with them had led to a relapse.

Becky sighed, closing the cupboard. "We're runnin' low on flour. Again. It's startin' to feel like the old days."

Lauren glanced at her. "The old days?"

"You know, before Hope House. Before ..." Becky's voice trailed off, her brow furrowing.

Lauren moved to her side, putting a hand on her arm. "Was it all the wedding talk last night bringing back memories?"

Becky gulped, her eyes shining. "I just wish I knew where Luke and Matt were. Ma and Donnie, they stayed at the Home for the Feeble Minded, but my brothers ..." Becky glanced out the window toward the mountains. "They could be anywhere. Before Hope House, I never thought I'd have this." Becky turned toward Lauren. "Now I look at Will, and I see somethin' real, somethin' worth building. It took me so long to see that." Becky hesitated. "They always liked Will. Matt used to say Will needed to be as stubborn as a goat to take me on. I guess he was right. Will's the kind of man who doesn't care how much I've been through. He just cares I made it through." Becky sniffed before straightening her shoulders. "You should be on the road already. Go."

Lauren gave her arm a quick squeeze, knowing Becky wouldn't welcome a hug at that moment.

SNOW STRETCHED ENDLESSLY AHEAD, a frigid, unbroken expanse. Lauren gripped the truck's wheel tighter, the icy chill in her fingers mirroring the knot tightening in her chest. The heater groaned, but no warmth reached her. Her thoughts felt just as frozen, stuck on the letter to Mary she'd left half-written on the kitchen table. *Edward's recovery is going well.* She'd written. But was it true? His bruised eyes and trembling hands, a week prior, left her worried.

The truck lurched over a patch of ice, yanking her from her thoughts. She blinked hard, focusing on the road ahead. Her route: sanatorium, then hospital.

THE SHARP STING of antiseptic greeted her the moment she stepped inside the hospital. She smoothed her skirt out of habit, her fingers brushing over her engagement ring.

Her heels clicked on the tile floor as she approached Edward's room, her breath catching as she paused at the door. *Don't look worried,* she told herself. *Be strong.*

She stepped inside. Edward's smile sent the butterflies in her stomach into a whirl.

His eyes gleamed as he teased her. "There you are. I was starting to think you'd forgotten me."

"Not a chance." She leaned down and pressed a quick kiss to his forehead, the cold of his skin startling her. *He looks thinner.*

She settled into the chair beside his bed, her knees brushing against the metal frame. "How are you feeling?"

Edward tilted his head toward the radiator in the corner, which let out a pathetic clank as it tried to do its job. "Better than that thing, at least."

A smile tugged at her lips despite the ache in her chest. "That's hardly a glowing report."

"I'm getting there. I'm walking now. Not far, but enough to make the nurses nervous. They keep threatening to tie me down." His joke didn't hide the frustration in his voice.

Lauren reached for his left hand, threading her fingers through his. His palm felt cool against hers, his grip faint but steady. "Walking is good. With practice, you will get faster. What about your hand?"

The question hung there. Edward glanced at the splint covering his dominant hand, his fingers twitching slightly before falling still. "No improvement yet, but the doctors said they expect excellent results when they remove the splint. I'll be writing again before you know it." His eyes flicked toward the stack of newspapers on the bedside table. "I have so many stories to tell."

Her throat tightened, but she forced the tears back. He would resent any sign of pity. She squeezed his good hand. "I stopped at the sanatorium to drop off Sophie's pictures and a letter from Clarissa for Bart."

Edward's brow furrowed, concern flickering in his tired gaze. "How is he holding up?"

"We aren't allowed to see him, just drop things off, but the staff give us updates. About as well as expected. Tuberculosis isn't easy, but the doctors are hopeful. He's been writing letters to the girls, trying to keep their spirits up. They miss him, of course, but Becky and I are doing our best to keep them distracted."

Edward's expression clouded. "And the girls? Clarissa is always protective of Sophie, even though she's only two years older."

"Clarissa hides it well, especially for a nine-year-old. She's strong, like Bart, but I can tell she worries. And Sophie has poured her heart into her drawings. Rachel has been helping her get them just right. They're both braver than they realize."

Edward's hand tightened around hers. "It's good that Bart has you and Becky looking after them. How are the other children?"

"Wonderful. It's hard to believe they're all growing so fast. Maisie is walking and talking a little. Nanny says she should be talking more for an eighteen-month-old, but I guess she finds it hard to speak up in the crowd. Joey is four and still Shelley's pet. She's really come out of her shell, although thirteen is a difficult age for a girl. She's taller than Fred, despite being the same age. Cal teases him badly, but he is still taller, even though he's a year younger."

"Are Carly and Terry still in love?"

Lauren nodded. "I still think Carly, at fifteen, is too young, but Nanny Kat and Becky remind me that's old for some couples up on the mountain. Terry is still very protective of her. Their feelings seem real."

"You and Becky are young to have such a large family." His eyes sparkled as he teased her.

Lauren shifted on the hard hospital chair, the cold metal pressing against the back of her legs, and smiled. "There are lots more children who need help, I think we should take in more."

He didn't laugh like she expected him to. Instead his gaze held hers for a moment before he looked away, his expression growing pensive. "Seeing families like Bart's and of course, the Hope House children. It makes me think about what's happening in Europe. The Nuremberg rallies, the propaganda. It's not just soldiers, Lauren. It's families. Ordinary people cheering for something that'll destroy them." The tormented expression in his brown eyes made her want to take him in her arms and hug him, reassure him he was safe now. But muted footsteps in the hallway reminded her they could be interrupted at any moment.

Lauren squeezed his hand, staring into his eyes. "You're

not in Germany, Edward. You're safe. Use your energy to concentrate on getting better, getting out of here."

He nodded, his lips quirking into a faint smile. "What would I do without you?"

"You'll never have to find out." Brushing a stray lock of hair from his forehead, she replaced it with a kiss. "Now, rest. We've got a wedding to plan once you're back on your feet."

His cheeks flushed. "Yes, ma'am."

As she drove back to Hope House, a fleeting thought crossed her mind. What would Edward think about living there? She couldn't imagine leaving the children or the life they'd built together, but they'd never spoken about it. Could he see himself calling it home, sharing in its joys and burdens? The idea of a life without him felt impossible, but so did asking him to change everything for her. Would he sit in the kitchen with Ruthie or Sophie on his lap, their drawings spread across the table? Or would he find the chaos too much, longing for quiet he'd never find there? The thought unsettled her, though she tried to picture him smiling, surrounded by the family they'd built.

Relieved to be home, she parked the truck and jumped out, her boots crunching in the frost. The chill bit through her coat, but it didn't dampen the relief that surged in her chest. Before she could reach the porch, the front door swung open. Becky appeared, wiping her hands on her apron, her face lighting up with a smile.

"Took you long enough! Did Edward get our love, or were you too busy makin' googly eyes at each other?"

Lauren rolled her eyes, unable to stop her own smile. "We did plenty of talking, thank you very much. He sends his love, especially to you."

Becky snorted, shaking her head. "That charmer. Now, get inside before you freeze your toes off. Nanny kept some stew back for you, it's warmin' on the stove along with fresh bread. That'll chase the chill out of your bones."

Lauren stepped inside, the heat of the house wrapping around her like a hug. The air carried the comforting scent of stew, mingled with the faint wood smoke from the fireplace. She shrugged off her coat and hung it by the door, glancing around. "Where are the children? It's awfully quiet."

Becky smirked. "Terry's tellin' them stories up in the girls' bedroom. He's gettin' good at it, too. They're hangin' on his every word. We figured you'd want some alone time before the questions start. We even bribed 'em with popped corn to stay put."

Lauren's chest tightened with gratitude. She reached out and hugged Becky. "Thank you. It was so good to see Edward. He's getting stronger, but ..." Her voice wavered, the weight of the day catching up with her.

Becky patted her back. "But nothin'. He's on the mend, and you're here, safe and sound. That's what matters." She pulled back, her smile softening. "Go on and eat while it's hot. Nanny Kat's in the kitchen pretendin' her cocoa is coffee. She'll want to see you before she heads to bed."

Lauren walked toward the kitchen, where Nanny Kat

was waiting. Should she talk to her about Edward? About where they would live?

Her steps slowed. Kathryn had been more than just a great-aunt. She had been a mother when Lauren lost hers. She had raised her, shielding her as best she could from Papa's temper. She had been the one to introduce Lauren to Becky and the whole Tennant family before Papa put a stop to it, banning Kathryn from Rosehall and from Lauren's life.

If not for Edward, they might have stayed apart forever. He had brought Nanny to Hope House, and Nanny loved him for it.

No, it wasn't right to burden the old woman with her worries. At least not yet. Not until she knew for certain there was something to worry about.

CHAPTER 2

The bell over the door jangled as Lauren stepped into the post office. She took a moment to brush the snow from the collar of her coat, her boots leaving damp prints on the wooden floor. Miss Chaney looked up from her ledger with a smile.

"Good afternoon, Lauren," Miss Chaney said, her voice as welcoming as the fire crackling in the corner. "What brings you in today?"

"Afternoon, Miss Chaney. I'm expecting a letter from Mary. I haven't heard from her in a while. Getting a bit worried about her, you hear the stories about things being tough in California."

"You do, but Mary is a good person. People like her will be looked after by the good Lord." Miss Chaney nodded, setting her pen down. "I haven't seen a Californian postmark, but there are bills waiting for you."

Before she could turn, the door swung open behind Lauren, the sharp gust of February air cutting through the room. She didn't need to look to know who it was; the heavy stomp of boots and muttered complaints were unmistakable. Mr. Harlan, with his scowl fixed in place, and Mrs. Simmons, who always seemed to carry an air of sour disapproval, filled the small space with their presence.

Lauren stepped to the side, hoping they'd handle their business and leave, but Mr. Harlan's voice cut through the room. "Miss Chaney, you got the latest Social Justice? Father Coughlin's paper?"

Lauren tensed, her stomach knotting. Of course, it would be about him. Every week, it seemed his name and his venom was on someone's lips.

Miss Chaney kept her hands steady as she sorted through the stack of newspapers. "I believe I do, Mr. Harlan. One moment."

"Do you listen to him on the radio, Miss Greenwood?" Mrs. Simmons asked, her gaze settling on Lauren like a cold draft.

Lauren glanced at her, meeting those narrowed eyes. What was it about Mrs. Simmons that made her feel as though she'd stepped into a courtroom without a lawyer?

"I haven't had the chance. I've been busy with the children."

"You should make time." Mrs. Simmons stepped closer, her voice dropping to a conspiratorial whisper that carried too well in the small room. "He tells the truth. Not like Roosevelt's lot. You heard about those international bankers, haven't you? The Jews? They're the ones behind this mess we're in. I'm sure they were to blame for all that nasty business with your father and you losing your inheritance."

Her skin crawled. It wasn't the first time she'd heard talk like this, but hearing it spoken so casually, as if it were the most natural thing in the world, turned her stomach. "My father and his business partners were to blame for their actions, Mrs. Simmons, nobody else."

Mrs. Simmons huffed. "I'd have thought you would set some store by family values."

Before Lauren had a chance to respond, Miss Chaney returned to the counter, setting the paper down with a quiet thud. "Here it is, Mr. Harlan. I'd appreciate it if we kept things civil. This is a public space."

"Civil?" Mr. Harlan scoffed, his hand slapping the counter loud enough to make Lauren flinch. "Father Coughlin's trying to save this country, and you're worried about bein' civil? What's civil about lettin' those people bleed us dry while Roosevelt gives away our money? It's a pity Coughlin is Canadian. If he were American, he could be president, and we'd get rid of Rosenfeld."

Lauren exhaled at the nickname Father Coughlin had given the president but bit down on the sharp words that rose to her lips. Arguing with men like Harlan was like trying to stop a storm with a broom.

Mrs. Simmons nodded in agreement. "Exactly. At least he's standing up for real Americans. More than I can say for some folks in this town."

Lauren's jaw tightened, the insinuation clear. She could feel their eyes on her, waiting for her to agree, to validate their venom. But she wouldn't. Couldn't.

"Real Americans stand up for fairness and decency." She forced her voice to remain steady despite her pounding heart. "At least, that's what I believe."

The silence that followed was as sharp as the cold outside. Mrs. Simmons' lips thinned, her face reddened, but before she could respond, Miss Chaney stepped in again.

"That's enough now. This post office is for letters, not arguments."

Mr. Harlan grabbed his paper with a grumble, muttering something about "soft-hearted women" as he stormed out. Mrs. Simmons lingered, her eyes narrowing before she sniffed and followed him.

Miss Chaney sighed, her shoulders sagging as she turned back to her ledger. "I'm sorry you had to hear that, Lauren."

"It's not your fault." She felt the chill of the air where their hatred had been, lingering like smoke in the corners. "It's everywhere lately. I heard someone say Father Coughlin's popularity is waning, but it doesn't seem that way. How can a man with his disgusting views set himself out as a man of God?"

Millions tuned in to his broadcasts each week, his voice carried into homes far and wide.

Miss Chaney shook her head, her kind eyes shadowed. "He claims to speak for God, but all I hear is hate. I know many Catholics who wish he'd disappear and take his views with him. It's a shame. There are good people in every faith, but men like him make it hard for folks to see that."

She hesitated before adding, "You and the children should come to Sunday services. We need to pray for hearts to change, for all of us to find a better way forward."

Lauren held back a sigh. She used to love church, the warmth of hymns lifting her spirits. But Pastor Curtis's sermons were heavy with judgment and fire, leaving no room for grace. She longed for the faith she'd known before, one that lifted her up instead of weighing her down.

She'd think about it for the children's sake, if not her own. They deserved the comfort she once found in faith, even if it felt so far away now. For now, she just wanted to get home.

Perhaps picking up on her discomfort, Miss Chaney changed topics. "How are the preparations for Becky's wedding coming along? Will mentioned the house-building's been slow."

Lauren clapped her hands, her eyes brightening. "You're a star, Miss Chaney! I almost forgot. Do you have the new Sears catalogue? Becky wants to order some bedding and other things."

Miss Chaney's expression stiffened, her lips drawing into a tight line. A pink flush crept up her cheeks as she spoke, her voice bristling with quiet reproach. "Bedding? Child, it's a tradition for mountain brides to have a wedding quilt, something made from scraps of old linen and family clothes, stitched with love, not bought from a catalog."

Lauren's smile faltered for the briefest moment, but she recovered quickly, her tone light and breezy. "Oh, look at the time! I'd better get back, or Nanny will send out a search party."

Miss Chaney opened her mouth, as if to say more, but Lauren had already turned toward the door, waving cheerfully over her shoulder. "Thanks for everything, Miss Chaney!"

LATER THAT EVENING, she told Nanny and Becky what had happened in town.

"I wish those two would get hitched and move to Richmond, or better yet, Europe." Becky gave the kitchen floor a vicious sweep. "How stupid do people have to be? And they call us mountain folk uneducated. Even we know it don't matter if it be a priest or a minister or anyone else, he ain't a man of God if he is spoutin' hatred toward anyone."

Nanny nodded in agreement before standing up. "I'm heading to bed, girls. The children are all asleep. Why don't you two go sit by the fire and enjoy the quiet? Becky, you should start thinking about your wedding dress or get working on the quilt. You can't be married without one or the other."

The fire crackled in the hearth, filling the sitting room with a comforting warmth. Lauren sat on the couch, a mug of tea cradled in her hands, enjoying the soothing scent of peppermint and honey. Across from her, Becky was fussing with some mending, her fingers deftly stitching the hem of a shirt for Big Will.

"Do you ever get tired of everyone calling him 'Big

Will'?" Lauren asked, the thought tumbling out before she could stop herself.

Becky glanced up, a flicker of surprise crossing her face, followed by a slow smile. "No, not really," she said, her voice light. "It suits him."

Lauren tilted her head, curious. "But he's not that big."

Becky laughed, the sound low and warm, and shook her head. "Oh, I know. It's not about his size." She set down her sewing and leaned back in her chair. "It started with Bertha."

"Bertha?" Lauren raised an eyebrow.

"The pig," Becky clarified, her grin widening. "Back when Will was just a lanky young lad working for the Thatchers. Bertha was the biggest, meanest sow this side of the Blue Ridge, and one day she decided she'd had enough of the pen. Broke straight through it and went tearin' off through the holler, leaving Mr. Thatcher shoutin' after her like a madman."

Lauren couldn't help but smile, already imagining the chaos.

"Will didn't even hesitate," Becky continued, her voice full of affection. "He grabbed a rope, ran after her, and somehow managed to wrangle her back. He was covered head to toe in mud, scratches, and well … let's just say it wasn't *just* mud, but he got her back in that pen."

Lauren laughed. "Let me guess. They started calling him 'Big Will' after that?"

"Mr. Thatcher started it," Becky said with a nod. "He was laughin' so hard, he slapped his knee and shouted, 'Big Will Strauss, wrangler of pigs and savior of barnyards!' It stuck." Becky's fingers traced the shirt in her hands. "At first, it was just a joke. But over time, the name came to mean something else. Will's laugh fills a room, his heart is big enough for everyone he loves. And when you really need him? He's always there. Folks around here noticed."

For a moment, the room was quiet, the only sound the soft crackle of the fire.

Lauren couldn't resist teasing. "Are you going to be known as Mrs. Big Will?"

Becky snorted, her cheeks reddening as she picked up her sewing. "You hush," she said, shaking her head, but there was laughter in her voice. "And if you breathe a word of this to Will, I'll make sure you're still single by Christmas."

Lauren laughed, leaning back in her chair, savoring the warmth of the moment. "Your secret's safe with me, Mrs. Big Will."

CHAPTER 3

"Mornin', Miss Lauren. How are things?"

Lauren whirled around to see Maisie's father, Tom, set a sack down just outside the barn door. "Some of the traps I set paid off. That's meat for Becky to work her magic with. The other bag is a couple of furs for you to sell at Hillmans. Thought I'd bring it by early."

Lauren pushed the hair back from her face and set her washing basket on the ground. She wasn't sure the clothes would dry in the chill, but the children were running low, so she had to try. "Morning, Tom. Thank you. I wasn't expecting you so early in the week. Becky took Maisie for a walk; she'll be back soon. Are you coming in?"

Tom shifted his hat from one hand to the other, avoiding her gaze. "I don't think you should hang out that washin'. Looks like rain to me."

Lauren glanced at the sky. He might be right, but she knew his concern wasn't the weather. She held his gaze until he looked away.

"Miss Lauren, I got somethin' to tell you, but I'm not sure I should. Feels like I'm stirrin' up trouble."

Lauren lifted the basket, intending to take it back inside. "Come in and have some coffee. I could use a break."

Tom took the basket from her, glancing toward the house. "Anyone inside?"

Her stomach tightened. "No. Nanny's still in bed, and the children are at school. Terry drove them into town and won't be back for a bit. Just us."

She opened the kitchen door and held it for him. Tom placed the basket on the table, pacing back and forth, hat clutched in his hands. His unease was infectious.

"Miss Lauren, I owe you and Miss Becky so much for lookin' after Maisie. I wouldn't bring this to you unless I thought it mattered."

"Tom." Lauren gestured to a chair. "Sit down and tell me what's going on."

"I can't sit. Got ants in my pants." He ran a hand over his face. "I seen Becky's brothers. Or at least one of them. Luke, I think."

Lauren's breath caught. "That's wonderful! Becky will be thrilled! She's never stopped hoping they'd ..."

She stopped short, reading the tension in Tom's face. "You've seen him? You're sure?"

Tom nodded slowly. "I know it was Luke. Recognized him from years back. But it's not just seein' him that's got me worked up." He faltered, his knuckles whitening around the brim of his hat. "It's what he was doin'."

Lauren's heart skipped a beat. "What do you mean? What did you see?"

"I saw him near the old mill with some men I don't recognize. They were movin' boxes of bottles. I heard 'em talkin' about trouble. I didn't stay long enough to hear more, but I reckon it's somethin' to do with moonshine."

Lauren swallowed hard. Despite Prohibition being repealed, illegal liquor still circulated, especially in the mountains. "And you're certain it was Luke?"

"As certain as I can be. It's him."

Lauren's mind raced. Becky's brothers had been gone for years, disappearing after their family's eviction. If they were mixed up in illegal activity? How would Becky handle it? "I need to tell her. She deserves to know."

Tom put his hat on the table and sat down, his shoulders slumping. "I just didn't want to cause no trouble. But I couldn't keep it to myself. I knows how much Becky misses her brothers."

Lauren poured him a cup of coffee, strong and hot. "You did the right thing."

The door creaked, and Becky walked in, her face bright from the crisp air and Maisie toddling at her side. "Paw-paw!" Maisie squealed, tottering over to Tom, who swept her up in a big hug.

Becky's eyes narrowed, catching the tension in the room. "Everythin' alright?"

Tom kissed Maisie's cheek and carried her into the living area. "I'll watch this one for a spell."

Becky turned back to Lauren, her fingers drumming on the table. "What's goin' on?"

Lauren hesitated. "Tom saw one of your brothers."

Becky froze, her face going pale. "One of my brothers? Who? Where?"

"He thinks it was Luke. Near the old mill."

Becky's voice rose. "The mill? What was he doin'? Why didn't he come to find me?"

Lauren reached for Becky's hand. "He was with some men. Tom thinks they were moving moonshine."

Becky's expression hardened, her color returning in a fiery flush. "If he's mixed up in somethin' like that, I'm goin' to find him and drag him out by the ear."

"Becky, wait ..."

"I've waited long enough. If he's been close all this time and hasn't come to find me ..." Her voice cracked, but she covered it with anger. "I need to see for myself."

"At least wait for Will."

"No. I'm going now."

Tom reappeared at the door, Maisie toddling ahead of him. He bent to scoop her up, kissing her cheek and whispering something that made her giggle before setting her down again. He stared at his daughter for a second or two before he straightened, his hand tightening on his hat.

"I'll go with you. But you can't just storm in and expect things to go your way."

Becky huffed, tugging her coat from the back of the chair. "Don't worry about me. I've got it handled."

Lauren caught a flicker of something in Becky's eyes. Doubt, maybe, or the faint shadow of fear. But just as quickly, it was gone, buried beneath her determination. Lauren shifted Maisie to her hip, her free hand stroking the girl's curls. Tom leaned down for another kiss, and something in his posture made Lauren's chest tighten.

"Becky, please be careful," Lauren called after them, her voice catching in her throat.

Becky didn't turn back. Her determined steps crunched against the frozen ground, Tom following close behind as they disappeared into the woods.

* * *

TIME PASSED SLOWLY, as Lauren tried to distract herself with chores. She was hanging damp clothes inside the barn when she heard the familiar rumble of Terry's truck approaching. She dashed outside, her heart pounding.

"Terry! I need you to fetch Will. Becky's gone up the mountain with Tom, and I think she's walking into trouble."

Terry climbed out of the truck, frowning as he adjusted his weight onto his good leg. "Trouble? What kind of trouble?"

Lauren wrung her hands, trying to steady her voice. "Tom saw one of Becky's brothers near the old mill. He's sure it was Luke, and there were men with him ... men moving moonshine. Becky wouldn't listen. She just grabbed Tom and headed straight up there."

Terry's frown deepened. "I'm glad Tom's with her, but if they're headin' near the mill, it could get messy. Moonshiners don't take kindly to visitors."

"That's what I'm afraid of." Lauren shivered as if

someone walked over her grave. "Will needs to know. He'll know what to do."

Terry nodded, his expression grim. "I'll fetch him. Should I go to the sheriff too?"

Lauren hesitated, biting her lip. The last thing Becky would want was the law involved, but if things turned dangerous ... "Not yet. Just Will and Earl. Will knows the mountain better than anyone."

"Got it. I'll be quick." Terry climbed back into the truck, the engine roaring as he pulled away.

Lauren lingered by the barn after Terry left, staring toward the woods where Becky and Tom had gone. She tried to picture the footpath winding up toward the old mill, but the thought made her stomach twist. What had Becky and Tom walked into?

She turned back toward the house, where Nanny stood framed in the kitchen doorway, her arms crossed and concern etched into her face.

"What's all this coming and going about?" Nanny asked.

Lauren sighed, stepping into the kitchen. "Becky got news of her brothers. She's gone up the mountain to find out the truth."

"Gone where?"

"Up the mountain," Lauren repeated.

"Alone?" Nanny's voice sharpened.

"No. She wouldn't wait, so Tom agreed to go with her, but I asked Terry to fetch Will. He'll follow her as soon as he gets back."

Nanny's sharp gaze narrowed. "What does Tom think those boys are involved in? Don't give me that look. They aren't with the Civilian Conservation Corps or doing anything honest. Not with you looking like that."

"It could be nothing."

"Or it could be a whole pile of trouble." Nanny's hands tightened around the edge of the counter.

Lauren hastened to reassure her. "For now, we need to stay calm and hope Will gets there in time."

Nanny nodded reluctantly, though the worry in her eyes lingered. She busied herself gathering ingredients for bread, her movements brisk and deliberate.

Lauren tried to focus on her tasks, but her mind refused to settle. Every creak of the wind and shadow of movement beyond the window sent her heart racing. The minutes crawled by until the crunch of gravel announced Terry's return.

She rushed outside, her heart pounding as he climbed out of the truck, his limp more pronounced as he adjusted his weight.

"Will and Earl drove up the mountain in Earl's truck," Terry said, his voice steady but grim. "Victor Meyer was at Hillman's, so he took over the shop with Ginny Dobbs to free Earl up. Ginny said it was a quiet day. Will sent me back. Said I'd be more useful here."

Lauren's frustration at Terry being dismissed due to his leg simmered. "Will's just protective of me and Nanny Kat. He knows how much we depend on you, Terry. It wasn't for any other reason."

Terry's gaze darkened. "Lauren, when you told me to stop callin' you Miss Lauren, you said I was an adult. Don't start treatin' me like a child now." Without waiting for a response, he turned and limped toward the barn.

Lauren opened her mouth to protest, but Nanny placed a gentle hand on her arm. "Let him be. He knows Will would have him at his side if not for that leg."

Lauren's frustration didn't subside. "Will's wrong. Terry's a good shot, if it comes to that."

Nanny raised an eyebrow. "Let's hope it doesn't." She paused, her expression softening. "What are you thinking, Lauren?"

Lauren took a breath, steadying herself. "I'm not staying here, Nanny. I'm going after Becky."

Lauren gave Nanny a tight hug before heading for the barn. The wind had picked up, swirling dry leaves around her feet as she pulled on her boots. She wasn't sure what she'd find up there or whether she'd be able to help when she got there. But staying behind wasn't an option. Not when Becky might need her. She walked farther into the barn, climbed the ladder to the loft, and removed her guns from their hiding place. Climbing back down, she handed one to Terry.

"Come on, we're going to help Becky."

He took the gun without a word and headed outside to the truck.

"Lauren!" Nanny called after her. Lauren turned back to see the older woman standing in the doorway, her apron dusted with flour. Nanny tutted, shaking her head. "You've got responsibilities here."

"So does Becky. But if she's walking into trouble, I'm not leaving her to face it alone."

Nanny's jaw worked, but she didn't argue. "Be careful, Lauren. You too, Terry." Nanny Kat hesitated for a second. "If I was younger, I'd go with you."

Lauren nodded, her throat tight. "I know."

She climbed into the truck beside Terry, her hands gripping the seat as he started the engine. The roar of the truck filled the stillness, and Hope House grew smaller in the rearview mirror as they drove toward the unknown.

CHAPTER 4

*A*s Terry drove up the mountain, the air turned sharper, the remnants of winter lingering stubbornly despite the thaw that had begun to awaken the landscape. The truck rattled over the uneven dirt road, its tires kicking up stones and leaving a fine cloud of dust in their wake. Patches of snow clung to the shaded corners, dirty and stubborn, while the higher elevations shimmered with frost under the weak sunlight.

Tall trees lined the road, melting snow dripping from their branches. Lauren spotted the first buds of spring, tiny bursts of green against the dark bark. The occasional caw of a crow echoed overhead, stark against the rattle of the creaking truck.

She glanced at Terry, his jaw clenched as he focused on the winding road. Her stomach cramped with worry, the unknown pressing on her chest like a heavy weight. "Do you think Becky found them?" she asked, breaking the silence.

Terry shook his head slightly, his hands gripping the wheel. "Hard to say. But if she did, let's hope it didn't turn into somethin' worse."

As they climbed higher, Terry slowed the truck, pulling it off the main path into a small clearing. "We should walk the rest of the way," he said. "Drivin' up to the mill might spook anyone there."

The silence of the forest was deafening as they stepped out, frost crusted leaves crackling under their boots. Lauren adjusted her coat, the weight of the gun grounding her nerves. Terry did the same, glancing toward her. "Stick close," he muttered.

Despite the tension, she hid a small smile. She was the one who'd taught Terry how to shoot.

A shout cut through the stillness. "Get off me! You don't know what you're doin'!" Becky's voice, sharp with fury, carried across the clearing.

Lauren's heart jumped into her throat. She exchanged a look with Terry, and they moved cautiously toward the sound. As they reached the edge of the clearing, the scene came into view: Becky struggling against the grip of a tall, rough-looking man, while a boy with the trademark Tennant fiery red hair stood nearby, a rifle shaking in his hands. Nearby, Tom lay motionless on the ground, blood trickling from a gash on his forehead.

Where were Will and Earl?

Lauren's stomach clenched. She recognized the man instantly. Foxy Flannery. The smug set of his mouth, the scruffy beard, the way his belly jutted out as if he owned the world. Foxy had earned his nickname for evading the law during his moonshining days, but his temper and cruelty had earned him something else: fear.

"Shut your mouth, girl!" Foxy growled, shoving Becky hard. She stumbled but didn't fall, her glare burning with defiance.

"Set her free!" Luke shouted, his voice trembling but his words clear. The rifle wavered as he stepped forward. "She ain't done nothin' wrong."

"I said let me go!" Becky demanded, twisting in the older man's grip.

"Shut up!" Foxy Flannery snapped, shaking her violently. The red-haired boy flinched, his gaze darting between Becky and the menacing older figure.

"Luke, think about what you're doin'. I came up here to find you; I've never stopped lookin' for you and Matt. Not once."

"Why should I listen to you? Matt said you ran off and didn't look back. We were on our own." Luke shot back, his voice cracking with uncertainty. "Foxy told us you was livin' in a big house with loads of kids. You replaced our family. You didn't care. That's what Matt believed!"

"Luke, I swear I tried everythin' to find you. I tried to get Ma and Donnie out of the asylum too. The house I live in..." Becky's voice stopped at a slap from Foxy.

Lauren's mind raced as she assessed the situation. Luke seemed conflicted, but Foxy exuded an air of desperation; he had nothing to lose. If they didn't act soon, someone could be hurt, or worse.

Lauren caught Terry's eye and mouthed, three, two...

"Now!" Lauren shouted, bursting from the underbrush.

They dashed forward, guns raised. "Let her go!" Lauren commanded, aiming her weapon at Foxy Flannery.

Foxy turned, surprise flashing across his face, but his grip on Becky remained ironclad. "You think you can threaten me?" he growled, eyes narrowing as he assessed the newcomers. His lips curled in a slow, cruel smile of recognition. "Well, well, if it isn't the poor little rich girl and Hopalong Cassidy. How quaint."

"Let her go, or you'll regret it," Terry warned.

Becky seized the moment, shoving against Foxy with all her might, but his grip remained firm.

Luke's eyes darted to the trees, his steps faltering, breath coming in short, quick bursts. His jaw tightened, and he stepped back, conflict flickering in his eyes. He looked like a boy torn in two, caught between loyalty and self-preservation.

"They'll be back any minute," he hissed. Without waiting for a response, he turned and bolted into the forest, the rifle nearly slipping from his grasp as he disappeared into the underbrush.

"Luke, no! Don't run off. Not again." Wrenching against Foxy's hold, Becky tried to kick free. Luke didn't look back.

"Stupid kid!" Foxy spat, tightening his grip on Becky.

Becky reacted instantly, slamming her heel into his shin and wrenching herself free. She stumbled back, her eyes wild with anger.

"You'll regret that, girl," Foxy growled, reaching for her again.

"Not so fast!" Will's voice rang out as he and Earl

emerged from the opposite side of the clearing, their guns drawn. Earl's shirt was torn, and there was dirt on his face, evidence of a struggle.

Foxy froze, his face twisting with anger before he turned and sprinted for the treeline.

"Go after him!" Will barked. Earl didn't hesitate, taking off after Foxy.

Will moved quickly to Becky's side, cupping her face with one hand. "Are you hurt? You scared me half to death."

"I'm fine, Will," Becky snapped, brushing dirt from her coat. "Stop fussin'. I've got worse scratches from the hens."

Lauren pressed her knee into the damp earth, her hands steady as she tightened the torn strip of fabric around Tom's head. Blood seeped through the cloth, warm against her fingers. His eyelids fluttered, a low groan escaping his lips.

"Don't move yet," she said. "You took a nasty hit."

Beside her, Becky crouched, swiping dirt from Tom's coat with quick, restless strokes. "You're gonna be alright." But the way Becky's fingers lingered against Tom's sleeve betrayed the fear she tried to hide.

Tom blinked at them, his gaze unfocused. "I'm fine. " His attempt to sit up ended in a wince. "Just need a minute."

Earl returned moments later, dragging Foxy by the arm. His shirt was torn, and dirt smeared his face where he'd tripped in his escape. Lauren's stomach churned as she met his sneer.

"Where's Luke gone?" Becky demanded, stepping

beside Lauren. Her fists were clenched at her sides, her voice shaking with barely restrained anger.

Foxy's lip curled. "The boy made his own choices. He wanted in, and now he's in. If he can't handle it, that's on him."

Becky lunged forward, but Will caught her arm, pulling her back. "He's not worth it."

"You filled his head with lies, didn't you?" Becky snapped, her voice rising. "You dragged him into this!"

Foxy snorted. "Dragged him? The boy came runnin'. Guess he's got more sense than you give him credit for."

Lauren's hand itched to reach for her gun, but she forced herself to stay calm. She glanced at Earl, who was still holding Foxy. "We're taking him down the mountain. The sheriff can deal with him."

Earl nodded, giving Foxy a hard shake. "You heard the lady. Move."

Will wiped his brow, his voice low but urgent. "There are two more of Foxy's men tied to a tree about half a mile down the path. Earl and I ran into them while they were haulin' supplies. It looked like they were headin' to a deal. They put up a fight, but we managed to take them down."

Earl grunted, adjusting his grip on Foxy. "Didn't have much of a choice. If we'd let them go, they'd have warned the others. We'll need to pick them up before heading to the sheriff."

"I'll handle the two tied to the tree," Terry said, his jaw tightening. "Let's get them all to the sheriff before they try anythin' else."

Foxy grumbled under his breath but didn't resist as Earl

began marching him toward the truck, Terry following behind him.

Will turned back to Becky, his expression torn. "No way am I lettin' you go back to Hope House with just Lauren and Tom. But we can't leave those two up there either."

Becky stepped closer, her voice firm. "We'll be fine, Will. Get the others to the sheriff. Lauren and I can handle gettin' Tom home." She glanced toward the trees, her gaze sharpening with determination. "But I'm not givin' up on Luke. I'll find him."

Lauren stayed quiet, watching the unspoken exchange between Will and Becky. She could see the worry etched in Will's brow and the resolve in Becky's stance. They were both stubborn, but this time, Becky wasn't backing down.

"You will," Will said, stepping closer. His voice was low and sure, each word steadying. "He ran, but that doesn't mean he's gone for good. You've been waitin' for this moment a long time, and you won't lose him now."

Becky looked at him, her jaw tightening as her eyes glistened with unshed tears. "I don't need sweet talk, Will."

"It's not sweet talk, it's the truth," he replied, his gaze holding hers. "You'll find him, Becky. I know you will."

For a moment, Becky didn't reply. Then she nodded briskly, brushing at her coat again. "Let's get goin' then. We've got work to do."

Will's jaw tightened as he nodded. "No stops. No chances. Get straight to Hope House."

Lauren and Becky each took one of Tom's arms helping him to the truck. Becky clambered into the back, putting a blanket down so Tom could lay on it. Then she helped Lauren get Tom into the truck. Lauren handed her a second blanket to cover their injured friend.

"I'm alright." But even as he protested, his face paled.

"We'll fix you up," Becky said, tucking the blanket snugly around him before taking a seat beside him. "We've got plenty of experience doctorin'. Lauren, get us home."

The ride back down the mountain felt heavier than the truck itself, each bump in the road jarring against Lauren's unease. The creak of the suspension filled the silence, the only company her own thoughts. As she neared Hope House, its lights flickered through the trees, warm and welcoming. But the chill clung to her, as if the danger from the mill had followed her down the mountain.

She'd always imagined Becky's missing family finding refuge at Hope House, their lives rebuilding within its walls. But as she turned into the lane, a new worry took root.

What if Luke had come seeking safety—but brought trouble with him?

CHAPTER 5

Lauren halted the vehicle with a loud creak, boots crunching on the frosty ground as she jumped out. Tom lay on the blanket, pale but awake. Lauren and Becky helped him get out of the truck.

Nanny Kat appeared on the porch, her shawl wrapped around her shoulders. "Thank the Lord," she called, descending the steps. "I've been worrying all afternoon. What on earth happened up there?"

Lauren met her halfway, saying, "It's a long story, Nanny, but the short version is we found Luke, or at least Becky did. He ran before we could talk to him. And Tom got caught in the middle."

Nanny's eyes flicked to Tom, her brow furrowing. "He looks terrible. Let's get him inside where it's warm."

"Easy now," Becky said, slipping his arm over her shoulders and guiding him to the door. "You took a bad knock, Tom. Don't try to argue."

"I'm fine," Tom muttered, though he leaned heavily on her. "Maisie, she's alright, isn't she?"

"She's fine," Nanny Kat reassured him. "Sleeping soundly, thank goodness. You'll see her in the morning. Right now, you need to rest."

Together, they helped Tom into the house, where Carly had just finished setting the table for supper.

Carly went still, her fingers brushing the edge of a plate but not picking it up. The color drained from her face. "What happened?" Her voice barely rose above a whisper. "Where's Terry?"

Lauren hastened to reassure her. "Don't worry, sweetheart. He's with Will, Earl, and the sheriff."

Lauren caught the sharp breath Carly let out, the way she blinked fast, as if trying to push back the fear threatening to spill over. "Terry wasn't injured but Tom's hurt. We need hot water and Old Sally's salve."

Carly swallowed hard, relief flickering across her face as her shoulders lost some of their stiffness. Fifteen, but already carrying love like a grown woman. She nodded quickly, her movements brisk, as if staying busy could push away the fear still lingering at the edges. "I'll get water heated up."

In the sitting room, Lauren gently unwrapped the makeshift bandage from Tom's head, revealing a shallow but angry-looking gash. She wrinkled her nose at the sight of dried blood streaking his temple. "It's not deep, but it needs to be cleaned."

Becky returned with a basin of warm water, a clean cloth, and the familiar jar of Old Sally's salve. "Here," she said, kneeling beside Tom. "Let's get you patched up. It might sting a bit." Becky carefully dabbed at the wound, cleaning away the blood and dirt.

Tom winced but didn't flinch, his fingers curled into his palms. "I've suffered worse."

"Shush," Becky replied, her tone sharper than usual. She applied a thin layer of the salve to the cut, its dreadful scent filling the room proving a sharp reminder of days gone by.

Lauren ran up the stairs and returned with a blanket and pillow. "You are staying here tonight, Tom."

He opened his mouth, but she didn't let him speak. "I don't want any arguments. You need to rest."

"I don't have the energy to argue with you, Miss Lauren."

"That's the first sensible thing I've heard today." Nanny Kat appeared with a fresh bandage and secured it snugly around Tom's head. "Let's get some soup into you before you pass out altogether."

Becky stood back, brushing her hands on her skirt. She lingered for a moment, watching Tom settle back on the couch with the bowl of soup Carly brought over. Then, without a word, she turned and walked out the back door.

Lauren hesitated only a moment before following her to the barn. The faint scent of hay and animals lingered in the cool air, mingling with the earthy tang of damp soil. She found Becky sitting on a bale of hay with Shadow resting his head on her knee. The dog's tail wagged as Lauren's boots scuffed against the dirt floor, but Becky didn't look up.

"You okay?" Lauren took a seat beside her.

Becky shook her head, her hand absently stroking Shadow's fur. "I don't get it, Lauren. Why was Luke alone? Where was Matt? They were inseparable when we were kids."

Lauren's stomach tightened. She'd wondered the same thing. "Maybe he stayed behind. Or maybe ..." She hesitated, not wanting to say what they were both thinking.

"Maybe he's dead," Becky finished flatly. Her voice was calm, but her eyes glistened with unshed tears. "Why else wouldn't he be there? Luke wouldn't have just left him."

"We don't know that." Lauren squeezed Becky's hand. "There could be any number of reasons why Matt wasn't there. We'll find out. You'll get your answers."

Becky let out a bitter laugh. "Will said the same thing. You two really are peas in a pod. Always so sure about everythin'."

Lauren studied her closely, the defeat in her voice unsettling. This wasn't like Becky at all. She was usually so fierce, so determined, even in the face of impossible odds. Seeing her withdrawn and defeated made Lauren's chest ache.

Taking a deep breath, Lauren forced herself to stay calm. "You're right. I am sure. Because I know you. You've been fighting for your family your whole life, and you're not going to stop now. Luke ran because he was scared, not because he didn't care. You'll find him. And when you do, you'll find out what happened to Matt too."

Becky swiped at her eyes, frustration evident in her movements. "I don't know. Every time I think I'm close to somethin' good, it slips away. I feel like I'm always climbin' uphill, fightin' for every inch."

Lauren pulled a clean hanky from her pocket and handed it to her. "That's not true. You've built something here no one can take away. The kids adore you, Will's building you a home, and you've fought harder than anyone I know. Don't forget that."

Becky let out a shaky breath, her hand tightening on Shadow's fur. "I just wanted them here for my weddin'. Is that too much to ask?"

"It's not. And you're not in this alone. We'll do everything we can to make your wedding special. You know that."

As they sat in silence, Shadow let out a gentle whine, nuzzling Becky's hand. Becky sat up straighter, her grip tightening on Shadow's fur. "Tomorrow, I'm goin' to the sheriff's office and gettin' some answers." Her voice was steadier now, and the faintest glimmer of fire returned to her eyes.

WHEN THEY RETURNED to the house, supper was already on the table, and the children had gathered around, their chatter filling the room. Becky slipped into her usual seat beside Sophie.

Sophie pushed her blonde bangs back. "You look funny Miss Becky. Your eyes are all red. Were you crying?"

"Sophie, shush now and eat your food." Carly offset her reprimand with a brief pat on Sophie's head.

Sophie put her spoon down, stood up and leaned over to kiss Becky on the cheek. "Miss Lauren does that when I'm sad. It always helps."

Becky's eyes shone with unshed tears as she flashed a weak smile at the five year old. "It does, Sophie. Thank you."

Shadow barked as if adding his agreement making the children laugh.

"I'm just checking on Tom." Lauren excused herself, struggling to keep her tears at bay. She walked into the living room to find Tom asleep. She adjusted the quilt to cover his shoulders.

Tom stirred before whispering, "Thank you."

Lauren swallowed hard, forcing her voice to sound normal. "Get some rest, Tom. You'll need your strength for Maisie in the morning."

Lauren returned to the kitchen and took her place at the table. Nanny Kat, who caught her glance at Becky, leaned over and whispered, "She'll bounce back. She's a tough one, that girl. Life's experiences have turned her into a survivor."

Lauren nodded, but her gaze lingered on Becky, who sat beside Sophie. Sophie leaned against her shoulder, chattering away as Becky stared blankly at the table, absently turning her spoon in her hand. Shadow was stretched out at her feet, his head resting against her leg, perfectly still.

Lauren wrapped her hands around her coffee mug, her knuckles whitening as she gripped it. "She's tough.

Tougher than most. But even the strongest of us can only take so much before they break."

"Then it's our job to make sure she doesn't."

Lauren didn't respond. Her eyes remained on Becky, who seemed utterly unaware of the concern surrounding her. Sophie giggled, her words dissolving into the chatter of the other children. Shadow stirred at Becky's feet, but she didn't move.

CHAPTER 6

The wooden steps of the sheriff's office groaned beneath Becky's boots as she stormed ahead, her stride as sharp as her resolve. Lauren hurried to keep up, her own steps hesitant compared to Becky's determined pace. Becky reached the door first and yanked it open.

Inside, the air was thick with stale coffee and damp wood. Lauren's nose wrinkled. It felt colder than it should have, the potbelly stove in the corner churning out warmth that barely reached the edges of the room. The peeling paint on the walls was gray with age, the ceiling sagging slightly. Even the light from the single, flickering bulb seemed tired, pooling unevenly on the scuffed floorboards. She tried not to look at the cell that had once held Cal, a bitter memory best left in the recesses of her mind.

Sheriff Dillon glanced up from his desk, his lined face betraying a flicker of surprise before settling into its usual stoic calm.

"Well, good morning, ladies," he said, leaning back in

his chair. His boots scraped against the scuffed floor. "What brings you here?"

Becky didn't even pause. "We're here to see Flannery." Her tone brooked no argument.

Lauren lingered a step behind, her gaze darting to the sheriff's face. Calm, almost detached. If he was annoyed by Becky's bluntness, he didn't show it. She stepped forward, her voice softer than Becky's. "It's important, Sheriff. Please."

He studied her for a moment before standing. He took his time, his movements deliberate. "Can't say no to you, Miss Lauren, but don't expect much. Flannery's not exactly cooperative."

The keys jingled in his hand as he led them to the cells. Lauren followed, trailing behind Becky, whose tension rolled off her in waves. The small, claustrophobic cells reeked of sweat and unwashed bodies. At the far end, Foxy Flannery sprawled on his cot, scratching his rotund belly, one leg stretched out, the other swinging lazily. He grinned when he saw them.

"Well, if it ain't the Queen of Hope House," he drawled, his tone a dagger wrapped in silk. "And her loyal lapdog."

Becky's fists clenched. "Where's Luke?"

Foxy leaned back, folding his hands behind his head. "Luke? That boy's always been a wanderer. Hard to keep track of him."

"Don't lie to me." Her grip on the iron bars tightened, her knuckles white. Her fiery hair, usually neat, had fallen loose from her braid, and it framed her face like a storm. For a split second, Lauren thought she saw something flicker in Becky's green eyes—fear, or maybe guilt—but it vanished as quickly as it came. "You were with him when we found you. Tell me where he went!"

His grin widened, sharp and cruel. "Why would I do a thing like that? Luke's swimmin' in waters even I wouldn't dare tread. Best leave him to his fate, sweetheart."

Lauren winced at the venom in his voice. Becky stiffened beside her, as taut as a wire ready to snap.

"And Matthew?" Becky pressed, her voice breaking just enough for Lauren to hear. "Did you see him after the boys ran off all those years ago?"

Foxy's smile twisted. "Matthew?" He stretched the name out like a taunt. "Who's to say? Could be he's out there livin' it up. Or not. Life's funny that way."

The words hung in the air, a cruel echo. Becky's breath hitched, but she didn't look away.

"What do you mean?" she demanded, her voice barely above a whisper. "Is he alive or not?"

"Ask Luke," Foxy said, his tone growing bored. "If you can find him. But if I were you, I'd let it be. Boy's hitched his wagon to trouble you can't outrun."

A low chuckle echoed from the next cell, sharp and cutting. Lauren's gaze flicked toward the source. A tall, wiry man with a scar snaking down the side of his face, his eyes like dark pits. He was leaning casually against the bars, but something about the way he watched them made her want to take a bath. In bleach.

"You think you're some kind of savior," the scarred man sneered, his voice low and venomous. He stepped closer to the bars, his fingers curling around the iron as though he might rip it apart. "But saviors die just like the rest of us."

Lauren's stomach dropped, a chill prickling along the back of her neck. She instinctively shifted a step closer to Becky, though her friend didn't seem to notice. Becky's glare sharpened, her fists clenching at her sides. For a moment, Lauren thought she might lash out with words, fists, anything to release the pressure radiating off her.

Before Becky could respond, Sheriff Dillon's voice cracked through the air like a whip. "That's enough!"

The sheriff's boots scuffed against the floor as he stepped forward, his presence a sudden wall between them and the prisoners. His hand hovered near his belt, fingers brushing against the keys. The scarred man's sneer melted into something colder, calculated, and watchful. But he backed away from the bars without another word.

Lauren exhaled, not realizing she'd been holding her breath. Her pulse pounded in her ears, and for a second, the room felt smaller, the walls closer. She looked toward Becky, whose chest rose and fell in sharp, measured breaths.

"We're done here." The sheriff gestured for them to follow.

Lauren cast one last look at Foxy. His smirk had faded, but his eyes remained as defiant as ever. As the sheriff locked the cell, she spoke, her voice low but steady. "You won't get away with this."

For the first time, Foxy's grin faltered. His gaze darted toward the floor, just for a moment, before snapping back to meet Lauren's. It was enough. A crack in the armor. He wasn't as untouchable as he wanted them to believe.

Sheriff Dillon led them back toward the office's front room. Becky stayed close behind him, her steps brisk and charged with frustration. Lauren trailed, glancing back once toward the cells. The other two prisoners hadn't moved, but their eyes followed her, dark and unyielding.

In the main room, he gestured to the chairs by his desk. "Sit, if you like."

Becky ignored the offer, pacing near the window instead, her hands stuffed into the pockets of her coat.

Lauren settled hesitantly into a rickety chair, its legs creaking beneath her slight weight. "Who are the men in the next cell?"

He leaned against his desk, his arms crossed, his lips pursed and the expression in his eyes causing Lauren to swallow hard.

"They're trouble. Both have long rap sheets including suspected murder."

Becky groaned, putting her hands to her mouth. Lauren's gaze stayed locked on the sheriff, her stomach tightening. There was more. She could feel it.

"They're not Flannery's men. If anything, he's a small piece on someone else's board. I had to keep Flannery in the other cell to keep him alive." His jaw tightened. "Their own mothers wouldn't be safe with those two."

"You're sayin' Luke," Becky swallowed hard. "Might be mixed up in somethin' bigger?"

Sheriff Dillon nodded grimly. "If Luke's tangled with the folks who keep Flannery in business, we're talking smuggling routes that stretch clear across the border. Those people don't take kindly to loose ends."

Becky's shoulders stiffened, her jaw working as if she were grinding her teeth. "But Luke's just a kid. He wouldn't …" She trailed off, her hands clasped together as in prayer.

Sheriff Dillon rubbed the back of his neck, exhaling slowly before speaking. "I know you want to believe that, but people get caught up in things they don't understand."

Becky's pacing resumed, more agitated now. "He's not like them. He's not." Her words sounded as much like a plea as a declaration.

Lauren leaned forward, her hands in her lap. "Sheriff, what happens to Luke if he's found? Legally?"

Sheriff Dillon dragged a hand down his face, exhaling through his nose. "Depends on what he's done. If he's just been keeping company with Foxy, running supplies or keeping lookout, he might get a light sentence or probation. But if it's smuggling, theft, or worse." He looked at Becky. "It'll be harder to help him. Especially if he's involved with whoever's behind Flannery."

Becky stopped mid-stride, her voice sharp. "Flannery said Luke's in deeper trouble than we could handle. What does that mean?"

"It means trouble," he replied bluntly. "Flannery talks big, but he's not the one pulling the strings. If Luke's tied to someone higher up, it's bad news. And Flannery's the type to throw anyone under the bus to save himself."

Lauren gripped the chair's armrest, a cold weight settling in her chest. The image of Luke, wide-eyed, nervous, barely fourteen, flashed in her mind. How could he be part of something so dangerous?

Becky's voice dropped to a whisper. "And Matthew? Did you find his name in any records? Hear anythin' about him?"

Sheriff Dillon shook his head slowly. "No records, no sightings. It's like he vanished after the boys left." He held Becky's gaze. "I wish I had better news, but there's nothing."

Becky's shoulders slumped for a moment, but then she straightened, her chin lifting. "I'll find Luke. And if he knows what happened to Matthew, I'll bring them both back."

Lauren nodded, pressing her hands against her lap to keep them from trembling. "Thank you, Sheriff. If you hear anything, please let us know."

He inclined his head. "You have my word. But be careful. You're stirring up a hornet's nest."

Lauren caught a flicker of something in his tone and it sent a shiver down her spine. *He knows more than he's saying,* she thought, but she didn't press. Not yet.

Becky didn't respond. She was already moving toward the door, her movements brisk and determined. Lauren hesitated, this man had tried so often to help them. "I'm sorry... she's upset. Thank you."

Becky stopped just beyond the door, staring out at the horizon, her breath misting in the air. Lauren studied her friend for a moment. The tension in Becky's shoulders hadn't eased, and her gaze burned with the same fire that had driven her through every trial they'd faced together.

Lauren knew Becky's stubbornness could be her greatest strength, but also her most dangerous weakness. That determination, the fire in her green eyes, had pulled them through countless trials before.

"I know you're worried, annoyed, and frustrated, but we have to listen to the sheriff," Lauren said, stepping closer. "He has more experience in that world than we do."

Becky exhaled, the sound shaky. "Luke's just a kid, Lauren. And Matt ..." Her voice broke. She folded her arms, as if trying to shield herself from the weight of her own words. "What if we're too late? What if I never know?"

Lauren placed a hand on her shoulder. "We can't think like that. Let's go home and see if Tom has remembered anything more. Will may have heard something."

Becky nodded, her jaw tightening as she pushed back tears. Without another word, she strode toward the truck. Before she opened the door, she glanced at the mountain. Lauren followed her gaze wondering what secrets lay hidden up there.

THE WARMTH of Hope House enveloped Lauren as she stepped inside, a welcome reprieve from the chill that clung to her from their trip to the sheriff's office. The scent of fresh bread and wood smoke drifted through the air, accompanied by the high-pitched giggles of children from the sitting room.

Lauren paused in the hallway, listening.

"And then the bear said, 'You can't catch me. I've got

boots!'" Cal's dramatic declaration earned an eruption of laughter.

Lauren shook her head, a faint smile tugging at her lips despite the heaviness pressing on her chest. Only Cal could convince the children that bears not only wore boots but had personalities to match.

Behind her, Becky hung her coat on the peg with sharp, jerky movements. "Least they're happy."

"They don't know to be anything else," Lauren replied gently. She caught sight of Nanny Kat peering out from the kitchen doorway.

"You're back," Nanny said, her sharp eyes scanning their faces. "How did it go?"

Lauren hesitated. Becky's shoulders stiffened, and she knew her friend wasn't ready to discuss it yet. Lauren gave Nanny Kat a look. "We'll tell you after supper."

"Fair enough. Supper's ready, and I won't have cold food because you're standing about."

Lauren smiled, following Becky into the kitchen.

Supper was its usual mixture of chaos and comfort. The kitchen was warm with steam from the stove, the clatter of dishes blending with the children's chatter. Lauren ladled out bowls of collard greens with fatback, handing them to eager hands as Nanny put baskets of bread rolls on the table.

"Boys!" Lauren called over the din. "Let the little ones go first."

"I was just gonna ..." Cal began, but Fred's triumphant grin and the extra roll tucked under his arm told a different story.

"Fred, the rolls are for everyone," Lauren said, raising an eyebrow.

Fred's grin faltered, and he reluctantly handed the roll to Maisie, who accepted it with a solemn nod. Lauren ruffled his hair. "Good boy."

Terry, seated at the far end of the table, chuckled as he took a bite of his bread. "Cal, I hear you've been tellin' stories again."

"I only tell the truth!" Cal said, his chest puffing out. "You did get chased by a goat!"

"Maybe, but you make it sound like the goat had a personal grudge."

"It did!"

Lauren hid her smile, focusing on her bowl. Across the table, Becky sat silently, her eyes distant. The weight of the day hadn't lifted for her.

After supper, the children's energy waned, their yawns growing frequent as they began to drift toward the stairs. Nanny Kat rounded them up with practiced efficiency, sending Cal upstairs with a nudge and steering Fred away from the breadbasket before he could pocket another roll.

"Maisie, time for bed," Lauren scooped the toddler into her arms.

Maisie rested her head on Lauren's shoulder, her small hand clutching at her dress. "Story?" she mumbled.

"Not tonight, sweetheart. But I'll sing you a song."

Upstairs, Lauren settled Maisie into her crib, humming until the little girl's eyes drifted shut. Becky moved quietly through the room, tucking blankets around the older girls.

Back in the sitting room, the adults gathered, the air

quieter now but heavier with unspoken tension. Terry stoked the fire, sending shadows dancing across the walls, while Nanny poured tea with steady hands. Tom sat in his chair, adjusting his bandage with a wince, and Will perched on the arm of Becky's seat, his presence calm but alert.

Lauren took her place beside Nanny, watching Becky as she stared into the fire. The flames flickered, their light casting her friend's features into sharp relief.

Finally, Becky spoke. "The sheriff thinks Luke's tangled up with somethin' bigger than Flannery. And there's still no sign of Matt."

The room fell silent. Lauren could feel the tension thrumming through Becky, her hands gripping the edges of the chair as if holding herself together.

Will broke the silence, his voice measured. "Becky, if Luke's involved with a bigger group, runnin' up the mountain to find him might not be the best idea. Not yet."

Becky's head snapped up, her eyes blazing. "We can't wait! What if they pull him in deeper? What if they ..." She trailed off, her voice breaking slightly.

"Darlin'," Will said, reaching for her hand, "it's still winter up there. The thaw hasn't set in, and the trails are dangerous. You know that better than anyone. We'd be riskin' a lot by goin' now."

Tom leaned forward, his voice quiet but firm. "Will's right. Luke and Matt know the mountains better than anyone. If Luke's scared or caught up in somethin', he'll go to ground. And if there's truth to what Flannery said, Luke might be hidin' from the gang as much as from the law."

Becky's anger disappeared giving way to something

more vulnerable. Lauren knew Becky didn't want to wait, but the reality of the risks was sinking in.

The words came out raw, trembling with emotion. "So what am I supposed to do?"

Will squeezed her hand. "We'll spread the word. Tom and I know plenty of folks in the mountains. We'll tell 'em to keep an eye out for Luke and to let him know he's got a home here. That his sister loves him and that Foxy was lyin'."

Tom nodded. "I'll talk to folks once I'm back on my feet. They trust me." He glanced at Becky, his tone softer. "If that doesn't work, we'll search. But not until it's safer."

Becky looked from Tom to Will, her shoulders sagging slightly. "And what if it doesn't work? What if he's too far gone?"

Will's voice was steady. "Then, when it's safer, I'll take you up there myself. We'll search until we find him. But Becky, you have to trust us on this."

Lauren felt a flicker of relief as Becky nodded slowly, though the tension in her frame hadn't completely eased.

"All right. But we'd better hear somethin' soon."

CHAPTER 7

*L*auren had to see Edward, to tell him the news about Luke. He had a way of making her feel better and always gave her good advice.

She stepped inside the foyer nodding in response to a smile from the man behind the main reception desk. It was eerily quiet, save for the faint clatter of a nurse's trolley somewhere in the distance. Lauren pulled her coat tighter against the chill that seeped through the walls, her boots tapping softly on the tiled floor as she made her way to Edward's room. Even with the floral arrangements scattered along the hallway, the clinical smell seemed inescapable.

Her heart was racing, her stomach twisted into tight knots. What would Edward say about Luke? Would he have the words that she couldn't seem to find? He always had a way of grounding her when everything else felt like it was slipping through her fingers.

Pushing the door open, she stepped inside. The room greeted her with the same stark, sterile air, colder than she expected. A draft from the window snuck in despite the radiator's best efforts. Edward stood at the far side of the room, hunched slightly over his crutches, the muscles in his arms visibly straining as he balanced his weight. His hair was damp at the edges, sweat slicking his brow.

He glanced up as the door creaked shut behind her. A smile broke across his face, warm and familiar despite the effort etched into every line of his features.

"Lauren," he said, his voice tinged with the breathlessness of exertion. "You're just in time to see a miracle. Or at least, a very determined attempt at one."

She managed a small smile, though her fingers tightened on the edge of her coat. "Edward, you should be resting."

"Resting is overrated." His crutches clicked against the floor, his movements slow but purposeful. "Watch this."

Lauren's breath misted in the cold air as she exhaled, her chest tight with conflicting emotions. Pride flickered in her heart, but it was quickly followed by that familiar ache. The one that came every time she thought of everything he'd endured and everything he still faced.

When he reached her, he stopped, his grin widening with boyish triumph. "Well? Impressed?"

Her throat tightened as she forced the words out. "You've made incredible progress. I'm proud of you."

"And yet, you're frowning," Edward said, tilting his head slightly. "What is it this time, Lauren? My hand?"

She shook her head. "No, it's not that."

Crossing the room, she gently placed her hand on his arm and guided him toward the chair by the window. The familiar scrape of the crutches followed, grating softly against her nerves. He sank into the chair with a quiet groan, leaning back with visible relief.

"Becky found Luke."

Edward's brows shot up, his posture straightening. "She did? Where?"

"At the mill," Lauren replied, perching lightly on the edge of the chair opposite him. Her hands twisted in her lap, her words coming out haltingly. "Tom saw him there and told us. You know Becky, she wouldn't wait for anyone. She went right after him."

Edward nodded, his lips pressing into a thin line as he waited for her to continue.

"Luke was there," Lauren said, her throat tightening as the words caught. "But he ... he ran." Her voice broke, trembling as her hands gripped her skirt. "She saw him for only a moment before he disappeared into the woods. She tried to follow him, but Foxy Flannery stopped her. Things turned violent. Tom was hurt, and we had to intervene. Will and Earl helped, but Luke's gone."

Edward exhaled. "The poor girl. She's waited so long for this, only to lose him again."

"She's devastated." Lauren's gaze drifted toward the window, where bare branches swayed in the biting February wind. "She barely eats. She barely sleeps. And Foxy told Luke lies about her. Lies about her forgetting her brothers, about only caring for the children at Hope House. He poisoned him against her, Edward."

Edward's hand reached out, his good fingers brushing against hers. "Becky loves Luke, they grew up in a loving family. That kind of love doesn't vanish, no matter what someone says. Luke will come back when he's ready. He just needs time."

Lauren turned to him, her chest aching. "What if he doesn't come back?"

Edward held her gaze. "Then she'll have to find peace with that, too."

Lauren gave him a faint, sad smile, the warmth of his hand on hers grounding her momentarily. The room lapsed into silence, the only sound the soft tick of the clock on the wall.

Beyond the window, the skeletal branches of the trees scraped against one another in the wind, a hollow sound that only deepened the chill in the air.

"I've been thinking about what I'll do when I leave here." His gaze still fixed on the bleak horizon beyond the glass.

Lauren stilled, her heart skipping a beat. Something about his tone sent a shiver racing down her spine. "And?"

"I'm going back to Germany."

Her breath caught, sharp and involuntary, as though the air had been knocked from her lungs. The words hung between them.

"To Germany?" Her pulse thundered in her ears, drowning out the faint tick of the wall clock. The room felt smaller, colder, as if the draft from the window had seeped into her very bones. "Edward, why?"

"You know why." The quiet determination in his voice carving a hollow ache in her chest. "There's work to be done, Lauren. People like my Aunt Rae are still there, hiding, running, barely surviving. The Nazis are destroying lives, it will only get worse and I can't sit here and do nothing."

The air caught in her throat, and her stomach churned as the room spun around her. "You nearly died last time," she said, her voice trembling as she fought to keep it steady. "They arrested you. They beat you within an inch of your life. Do you think they'll hesitate to do it again?"

Edward leaned forward. He tried to take her hand in his good one but she moved back. He clasped his hands in his lap, the knuckles of his left hand whitening. "I know the risks. I'm not stupid. But Hans and Rachel made it out because I, and people who feel like I do, helped them. There are more like them, Lauren. Children, families, men, women who won't make it unless someone steps in."

Lauren's jaw tightened, and a flush of anger swept through her. She stood and paced the room before turning to him. "And you just decided this on your own? Without me?"

Edward blinked, his expression faltering for the first time. "I didn't ..."

"You didn't think to tell me." She interrupted, her chest tightening as her composure began to slip. Keeping her tone below a scream was an effort. "We're supposed to be building a life together, Edward. We're engaged. How am I supposed to fit into this decision of yours? Where do I come in?"

Edward leaned back slightly, his shoulders stiffening. The warmth in his expression ebbed, replaced by something colder. "This isn't about us, Lauren. It's about what's right."

"It should be about us!" she snapped, her voice rising before she caught herself. She glanced toward the door, her heart pounding, and forced herself to lower her tone. "We've waited so long, Edward, and now you're willing to throw it all away? For what? A cause that could get you killed?"

Her voice cracked on the last word, and the emotion hit her in a wave, surging past the walls she'd tried so hard to keep intact. She brushed the tears from her eyes, determined not to start wailing like a baby. She'd come here for comfort and instead had her heart ripped open.

Edward's expression darkened, though his voice grew quieter, the intensity in it sharper for the restraint. "You would risk everything for the children at Hope House. You'd walk into fire for them without a second thought. And I would never stand in your way."

"That's different."

"Is it?" His gaze held hers, piercing through every argument she wanted to make. "Because I love Aunt Rae just as much as you love those children. I've waited years for you to admit you loved me. And now, when I'm asking for your support, you're telling me no?"

Her chest ached as his words struck home, sharp and unrelenting. Her breath came quicker, the room spinning as guilt and frustration twisted together in a painful knot. She dropped her gaze to the floor, her hands twisting in the fabric of her skirt. "It's not that simple." She took a seat, afraid she was going to faint.

Edward exhaled, the sound heavy with frustration. "It is to me. I can't stay here safe in America and live with myself, knowing I could have made a difference."

The silence that followed was suffocating, thick with the weight of everything left unsaid. Lauren's vision blurred as she stared out the window, the skeletal branches of the trees swaying in the cold February wind. She wanted to tell him he was being reckless, that his place was with her, but the words caught in her throat. No argument would change his mind. She could see it in the hard set of his jaw, in the resolve that had replaced his usual warmth.

"What happens to us?" She whispered. "If you go, what happens to us?"

Edward hesitated, reaching out for her hand. The regret that flickered in his eyes did nothing to soften the blow of his next words. "I don't know. But I do know I love you. And I hope, in time, you'll understand."

Lauren stood abruptly, the legs of her chair scraping against the cold, tiled floor. The sudden motion made her head swim, but she forced herself to stay upright. "I need to go."

"Lauren," Edward began, reaching for her, but she stepped back, her hands rigid at her sides.

"I need time." Tears brimmed in her eyes, but she refused to let them fall. "That's all I can give you right now."

Edward didn't try to stop her, his hand falling back to his lap. As she turned and walked out, it took every ounce of her strength to take each step. Away from him. She had to get to the truck without losing her restraint. She'd thought the only hurdle they faced was choosing where they would live. Not for one second did she believe he would rush into danger as soon as he was released.

CHAPTER 8

The next week passed in a blur. She barely slept, tossing and turning, wondering how she could make him change his mind. She didn't go and visit him as usual on Sunday but when Becky queried why, she told her she had a headache.

"Lauren, what is the matter with you? You will make a hole in the floorboards with all that pacing."

Lauren barely heard Nanny Kat as she paced up and down, twisting the diamond ring on her finger. How could she wear such a beautiful piece of jewelry when her family and so many others were going without? How could she wear it when he wanted to throw away their future?

"Sit down, Lauren. Now."

Lauren sat at the side of Nanny's bed. She stared at her fingers before looking up into Nanny's face. She couldn't talk about Edward but had to tell the old woman something.

"I don't know what to do. I'm worried about Becky.

Despite what she said about waiting for Will and Tom, not to mention the sheriff to find news about Luke, she keeps disappearing for long periods of time. I think she is doing her own searching. What if she gets hurt? Sheriff Dillion hinted those smugglers aren't going to take kindly to anyone interfering in their business."

"It's not just Becky on your mind, is it?"

Lauren couldn't look Nanny Kat in the face. How could she confess she was worried about Edward's plans? How his love for her was not enough to keep him safe.

"Lauren, talk to me."

Lauren stood up and paced again. "There are so many bills. Becky will need money to set up home, you know she never took any wages from Hope House. We need to replace Norma, God rest her soul and find the seven dollars a week to keep Bart at the sanatorium. He's family just as much as any of the children. We can't desert him at a time like this. I just … I feel helpless."

"Helpless is not an attractive look on anyone, least of all you, Lauren. Stop fretting and think clearly. Sit down." Nanny took Lauren's hand in hers. "Edward gave you his grandmother's ring. It clearly has a lot of sentimental value and it isn't yours to sell."

Lauren gaped at her Nanny. "How did you know that's what I was thinking?"

"I've known you all your life, Lauren. You'd never make it as a hustler." Nanny patted her hand. "The answer to part of your problem is staring you in the face."

"It is?"

"Invite the Meyers to move in. The children loved

having them here over Christmas and New Year, especially Hans and Rachel. Chana is more relaxed out here than in Delgany. She doesn't jump at every loud noise, not like she used to. She loves the children and they love her. Victor is no Bart, at his age you can't expect him to be climbing ladders and fixing roofs, but he has other qualities. They won't expect a wage or at least not a large one. They will be happy with room and board. Chana could do what Norma did. Make some of her delicacies and sell them down at Hillman's."

Lauren sighed. She'd thought of the same solution, but it didn't really solve all her issues. She still needed money for Becky.

As if she'd read her mind, Nanny continued, "Becky is a mountain girl and knows that land like the back of her hand. Telling her not to search for her brothers is like telling you not to use your brain. It's part of her nature. As for the other worries you have about Becky, she knows you can't make a penny into a dollar, no matter how you stretch it. You have signed over the land for their house with enough for a small garden. They don't expect more than that. Becky is resourceful, she'll find a way to make things work just as you will." Nanny squeezed her hand before letting it fall back on the bedspread as they heard a car driving up. "You expecting someone?"

Lauren shook her head. Standing up, she walked over to Nanny's bedroom window and looked out. "It's Mr. Stewart. I'll go and let him in while you make yourself presentable."

Without waiting for a reply she walked out of the room,

closing the door behind her so Nanny could get dressed. Smoothing down her own hair, she walked out to greet their guest.

"Morning, Lauren. How are you this beautiful morning?"

Lauren glanced at the snow covered mountains, shivering in the freezing air. It might be picturesque, but it was cold. "Fine, thank you. How are you?"

Mr. Stewart rocked back on his feet, passing his hat from one hand to the other. They were rescued from the awkward silence by Cal coming out the front door. "Morning, Mr. Stewart. What are you doing here? Did you come to give us a ride in your motorcar?"

Lauren opened her mouth to tell Cal off for being cheeky, but Mr. Stewart just laughed. "That wasn't part of my plan young Cal, but I might be persuaded to take you and some of the other children for a spin later on. But first I have some business to see to."

Was it her imagination or was Mr. Stewart blushing? He certainly looked uncomfortable.

"Where are my manners? Come in please. Would you like a cup of coffee? Earl Hillman dropped by yesterday with a box of provisions, courtesy of John Thatcher."

"I'd love some, thank you. How are the Thatcher's doing?"

They walked into the house chatting as they went.

"Very well. Katie, I mean Cassie, is blossoming now the truth has come out about what happened. The adoption is proceeding despite some ridiculous claim made that John and Alice only wanted to adopt her due to her being an heiress, but Edward's solicitor friend sorted that out. It will soon be official, and John will assume the role of trustee."

"Will they return to Delgany or stay in Washington?" Mr. Stewart set his hat on the counter before taking a seat at the table. Lauren put the water on to boil.

"I think the plan is to return. Cassie doesn't want to live with the constant reminders of what happened, but as of yet no firm plans have been made."

"I'm sure Kathryn hopes they will return to live here, she misses them."

"Who misses who?" Becky asked, coming down the stairs with a basket of dirty laundry in her arms. "Mornin' Mr. Stewart, I mean Ian, you are out and about early."

He stayed quiet, so Lauren spoke up. "Can you make the coffee please, Becky, while I check on Maisie? She was running a slight fever earlier and she never sleeps this late."

Lauren left the kitchen, walking upstairs while letting her thoughts whirl. What could he want to speak to them about? He looked nervous. Oh, please God, let it not be more bad news.

BY THE TIME Lauren returned downstairs, Nanny had joined Becky and Ian in the kitchen. Becky poured out the coffee as Lauren took a seat.

"I was passing as I have an appointment up the road so thought I would call in. I brought you the newspapers although I'd rather bin them. Perhaps don't let Hans read them."

Intrigued, Lauren reached for the paper as Becky asked, "Why?"

"You know the Friends of New Germany was investigated?"

"Yes. It was disbanded and Rudolf Hess recalled all the leaders to Germany. Good riddance. We don't need the Nazis here." Becky stirred her coffee.

"We might have been better off leaving them alone."

"Ian! They were hateful. Why would you think that?" Nanny Kat stared at him.

"The devil you know is better than the devil you don't. They've been replaced by a new outfit, they call themselves the German-American Bund. They have divided the USA into three so called districts, each with their own chain of command. They intend setting up training camps and holding rallies displaying the Nazi insignia."

"That is disgusting." Lauren wanted to burn all the Nazi flags. "Why does our Government allow it?"

"Freedom of speech is laid down in our constitution. It's ironic, the very element of our society which protects its citizens is being used by those who want to destroy the idea of a democracy. Or at least the members of that civilization they deem to be unworthy. Anyway, the Bund is mainly concentrated in bigger cities such as New York and elsewhere, but I think it could mean trouble. When people have too much time on their hands and little hope for the future they make bad decisions."

"You mean you are afraid they will start marchin' through our streets?' Becky asked.

"That's the least of it, Becky. I think they will turn

people against what Cal calls good Germans. Those who are proud of their backgrounds and have nothing to do with the Nazis. Just last week, there was a rally over in Riverhaven," Ian said grimly. "They were passing out pamphlets, talking about 'American purity' and other nonsense. Some local boys got swept up in it. Good kids from hardworking families, but they don't know any better. That's what worries me. Desperate people will believe anything if it promises them hope."

He stared into his coffee as if the answers were at the bottom of the cup. "There are many immigrants who came to the USA in the last century. Like the Irish or," he glanced at Nanny, "Scottish, they are proud of their origins. But some people will just hear the German names and lump them all in as being Nazis. And then there is the matter of Bund's beliefs. They share the same hatred for Jews and are bound to cause trouble for the Jewish population living here."

"If anyone touches Hans and Rachel or even the Meyers, they will have me to deal with." Becky pushed the newspaper across the table. "They shouldn't be printin' anythin' about those horrible organizations but instead make them illegal and lock the members all up."

"And make martyrs out of them? There is nothing better for a cause than a martyr, particularly if he is wearing a suit and looks normal. They try to show the world they are good Americans by flying the flag alongside the Nazi flag."

Lauren's stomach tightened as Ian's grim words sank in. The hatred consuming Germany was seeping into their own soil, spreading like a disease. She pictured Foxy and Mrs. Flannery, their faces twisted with disdain, and a chill ran through her. Would people like that turn their anger toward Hans, Rachel, or the Meyers? And what about Edward? If he went back, wouldn't he face the same hatred magnified a thousandfold?

"Just this morning, Lauren and I were talking about the Meyers. We had yet to discuss it with Becky but wondered if it might be an idea for them to move in here." Nanny glanced at Lauren. "We all know Chana is worried because of her experiences before the War and also the news from Germany is reminding her of the loss of her son. These articles are only going to heighten her fears."

"That's a great idea, but where will we put them? Christmas and New Year were lovely, but the house is more than a little crowded and with the young girls growin' up that bathroom is never free." Becky pushed back her hair. "They could have my room, I guess. I'll be movin' out just as soon as our house is built, but that may take a while. Maybe we could share?" Becky looked toward Lauren.

Lauren bit her lip. She wanted to help, but long ago she and Becky had decided them sharing a room was a bad idea if they wanted harmony in Hope House. But then with both of them getting married and soon moving out, it might be a short term solution.

"Oh, I forgot. I have something else for you. You talking about weddings reminded me. Excuse me." Ian stood up and went outside to his car returning with a large box.

"What's that?" Lauren asked as he placed it on the table.

"I know how pushed you are for time. With all the work you have to do to keep Hope House going, you have little to spare for making wedding trousseaus. I thought this might help. Go on, open it."

Excitement lit up Becky's eyes as she opened the box to display a Singer machine. "I seen these in the catalogues but never thought we'd have one. You are such a lovely man. Thank you." Becky moved to kiss Ian on the cheek making him blush.

"Miss Chaney helped me a little bit. She chose the fabric."

Becky's eyes widened. She opened the smaller brown parcel revealing some beautiful material. "For us?"

"Yes. The cotton is for practice and the rest is for whatever you decide to use it for. Miss Chaney said she would show you how the machine works."

Becky held the package against her chest, her eyes filling with tears. "I feel just like I did when Lauren brought the coat to our old house. Remember how Sarah got upset as she wanted somethin' for herself and you came back with that coat for her. It was the first time my sister ever owned somethin' new."

Lauren stood and gave Becky a hug, her eyes watering as she remembered the poor child who had died shortly afterwards from fever. "I remember. I'm sure Sarah is looking down now and smiling."

Nanny Kat put a hand on Becky's shoulder. "Ian, Becky heard some news about her brothers. Luke was seen up on the mountain. Tom and Will have volunteered to go looking for him when the thaw comes. For now, we just have to wait and try to concentrate on happier events like the wedding."

Lauren wondered if Becky would take offense at Nanny Kat's explanation. Becky's green eyes flashed with determination, but with a flick of her hair she leaned in and gave Ian a kiss on the cheek.

"Thank you Ian, you are so generous."

"My pleasure." A faint flush crept up his neck. He lifted the coffee to his lips, but his hand hesitated for half a second before he took a sip. "I think you should speak to the Meyers. They will jump at the chance at moving in here. As far as I know they own their house so maybe they will consider selling up and investing the money into this place. You could build on an extension, maybe give them a room on the ground floor with its own bathroom. Given their ages, the stairs may prove a challenge in the future."

"They are younger than both of us!" Nanny Kat reminded him.

"I'm planning ahead." He retorted as they all laughed. "How is Bart doing?"

Lauren swallowed the lump in her throat. "He's ill and instead of concentrating on his recovery, he is worrying about bills. He is worrying about his girls, too."

"I may have a solution to some of his issues. I have a friend who works in the Blue Ridge sanatorium. He may be able to get us a discount on Bart's fees. It wouldn't hurt to ask. That would take a little bit off his mind, perhaps?"

"Anything you could do, Ian, would be welcome. We were going to try to visit him next month. The girls can't go, they don't allow children for fear they will catch TB."

"I've met Bart only a couple of times but I like him. I can go see my friend and catch up with Bart at the same time and report back."

Becky stood up. "I'll put on more coffee. Can you let us know when you go so we can pack a box for him? Make him a few of his favorites and also include some pictures from his girls."

"Of course. No more coffee for me." Ian coughed. "I was wondering if I could borrow Kathryn for a minute?"

Lauren saw Becky glance at her, but she couldn't look at her friend or she would laugh. It was almost a reversal of roles. Instead of asking for the date's parents permission, Mr. Stewart was asking them.

"I'm quite capable of making my own decisions, Ian Stewart. There is no need to ask Lauren and Becky for permission.'

"Of course not, I mean, that's not what I intended. I didn't mean to cause offense. I just..."

"Why don't you ask me to take a walk to the porch?" Nanny stood and walked toward the porch. Ian nearly fell over his own feet in his haste to beat her to the door so he could open same. Only when it closed behind them did Lauren catch Becky's eye and they both burst out laughing.

Becky wiped a tear from her eye, still grinning. "Did you see the look on his face? Poor Mr. Stewart. He was terrified."

Lauren nodded, her smile fading slightly as her thoughts turned inward. "Do you think he wants to go courting? Nanny won't tell me, but I got the impression there was history between them. Didn't you?"

Becky nodded.

Lauren moved the empty cups to the sink before retaking her seat at the table. "I never imagined Nanny Kat with a beau. She's always been so fiercely independent."

Becky poured more coffee into Lauren's cup, her expression thoughtful. "Maybe she's considerin' it now. She's been strong and independent all her life, takin' care of everyone else. Maybe she's finally ready to let someone take care of her, even if just a little."

"I suppose you're right. And if anyone deserves a bit of happiness, it's Nanny Kat. She's done so much for us all these years."

* * *

THEY HEARD the car drive away but Nanny Kat didn't return to the kitchen. Lauren went to find her while Becky examined the sewing machine.

Nanny was sitting on the porch staring out at the mountain ridges cloaked in hues of deep green as winter slowly loosened its grip. Patches of snow still clung stubbornly to the higher elevations, but it was clear spring was emerging. The brilliant blue sky held only a few wisps of white clouds.

"It's beautiful, isn't it?" Lauren whispered taking the seat beside Nanny. "I never get sick of looking at those mountains."

Nanny wiped her eye before turning to smile at Lauren. "I love them too. I was thinking of all my friends who lived there, past and present. Hetty Tennant among them. Ian has been trying to find out more about what happened to her. Did you know that?"

Lauren shook her head.

"I didn't want Becky to know, but I asked for his help to trace her family. The Home for Feeble Minded is not cooperating. I thought maybe now Luke has been spotted but fled, we could find out some good news."

Lauren grasped Nanny's hand. She hated to think about how badly Becky's mother and brothers had been treated.

"Hetty Tennant was a wonderful woman and a good friend." Nanny Kat closed her eyes as another tear escaped.

"Nanny, I hate seeing you so upset. Please don't cry. It's horrible what happened, but Becky is happy now. She can't wait to marry Will."

"Yes, darling, but she should have her family by her side when she gets wed."

"She does. She has all of us. We're her family."

Nanny Kat patted her hand and leaned in to kiss her on the cheek. "You're a wise young woman, Lauren. I'm so proud of you."

Lauren forced her voice past the lump in her throat. "Would you like to drive into Delgany and speak to the Meyers about moving here?"

Nanny nodded as she stood up. "I'd like that. Thank you. You won't tell Becky what Ian is up to, will you?"

"No. I don't want to raise her hopes. I'm just going to check with her if she needs anything in Hillman's."

* * *

As the truck rattled along the gravel road, Lauren gripped the wheel tighter, her thoughts drifting toward Edward like a storm cloud she couldn't shake. The hum of the engine faded to the background, replaced by the echo of his words the last time they'd spoken.

"I need to go back, Lauren. I can't just sit here while they suffer."

Her stomach twisted at the memory, Edward's calm conviction echoing in her ears. She understood him. How could she not? That unshakable drive to fight injustice was one of the things she admired most about him. But the thought of him walking willingly back into Germany, where his scars had been etched into his skin, felt like a knife twisting in her chest. Would his principles always demand so much? Would they always come first, before their future, before her?

Lauren tightened her grip on the steering wheel, her knuckles pale against the worn leather. She wanted to support him. She wanted to be the kind of woman who could stand by her fiancé no matter what. But what if standing by him meant losing him?

She blinked hard against the sting of tears. She didn't want to be selfish. She didn't want to hold him back. But the idea of Edward leaving again, this time to do something even more dangerous than before.

"Lauren?" Nanny's voice cut through her thoughts, pulling her back to the present. She glanced at the older woman, who was watching her with a look of quiet concern.

"Hmm?" she murmured, feigning nonchalance as she focused on the road.

"You've been quiet," Nanny said, her tone matter-of-fact. "What's on your mind?"

Lauren hesitated, the words forming on her lips but refusing to take shape. She wanted to tell Nanny everything. To spill her fears and frustrations the way she had as a girl. But something stopped her. Maybe it was pride, or maybe it was the knowledge that Nanny, practical as ever, would tell her what she already knew: that this was Edward's choice, and hers was to either accept it or not.

"Nothing really. Just thinking about how much there is to do."

Nanny gave her a long, measured look, one that said she didn't believe her but wouldn't press the issue. "Well, stop thinking so hard," she said lightly. "You'll give yourself a headache."

Lauren managed a weak smile, but her chest still ached. She focused on the road ahead, but Edward's voice lingered in her mind. *I need to go back.*

Beside her, Nanny stared out of the window, her jaw tight, lips pressed into that thin line that always made Lauren feel like a little girl again. She wanted to ask about Ian Stewart, about what he had said but the words clung to the back of her throat.

"Ian asked me to go see a movie over in Charlottesville."

Lauren kept her eyes on the road, her lips twitching.

"Has God struck you dumb?" Nanny's sharp words cut through the hum of the engine.

"Not at all," Lauren bit back a laugh. "I was just waiting for you to tell me what movie you were going to see."

Nanny shifted, the fabric of her dress rustling, muttering, "That's not all you were waiting for."

Lauren's grip tightened on the steering wheel. "I wondered if you had a history with Ian, I mean." She tried to sound casual, but her words hovered between them like a breath held too long. "He's a lovely man, and he certainly remembers you fondly."

From the corner of her eye, Lauren saw Nanny's fingers twitch in her lap, her shoulders stiffen beneath her coat. When she finally spoke, her voice was softer, tinged with something Lauren couldn't quite place—regret, maybe, or longing.

"We met at a Christmas ball," Nanny said, her words slow and deliberate, as though pulling them from a place she rarely visited. "He said he'd ask my father if he could see me again." Her voice softened, barely audible over the steady hum of the truck. "He didn't, and that was that."

Lauren exhaled, her breath fogging the window momentarily. The silence returned, stretching between them as the truck bumped along the uneven road.

"Did you say yes?" Lauren asked. "To the movie?"

"I did."

Lauren risked a smile.

"Ian's a good man," Nanny said, her tone clipped. "But I don't need you meddling in my business, young lady."

Lauren raised an eyebrow, fighting a grin. "So you're saying there's business to meddle in?"

Nanny glared, but the corner of her mouth twitched. "Just drive, Lauren."

CHAPTER 9

*L*auren parked the truck, the engine sputtering to a stop just outside the Meyers' home. Before she could help Nanny out, Victor appeared, his shoes echoing on the sidewalk. His broad shoulders seemed stooped today. He looked older than he had at Christmas. "Come in, come in! Chana's been baking," he said, his voice booming with forced cheer that didn't match the weariness in his eyes. "Chana! Put the kettle on! We have visitors!"

Lauren stepped down from the truck, the cold air biting at her cheeks. Victor kissed her on both cheeks, but his hands trembled slightly, betraying the unspoken worry he carried. "How are the children? Becky and Will? Their house?" His questions tumbled out fast and insistent, like a dam about to burst.

"Victor, let them sit down before you wear them out," Chana called from the door, her voice warm but thin. Dark circles under her eyes etched a map of sleepless nights.

Lauren settled onto the couch, but the faint crinkle of

paper met her ears. She shifted, pulling out a folded letter from beneath her.

"Sorry, I ..."

"I'll take that." Chana darted forward, almost snatching the letter from Lauren's hand.

Lauren blinked, startled, as Chana turned quickly to the kitchen, stuffing the letter into a drawer.

Victor sighed, sinking heavily into a chair beside her, his bulk making the wood creak. "We get one or two of those papers a week now," he said, his voice low. "Sometimes it's clippings about the Friends of America. Other times, it's the travel notices. Subtle reminders that we're not welcome here."

Victor's gaze turned toward the window. His eyes darkened, his jaw tightening. "But this is our home," he muttered, defiance hardening his voice. "They won't drive us out."

Lauren exchanged a glance with Nanny, who gave a slight nod, as if confirming what they'd both suspected. Ian had been right. Life for the Meyers was becoming untenable. But how could they convince such a proud couple to come to Hope House without making it seem like charity?

Chana returned with the tea tray, her hands trembling slightly as she set it down. The delicate china rattled, the sound punctuating the quiet murmur of Nanny's voice as she began spinning stories about the children.

"Cal told the teacher he had to help Will set the roof on the new house," Nanny chuckled, her eyes gleaming with amusement. "Probably would've gotten away with it too, if the teacher hadn't bumped into Will while he was telling Earl how hard it was to set the foundations."

The room filled with laughter, rich and comforting, and for a moment, the tension eased. Victor leaned back in his chair, his belly shaking with mirth. "Got to give that boy credit for his imagination. He should be a writer like Edward."

Lauren's smile faltered as Victor's words hung in the air. Edward. Her thoughts drifted to him, and the tight knot in her chest returned.

"How is Edward?" Chana asked, her voice holding a note of hope even as her hands trembled over her teacup. "Is he recovering?"

Lauren hesitated, her throat tightening. "He's ..." She glanced at Nanny, but the older woman stayed quiet, letting Lauren find the words. "He's still healing. It's going to take time, for his body and his mind."

Chana's hand faltered, spilling a few drops of tea onto the tray. Her face tightened, the color draining from her cheeks. "I see," she murmured, her voice trembling. "We get letters," she continued, her hands twisting the handkerchief she kept tucked in her sleeve, "from friends and family still over there. They tell us terrible things. They want our help to come to the USA but we can't ... we don't have the money or the power..."

Her voice broke, and she pressed the handkerchief to her face as her shoulders shook.

Lauren leaned forward, resting her hand gently on Chana's arm. "Please, don't cry. I'm so sorry. I didn't mean to upset you."

Chana shook her head, her handkerchief trembling against her lips. "It's not you, Lauren. It's just ... the things we hear. The things happening there ... I can't believe it." She swallowed hard as her voice trembled. Taking a second to steady herself, she said, "Edward is brave, but did he have to go looking for trouble?" She hesitated, guilt flickering in her eyes. "Sometimes bravery takes too much. Sometimes it asks more than we can give."

The words cut through Lauren, leaving her silent. Edward's bravery had already cost so much, his health, his peace of mind, and yet he still felt the pull to return to Germany. He couldn't give up the fight, even if it meant losing himself in the process. The thought left Lauren's chest tight, her own guilt clawing at her throat. She wanted to defend him, to tell Chana that he was doing the right thing, but she wasn't sure if she believed it herself.

Victor stood, crossing the room with slow, deliberate movements. He placed a hand on Chana's shoulder, pulling her gently into his embrace. "Darling," he said, his voice steady but full of pain. "Everyone knows you don't blame Edward. Just as you didn't blame our boy."

Lauren's gaze followed Victor's to the mantle, where a photograph of their son, Pieter, sat, young, bright-eyed, full of life. Before the Nazis took that from him. The image seemed to watch over the room, a silent reminder of all they'd already lost.

Victor's voice dropped to a near whisper. "Evil persists when good men do nothing."

The room fell silent, save for the crackle of the fire. Lauren swallowed hard, the lump in her throat making it difficult to breathe. How could one family endure so much and still stand so tall?

It was Nanny who broke the quiet. Her voice was calm but resolute. "We were hoping you'd consider moving to Hope House."

Victor turned sharply, his eyes narrowing. "Move? To Hope House?" His voice was careful, guarded. "Kathryn, we could never..."

"Before you say no," Nanny interrupted gently, "hear me out. Hope House is bursting at the seams. We need help, Victor. And I don't just mean with the children or the chores. I mean we need a family like yours, strong, steady, and full of love. That house has always been about more than just providing for the children. It's about community. And right now, the children need you as much as you need them."

Victor's lips pressed into a thin line, his pride obviously warring with the reality of their situation. Chana remained silent, her teacup trembling slightly in her hands.

"You don't have to decide now," Lauren said. "But Nanny's right. Hope House isn't charity. It's a place to build something new. And right now, we need you."

Chana's voice broke the quiet. "It's not the house we'd miss," she whispered, her gaze dropping to her hands. "These are only walls. It's the memories..." Her voice cracked as tears welled in her eyes. "But perhaps it's time to make new memories. Kinder ones."

"Our landlord wants us out, so now is a good time to move." Victor nodded slowly, his hand tightening over hers. "Let's make new ones."

Lauren exhaled a breath she hadn't realized she'd been holding. The Meyers would come to Hope House. It was the right thing to do. But without a house to sell, the Meyers weren't in a position to fund an extension at Hope House. They'd have to find a way to fit them in. There was no way to go back on the invitation.

The road home felt longer than usual, and as the truck rumbled along, Lauren found herself glancing out at the trees. Their branches swayed in the breeze, budding with spring's new leaves. Nanny's words echoed in her mind, tangled with thoughts of Edward's struggle and the ever-growing costs of Hope House.

She let out a bitter laugh. Maybe the trees would start sprouting dollar bills, but until then, she'd have to find another way.

CHAPTER 10

Becky scrubbed the kitchen table in frantic, circular motions. The coarse bristles rasped against the wood, her nails occasionally screeching as they caught the surface. A faint smell of vinegar hung in the air, mingling with the metallic tang of cleaning products. The table wasn't even dirty anymore except for the faint discolorations etched into the grain of the table. The kind of stains that spoke of years of use, and no amount of scrubbing could erase them.

A stray crumb or two had long been swept into oblivion, but Becky kept scrubbing, her jaw tight.

Lauren exchanged a look with Nanny Kat, who sat near the window with her cane resting against her chair. Lauren's hands tightened on the edge of the sink before she turned to face Becky.

"Becky, are you going to tell us what's wrong?"

Becky didn't stop scrubbing. Her voice was clipped, strained. "Look at the state of this table. It's a wonder nobody dies from contamination. The dirt is part of the wood now. I should sand it down. Refinish it. Maybe paint the whole thing."

Lauren crossed the room and gently took the scrubbing brush from Becky's hands. Becky let it go without a fight, her hands trembling.

"Sit down," Lauren said. "I'll make you something to eat. You're wearing yourself into the ground. I hear you pacing every night. And every day, you're pushing yourself harder."

Becky shook her head, her expression fraught. "I can't sleep. There's too much to do. We can't expect Chana and Victor to move into a grubby house." She gestured vaguely around the spotless kitchen. "They..."

Lauren cut her off mid sentence. "The house is fine. The Meyers have stayed here before."

"For a visit. This is different." Becky pulled away, her voice rising as she turned toward the door. "They're movin' in. I must get their room ready."

"Enough."

The sharp crack of Nanny Kat's cane striking the wooden floor cut through the air like a whip. The room fell into silence, save for the rhythmic ticking of the clock on the wall. Becky froze mid-step, her back to them. Lauren stood rooted, her hands curling into fists as she glanced at Becky and then at Nanny Kat.

The old woman rose to her feet, leaning heavily on her cane. Her knuckles were pale where they gripped the handle, but her voice was firm, even as it quivered with the weight of emotion. "Becky, you making yourself ill isn't going to bring Luke home any faster. The boy may only be fourteen, but he's been surviving out there for the last three years. He knows where you live, and if he wants to come back, he will do so when he's good and ready. Meanwhile, you have a life to live here. The children need you. The real you. They already have enough to deal with without feeling like they're stepping on eggshells in their own home."

Becky turned slowly to face Nanny Kat. Her mouth opened, but no sound came out. Her face crumpled, her eyes glistening.

Lauren looked away, her throat tightening at the sight of her friend's grief. She focused on the scuffed edge of the counter instead, blinking hard to keep her own tears in check.

Nanny Kat softened as Becky's shoulders sagged. She set her cane aside and pulled Becky into a hug, her gnarled hands firm but gentle. "I love you. Just like I loved your mother. I know you're hurting, and I'd do anything to take away your pain. But wallowing and tormenting yourself with what-ifs isn't helping anyone, least of all you. Goto bed and get some rest. Have a cry if you need to. Then put your best face on, because you have a wedding to plan on top of everything else around here."

Becky let out a choked sob, her hands clutching her apron. She pressed the fabric to her eyes, then turned and bolted from the room. Her footsteps pounded up the stairs, and the sound of a door slamming echoed through the house.

The tension seemed to drain out of Nanny Kat's body

all at once. She shuffled back to her chair, lowering herself slowly, her breathing shallow and uneven. Lauren crossed the room and kneeled beside her, gripping the old woman's hand.

"She'll be okay," Lauren said, more to reassure herself than Nanny Kat.

Nanny Kat gave a small nod, though her eyes betrayed her weariness. "I know her heart is breaking. But she can't keep going like this. She'll be skin and bone before long."

Lauren squeezed her hand, then stood. "You did the right thing. She'll understand, maybe not right away, but in time."

Nanny Kat stayed silent, her gaze distant. Her fingers absently traced the worn wood of the cane by her side, and Lauren wondered if her thoughts had drifted back to the past. Memories of Becky's mother and siblings, of grief that time hadn't fully mended.

Lauren hesitated, the weight of the moment pressing down on her. Should she stay home? Keep her promise to the boys? She had so much to do—shopping, bills to pay, and she wanted to catch the sheriff to check for news. But leaving felt wrong. What if Becky spiraled further? What if Nanny Kat needed her?

Before she could decide, Nanny Kat cut through her thoughts. "Stop standing there staring at me as if I'll evaporate," she said, her voice sharp but laced with a faint smile. "I'm stronger than I look."

The old woman pushed herself to her feet, the familiar steel returning to her spine. "Don't you have to go to town?"

Lauren relaxed, just a little, though the knot in her chest didn't fully loosen. "I promised Cal and Hans a treat for their extra effort cleaning out the pigsty yesterday. Will you be all right here for a bit?"

Nanny Kat gave a small huff, her eyes bright with determination. "Yes, child. I'll be fine. Go on now."

Lauren gripped the steering wheel tighter as the truck rattled over the uneven road into the center of Delgany. The engine sputtered, its usual protests louder in the biting cold. She muttered under her breath, "Just a little farther, old girl."

The truck wheezed and shuddered as she parked it in front of the sheriff's office. For a moment, Lauren just sat there, her breath fogging the icy air inside the cab. Fixing the truck wasn't impossible, it was laughable. A problem for another day.

The sudden slam of a door startled her. Hans and Cal were already out, bounding up the street.

"Come on, Cal!" Hans called. "I bet Hillman's has Clark Bars!"

"Clark Bars are good, but peppermint sticks last longer!"

Lauren climbed out, pulling her scarf tighter against the wind. The boys' chatter brought a flicker of warmth to the cold morning, even if their boundless energy left her trailing in their wake. Tucking her hands into her coat pockets, she glanced toward the sheriff's office.

Sheriff Dillon stood on the porch, hat tipped back as he shuffled through a stack of papers. He looked up as she approached, his weathered face cracking into a brief smile.

"Morning, Miss Lauren," he said, his gravelly voice cutting through the quiet.

"Morning, Sheriff." She nodded, though her focus lingered on the boys already barreling toward Hillman's.

"Running errands?" he asked, tucking the papers into his coat.

"Just some bits and pieces. Cal and Hans did all their chores, so it's their turn to pick out a treat. It's just a small one, but you'd think they had a million dollars to spend."

He chuckled, watching the boys for a moment. "I'm looking forward to spring, so I can get back to fishing."

Lauren hid a smile. He'd never admit how much he enjoyed taking the boys fishing.

"I'm getting things squared away here," he said, stepping off the porch. "We're moving Foxy Flannery to Charlottesville."

Lauren suppressed a small sigh of relief. The Flannery name had caused more trouble in Delgany than most families managed in a generation. "Good riddance. Will there be a trial?" Her stomach tightened. "We won't have to give evidence, will we?"

Dillon scratched his chin. "Doubt it. The Revenuers want their money more than anything. Flannery's no Capone. Still, I wouldn't lose sleep over him coming back anytime soon. The Feds don't mess around."

Lauren nodded, but the tension in her chest didn't ease. What if he did come back? People like Flannery didn't forget grievances, and he'd never been fond of Hope House.

"Don't worry, Miss Lauren," he said, reading her face.

"Even if he sings, he's still looking at time. Those interviewing him know of his connections to ..." He hesitated as if forgetting who he was taking to.

"To?"

His neck flushed. "The same investigators who seized your father's property are investigating Flannery. They think they were all working for the same people."

Lauren held back a groan. She didn't want to hear the history behind her father and Justin Prendergast. Living through it had been enough.

He coughed, no doubt to cover his embarrassment."Still there is a ray of hope in all this."

She glanced at the sheriff waiting for him to elaborate.

"If the Revenuers seize his property, we might lose Mrs. Flannery too."

A pang of pity surged through her. "That's not fair. I don't like Mrs. Flannery, but she's not responsible for what her husband does."

"Life ain't fair, Miss Lauren. You know that better than most."

The truck let out a creak as it settled, drawing the sheriff's gaze. Lauren followed his eyes, her stomach sinking.

"Sounds like she's about ready to give up on you," he said with a half-smile, nodding toward the truck.

Lauren forced a small laugh. "She's just cranky."

His jaw tightened, the muscles flickering under his skin. "You might want a mechanic to take a look. Better to catch the trouble early than end up stranded."

Lauren nodded, but the suggestion sat like a stone in

her stomach. She barely had enough money for necessities, let alone repairs. "I'll think about it."

He studied her for a moment but didn't press. Instead, his tone shifted, growing more serious. "I saw Becky near the old mill yesterday. Despite my warning, she's still chasing after her brothers."

The knot in Lauren's stomach tightened. "She's not going to give up on them."

"That mill's trouble. Always has been. Moonshine, fights, even worse. You might want to remind her of that." He adjusted his coat, his expression softening. "You're steady, Miss Lauren. She listens to you, even if it doesn't always seem like it."

Lauren nodded, her throat tight. Becky wasn't reckless, at least, not in the obvious sense. But she had a way of throwing herself into things headfirst, ignoring risks until it was too late. Lauren had seen it before and knew how easily determination could turn dangerous. "I'll talk to her."

"Good." He tipped his hat, his boots thudding against the frosted dirt as he turned back toward the jailhouse. "And don't forget about that truck."

"Miss Lauren!" Hans called, his grin wide as he waved her over. "Can we pick our candy now?"

Thankful for the interruption, Lauren quickened her steps to catch up with the boys. "Only if you don't argue about it."

"Peppermint lasts longer," Cal insisted as he stomped inside ahead of her.

Hans had to have the last word. "But chocolate tastes better."

Lauren paused at the door, watching the boys dart toward the candy counter. Their chatter bounced off the store's wooden walls, carefree and light. For a moment, the warmth of their voices made her forget the cold pressing against her skin and the weight she carried in her chest.

She glanced back over her shoulder, catching sight of the sheriff climbing the steps to his office. His figure, solid and steady, disappeared inside, leaving her standing alone in the street.

CHAPTER 11

*L*auren stepped into the store, the door creaking shut behind her. The warmth inside felt foreign against her cold cheeks, but it didn't thaw the knot in her stomach.

Hans's laughter snapped her from her thoughts. She spotted him and Cal squabbling good-naturedly over the shelves, their faces alight with excitement.

Lauren let out a breath, her chest tightening. She envied their innocence, their ability to live only in the moment. For them, this was just a candy run. For her, it was one more day to get through. One more list of things to juggle before something, maybe the truck, maybe Becky, maybe everything, fell apart.

She closed her eyes for a beat, willing herself steady. One thing at a time, Lauren. One thing at a time.

"Miss Lauren!" Hans called again, his voice pulling her back. "Can I get a Clark Bar and a peppermint stick?"

"Not a chance."

Earl, tall and lanky with a mop of unruly hair, looked up from behind the counter and grinned.

"Morning, Miss Lauren. Boys."

"Morning, Earl." Lauren pulled out her shopping list from her pocket.

The boys darted to the candy jars, their voices rising in friendly debate.

"Have you ever tried a Clark Bar?" Hans asked, leaning close to peer at the rows of chocolate. "They're amazing!"

Cal wrinkled his nose. "But peppermint sticks are bigger! You can make them last all day!"

Earl chuckled as he bagged sugar for another customer. "You boys better decide quick. Miss Lauren doesn't look like she's got all day."

Lauren smiled but kept her focus on the shelves. She added flour and salt to her basket, though her mind wandered back to Becky. So she'd been looking for Luke alone? She was closer to her breaking point than they'd realized if she was taking risks like that.

The familiar murmur of conversation rose from near the fabric section. Lauren wasn't one to eavesdrop, but a sharp laugh caught her attention.

"Well," came Mrs. Curtis's clipped voice, "it's no wonder this country's in such a state. Father Coughlin says it plainly. These foreign influences have been dragging us down for years."

Lauren froze, her hand tightening around the basket.

"And right here in Delgany," Mrs. Simmons added, leaning closer. "The Meyers, for example. They've been here for years, sure, but have you ever seen them in church? Makes you wonder what they believe in."

Lauren set her basket down and approached, her pulse racing. She hoped her voice wouldn't betray her. "Good morning, ladies. I couldn't help but overhear."

Mrs. Curtis turned, her thin smile faltering slightly. "Miss Greenwood. Good morning. We were just discussing general matters of community concern."

Lauren met her gaze. "If you have concerns about the Meyers, I'd suggest speaking to them directly. They've been nothing but kind and hardworking, and they deserve the same respect as anyone else in this town."

Mrs. Simmons folded her arms, clearly bristling. "They don't even go to church, Lauren. Surely you understand how that looks."

"What it looks like," Lauren said, keeping her voice steady, "is a family doing their best to live quietly after facing unimaginable hardship. We really enjoyed having them to stay over Christmas and New Year at Hope House."

Mrs. Curtis raised an eyebrow. "Hope House, you say?"

"Yes," Lauren said. "I've invited the Meyers to move in. They'll be joining us soon."

Mrs. Simmons blinked, her jaw slack. Mrs. Curtis recovered faster, though her eyes narrowed. "That's certainly unexpected."

You will catch more bees with honey than vinegar, Lauren. Nanny Kat's voice echoed in her head. She softened her tone determined to convince these ladies they were wrong. "Chana and Victor have so much love to share, and I know it will help the children. Hope House isn't just a roof over their heads. It's a community. One where kindness matters more than where someone prays."

Mrs. Curtis pressed her lips together. "Well, I'm sure you mean well, Miss Greenwood. But you might find this town less accommodating than you think."

Lauren didn't flinch. "Then it's time Delgany remembered what being a community really means."

Mrs. Curtis's cheeks colored, and she turned abruptly to Mrs. Simmons. "Shall we go?"

As the two women left, Lauren spotted Mrs. Flannery coming in the door. She braced herself for more cutting remarks, but instead, Mrs. Flannery hesitated, casting a wary glance at Lauren before following the women out. The bell jingled as they disappeared into the cold.

Lauren let out a slow breath as she turned back toward the counter. Miss Chaney was standing nearby, having arrived unnoticed during the exchange.

"Well done," the postmistress said, setting her basket down. Her sharp eyes twinkled with quiet approval. "Not everyone would've had the nerve."

Lauren gave a faint smile. "It needed to be said."

Miss Chaney tilted her head slightly. "So, it's true about the Meyers, then? You've asked them to move in?"

"Yes. They were hesitant at first, but I think it's the right decision. For them and for the children."

Miss Chaney nodded slowly. "It is. Don't let anyone tell you otherwise."

Lauren felt the tension in her chest ease. "Thanks, Miss

Chaney. That means a lot." She glanced toward Earl, who was serving the boys. "Have you heard anything from Gene or Vivian?" Earl's parents had moved closer to their daughter, along with their two adopted children, Ellie-Mae and Dalton.

"Not recently. I don't like to ask Earl. I know he hopes they will return." Miss Chaney stopped talking as Hans and Cal returned, their faces alight with triumph. Hans held up a Clark Bar like a trophy.

"Look, Miss Lauren!" he exclaimed. "I told you chocolate's the best!"

"Peppermint sticks last longer," Cal muttered, though his grin betrayed that he didn't really mind losing the argument. He pulled a small paper bag from behind his back and held it out to Lauren. "Me and Hans put the rest of our money together and bought some candy for the others. We got everyone a piece each, even Shelley."

Lauren's chest tightened with warmth as she took the bag. "That was very thoughtful of you both," she said. "You've got kind hearts."

She glanced toward the counter where Earl stood, watching them with a knowing smile. She caught the way he'd slipped a few extra coins from the boys' pile back into their hands while ringing up the candy. The quiet generosity wasn't lost on her.

"Thank you, Earl," she said, her voice sincere as she met his eyes. "I think you made their day."

Earl waved a hand, his grin widening. "Ah, it's nothing, Miss Lauren. Just making sure good kids like them get a fair deal."

"Goodbye, Earl, Miss Chaney," Lauren said, her smile lingering as she guided the boys toward the door.

"See you soon, Miss Lauren," Earl called after them, the bell jingling as they stepped outside.

Lauren ruffled Cal's hair as they started down the street. "Come on, you two. We've got chores waiting at home."

Hans and Cal exchanged a quick glance before racing ahead, their laughter echoing in the crisp morning air. Lauren watched them for a moment, clutching the small paper bag in her hand. Why couldn't adults be as kind as children?

LAUREN PUSHED OPEN the heavy front door of Hope House, the faint, sweet scent of baking fruit filling the air. She set her basket on the entryway table, pausing to tug off her gloves and hang her coat. The warmth of the house seeped into her bones, chasing away the morning chill.

"Lauren?" called Nanny Kat's voice from the kitchen. "That you?"

"It's me," Lauren replied, her voice carrying over the faint hum of activity upstairs. The clatter of wooden blocks and the occasional peal of laughter told her the children were entertaining themselves for now.

She found Nanny Kat in the kitchen, standing at the counter, her hands expertly crimping the edge of a pie crust. A mason jar sat open nearby, the syrupy remains of canned peaches glistening inside.

"Using up the last of Norma's canning?" Lauren asked, leaning against the doorframe.

Nanny Kat nodded without looking up. "We had just enough peaches left to make one pie. Figured it'd be a nice treat for the little ones, and a reminder of her."

Lauren smiled. "They'll love it. You always know how to make something out of nothing."

Nanny Kat snorted lightly. "Comes with the job. You're back later than I expected. Everything alright?"

Lauren crossed to the table and sat down, her shoulders slumping. "It was a morning. I ran into Mrs. Curtis and Mrs. Simmons at Hillman's. They were gossiping about the Meyers, spouting off Father Coughlin's hateful nonsense."

Nanny Kat's hands stilled. She looked up, her sharp gaze locking onto Lauren. "What did you say to them?"

"I told them I'd invited the Meyers to move into Hope House," Lauren said simply.

Nanny Kat blinked, her hands dropping to her sides. "You told them? What'd they have to say about that?"

"They were shocked," Lauren admitted. "Mrs. Curtis warned me that the town might not be as welcoming as I think."

"Hmph," Nanny Kat huffed, turning back to the pie crust. She pressed the edges a little harder than necessary. "People like her don't need reasons to keep others out. They just like to feel important. But this house isn't the town. It's yours. And you're doing the right thing."

Before Lauren could respond, a small voice interrupted them from the doorway. "Miss Lauren? Why do people hate us?"

Lauren turned to see Rachel standing there, her small hands twisting the hem of her dress. Her brown eyes, so wide and full of uncertainty, stopped Lauren in her tracks. Behind her, Hans peeked out, his expression unusually serious.

Lauren's heart hurt. She glanced at Nanny Kat, who had frozen, her hands still resting on the counter.

"Nobody hates you, darling. Why would you say that?"

Rachel held her gaze. "Hans heard what those ladies in the shop said. That's what people in Germany said too. They were talking about Jews. They hate us."

Lauren patted the chair beside her. "Come here, Rachel."

Rachel hesitated, then shuffled over and climbed into the seat. Hans followed, standing close behind her like a quiet sentinel.

Lauren leaned forward, resting her forearms on the table. "They don't hate you sweetheart or your brother. Or the Meyers."

Confusion clouded Rachel's eyes.

"Sometimes, people believe things that aren't true," Lauren said carefully. "And instead of questioning those ideas, they hold onto them because it's easier than trying to understand someone different from themselves."

Rachel frowned, her small brow furrowing. "But why us? We didn't do anything wrong."

Lauren reached for her hand, squeezing it gently. "You're right. You didn't do anything wrong. And it's not about you. It's about their fears and prejudices. But what matters is that there are people who see the truth. People who care about you and your family, who know how kind and brave you are."

Hans looked up at her, his voice quiet but firm. "Like you?"

Lauren smiled. "Yes, like me. And Nanny Kat. And everyone here at Hope House. We're a family now, and families take care of each other."

Rachel's eyes glistened, but she gave a small nod. Hans placed a protective hand on her shoulder.

Lauren gave them each a hug, "Why don't you two check on the little ones upstairs? I'll be up soon."

Hans nodded and tugged Rachel's hand, leading her out of the kitchen.

When they were gone, Lauren let out a slow breath and glanced at Nanny Kat.

Nanny Kat wiped her hands on her apron. "Poor girl. It's not right for children to carry such heavy questions."

"No," Lauren agreed, rubbing her temples. "But if they're asking, they're already carrying them. All I can do is help lighten the load."

Nanny Kat gave a small hum of approval before tilting her head toward the clock on the wall. "I wonder if Becky will come down soon?"

Lauren hesitated for a second. "Sheriff Dillon saw her near the old mill yesterday."

Nanny Kat's lips pressed into a thin line. "I was afraid of that. No matter how often we tell her, she won't give up."

Lauren began unpacking her shopping. "He warned me the mill's dangerous. I'll, I mean, we'll have to talk to her again."

Nanny Kat rolled her eyes. "That girl's got a head full of stubbornness and a heart full of fire. Not an easy combination."

Lauren stood, smoothing her skirt. "No, it's not. But it's who she is."

"And she's lucky to have you looking out for her."

CHAPTER 12

"Miss Becky, will you come and see our surprise? Rachel said we should wait for Nanny Chana to arrive, but I'm too excited!" Lottie hopped from one foot to the other, her braids bouncing with each movement.

Becky wiped her hands on her apron, leaving faint traces of flour on the fabric, before taking Lottie's outstretched hand. "Did you and Rachel draw some pictures for the Meyers?"

The five year old nodded eagerly, her wide eyes sparkling with excitement. "Uh-huh. We wanted to make their room feel special!"

Lauren leaned against the counter, arms crossed, a playful smile tugging at her lips. "Why don't you bring your drawings down here to Miss Becky so she can finish her baking, Lottie?" she suggested, knowing full well Becky's cinnamon bread wasn't about to bake itself. There was no point in offering to help. Lauren knew the kitchen was strictly off-limits for her, except when it came to washing dishes.

Lottie shook her head vigorously, her determination unshakable. "Can't, Miss Lauren. It's not on paper. You have to come see it!"

Exchanging a bewildered look with Becky, Lauren set down the towel she'd been holding and followed the little girl out of the kitchen.

Lottie's excitement was infectious as they climbed the stairs toward the newly renovated rooms meant for the Meyers. The faint smell of fresh paint lingered in the hallway, mingling with the scent of cinnamon wafting up from the kitchen below.

"Close your eyes," Lottie instructed, stopping just outside the doorway. She clapped her hands together as if conducting a grand performance. "And no peeking! Open them when I say so."

Lauren exchanged an amused glance with Becky before obediently closing her eyes. She could hear Lottie's small footsteps padding across the floorboards as the child positioned herself dramatically in the middle of the room.

"Okay," Lottie chirped, barely containing her excitement. "You can open them now!"

Lauren opened her eyes and blinked, scanning the room. At first glance, everything appeared normal. The neatly made bed, the freshly painted white walls, the newly hung gingham curtains fluttering slightly in the breeze from the open window. She was about to ask what the "surprise" was when she noticed Becky standing frozen beside her, one hand over her mouth.

Then Lauren turned toward the far wall and gasped.

"Oh my ..." The words escaped her in a whisper, her stomach sinking as she took in the sight before her.

There, sprawling across the freshly painted white wall, was a hand-drawn picture. Childish, uneven figures stood in a crooked line, each one wearing an almost comical smile. A lopsided dog sat at their feet, its tail painted mid-wag.

"That's me and Rachel," Lottie announced proudly, pointing to two smaller figures holding hands near the center. "The dog is Shadow. And there you are, Miss Becky! And you too, Miss Lauren, with the dark hair."

Lauren squinted, barely making out what must have been her "figure," distinguishable only by the black scribbles that seemed to represent her hair. Next to her stood a crooked figure labeled "Nanny Kat," and beside that, a group of slightly taller shapes.

"And that's the Meyers! We didn't have time to draw Fred and the other boys, but ..." Lottie's voice trailed off when she noticed Becky's shoulders shaking.

Lauren wasn't sure whether Becky was laughing or crying. As for herself, she didn't know what to feel. Laughter bubbled at the edges of her throat, but it was overshadowed by the rising panic in her chest. The wall, the freshly painted, pristinely white wall, was ruined. And the Meyers were due to arrive that very afternoon.

The room was silent, save for the sound of the breeze rustling the curtains.

Becky's hand remained clamped over her mouth as she turned slightly away, her shoulders still trembling.

Tears welled in Lottie's eyes as the silence dragged on. Her lower lip quivered. "You don't like our picture, do you?" she whispered. She stepped back, looking from Lauren to Becky, her earlier excitement crumbling into confusion and hurt.

Lauren's heart twisted. She crouched down to Lottie's level, resting her hands lightly on the child's shoulders. "Lottie, it's not that we don't like it. It's a beautiful picture, and you worked so hard on it. But …"

"But we needed to keep the wall plain for the Meyers," Becky finished gently, stepping forward and kneeling beside Lauren. She reached out, brushing a stray tear from Lottie's cheek. "They'll need the space to make it their own. Do you understand?"

Lottie sniffled, looking back at the drawing as if seeing it in a new light. "We just wanted to make it special for them."

Lauren couldn't be angry with the child. "And you did, sweetheart. It's special because it shows how much you care. But we'll find another way to welcome the Meyers, one that won't get us in trouble with Terry for messing up his paint job." She gave Lottie a playful wink, trying to coax a smile from her.

"Maybe we can paint over it and put your drawin's on paper instead," Becky suggested. "That way the Meyers can hang them wherever they like."

Lottie hesitated, then nodded slowly, wiping at her eyes with the back of her hand. "Okay … but Shadow looks really good, doesn't he?"

Lauren and Becky exchanged a glance before nodding in unison.

"He's the best-looking dog I've ever seen," Lauren said.

A small smile crept back onto Lottie's face, and Becky ruffled her hair gently. "I'll find Terry and ask him to repaint the wall," she said. "But first, you and Rachel can draw Shadow on paper so he doesn't disappear forever."

Lottie perked up at the idea, her earlier sadness fading as she dashed out of the room to find Rachel.

Once she was gone, Lauren stood and turned to Becky, letting out a heavy sigh. "Terry's going to have a fit."

Becky smiled, shaking her head. "He'll get over it. It's Hope House. We're used to fixin' a little chaos."

Lauren chuckled, glancing back at the wall one last time. "I'll never forget this one."

Terry painted the last stroke onto the wall, stepping back to survey his work. He held the wide brush loosely in one hand, its bristles stained white from the fresh coat. A bucket of paint sat at his feet, a few smudges already dotting the floor despite his careful efforts.

"I nearly feel bad for removin' the children's picture. It did add some character to the walls." Becky rubbed her arms. "The white makes the room look bigger but it's a little cold, don't you think?"

Lauren agreed but there was no point in worrying about the color choice now. "The Meyers will have their own things. They'll soon brighten up the place." She turned to Terry, "Thank you again, Terry. You were kind not to tell the girls off for damaging your paintwork."

Terry shrugged, his ears turning pink as he began cleaning the paintbrush, dunking it in a tin of turpentine on the floor. "They were just tryin' to be nice."

He disappeared through the doorway, his arms full of brushes and the bucket of paint. Lauren lingered for a moment, watching him go. He'd grown so much since she'd first come to Hope House, and she felt a small swell of pride at the man he was becoming. Turning back to the room, she crossed to the window and pushed it open as wide as possible, letting in a gust of fresh air to carry away the lingering smell of paint and turpentine. She couldn't help but think of the first time they had remodeled this space. Norma and Bart had been so excited about living in Hope House.

"They'll be happy here," Becky said softly, almost as if reading Lauren's mind. "A fresh start in a safe place. That's what Hope House is all about."

Lauren nodded but stayed silent, her throat tightening with a mix of emotions.

"Stop lollygaggin'," Becky teased, tossing a cleaning cloth at her. "This room isn't goin' to clean itself."

Lauren caught the cloth, a small smile tugging at her lips. For a moment, she was tempted to throw it back, but Becky's expression stopped her. Beneath the teasing glint in her friend's eyes, there was understanding.

"Let's concentrate on the happy memories." Becky grabbed her own cloth and started wiping down the windowsill. "Not the sad times, like when you hadn't cleaned a day in your life."

The cloth sailed back at her before she could duck, smacking her square on the shoulder. Becky let out a laugh, holding up her hands in mock surrender. "All right, all right, truce!"

Lauren grinned, the knot in her chest loosening just a little. Together, they set to work, their laughter and banter filling the empty room.

Terry arrived back sometime later. "I think I should head into Delgany and collect them, Lauren. Those clouds look like we are in for a downpour. The weather man has been threatenin' heavy rain for days now."

Lauren gave the room a quick glance over. "The wall isn't quite dry but we'll just tell them to be careful. Thank you, Terry, for collecting them."

He nodded and headed off. Lauren picked up the cleaning tools and headed back downstairs. In the kitchen, under Becky's supervision, the girls were happily recreating their drawings, this time on paper.

* * *

TERRY RETURNED with the old truck packed so high with mismatched furniture and boxes that Lauren wondered how it hadn't tipped over on the drive from Delgany. She tucked a strand of hair behind her ear, adjusting the hem of her cardigan, and braced herself for what was to come. Where were they going to put all their stuff?

The thought made her chest tighten. She had wanted

this, hadn't she? For Chana and Victor to feel safe enough, welcome enough, to call Hope House their home. And yet, she worried. Would they be able to adjust? Not just to the cramped space, but to the constant noise and bustle of the children. Hope House was a sanctuary, yes, but no one would ever accuse it of being quiet or peaceful.

Lauren stepped off the porch as the truck came to a groaning halt. Victor climbed down from the driver's side, moving with the careful deliberation of a man who had carried too many burdens for too long. His gray hair was combed neatly back, and his coat, frayed at the cuffs, was buttoned as tightly as the stiff expression on his face. He nodded politely to Lauren but didn't smile. His pride, Lauren thought, was a shield he carried everywhere, armor against a world that had given him every reason to distrust it.

Chana, by contrast, emerged more slowly from the passenger seat, smoothing the folds of her dark skirt as she stood. Her eyes, dark and intelligent, carried the weight of a life turned upside down, but when she saw Lauren, Becky, Nanny Kat, and the children waiting to greet them, her lips curved into a small, genuine smile.

"Hello, everyone," Chana said warmly, her voice steady despite the evident weariness in her posture. "It's good to see you again."

Lauren stepped forward, opening her arms for a hug. "Welcome to your new home. We all hope you'll be very happy here."

The children moved forward in a chattering wave, their enthusiasm bubbling over before anyone could stop it.

They bombarded Chana and Victor with questions about the truck and its contents, their voices overlapping in an uncontainable cacophony. Chana's smile faltered, her gaze darting nervously between the small faces.

Lauren caught the flicker of overwhelm and quickly raised a hand to Carly. "Carly, can you round up the others and get them started on chores? I think it's a little too much excitement for now."

Carly nodded, stepping in with a reassuring smile. "Come on, everyone. Let's give Mr. Victor and Nanny Chana some space to settle in."

The children groaned in unison but obeyed, scattering toward the barn and kitchen. Lauren let out a quiet breath of relief as the noise dissipated. Chana offered a grateful smile, while Victor's shoulders eased, just slightly.

"Come inside," Nanny Kat said briskly, opening the door. "Let's get you some coffee and cinnamon bread before we even think about unloading that truck. Becky baked it this morning, and it's still warm."

Lauren followed them into the house, sparing one last glance at the overloaded truck before stepping inside.

VICTOR SET down a heavy trunk in the corner of their new room, his breathing steady but labored. He surveyed the space, his expression unreadable, the silence pressing against Lauren's nerves. Chana, meanwhile, opened one of the smaller boxes, her movements careful and deliberate. Piece by piece, she unwrapped its contents: a chipped porcelain teacup, a pair of candlesticks, a photograph in a silver frame. Each item seemed to carry the weight of memory.

Lauren watched as Chana placed the photo on the nightstand. It was a black-and-white image of three young children; a young man with dark hair and a confident, boyish grin, a girl on either side of him. The glass was cracked, but the frame gleamed from careful polishing.

"Your children?" Lauren asked.

Chana stilled, her fingers resting on the edge of the frame. Her expression betrayed nothing, but her gaze lingered on the photograph longer than it needed to. Finally, she pointed. "Rebecca, like Becky but we call her Rivka, our eldest. Hannah, our middle child and Pieter. Our youngest."

Lauren's throat tightened at the sorrow in Chana's voice. She knew the story, how Pieter had rushed to the aid of a friend and was killed by Hitler's men in the early 1920s. She began unpacking another box, giving Chana the space to collect herself. The silence in the room felt heavy, filled with unspoken pain.

Victor finally broke it, his voice clipped and terse. "This will do. Better than do. We'll make it work." His tone was gruff, and Lauren could hear the pride layered beneath his words. Accepting charity clearly chafed him, even here, at Hope House, where everyone understood what it was to need help.

"We're glad you're here," Lauren said, meeting his eyes. "Hope House is your home now."

Victor gave her a curt nod, but it was Chana who

reached out, her hand brushing Lauren's arm. "Thank you," she said. The sincerity in her voice left no room for doubt.

Just then, the door burst open, and Cal bounded in, his face alight with curiosity. "Mr. Victor! Nanny Chana!" he exclaimed, skidding to a halt. "You're really staying this time, huh?"

Victor raised an eyebrow at the boy's boldness, while Chana smiled warmly. "Yes, Cal. We are."

"Good," Cal declared, plopping himself onto the edge of their bed without hesitation. "Because I've got about a million questions for you."

"Cal..." Lauren began, her tone warning.

But Chana held up a hand. "It's all right." She turned to Cal, her smile patient. "What would you like to know?"

His grin widened. "Can you teach me German? Hans said he would but all he wants to do is learn English. I already know enough English."

Victor chuckled, a warm, unexpected sound that softened the tension in the room. "Why would you want to learn German?"

"Because it sounds cool!" Cal said, as if the answer were obvious. "And Hans told me about that Krampus guy! He's not allowed to come here, right? We're not that naughty. But we like the guy who comes and puts candy in our shoes. And the food like strudel! It's the best thing I've ever tasted."

Victor's chuckle deepened, but Lauren noticed the way Chana's smile faltered, just for a moment. The boy's enthusiasm, innocent as it was, seemed to strike a chord.

Lauren stepped in. "Come on, Cal. Let the Meyers settle in. I'm sure you've got chores waiting for you."

Cal groaned but obeyed, trudging out of the room. Lauren glanced back at Chana and Victor. "Sorry about that. I'll ask Terry to put a lock on your door, just to make sure you get some privacy."

Chana's smile returned, faint but genuine. "Thank you, Lauren. That would be appreciated."

Lauren nodded, stepping back. "We hope you'll be happy here. But no matter what, you're part of our family now. Whether you stay here or decide to live on the moon."

* * *

Lauren found Chana in the kitchen, scrubbing the counters long after everyone else had gone to bed. She hesitated in the doorway, unsure whether to interrupt.

"You don't have to work so hard, you know," Lauren said finally, stepping inside.

Chana didn't look up immediately. When she finally spoke, her voice was low and measured. "Cal ... he reminds me of Pieter."

Lauren leaned against the counter, waiting.

"When Pieter was Cal's age, he was the same. Curious about everything. Always asking questions, always imagining a better world." Her hands stilled on the cloth. "I never imagined that same world would take him away."

The words settled heavy in the air. Lauren wanted to say something, but nothing seemed adequate. She placed a hand on Chana's arm, her touch gentle. "Germany didn't take Pieter. People who chose hate over humanity did."

Tears welled in Chana's eyes. "How do I teach Cal about my culture, Lauren? About my language, my traditions? When I don't even believe in them anymore?"

Lauren squeezed her arm. "Teach him about the Germany you loved. The one that gave you Pieter. Share the memories that mattered. That's the Germany he should know."

CHAPTER 13

*A*fter what felt like hours of tossing and turning, Lauren finally gave up on sleep. She swung her legs over the side and slipped her feet into the worn slippers waiting on the floor.

Pulling her dressing gown tight around her, she opened the bedroom door carefully. The house was still, wrapped in the kind of deep, quiet stillness that only came in the dead of night. Rain pattered softly against the shutters, a steady rhythm that seemed to amplify the silence.

Lauren descended the stairs slowly, avoiding the middle step that always creaked. At the bottom, the chill of the stone floor seeped through her slippers, sharp and bracing. She was reaching for the kitchen door when she noticed a faint light spilling through the crack, pooling on the wooden floor.

She froze. Was someone up? It wasn't unusual for Becky or Nanny Kat to have restless nights, but something about the stillness felt different.

Pushing the door open wider, she stepped into the kitchen and stopped abruptly.

Victor sat at the table, hunched over a letter he held in both hands. His glasses rested on the table beside him, and his face was etched with an emotion she couldn't immediately place. Sorrow? Weariness? A little of both, perhaps. He glanced up, startled, and brushed at his eyes, his movements stiff and self-conscious.

Lauren's first instinct was to retreat, to slip back up the stairs and pretend she hadn't seen him. It felt wrong, almost intrusive, to witness such a private moment. But something in the slump of his shoulders rooted her in place.

She cleared her throat. "Victor? Are you all right?"

He straightened, slipping the letter onto the table. "Ja, I'm good," he said, though his voice was thick with something unsaid. He began to rise. "Did I wake you?"

Lauren waved him back into his seat. "I couldn't sleep," she admitted. "I was going to make some coffee. Would you like a cup?"

"Coffee won't help you sleep," he said, a faint smile tugging at his lips. "My Chana would suggest hot milk."

Lauren smiled back. "Nanny Kat would, too. But sometimes nothing but coffee works. Can I get you a cup?"

He nodded. "If it's no trouble. Perhaps you wanted privacy?"

Lauren shook her head as she moved toward the stove. "No, I don't mind the company." She glanced at the letters on the table. "You picked up some post from Miss Chaney?"

"Ja. We have some good friends still living in Germany. They write letters telling painful stories. I ... I read them first and the less upsetting ones I share with Chana." He scratched his head. "Maybe you think that is wrong. That I am being deceitful."

Lauren set the kettle on the stove and turned back to him. "That doesn't sound deceitful to me. You're protecting her."

Victor's shoulders sagged, relief flickering across his face. "I hope so. She has been through so much already. I do not want her to carry more than she has to." He paused, his expression softening. "She is happier now. Being here, with you and the children, has given her ..." He gestured, searching for the words. "A new life. How do you say it?"

"A fresh start," Lauren supplied. "We love having her, both of you, here." Lauren set out two cups and poured the coffee into them. "Would you like something to eat?"

He patted his stomach. "No thank you. I have enough."

Victor leaned back slightly, studying her with a quiet, perceptive gaze. "You've been distracted lately," he observed. "Is everything all right?"

Lauren hesitated, her fingers brushing the edge of the cup. She hadn't meant to burden Victor with her troubles. But something about his calm demeanor, the wisdom etched into his features, made her want to talk.

"It's Edward," she admitted, her voice barely above a whisper. "We had a fight."

Victor nodded slowly, removing his glasses and setting them on the table. "I see. May I ask what about?"

Lauren exhaled, the words spilling out in a rush. "He

wants to go back to Germany. To help people like your family like Aunt Rae. But it's so dangerous, Victor. The last time, they arrested him. They ..." Her voice caught, and she swallowed hard. "They nearly killed him. I can't let him do that again."

Victor's brow furrowed, his expression growing thoughtful. He clasped his hands together, leaning forward slightly. "Edward has a strong sense of duty," he said gently. "I understand his desire to return. But you are right to be concerned. Germany is not safe. Not for someone like him."

Lauren nodded, her chest tightening. "I tried to tell him that, but he's so determined. He said he can't live with himself if he doesn't try to help."

Victor tilted his head, a faint smile playing at the corners of his lips. "That sounds like Edward. I do not know him well, but I could see from Christmas, he is stubborn and very much in love with you."

She blushed, lifting the cup to her mouth and blowing on the contents.

"He put his health at risk by coming to Hope House to propose to you. That kind of love doesn't just go ... poof." Victor gestured with his hands, smiling at her. Then he glanced at the pile of letters. "He is also a man of honor, one who will not desert his people at their time of need. If I was younger, I would hope I could be as brave as him."

"So you agree with him? You think I am being selfish?"

"Nein, no. Not selfish, but a woman in love." He took a sip of his coffee, his forehead clenching in thought. "Perhaps there is a better way. A compromise, if that is the correct word."

Lauren's heart quickened, and she leaned forward. "What do you mean?"

Victor reached for the envelope on the table, his fingers brushing the edge of the parchment. "I have a friend in France. He works to help Jewish families escape across the borders into Switzerland. It is dangerous, yes, but not as dangerous as remaining in Germany itself. My friend, if he is caught, risks French prison, but most people do not end up needing treatment for vehicular injuries on release from French captivity."

Lauren shuddered, remembering how the doctors had scoffed at the explanation the Germans had given for Edward's condition.

"Edward could base himself in a place like Switzerland or France. Somewhere he could help without putting himself directly in harm's way."

Lauren blinked, her mind racing. "Switzerland? France?"

Victor nodded. "Switzerland is neutral, and there are already individuals and small groups working to assist refugees. France, while not neutral, is still safer than Germany—for now, at least. Edward could work with people like my friend. He could help organize escape routes, provide resources, and save lives without stepping directly into the lion's den."

The weight in Lauren's chest eased slightly, and she clung to the idea like a lifeline. "That could work," she murmured, more to herself than to Victor. "It would be safer. He'd still be helping, but he wouldn't be ..." She trailed off, unable to finish the sentence.

Victor's gaze softened. "You love him very much."

She looked up, her eyes brimming with tears. "More than anything. But sometimes it feels like his love for me isn't enough to keep him safe."

Victor shook his head. "It is not a question of love, Lauren. Edward's actions come from his heart, from the same place as his love for you. But you are right to want to protect him. And if he listens to you, perhaps this compromise will be enough."

Lauren reached across the table, squeezing Victor's hand. "Thank you," she said, her voice thick with emotion. "I don't know what I'd do without you and Chana."

Victor smiled warmly. "You would manage, as you always do. But I am glad to help."

* * *

THE NEXT AFTERNOON, Lauren stood outside Edward's hospital room, her hands clutching the strap of her purse. She drew in a shaky breath, her pulse fluttering like a trapped bird. After her talk with Victor, hope had started to bloom in her chest, fragile and tentative. But the thought of facing Edward again, of convincing him, still made her stomach churn.

Steeling herself, she pushed the door open.

Edward was seated in his usual spot by the window, sunlight brushing the sharp planes of his face. A book rested on his lap, his good hand idly turning the corner of a page. He glanced up as the door creaked, and his expression shifted from surprise to cautious warmth.

"Lauren," he said, his voice tinged with relief. "You came."

She closed the door behind her, forcing a small smile. "I couldn't stay away forever."

He gestured to the chair across from him. "Sit. Please."

Lauren crossed the room, her heart hammering in her chest, and lowered herself into the chair. The silence that followed was thick with the weight of their last conversation, the faint ticking of the clock amplifying her unease.

"I've been thinking." Her fingers curled around the edge of her purse. "About what you said."

Edward leaned forward slightly, his gaze searching hers. "And?"

"I understand why you want to go back. I do. But I can't. I can't let you walk into Germany again, Edward. Not after what happened to you there."

His shoulders tensed, but he didn't interrupt, his jaw tightening as he waited for her to continue.

"There has to be another way," she said, her voice firm despite the lump in her throat. "Victor and I were talking. He told me about people in France and Switzerland. People helping refugees escape. You could base yourself there. It would still be dangerous, but not as dangerous as going back into Germany itself."

Edward tilted his head, his brows drawing together. "France? Switzerland?"

Lauren's heart pounded. "Yes. You'd be close enough to help, organizing routes, funding escapes, but you wouldn't be walking straight into the lion's den. You'd be saving lives, Edward, just like you want to. But you'd be safer. And you'd be closer to me."

Edward leaned back slightly, his gaze drifting to the window. For a long moment, he was silent, the muted hum of the radiator and the soft rustle of curtains filling the quiet.

Finally, he looked back at her, his expression quizzical. "You'd be all right with that? If I went to France? Or Switzerland?"

Her breath hitched, and she nodded. "I'd miss you every second. But I'd rather miss you than lose you."

Edward's lips curved into a faint, rueful smile. "You've always been stronger than I deserve."

Lauren reached across the space between them, taking his hand in hers. "I'm not strong, Edward. I'm terrified. But I love you, and I'll do whatever it takes to keep you safe."

His fingers tightened around hers, warm and steady despite the faint tremor in his hand. "I'll think about it. I promise."

Lauren's chest ached with relief, though she knew the road ahead would still be difficult.

Edward's eyes twinkled, the corners of his mouth quirking up. "Would it be too soon to ask for a kiss? My walking has improved, but getting to my feet unassisted is …"

She cut him off with a soft kiss, her lips brushing his before she leaned her forehead against his. "We are both very stubborn. That doesn't bode well for the future."

He grinned and curled his good arm around her waist,

dragging her onto his lap. She shrieked, her laugh spilling into the quiet room. "What if someone comes in?"

"Let them. We're a newly engaged couple planning our wedding." He leaned in and stole a kiss. "At least I hope you still want to marry me?"

"Very much so." She kissed him again but, fearing a nurse might interrupt them, reluctantly slipped off his lap and back into her chair.

She held his hand, their fingers entwined.

"Tell me about Hope House," Edward said, his tone soft but curious. "How are the children? Becky? Any news? Tell me everything."

Lauren hesitated, her thumb brushing across the back of his hand. "The children are fine. Well, mostly. Maisie's been fighting a fever, but Nanny Kat's keeping a close eye on her." She paused, her gaze drifting toward the window. "It's Becky I'm worried about."

Edward's brows knitted. "Becky? Why?"

"She's restless," Lauren admitted. "She keeps disappearing for hours, sometimes longer. I know she's out searching for Luke. Even after what happened at the mill, she won't let it go."

Edward frowned, his thumb tracing a thoughtful line along the edge of her hand. "She's grieving in her own way. But heading into danger, especially with smugglers involved, isn't the answer."

"I've tried to tell her that," Lauren said, her voice tinged with frustration. "But you know Becky. She won't listen. She's convinced that if she doesn't keep looking, she'll lose him forever."

Edward sighed, leaning back in his chair. "She might be right, but it doesn't make it any less dangerous. If Luke's involved with those men, they won't take kindly to interference."

Lauren nodded, the ache in her chest deepening. "That's what Sheriff Dillon thinks too. He said Foxy Flannery has been involved with smugglers for a long time. He hinted since before my father ... and Justin's time."

His silence confused her. "You aren't surprised?"

He shrugged his shoulders. "Nothing surprises me when it comes to your father or that man. And Foxy isn't a good judge of character."

Lauren sensed he knew more than he was letting on but the last thing she wanted to talk about today was her father or him.

"With Becky being so stubborn, I'm afraid she's going to get herself hurt."

Edward clasped her hand. "She's lucky to have you. You'll find a way to help her."

Lauren managed a faint smile, though her chest remained tight. "I hope you're right."

Edward's gaze drifted toward the window, his jaw tightening. "And what about Ian? How's his investigation coming along?"

She tilted her head, surprised. "How did you know about Ian's concerns?"

He gave her a faint smile. "I have my ways. Besides, it's not hard to guess. Ian's got connections in law enforcement. They've been worried about Nazi sympathizers for a while now."

Lauren exhaled, the weight of the conversation settling over her. "He's been talking about the German-American Bund. Apparently, they've started organizing rallies, even in places like Riverhaven. He said they're passing out pamphlets, talking about 'American purity' and other nonsense."

Edward's expression darkened, his lips pressing into a thin line. "It's not nonsense to the people who believe it. The Bund isn't just spreading propaganda. It's laying the groundwork for something more dangerous. Hatred has a way of growing roots if it's left unchecked."

"That's what Ian said," Lauren murmured. "He's worried it'll turn people against families like the Meyers. Against Hans and Rachel." Her voice trembled slightly. "I can't let that happen. I won't."

He squeezed her hand, his grip firm despite the faint tremor that lingered in his fingers. "We won't," he said. "But it won't be easy. The world's changing. It's growing darker every day."

She looked at him, her chest tightening at the weariness in his eyes. "And that's why you feel you must go. To fight back."

He nodded, his gaze steady. "Exactly. But it's not just me. You're fighting too, in your own way. Hope House, the children, it's a kind of resistance, even if it doesn't look like it."

Lauren blinked back the sting of tears, her voice steady despite the emotion rising in her chest. "And what about you, Edward? If you go to France, or Switzerland, how do you fight without losing yourself?"

His lips curved into a faint, rueful smile. "I'll find a way. With you beside me, even from here, I'll find a way." He hesitated before adding, "I know it is a lot to ask of you. I have thought and thought about it. "I love you, I do. More than you will ever know."

Her heart almost stopped, making it difficult to breathe, "But?"

"This is something I must do. I can't just turn my back. That would be like asking you to walk away from an injured child, in a burning house, about to fall into a flooding river."

She smacked him lightly with her hand. "I get the picture." She stood and leaned down to kiss him again. "I might understand, but it doesn't mean I have to like it."

Lauren stood in the kitchen doorway, the cold wet air creeping in as she watched Becky and Will on the porch. Becky sat on the top step, gripping something in her hands, while Will leaned against the railing, his arms crossed. The tension between them was almost palpable.

Lauren hesitated before stepping outside, the screen door creaking behind her. "It's getting colder," she said, glancing at Becky. "You'll both catch your death sitting out here."

"I'm fine." Becky's voice lacked its usual sharpness.

Will straightened, his expression grim. "She wants to charge back up the mountain without a plan, just because she thinks she can handle it on her own."

"I'm right here, Will," Becky snapped. "Don't talk about me like I'm some stubborn mule."

Will arched an eyebrow. "You're actin' like one."

"Enough," Lauren cut in, stepping between them. "What's going on?"

Will huffed, pushing off the railing. "She wants to rush back up the mountain, no matter the risks."

"Because Luke's my brother," Becky said fiercely, rising to her feet. "He's in trouble, and I'm not sittin' here waitin' for someone else to fix it."

Lauren's eyes darted to Becky's hands, noticing for the first time the object she was clutching. "What's that?" she asked.

Becky hesitated, her fingers tightening around the item. Finally, she held it out, revealing a knife with a worn, carved handle. The initials M.T. were etched into the wood, faded but unmistakable.

Lauren's breath caught. "Is that—"

"Matthew's," Becky said, her voice trembling. "Pa gave it to him on his 12th birthday. They went huntin' together for the first time, just the two of them. Ma was worried but Pa said Matt was a man not a child. And he needed to learn how to provide for the family."

Lauren reached out, touching the knife gingerly. The wood was smooth, worn from years of use, and the sight of it made her chest ache.

"Where did you find it?" Lauren asked.

Becky blushed, her eyes not meeting Lauren's. "I found it when I went back to the old mill. I hoped Luke would be there. But all I found was this." Becky rubbed her finger against the wooden handle. "But it means Matt was there. Or Matt gave this to Luke."

Will's face softened slightly, but his tone remained firm. "Becky, I know this means somethin' to you. I get it. But runnin' back up there tonight or tomorrow isn't going to solve anythin'."

Becky glared at him. "You don't get it, Will. That knife. It's proof he hasn't forgotten. It means he's still Luke, no matter what mess he's gotten into. And I'm not goin' to sit here while he's ..."

"While he's what?" Will interrupted. "Alive? Becky, if you rush in without thinkin', you could get yourself hurt, or worse, push him farther away."

"That's not your decision to make!" Becky shot back, her voice rising.

"It's not yours alone, either!" Will countered, stepping closer. "You're not the only one who cares about him. And if you'd stop bein' so bullheaded for once, you'd realize you've got people who want to help you."

Becky's jaw worked, and for a moment, Lauren thought she might slap him. But instead, she turned sharply, her shoulders heaving as she fought for control.

Becky didn't look up. "It was the only thing Daddy ever gave him," she murmured. "And now he's runnin' with men who'd spit on everythin' Daddy stood for."

Will crossed his arms, his voice steady. "Maybe he's not runnin' with them because he wants to. Maybe he doesn't have a choice."

Becky's head snapped up, her glare sharp. "And maybe he does. Maybe he's just like them now."

"You don't believe that," Lauren said.

Becky hesitated, her fingers brushing the knife. "I don't know what to believe anymore."

Lauren reached out, placing a hand over Becky's. "Then believe this: He's still your brother. And you're not going to lose him. Not while we've still got a chance to bring him back."

Will nodded. "She's right. And when we go back up that mountain, we're goin' together. No more runnin' off on your own."

Becky looked at him, her expression wavering between defiance and something softer. Finally, she nodded.

CHAPTER 14

"Isn't that the children? What are they doin' home so early?" Becky asked, pausing mid-sentence as the sound of Will's truck rumbled up the driveway.

Lauren set her cup down and moved to open the front door. A burst of damp, cool air greeted her as she watched the children spilling out of the truck, their chatter mingling with the steady patter of rain.

Will climbed down from the cab, calling over the sound of the downpour. "School's closed. Sheriff's orders. Seems the flood warnin's are getting worse."

Lauren nodded briskly, shooing the children inside as they dripped rainwater onto the porch. "Go on, all of you! Up the stairs and change into dry clothes before you catch your deaths. Leave your boots by the door!"

She turned back to Will, who stood on the porch, removing his coat and hat. Becky walked up beside her, hands on her hips. "Come in and have somethin' hot to eat." She leaned in, giving Will a quick kiss before turning toward the kitchen. "I've got soup on the stove," she called over her shoulder, disappearing inside without waiting for a reply.

Will hung his wet coat on the swing and set his hat beside it, pausing to take off his shoes. "They're soaked through," he said, shaking his head. "No point in bringin' them inside."

Lauren glanced down as he removed his second shoe, catching sight of a small hole in the toe of his sock. One damp toe peeked through. Will froze when he noticed her looking, a flush creeping up his neck. "Sorry. Wasn't expectin' anyone but me to see that," he muttered, sheepishly rubbing the back of his neck.

Lauren smirked, nudging him playfully. "Soon, you'll have a wife who won't let you out of the house without being properly dressed. Come inside before she comes looking for you and sees it herself."

Will chuckled, shaking his head as he stepped inside. "Becky already has enough ammunition to tease me. No need to add to it."

Lauren rolled her eyes and handed him a towel. "Go sit down in the kitchen before you drip all over the place. I'll leave Becky to warm you up." Laughing as the red flush covered his neck and face, Lauren headed up the stairs to check on the children.

* * *

By late afternoon, the rain hadn't let up, the steady drumming against the windows casting a soft rhythm over the house. In the kitchen, however, the sound was barely noticeable amid the quiet hum of activity.

Victor sat at the long table, his posture straight, his hands moving with deliberate precision as he measured a length of paper. Beside him, Fred hunched over a drawing, his pencil poised as he concentrated on the sketch of a small table. Carly and Shelley leaned in, their eyes wide with curiosity as they watched Victor guide Fred's movements.

Lauren paused in the doorway, unnoticed at first. She had never seen Carly and Shelley volunteer for extra lessons, particularly math.

Victor tapped the ruler on the table lightly, drawing Fred's attention. "Now, Fred, if you're building a table, what's the first thing you need to know?"

Fred blinked, his brow creasing. "The size?"

Victor nodded approvingly. "That's right. And what happens if one leg is even half an inch too short?"

Fred's expression brightened with understanding. "It wobbles!"

"Exactly. Measurements are the foundation of everything. They have to be precise."

Fred leaned forward eagerly, pointing to the ruler. "And that's what this is for, right?"

"Yes," Victor said, lifting the ruler. "But do you know why an inch is the size it is?"

Fred shook his head, and Carly, her curiosity bubbling over, piped up. "Someone just made it up, didn't they?"

Victor chuckled softly. "Not exactly. An inch was originally based on the width of a man's thumb. People used what they had, something they could see and feel, to measure."

Fred held up his own thumb, inspecting it with exaggerated seriousness. "So if I was building something back then, I could just use my thumb?"

Victor's eyes glinted with humor. "In theory. But you'd have to make sure it was always the same thumb. That's why we have tools now, to keep things accurate."

Fred's lips quirked into a grin as he studied the ruler again. "And are inches the same everywhere?"

"Ah, good question," Victor said, picking up a measuring tape. "No, most of the world uses the metric system, centimeters and meters. Those are based on decimals, which make them easier to calculate. But here in America, we use inches and feet."

Fred frowned thoughtfully. "Which is better?"

Victor spread his hands. "Neither is better. They're just different systems. What matters is knowing how to work with the tools you have, and being precise no matter the system."

Shelley tilted her head, her tone curious. "You can't measure one side in inches and the other in centimeters?"

"Absolutely not," Victor replied with a chuckle. "Unless you want a table that wobbles, falls over, or doesn't fit together at all."

Lauren finally stepped into the room, her voice warm as she teased, "Looks like you've got quite the workshop going here."

Victor leaned back in his chair, satisfaction evident in his expression. "Fred's a quick learner. He's got a natural talent for this."

Fred's cheeks turned pink, though he didn't look up from his sketch. "Victor's good at explaining it. Makes it make sense."

Lauren moved closer, glancing over Fred's shoulder. "That's going to be a fine table. Shelley, are you taking notes for your own project?"

Shelley grinned. "Maybe. I think I'll carve flowers into my table legs."

Victor chuckled, shaking his head. "One step at a time, Shelley."

CHAPTER 15

A week went by and still the rain drummed steadily against the windows. Chana stood at the kitchen counter, her hands deftly working the dough with rhythmic, practiced motions. Each slap and push seemed purposeful, coaxing the flour and yeast into submission. The warm air carried the scent of cinnamon, mingling with the earthy tang of yeast.

From the corner, Cal leaned against the wall, arms folded tight across his chest, his face screwed into a skeptical frown. "I don't see why you have to slap it like that," he muttered. "Looks like a lotta work for bread. Can't you just buy it?"

Becky let out an exaggerated gasp from the table, where she was peeling apples. "Cal! You sound like a city boy. Around here, we've always made bread from scratch. You've seen us do it."

"Never paid attention before," Cal grumbled. "But now you've got me stuck in the kitchen instead of playing with the others..."

Lauren, rolling up her sleeves, shot him a pointed look. "When you learn how to behave and stop pulling Shelley's hair, you can go back with the others. For now, you stay here where we can keep an eye on you."

Cal's mouth opened, probably to argue, but as Lauren's gaze held steady, his shoulders slumped. "She deserved..." he muttered, before catching himself and glancing away, his ears pink.

Chana, oblivious or intentionally ignoring the tension, glanced up from her dough. Her dark eyes glimmered with something mischievous. "Bread made with your hands tastes better," she said lightly. "And it's good practice."

"For who?" Cal shot back, wrinkling his nose. "Looks like women's work to me."

Lauren nearly dropped the mixing bowl she'd picked up. "Cal!" she exclaimed, half-shocked, half-laughing. "Do you want to dig yourself into a bigger hole?"

Chana paused, brushing a stray strand of hair from her forehead. "If it's women's work, Cal, perhaps you should try it. Then you can see for yourself how easy it is."

She reached for a smaller lump of dough and placed it on the counter in front of him with a soft thud. "Go on. Show me how it's done."

"What? Me?" Cal straightened, staring at the dough like it was a coiled snake. "I don't know how to do that."

"Then it's time you learned," Chana said, her tone sweet but unyielding. She stepped aside, brushing the flour off her hands onto her apron. "First, you fold it. Then press down. Like this." She demonstrated, her hands moving with effortless precision, coaxing the dough into shape. "Your turn."

Becky smirked, her knife pausing mid-peel. "This'll be good."

Cal muttered something inaudible but reluctantly rolled up his sleeves to wash his hands. Approaching the counter, he eyed the dough warily before placing his hands on it.

"Like this?" he asked, pressing his palms against it with an exaggerated slap. A cloud of flour exploded into the air, landing squarely on his face.

Becky burst into laughter, dropping an apple in the process. "Cal, you're a natural."

Cal coughed, waving a hand in front of his face. "Yeah, yeah. Real funny."

Chana smirked but gestured toward the dough again. "Alright, now actually knead it. Fold, press down, turn. Like this." She demonstrated again, slow and patient.

Cal copied her movements, but his touch was clumsy and uneven. He pushed too hard, squishing the dough into an unrecognizable lump, then pulled at it like he was wrestling a stubborn mule. "This thing's fighting back," he grumbled.

Becky leaned on the counter, chin in her hand. "Imagine that. Dough that requires effort."

Cal scowled but kept at it, though his movements were more dramatic than necessary, as if he were proving some grand point. Finally, after several attempts and a few exaggerated sighs, he threw up his hands. "Alright, there. It's kneaded. Happy?"

Chana pressed a finger into the dough, inspecting it with mock seriousness. "Hmm. Well, it's...unique. A little overworked in spots, underworked in others."

"Perfect," Becky quipped. "Just like Cal."

Cal shot her a glare, but Chana patted the dough into a more even shape and slid it onto a tray. "Not bad for a beginner," she said with a wink. "Maybe next time, you'll get it just right."

"Next time?" Cal groaned, wiping his flour-dusted hands on his shirt.

Lauren grinned. "Oh yeah, Becky. You better write this down. Cal *actually* made bread."

Becky let out a snort of laughter. "I can't wait to tell Fred and Hans."

Cal's head whipped around, his glare sharp. "Don't you dare."

Becky's smirk widened, but Chana intervened with a soft laugh. "That's enough teasing for one day. Cal, you did well for your first time. And who knows? Maybe someday, you'll be making bread better than me."

Cal grunted, but Lauren didn't miss the flicker of pride in his eyes as he helped carry the tray to the oven.

* * *

THE PORCH WAS dark except for the dim glow of a lantern Lauren had left burning on the windowsill. She sat on the swing, her shawl wrapped around her shoulders, her gaze fixed on the distant woods. The night was unusually quiet, only the pitter-patter of raindrops hitting the trees.

Becky hadn't returned for supper. Lauren had noticed her absence immediately, though no one else had remarked on it. Becky had left a note in the kitchen, but its curt explanation, "Gone for a walk", did little to ease Lauren's concern, despite Becky's promise not to go back up the mountain alone.

Now, as the minutes dragged on, Lauren's unease grew. The crunch of footsteps broke the stillness. Lauren straightened, peering into the shadows. A moment later, Becky emerged from the woods, her figure stark against the lantern's glow. Her steps faltered slightly as she climbed onto the porch, her breath uneven, as though she'd been running or crying.

For a fleeting moment, Lauren thought she saw movement behind her, but the shadows remained still. "Becky?"

Becky froze, her hand gripping the porch railing as she looked up. "You're still awake?"

"I couldn't sleep," Lauren kept her voice calm despite the pounding in her chest. "Where have you been? You're wet through."

"I went to see Luke."

Lauren's breath hitched. "Luke? How?"

"It doesn't matter," Becky snapped, then sighed. "I got a message. Someone left it at the tree line near the old mill."

"And?"

Becky sank onto the step, her elbows digging into her knees. She buried her face in her hands. "He wasn't there but he left a note, told me to stay away," she said, her voice muffled. "He's scared, Lauren. Of them. And now, he's pushin' me away, thinkin' it'll protect me."

Lauren placed a hand on Becky's shoulder. "Who are they?"

Becky lifted her head, her eyes flashing with anger. "Moonshiners, smugglers, I don't know. But they've got their claws in him, and he's too afraid to fight back." Her voice cracked. "He thinks this is all he has now. That there's nothin' left for him. I should have tried harder to find him. And Matt. Instead of livin' here lookin' after orphans, I should have been up there findin' my own flesh and blood. What kind of sister am I? I abandoned them when they needed me most. I ...," She put her head in her hands and cried.

Lauren squeezed her shoulder gently. "He's wrong, Becky. You've done everything you can. But if he's in danger, we have to be smart about this."

Becky looked up, holding Lauren's gaze. The misery in their depths made Lauren pull her closer. "I just ... I can't lose him. Not again."

Lauren wanted to promise she wouldn't but given his history and his choice of friends, that was a promise she couldn't make.

For a long moment, neither of them spoke. The lantern flickered, casting shadows across the porch. Finally, Becky stood, brushing off her skirt. "I'm goin' to bed."

Becky's steps faltered as if exhaustion weighed her down with every movement. When the door clicked shut, the silence settled heavier than before, pressing against Lauren's chest. She took a seat in the swing, its faint creak the only sound breaking the stillness.

The lantern's flickering light cast restless shadows

against the porch, mirroring the churn of unease in her mind. Lauren's fingers tightened on the edge of the swing as she stared toward the woods. Somewhere out there, Luke was caught in a world of danger. And now, that world was bleeding closer to Hope House, threatening to pull them all under.

CHAPTER 16

"I can't believe God has any more tears left. He's been crying forever."

Lauren glanced up from her letter to Edward at Ruthie's words. "What do you mean God is crying?"

"That's what Nanny Kat said when I asked her why it was raining so much. She said God had a lot to cry about."

Lauren loved her great-aunt but sometimes she could throttle her. "Come here, sweetie."

She pulled Ruthie onto her knee. "Rain isn't God's tears. It is just something that happens when hot air and cold air meet in the skies. Nanny Kat was just teasing."

"She was? But she sounded serious."

Cal looked up from the floor where he was reading another newspaper report, this time on the Tri State gang. "She always does."

A single drop fell from the ceiling into the waiting tin bucket below, its sharp *plink* breaking the silence.

Three buckets were already scattered around the sitting room, each catching rhythmic drips that echoed through the house.

"Another one, Miss Lauren!" Joey called from the window, his finger darting toward a fresh trickle winding its way from the corner of the room.

Lauren sighed as she gave Ruthie a kiss and gently pushed her from her lap. She stood up. "I'll grab another bucket. At this rate, we'll be swimming by morning." She gave Joey a wink, though her shoulders sagged as she disappeared into the kitchen.

The smell of soap greeted her as she entered. Becky stood at the sink, hands buried in sudsy water, her face turned toward the rain streaking the window. Her shoulders tensed as Lauren came in, but she didn't turn around.

"Why are you doing the dishes?" Lauren set the bucket down by the counter. "The children should be helping."

Becky let out a shaky laugh, though it didn't reach her eyes. "You gave me a fright, creepin' up on me like that."

"I wasn't creeping," Lauren said, crossing her arms as she leaned against the counter. "You're brooding. About Luke."

The water swirled around Becky's hands, but she didn't answer.

"Does he have shelter?" Lauren pressed, her voice softer now. "Maybe with whoever left you that note?"

Becky's cheeks flushed, and her hands stilled in the water. Silence stretched between them, broken only by the drumming rain against the windows and the faint splatter of drops hitting the buckets in the next room.

"Who's helping him? Will? Earl?"

Becky shook her head, as though trying to cut off the question entirely.

"I need to know," Lauren said, stepping closer. "If there's someone helping him, we could all be in danger. You heard what the sheriff said. These gangs don't leave loose ends, Becky. If Luke brings them here ..."

The plate slipped from Becky's hands, clattering back into the water. Suds splashed across the counter as she turned, her eyes blazing.

"For years, I've put this place and these kids ahead of my own flesh and blood," Becky said, her voice trembling with fury. "I ain't doin' it no more. Not this time."

Lauren stiffened, the words cutting deep. She wanted to argue, but Becky's pain was raw, exposed, and undeniable. The laughter of the children floated in from the sitting room, a distant melody that only heightened the tension in the kitchen.

"Do you hear that?" Lauren said, her low voice laced with steel. "That's the sound of the children you love. The ones you've helped raise. Are you really so willing to risk their safety?"

Becky's hands gripped the edge of the sink, knuckles whitening. Her back was rigid, her gaze fixed out the window. For a long moment, she didn't move, didn't speak.

When she finally did, her voice was low, almost broken. "I can't lose him."

The words hung in the air, heavy with grief.

Lauren hesitated. She wanted to push, to make Becky see reason. But that pain, so raw and desperate, held her back. Slowly, she reached for the bucket she had come for.

"You can't save him alone." She turned toward the doorway.

"Wait." Becky's voice cracked, pulling Lauren to a stop. "Please."

Before Lauren could answer, the back door banged open, letting in a gust of cold wind. Chana Meyer bustled in, clutching a dripping newspaper over her head like a makeshift umbrella.

"What a mess!" Chana exclaimed, brushing rain off her shawl. "I thought I dropped my bracelet in the barn when I collected the eggs this morning, and now I'm soaked through. Like a drowned dog, ja?"

Lauren blinked, the tension in the room colliding with Chana's disheveled, cheerful entrance.

Becky grabbed a towel from the counter, stepping forward with a faint, shaky laugh. "Did you find it?"

"Ja, ja. But not before I got wetter than the leaky roof!" Chana rubbed at her hair with the towel, then paused, her gaze flicking between the two women. Her sharp eyes narrowed. "What's going on here? You both look like the rain followed me inside."

"It's nothing." Lauren held the bucket in front of her.

Chana tutted, waving her hand. "Nothing is never nothing. Sit, both of you. When my daughters fought, I made them sit until they talked it out. Now sit." She gestured toward the chairs around the kitchen table.

Lauren hesitated, but Becky, still holding the towel,

gave a faint smirk. "Not sure we should've let you move in if you're goin' to boss us around."

Chana's eyes twinkled as she pulled out a chair. "Good! Then you'll listen. Sit."

Reluctantly, Lauren settled into a chair, and Becky followed. Chana sat with them, folding the towel neatly on the table.

"You are worried about your brother," Chana said, turning to Becky. Then, to Lauren: "And you are afraid for the children, afraid of what the sheriff's warning means."

Lauren stiffened, her fingers curling around the bucket. "You don't understand."

"I understand plenty," Chana said. "You are both letting fear make decisions for you. And fear is a bad friend. It keeps you from trusting, from seeing clearly."

Becky looked down at her hands, her fingers tightening into fists. "I'm not afraid for myself."

"Of course not," Chana said gently. "But you're afraid of losing him. And you, Lauren, you're afraid of losing what you've built here. The children. Your family." She leaned forward. "But if you don't find a way to trust each other, you'll lose more than you think."

Lauren glanced at Becky. The tension in her chest loosened, if only slightly. "We'll figure it out," she said, reaching for Becky's hand. "But we'll talk after the children are in bed. The less they know, the better. Tomorrow night. We will ask Will and Tom to join us."

"Good idea," Chana said, standing. "And excuse me while I go change. I'm bringing in more rain than the cracks in the ceiling."

* * *

THE FIRE CRACKLED in the hearth, its warm light stretching across the sitting room and softening the worn edges of the furniture. Rain still tapped against the windows, but inside, the children of Hope House were gathered on the rug, their faces glowing in the flickering light. The older ones leaned back against the chairs, their postures casual but their eyes watchful. The younger ones sat cross-legged, knees pulled close to their chins, wide-eyed and waiting.

Nanny Kat sat in her usual spot, a creaky rocking chair near the fire. Her knitting needles clicked, their rhythm steady as she listened to the children settle into the circle. Across the room, Chana Meyer sat on the small couch, her back straight and her hands neatly folded over a worn book she hadn't opened. She watched the children intently, her brow slightly furrowed, as if their enthusiasm needed careful monitoring. Beside her, Victor sprawled comfortably, his arm draped over the back of the couch and his ankle crossed over one knee. His shirt was unbuttoned at the collar, and his grin came easily as he waited for the story to begin.

Lauren settled herself in an armchair near the fire, her knitting forgotten in her lap. She watched the group with a quiet smile, her heart warming as the children shuffled closer together, their laughter and murmurs fading into anticipation. For a moment, the weight on her shoulders felt lighter.

"Who's startin' tonight?" Becky asked, tugging her braid over her shoulder as she perched on the edge of the couch.

Her tone was light, but her gaze flicked to Lauren, a silent acknowledgment of their earlier tension.

Cal's hand shot up, his grin already stretching ear to ear. "Me! Me! I've got a good one!"

Shelley groaned, rolling her eyes. "Of course you do. Go on, then."

Cal scooted closer to the center of the circle, the firelight catching the mischievous glint in his eyes. He spread his hands wide, his voice dropping into a dramatic whisper.

"There was a man who lived deep in the forest. And they said," he paused, his gaze sweeping the room, "he could talk to animals."

Ruthie giggled, hugging her knees. "What kind of animals?"

"Any kind," Cal replied with a wave of his hand. "Squirrels, deer, even bears. But he had a secret." He leaned in, his voice dropping lower. "He couldn't talk to people."

Lottie frowned, her chin resting on her palm. "That's sad," she said.

"Not too sad," Becky chimed in, her tone teasing. "Bet he liked animals better anyhow."

Cal gave her a mock glare, then turned back to his audience. "One day, he found a little boy lost in the woods. The boy didn't talk much either, but he had a dog. A big, shaggy dog. And the dog said ..."

"You're skipping!" Hans interrupted, leaning forward with a scowl. "What did the forest man do before he found the boy? He didn't just sit around waiting, did he?"

Cal scowled back at Hans, but his grin returned just as

quickly. "Fine. He was gathering herbs for his stew. Happy now? Can I finish?"

The room erupted in laughter. Victor threw his head back and let out a booming laugh, shaking his head as if Cal's story was the most entertaining thing he'd heard all day.

"Easy there, Hans," Victor said, his grin broad. "The boy's got a tale to tell. Let him spin it."

"Victor," Chana murmured sharply, her tone clipped as her gaze flicked toward him. "You're encouraging him."

"That's the point!" Victor grinned at her, then turned to Cal with an exaggerated wink. "Go on, lad. Tell us what the dog said."

Chana's lips pressed into a thin line, but she said nothing, merely shifting her posture and tucking her book closer to her chest as she returned her attention to the children.

"All right, Cal," Lauren said gently, breaking the tension. "Let's hear what the dog had to say."

Cal cleared his throat, clearly pleased with himself. "The dog said, 'You've got to help this boy. He's got somethin' the forest needs.' And then ..."

"Wait, wait!" Ruthie interrupted, her eyes sparkling. "Can I tell what happens next?"

Cal groaned but waved a hand. "Fine. But you better make it good."

Ruthie scooted forward, her voice dropping to a near-whisper. "The boy had a magic stone," she said, her words slow and deliberate, "but he didn't know it was magic. The forest needed it to stay alive. But there was someone else looking for it. Someone dangerous."

The group leaned in, spellbound. Even Shelley's sarcastic facade slipped as she tilted her head, her eyes narrowing with interest.

Lauren's gaze flicked to Becky. Her friend's fingers fidgeted with the fraying hem of her skirt, a telltale sign of her unease. Becky's face was calm, her expression soft as she listened to Ruthie's tale. But Lauren knew her too well. The words were hitting too close to home.

"The boy didn't know who to trust," Ruthie continued, her voice barely louder than the fire's crackle. "Not even the forest man. But the dog said, 'You have to choose. If you trust the wrong person, the stone will be lost, and the forest will die.'"

Lauren's breath caught, the words landing heavier than she expected.

"That's enough for tonight," Becky stood.

Ruthie blinked in surprise but sat back, a faint pout on her lips.

"Aww," Cal groaned. "But it was just getting good!"

"Tomorrow night," Becky promised, ruffling Cal's hair. "You can finish it then. All of you, off to bed."

The children groaned and protested, but they began to rise, their yawns betraying their exhaustion. Lauren stood as well, stretching the stiffness from her legs.

As the last of the children filed out, Lauren lingered by the hearth, staring into the embers. Becky moved to her side, folding her arms across her chest.

"You stopped her story early," Lauren said.

Becky shrugged, her gaze fixed on the dying fire. "Sometimes it's better to leave a story unfinished," she said. "At least until you know how it ends and who you can trust."

CHAPTER 17

For two weeks, the rain battered the roof of the orphanage, each drop a hammering reminder of the storm's ferocity. Inside, the living room was a symphony of anxious sounds. The plink of water pooling in tin buckets, the hiss of the wind through the aging window frames, and the low hum of WCHV on the radio.

Becky sat by the crackling radio, her foot tapping a frantic rhythm on the wooden floor. "WCHV says several rivers have breached their banks," she muttered, her voice tight. "Storm's not lettin' up anytime soon."

Lauren stood at the window, the dishtowel in her hands twisted into a knot. She stared out at the water cascading in thick sheets down the glass, the creek beyond the orchard swollen and angry. The lower field was no longer a field, it was a muddy expanse swallowing debris in its rush.

"Do you think the lake will flood? Should we evacuate?" Chana's voice trembled as she glanced at Lauren.

"Where would we go?" Becky cut in, rising from her chair. "Delgany's already under water, and they're warnin' folks not to travel unless it's life or death." She peered over Lauren's shoulder at the storm. "Kids were thrilled to miss school, but now they're climbing the walls. Reckon they'd welcome their lessons back now."

Before anyone could respond, the back door slammed open with a crash.

Will stumbled in, his boots caked in mud, water dripping from his coat in rivulets. His face was flushed with cold, but his eyes were sharp. "Flood's hittin' hard all over. Some folks up on the mountain are worse off."

He yanked off his scarf, tossing it toward the coat rack. It missed and landed on the floor with a wet slap. "There's a tree down by John's old place. No way through unless you've got an axe and all night to clear it."

Lauren hurried to pour him a mug of coffee, pressing it into his trembling hands. "You're soaked through," she said, her worry evident. "You should've stayed in town."

Will took a gulp of coffee, then set it down to haul a heavy box through the door. "Earl let me take what I could before they started rationin'. Told 'em it was for Hope House."

Becky flew at him, throwing her arms around his neck. "Thank you," she said, then leaned back and swatted his chest with her palm. "What were you thinkin'? You could've been killed!"

Will chuckled, pulling her close. "I'd do it again for my woman."

Becky shoved him, though her grin betrayed her affection. "You're impossible."

Lauren began unpacking the box, bags of flour, canned goods, and coffee, while Chana brought a towel to Will. "You need to change out of those wet clothes," Chana said, worry creasing her brow. "And eat something. You must be starving."

Will nodded, running a hand through his damp hair. "Earl's holdin' up for now. Floodwaters are higher on the other side of Delgany." He hesitated, his gaze meeting Chana's. "Your old place ... it's bad. A lot of damage."

Chana swallowed hard but nodded. "We're safer here."

At the window, Becky's said. "I hope Luke's safe."

Will's expression shifted, the humor fading from his face. "Luke knows these mountains. He'll stick to high ground, find shelter. He's smart enough to stay clear of the relief crews."

Becky's shoulders sagged as she turned back to the table, her arms crossed. She didn't speak, but Lauren could see the trembling in her hands.

A loud crash upstairs broke the tension, making everyone jump. Will's hand went to his belt, his fingers brushing the handle of his knife.

"It's the kids," Lauren said quickly, though her heart raced. "They've been cooped up too long. I'll check on them."

Will's jaw relaxed, but he muttered "This storm's got a bad feelin' to it. Like it's meanin' to do more than flood us out."

Lauren's gaze flicked back to the window. The creek was rising fast, its churning waters dragging debris downstream. Among the broken branches and scraps of wood, a small barrel bobbed in the current, carried from who-knows-where.

CHAPTER 18

Finally after what seemed like forever, the sun broke through the clouds. At first, it was just for a couple of hours at a time, but eventually it won the battle and the rain eased.

"Miss Lauren! Miss Lauren!"

Lauren came running out of her bedroom at Cal and Ruthie's calls. "What's wrong?" She held her hand to her heart.

"The rain's stopped. Can we put our shoes on and go outside?" Cal asked.

Ruthie hopped from one foot to the other, her face flushed. "Is school back now? I miss school."

"I don't, but if I have to stay inside one more day, I'm going to explode." Cal lifted his leg as if to kick the wall but lowered it at a glare from Lauren.

"Children, you know not to scream at me like that. You put the heart across me."

"Huh? We broke your heart." Ruthie started crying. "I'm sorry, Miss Lauren, we didn't mean to do it."

"Oh darling, come here. I meant you gave me a fright, that's all. Come and give me a hug and then you can get dressed. School won't be open 'til Monday though. It never opens at the weekend."

As Ruthie leaned in for a kiss, Lauren felt the heat coming off her in waves.

"Ruthie sweetie, you have a fever. You need to go back to bed. Seems you've caught the chill the other children have."

"Does that mean I'll miss more school?" Ruthie hiccuped as the tears flowed. "I don't want to."

"You will be better in a day or so. Rest is a wonderful cure." Lauren picked up the unusually fretful child and carried her back into the girls' bedroom. With a look over her shoulder, she addressed Cal. "You can get dressed and go help Becky with the chores. When they are done, properly mind, then you can go outside."

"Aw man."

She gave him a look and he ran.

"Sure you girls can manage without us?" Nanny Kat asked, standing near the front door with her coat draped over one arm.

"Yes, of course. Will offered to drive you into Delgany to check on Miss Chaney and the others. Chana and Victor are worried about their neighbors, even though they weren't too neighborly to them." Becky glanced at Nanny Kat. "Before you say it, I know. It doesn't cost anything to be kind."

Nanny Kat smiled as Becky repeated one of her sayings. "We should count our blessings, dear. We escaped with a few roof leaks, a mud invasion, and some soggy fields. Many lost their homes, their livelihood, and I heard on the radio there were several deaths in Johnston County."

Becky's sweeping brush scraped across the wooden floor. Lauren intervened before the younger girl could remind Nanny Kat that Luke was on the mountain somewhere and still unaccounted for. "Go on, Nanny Kat. Will can't wait forever."

The older woman hesitated, but only for a moment. "All right. Don't overwork yourselves, and keep an eye on the little ones." She smiled warmly at the two women before stepping out into the gray morning.

The next hour passed in a flurry of activity. The children clattered about, clearing the table, washing and drying the dishes, while their voices rose above the rhythmic swish of mops, as Becky and Lauren tackled the muddy floors.

Lauren wiped the sweat from her forehead and glanced around the room. "Despite everyone leaving their shoes at the door, I think there was more mud in here than out there," she said, gesturing toward the sodden fields visible through the kitchen window. She tossed a damp rag onto the counter, where a chipped bar of Fels-Naptha soap sat next to the basin, its scent sharp in the humid air.

Becky dumped the contents of her bucket into the yard

before filling it back up with clean, hot water. Grabbing another mop, she started at the opposite end of the kitchen, where the children had stacked the chairs on top of the tables after drying the last of the dishes.

"Miss Lauren, can we go outside and play now? We're bored." Cal stuck his head around the door, his mop of hair flopping into his eyes as he gave his most pleading expression.

"Bored?" Becky arched an eyebrow. "I've got more than enough chores to keep you busy." Despite her tone, she winked at Lauren.

"Aw, man. We've made our beds, cleaned our rooms, cleaned out the barn …"

From somewhere behind him, Terry coughed loudly.

"Alright, helped Terry clean out the barn," Cal corrected. "And I even dried the dishes, and that's uh. " He hesitated, looking to Fred for backup. "Well, you know. Women's work."

Fred snickered. "You might wanna stop digging that hole, Cal."

Cal flushed. "I just wanna be a real man, that's all."

Becky crossed her arms and gave him a look. "Real men know when to stop talkin'."

"Sorry, Miss Becky."

"I'm not sure it's safe out there just yet," Becky said. "The water's gone down, but there could still be some deep spots. Not to mention snakes and any other critters the waters may have uprooted."

"Aw, shucks, Miss Becky. You'd think we were babies,"

Cal protested. "We won't go near the lake. Terry can watch us. Can't you, Terry?"

Terry leaned against the doorframe, arms crossed, an amused expression on his face. "I've got enough work to do without keepin' an eye on you lot. The vegetable patch is a mess: branches, trash, mud everywhere."

"I can help!" Cal volunteered, perking up. "So can Fred!"

Fred raised an eyebrow. "Whoa, whoa, whoa. We can help? Who said I was helping?"

Lauren hid a smile. "You're helping."

Fred groaned. "Fine."

"Hans is staying in bed," Lauren added, wiping down the last of the counters. "He's got a bad cold, and so do Rachel and Joey. But the rest of you can go outside. If you help tidy up first, don't go near the lake or get in Terry's way. Got it?"

"Yes, Miss Lauren!" Cal scrambled out the door to tell the other children to get their coats and boots on.

Becky leaned on her mop and muttered to Lauren, "If the yard's anythin' like the kitchen was, I hope they don't come back even muddier than they are now." She tapped the bucket of soapy water with her foot, where a box of Borax sat nearby. "Otherwise, we'll need another box of this to clean up after them."

Lauren chuckled. "You really think that's possible? I think now would be a good time to have a break and enjoy a cup of coffee on the porch. We can keep an eye on them and get some fresh air. The ammonia fumes are making my eyes water."

* * *

LAUREN TOOK a deep breath as she assessed the damage. The water had mostly receded, leaving the orphanage's vegetable garden a soggy mess of fallen branches, mud, and who-knows-what swept in by the flood.

The kids stood assembled on the porch, boots mismatched, gloves too big for their hands, staring out at what could only be described as a swamp. Shelley, arms crossed and her nose wrinkled, was already grumbling. "This isn't cleanup. This is punishment."

"It's an adventure!" Cal shouted, already halfway down the steps, his too-large boots slapping awkwardly against the wooden boards.

Fred leaned lazily against the porch railing, chewing a piece of grass he'd picked up. "Adventure for you, maybe. For the rest of us, it's mud-wrestling with a field."

Lauren handed Becky her coffee before taking a seat beside her on the swing. "Cal offered your help, so the sooner you finish, the quicker you can go back to doing whatever it is you want to do."

"Will you keep an eye on Joey, Miss Lauren?" Shelley asked.

"Carly will. She's staying upstairs with Maisie, Joey, and the others. Off you go."

Fred groaned but reluctantly followed Shelley and Cal into the vegetable garden. As they worked, they came across a few tangled branches that seemed like perfect hiding places for snakes. At one point, Cal stopped dead in his tracks and poked a pile of debris nervously with his stick.

"You think there's a snake under there?" he asked, his voice dropping to a whisper.

"Probably," Fred said casually. "Maybe more than one."

"Fred! Don't joke about that!" Shelley barked, though she, too, took a step back.

Fred smirked, twirling his stick. "If there's a snake, it's probably more scared of you than you are of it. You're loud enough to scare off anything."

Lauren, watching from the porch, nudged Becky. "Look at Shelley's face. I think Fred's lucky he didn't land on his butt in the middle of the mud."

Becky chuckled. "She's come a long way, really, hasn't she? Havin' Joey around has helped soften her edges."

Shelley straightened up, clearly regaining her composure, and marched into the field like a general leading a very muddy army. "Alright, here's the plan: I'll supervise. You two," she jabbed a gloved finger at Cal and Fred, "pick up branches and... whatever that is." She pointed at what might have been a wheelbarrow, though it was mostly buried in mud.

"Why do you get to supervise?" Fred asked, smirking. "Because you're wearing boots like you're about to climb Mount Everest?"

Shelley lifted her chin. "Exactly. Leadership boots."

Fred rolled his eyes but grabbed a stick anyway, using it to nudge a piece of debris. Cal, meanwhile, had decided his "branch" was a heroic sword, swinging it wildly as he charged into a puddle.

"En garde!" Cal shouted, stabbing his "sword" into the mud. The puddle responded by swallowing his boot with a loud schlorp.

"Cal, quit fooling around!" Shelley barked. But as she took a commanding step forward, her own foot sank deep into the mud. "Oh, no. No, no, no."

The mud grumbled ominously as she tried to pull her foot free. "Fred! Help me!" she shouted, arms flailing for balance.

Fred snorted. "Looks like the mud likes your leadership boots."

"Just help!" Shelley growled, glaring at him.

Fred ambled over and grabbed her arm. With a dramatic tug, Shelley managed to free her foot, only to realize that her boot was still in the mud.

"My boot!" Shelley wailed, hopping on one foot. "It's stuck! Someone get it!"

"Don't worry, I've got this!" Cal announced, leaping into the mud like a knight charging into battle. His first attempt to grab the boot ended with him face-first in the muck. When he popped back up, grinning from ear to ear, Shelley shrieked.

"That's NOT my boot! That's, what is that?"

Cal held up a muddy object triumphantly. "It's a football! And it's mine now!"

Fred doubled over laughing, leaving Shelley hopping in place, arms crossed in fury. "You're both useless!"

After the boot fiasco, Shelley was back on the porch trying to scrub mud off her sock with an old rag while Cal and Fred roamed farther into the field.

"Hey," Fred called, stopping in his tracks. "What's that?"

"What's what?" Cal replied, swinging his branch-sword at a clump of weeds.

"That." Fred pointed to a long, mud-covered log half-buried in the muck. Its gnarled roots stuck out like claws, and its surface was so slimy it glistened in the weak sunlight.

Cal squinted. "It's a log."

Fred frowned. "What if it's not?"

Cal tilted his head. "What else would it be?"

Fred crouched down dramatically, his voice dropping to a spooky tone. "What if it's a monster? Like a swamp monster! Look at the claws!"

Cal's eyes widened. "You think it's a real monster?"

Fred shrugged, grinning. "Could be. You never know what comes out of the mountains during a storm."

"Should we? Should we poke it?" Cal whispered, gripping his stick like a knight facing a dragon.

Fred nodded solemnly. "We have to. It's our duty."

Cal crept closer, stick extended like a lance. "Okay, here goes." He gave the log a cautious prod.

It shifted slightly in the mud.

"It MOVED!" Fred shouted, stumbling back.

"IT'S ALIVE!" Cal screamed, dropping his stick and sprinting toward the house.

Fred, not one to be left out, turned and bolted after him, yelling, "RUN FOR YOUR LIVES!"

They tore across the field, screaming, boots splashing, as Shelley looked up from the porch in utter confusion.

"What's wrong with you two now?" she demanded as they skidded to a halt, panting and splattered with mud.

"Monster!" Cal gasped, pointing toward the field. "It's in the swamp!"

Fred nodded solemnly. "Big claws. Nearly got us."

Lauren, unable to look at Becky without laughing, adopted a serious expression. She crossed her arms. "What's this about a monster?"

"It's a log," Shelley muttered, giving up on cleaning her sock. "They're just being ridiculous."

"It MOVED!" Cal insisted, still catching his breath.

Fred leaned casually against the porch railing, a smug grin on his face. "Might've been a log. Might've been a swamp beast. Guess we'll never know."

Lauren groaned. "Fred, stop filling his head with nonsense."

"I'm not filling it. It's already full of nonsense," Fred said with a grin.

"Take that back!" Cal shouted, lunging at Fred, who darted off laughing.

"You two quit messin' around and help Terry clear that patch," Becky called, "or you'll be eatin' beans for the whole summer."

Later, as Terry returned from confirming the "monster" was indeed a log, Cal proudly declared, "We scared it off! You're welcome!"

Shelley, still annoyed about her missing boot, shot him a glare. "You didn't scare off anything, Cal."

"I did too!" Cal puffed out his chest. "Fred saw me! I was brave!"

"Brave? You screamed like a baby and ran faster than anyone!"

"That's called a tactical retreat," Cal said confidently.

Fred chuckled, nudging Shelley. "Hey, at least he makes us laugh."

"Great. Maybe he can make my lost boot laugh its way back out of the mud."

CHAPTER 19

Taking advantage of the older children being at school and the little ones napping, the kitchen of Hope House buzzed with activity.

Chana poured coffee, her movements quick and efficient. "Thank goodness the rain has finally stopped. Things can go back to normal."

"Normal?" Becky glanced around the room with a teasing grin. "What's that?" She gestured at the table, which was buried in fabric scraps, ribbons, and patterns—what Miss Chaney called "organized chaos." "I love how Terry and Victor practically ran out the door as soon as they heard weddin' talk."

"My Victor," Chana chuckled, "he is a romantic, but even this is too much for him."

Miss Chaney worked at the mannequin with practiced precision, adjusting the fit of Becky's wedding dress, pins sticking out of her mouth like a porcupine. Across the table, Carly's small hands guided fabric through the new

Singer sewing machine, her brow furrowed with concentration as Nanny Kat sat beside her, supervising her work.

Becky hovered by the mannequin, fingers brushing the hem of the dress. An expression of disbelief flickered across her face.

"Is it too fancy?" she asked hesitantly, holding up the fabric as if she were afraid of it. "I'm just a mountain girl."

"It's perfect," Lauren said from her spot on the floor, sorting through a box of buttons Joey had knocked over earlier.

Becky wrinkled her nose. "I'm not so sure. It looks more like somethin' you would've worn back in the old days, Lauren, when you were rich."

Lauren flashed her a reassuring smile. "Becky, you only get married once. Let us spoil you."

"I'll look like the Queen Bee," Becky said, but the delight in her voice betrayed her words.

"You won't," Carly said, giggling as she snipped a thread. "You're going to look like a princess. A proper princess."

Chana stood and excused herself with a mysterious smile. "I'll be right back."

The women kept working, chatting easily, until Chana returned a few minutes later with a round hatbox in her hands.

"I would be honored if you would use this as your 'something borrowed'. That is the American custom, ja?" An uncertain expression crossed her face. "But you can say no, if you think it is too old or fussy."

She placed the box carefully on the table. Becky's

mouth dropped open as she stepped forward. "You mean for me to open it?"

"Ja, of course! How else could you try it on?" Chana's smile lit her face. "Just be careful. It is old and handmade. Not always the best combination."

The room went quiet as Becky lifted the lid, a faint scent of lavender drifting out as she carefully unwrapped the tissue paper inside. What she revealed drew audible gasps.

It was a veil, delicate and impossibly fine, its lacework so intricate it looked like it had been spun from moonlight.

Miss Chaney was the first to speak. "Oh my word, just look at that craftsmanship." She leaned in for a closer look. "It's a blend of Chantilly and Brussels lace, isn't it? I recognize the floral motifs. See here, Carly, the vines cascade like real ones, and even the petals curl as though they're alive."

Becky's hands trembled as she held the veil up to the light. "It's … it's beautiful," she whispered, her voice thick with emotion. "I can't take this."

"You are not taking it," Chana insisted gently. "I am lending it. You, all of you, have been so kind to Victor and me. You've made us feel like family, something I thought we had lost forever. I would be honored."

Tears shimmered in Chana's eyes, and Lauren quickly handed her a handkerchief before pulling her into a warm hug.

"Chana," Becky said, her voice trembling. "This is too much."

"It is not too much. It is tradition," Chana said, recovering herself. "Now, put it on, please."

Becky hesitated. "Will you help me?"

Chana nodded and stepped forward, her hands steady as she arranged the veil over Becky's hair. "The embroidered medallion here at the crown—it features lilies and roses. They are symbols of purity and love."

"The seed pearls catch the light so beautifully," Carly murmured, stepping back to admire it. "It looks like it's glowing."

"It's a little long, and the edges are fraying, but …" Chana glanced at Miss Chaney, her brow raised in a question.

Miss Chaney shook her head. "I'd be terrified to touch it. What if I ruined it?"

"Leaving it in a box is the only way it would be ruined," Chana said with a sad smile. "Neither of my daughters wanted to wear it. They said it was old-fashioned and heavy." She turned her face away quickly, but not before Lauren caught the hurt in her eyes.

"But it's not heavy," Becky said, twirling around. "It feels like spider silk. Chana, it's absolutely gorgeous. Did you make it?"

"Me? No." Chana's hands hovered over the lace as if she could still feel the hands that had stitched it. "My mother, my grandmother, and several aunties, all the ladies of the neighborhood, came together to make it. It took months. Every stitch holds a piece of them."

The room fell quiet as Chana's words sank in.

After a moment, Nanny Kat stepped forward, running

her fingers over the frayed edges. "Miss Chaney and I can fix it. We'll shorten it, too. No sense letting it trail across the grass."

Chana clapped her hands, her smile returning. "Please, make it to suit Becky. I hope it brings you and Will the blessings of a happy marriage, as it gave me and Victor."

Lauren spoke up hesitantly. "Chana, I've always wondered. I mean, at a Jewish wedding, what does it mean when you stomp on a glass? I read about it in a book."

"You break a glass on purpose?" Carly asked, wide-eyed. "Wouldn't that be bad luck?"

"Oh, no," Chana said, plucking a pin from her mouth to gesture. "It is good luck for us. Breaking the glass seals the moment forever. The rabbi says it is to remember the fragility of joy, but also how strong love must be to endure."

Twirling a button between her fingers, Lauren sighed. "I like that. It's romantic."

"Romantic?" Becky snorted, twirling in her veil. "I'd probably trip over the glass and ruin the whole weddin'!"

The room burst into laughter, a warm, familiar sound that made the old kitchen feel cozier than ever. Chana's cheeks flushed. "I bet mountain folks have their own traditions for weddings."

"We sure do. Some are good, some a little old fashioned, others plain embarrassing." Becky lifted the veil from her head. "Can you help me put this away for now please, Chana."

Chana took the veil. "What's the most embarrassing?"

Becky glanced around the room before whispering, "The shivaree. But Will and I agreed we aren't havin' one."

"That's what you think." Miss Chaney put another pin in her mouth at the look Becky sent her.

"What's a ... what did you call it?' Chana couldn't get her tongue around the unfamiliar word.

Lauren came to the rescue. "Don't mind Becky, Chana. It's a little tradition where friends and neighbors gather to celebrate the newlyweds. They make a lot of noise, banging pots, singing, sometimes even playing pranks on the wedding night."

Becky put her hands on her hips, her glance landing on each person, finally settling on Lauren. "Nobody is goin' to ruin my weddin' night, you hear?"

Lauren glanced over at Shelley, who sat in the corner, unusually quiet, her fingers toying with the hem of her cardigan. Maybe the conversation was too adult for her to follow.

"That's enough of that talk. There are other traditions too." Nanny Kat chimed in, carefully threading a needle, "Every bride gets a quilt made from scraps, bits of cloth from her family and friends. It's meant to keep her warm on her wedding night and remind her of the home she came from."

Becky turned from the window, one eyebrow arched. "So you're sayin' I get to carry all of you with me *forever*? Sounds a bit heavy for one quilt."

"Careful, Becky," Nanny Kat said with mock sternness, winking at Shelley, "or I'll start stitching in a few pieces from Shelley's old flannel nightgown."

This earned a round of laughter, but the sound didn't reach the far corner of the room, where Shelley sat slumped on a stool by the cooker.

Lauren glanced at her, frowning slightly. Shelley's hands rested on her stomach, her face pale and drawn. She hadn't been feeling well all morning. Becky had insisted she go to school anyway, Shelley had groaned and complained until they relented. Stomach cramps weren't exactly rare for Shelley. She was prone to them when she got anxious, but today Lauren suspected something deeper was bothering her.

"Shelley," Lauren called gently, setting the box of buttons aside. "Do you want to come help us? Even just sitting with us would be nice."

Shelley didn't look up. "No," she muttered, her fingers toying with the hem of her cardigan.

Carly chimed in, always the optimist. "You don't have to sew, Shelley. You could just sort the squares for the quilt for us. No pressure!"

"I said no!" Shelley's head snapped up, and her voice cracked with sudden anger. "I don't care about stupid traditions! Or the stupid dress!"

The laughter in the room stopped cold. Miss Chaney straightened up, startled, and Becky froze with the veil still in her hands. Carly looked wide-eyed, unsure of what to say.

"Shelley," Lauren stood up and walked to the girl's side. "What's wrong?"

"What's wrong?" Shelley stood abruptly, her voice

trembling. "You and Becky are leaving! Getting married and leaving us behind. Just like everyone else!"

Lauren heard the echo of years of hurt in Shelley's voice. The rejection she'd suffered from parents who didn't want her, and the cruelty she'd endured under Matron Werth before Hope House became a place of love and safety.

"Shelley," Lauren began, but Shelley wasn't done.

"You said this was our home," she cried, her voice cracking. "You said you wouldn't leave. You said you would try to find me a home with real parents. But it was all lies! You're just like Matron Werth, saying things you don't mean!"

Becky took a step forward, her mouth opening to protest, but Lauren shot her a quick, warning glance. Becky stopped, her brow furrowing.

Lauren crouched slightly, lowering herself to Shelley's level. Her voice was calm and steady, even as her heart ached for the girl. "Becky is getting married but she will continue to be here every day. There's nothing decided about my wedding." Lauren pushed aside her own uncertainty. "I know it feels like everything is changing right now. And I know it's scary."

"It is changing!" Shelley blurted out, her face twisted with a mixture of anger and fear. "Becky's leaving! Edward wants to marry you when he gets better. What if you don't come back? What if we're stuck here alone again?"

Lauren let the girl's words wash over her. Shelley's pain was raw, and it had to be heard before it could be soothed. "Nanny Kat and the Meyers are here."

"That's not the same!"

"Do you remember the day I came to Hope House?" Lauren asked gently. "Becky, Carly, Terry, you and the other children showed me how brave you were."

Shelley shook her head, her hair falling into her face. "I'm not brave."

"You are," Lauren said. "You've survived so much. More than anyone your age should ever have to. And do you know what? This is your home. For as long as you want it. If you want to be adopted, we can work on that for you. But in the meantime, Hope House isn't just a building. It's all of us, together."

Shelley sniffled, her arms wrapping around her middle. "Matron Werth said we weren't worth keeping. My own parents didn't want me."

Lauren's throat tightened at the mention of that cruel woman. Even years later, her poison lingered in the hearts of the children she'd hurt. "Matron Werth was wrong. She was so wrong. You are worth keeping, Shelley. Every single one of you is. And neither I nor Becky will ever stop fighting for you to know that."

Shelley's shoulders slumped, and she wiped her face with her sleeve. When she finally looked up at Lauren, her voice was small and uncertain. "You promise?"

"I promise," Lauren said, her voice unwavering. "This is your home, Shelley. No one, not me, not Becky, not anyone can take that from you."

Becky stepped forward, her voice softer now. "Besides, who else is goin' to keep me in line around here? Carly? She'd let me get away with everythin.'"

"Would not!" Carly protested, making Shelley's lips twitch into the smallest of smiles.

Lauren reached out again. Shelley hesitated, her arms crossed over her chest, as though holding herself together. But when Lauren didn't move, didn't rush her, the tension in her shoulders began to melt. Slowly, she stepped forward and allowed Lauren to pull her into a hug.

"Why don't you come sit with us?" Lauren said as they pulled apart. "No sewing, I promise. Just rest."

Shelley hesitated, then nodded slowly. "Okay."

As Shelley joined Carly at the table, the chatter in the kitchen gradually resumed. Nanny Kat caught Lauren's eye and gave her an approving nod.

Lauren looked away. Heat flared at the base of her neck, spreading upward until her face burned. Her hands, though, felt like ice. Because, despite what she had said, things were changing. And it scared her. Hope House had always been her anchor, but what if Edward wanted her to leave? What if she had to choose between him and this, her family.

CHAPTER 20

*L*auren parked the truck outside the hospital just as a man held the door open for his wife, who carried a newborn baby. She watched the little family walk to their car, their faces alight with joy. Maybe someday that would be her and Edward? Shaking her head, she pushed the thought aside. They were a long way from babies. They still hadn't even set a wedding date, let alone discussed where they'd live. His newspaper was in Charlottesville, so would he want to move to Delgany? If he pursued his plan of traveling to France and other places, could she stay at Hope House? Would she have to choose between the man she loved and the home she'd built? She twisted her hands, the questions swirling, unresolved.

Reaching into the truck, she grabbed the basket of cookies Nanny Kat and Chana had prepared. She climbed the stone steps, gripping the iron railing worn smooth by years of anxious hands. The faint tang of coal smoke lingered in the air, mingling with the sharper bite of disinfectant wafting from inside. Pushing through the glass-paned doors, the smell of carbolic soap hit her, sharp and clinical, underscored by the low hum of hospital life. The murmurs of voices, the click of nurses' shoes, and the faint creak of a gurney's wheels. She nodded at the nurses as she passed.

Edward sat by the window, a blanket over his legs and a book resting on the arm of his chair. On the table beside him, a bowl of broth sat untouched, its surface congealing under the fluorescent light.

Lauren stepped inside, basket in hand. She looked at the food. "Two months of hospital food, how are you still alive?"

"Barely." He set the book aside and glanced at the basket. "What did you bring?"

"Nanny Kat's cookies. Don't tell the nurses. I'd hate to get caught smuggling."

"If I never see jello again, it'll be too soon." He took a cookie from the basket, his eyes lighting up with pleasure as he bit into it. "Tastes better than ever."

He finished the cookie and leaned back slightly. "I've got news."

"Good news, I hope."

"Great news. Doctor says I'm getting out of here in a few days."

Her chest tightened, her stomach flipping with relief. "Edward, that's wonderful! How do you feel?"

"Relieved. Excited. And ..." He turned back toward the window. "A little nervous."

"Nervous? Why?"

He shrugged his shoulders. "Don't mind me, I'm being silly."

She sensed it was more than that but he changed the subject.

"When I get out of here, I'm coming straight to Hope House. Roast beef, mashed potatoes, Nanny Kat's pie, and tea you can stand a spoon in. None of that watered-down milk they serve here."

"You might have to chop firewood to earn that supper."

"Deal. Just keep the jello away from me."

She laughed, her chest light with relief. "The kids will take your share. It'll be good to have you back. Everyone's missed you."

"I've missed you too."

They sat together until the bell signaled the end of visiting hours.

"Do you have to go? Stay a few more minutes."

She stood, brushing a strand of hair behind her ear. "You'd better get used to me hanging around. I'm not going anywhere."

"Good," Edward said, his voice softer now. "I'd hate to think I went through all this just to lose the one person who kept me sane."

The words hit her squarely in the chest, warm and certain, and before she could overthink it, she leaned forward and kissed him. It was quick, barely more than a brush of her lips against his, but it was enough to leave her heart pounding and her cheeks warm.

"I definitely can't wait to get out of here now," he said.

She laughed, her fingers trembling slightly as she reached for the door. "Save the poetic lines for your first article back. I'll see you Sunday."

CHAPTER 21

The moment the dark blue, 1929 Ford Model A rolled up the driveway, Lauren's heart stuttered. Edward's car. Her breath caught, a flicker of hope rising before doubt swept in just as quickly. He hadn't said anything about being cleared to drive again.

The engine rumbled to a stop, and Lauren stepped onto the porch, the crisp scent of damp earth and pine tangling with a faint trace of gasoline. The drivers door opened.

Not Edward.

"Sam!" The name burst from her lips, her pulse leaping.

Old Sam stood there, his weathered face folding into that familiar, steady smile. A lump formed in her throat, thick and unexpected. He wasn't just a friend; he was the steady hand, the voice of reason when everything else spun too fast. More a father than the one she'd been born to.

Lauren barely noticed herself moving, her arms wrapping tight around him. "You can drive now? It's so good to see you!"

"And what about me? Don't I get an hello?" Edward got out of the passenger seat. Lauren ran around to give him a kiss but came back to Sam and hugged him again.

A low chuckle rumbled in his chest as he patted her back. "You saw me at Christmas, Miss Lauren."

"That was four months ago," she shot back, stepping away but keeping hold of his arm, as if letting go might make him vanish. Her real father would be rolling in his grave, watching her fuss over Sam like this. She didn't care. Not then, not ever.

"How's Prince?" Her voice softened. "I miss him."

"He misses you too, Miss Lauren," Sam's eyes crinkled with warmth. "You should come visit. Take him for a ride. Or bring him here. He'd be good for the children."

Lauren's heart lifted, a smile tugging at her lips. "Sam, that's perfect!" She gestured toward the house. "Go in and see Nanny Kat and Becky. They'll be thrilled to see you."

But Sam's gaze drifted past her, toward the towering oaks lining the estate. His voice, when it came, was quieter. "I'd like to pay my respects to Patty first."

Lauren's chest tightened. She squeezed his hand. "Take your time, Sam. They'll be inside when you're ready."

Edward walked toward her, the crunch of gravel under his boots the only sound between them, the world around them seeming to fade away, leaving just the two of them in that moment. Edward leaned in, his lips brushing her cheek in a gesture so tender it made her knees weak. Then, with a quick glance around, as if to ensure they were truly alone, he stole a kiss on her lips—soft, brief, but filled with a promise that made her pulse race. "I thought you might like to take a drive with me?" Then he glanced down at his still splinted hand. "Maybe I should rephrase that as you might like to take me for a drive?"

"Seeing as you asked so nicely," Lauren's heart beat faster making her slightly dizzy. "Where are we going?"

"It's a surprise." His voice carried a teasing edge that sent a thrill down her spine. "But tell Becky you'll be at least an hour. I'll wait for you here."

Lauren glanced back at the house, "Aren't you coming in to say hello?"

"Not a chance," Edward chuckled, shaking his head. "If they get me inside, Becky and Kathryn will grill me over where we're going. I'll wait here."

"Anyone would think you were afraid of them." Lauren enjoyed the banter that always flowed so easily between them.

"Anyone with a brain should be." He leaned in for another kiss. This time, it was slower, more deliberate, as if he was savoring the moment, the taste of her lips, the feel of her close to him. Lauren's breath hitched, and she felt a warmth spread through her that had nothing to do with the sun peeking through the clouds above.

"Edward Belmont," she murmured, half in protest but mostly in affection.

She could feel her resolve melting away, replaced by a deep, yearning desire to be near him, to never let go. It had taken nearly four long years and the harrowing ordeal of almost losing him to Nazi torturers for her to finally embrace what he had always tried to show her: that love could be gentle and exhilarating, a source of magical feelings she had never imagined. Reality hit like a bucket of cold water. He was leaving again.

She drew back but he held her firm. "I won't live in France or Switzerland."

"You won't?"

"No. I love you and want to be with you."

She threw her arms around him, but he gently held her shoulders, his gaze serious. "I meant what I said, Lauren. I have to help my people. My parents may not practice, but I still feel Jewish, and even if I didn't, I can't stand by after seeing what the Nazis do to those who resist them."

She swallowed hard, unable to speak.

"I've asked Tim Egan to keep running the Charlottesville paper. I want to be a reporter again. It's what I love. I'll travel to France, Switzerland, maybe even England, and connect with Ian's friends from Germany, Aunt Rae's circle, and perhaps Victor's as well. We'll figure out the details, but what matters is that I want to marry you, live with you, and wake up by your side."

She blushed but her heart swelled at his words. His eyes darkened with desire as he leaned in to kiss her. Her lips met his, her arms moving around his waist. She didn't care who saw them. He loved her. He was the one to move away first.

"We should get going before the sun gets too hot." Grinning, she walked away. It hadn't been the sun and they both knew it. She glanced over her shoulder, catching one last glimpse of him standing by the car, watching her with a look that made her feel like the most important person in the world.

***

Nanny Kat was in bed but Becky was sitting at the kitchen table writing up a list. "I heard a car." Becky glanced up. "Someone lost?"

Lauren shook her head. "Sam drove Edward over to see us."

Becky stood up. "Sam? Edward? Where are they? Are they coming in?"

"Sam's visiting Patty's grave, and Edward's outside." Lauren grabbed her purse. "He wants me to drive him somewhere."

Becky sat back down and smirked knowingly. "And why didn't he come in? Hidin' somethin'?"

Lauren rolled her eyes, swiping at Becky's arm. "Stop teasing me! He just wants to show me something."

"Hmmm." Becky leaned back in her chair. "Nanny Kat won't like him stealin' you away."

Blushing, Lauren rushed out the door, Becky's laughter trailing after her.

Ten minutes into the drive, Lauren sighed. "Are we nearly there?"

Edward shot her a sideways glance, his lips twitching with amusement. "Almost."

She huffed impatiently, but a few miles later, he instructed, "Park here."

Lauren frowned as she stepped out, looking around at the wide-open field before her. It was beautiful, lush, green, dotted with tiny wildflowers, but it was just a field.

Edward reached for her hand, his touch grounding her. "Close your eyes."

She obeyed, barely containing her curiosity.

"No peeking," he warned.

"I'm not!" she giggled, though the temptation was unbearable.

"Okay, open."

Lauren blinked as her eyes adjusted to the soft light of the overcast day. She took in the field before her, a vast expanse of tender green, the blades of grass still glistening with the morning dew. The field stretched out before them, bordered by a line of trees that framed the landscape like a natural picture. The buds on the branches were just beginning to open, promising a burst of color in the coming weeks. She inhaled deeply, the air fresh and clean, carrying the faint scent of wildflowers that dotted the field like tiny jewels. She turned to Edward, a question in her eyes, trying to mask the hint of disappointment she felt. It was just a field. Beautiful, yes, but she had expected something more. But Edward's expression was soft, his dark eyes watching her with a mix of anticipation and love that made her heart skip a beat.

"What do you see?" he asked, as if coaxing her to look beyond the obvious.

Lauren took another look, this time trying to see the field through his eyes. It was then that she noticed the subtle details. The way the land sloped gently, the way the trees seemed to form a natural boundary, creating a secluded space. And then it struck her. This wasn't just any field. "This ... this is where?" she began, her voice catching with emotion as the realization dawned on her.

Edward smiled, a slow, proud smile that made her heart swell with affection. "I heard it was for sale and had a word with the owner. It's ours if you want it. To build our new home and start our life together."

Speechless, she turned in a slow circle, taking it all in. The field, the trees, the mountains in the distance. It was perfect. Wasn't it? *It isn't Hope House.*

Pointing towards the edge of the field where a small, winding trail disappeared into the woods, Edward said. "That path leads straight to Hope House. Or at least it will when Will and his team clear some of the trees. It's a short walk, so you can be close to the children whenever you want, but far enough that we'll have our privacy."

"But it took ages to drive here."

"There is a much shorter route, but I know how you have lots of patience." Lauren slapped his arm gently for teasing her, as tears prickled at the corners of her eyes, but they were tears of happiness, of relief.

"What about your home in Charlottesville?"

"You mean my parent's house? I'll keep a small place in town near the newspaper. But home is where family is and that's you. I know you could never leave Hope House and while I don't want to live in the actual house, I have no issue living near it. So long as we install a telephone, and I have an office in our new house."

He continued talking but all she could focus on were the words. *I don't want to live in the actual house.*

Edward stepped closer, his hand lifting to brush a

strand of hair from her face, his touch light but filled with meaning. "Say you'll be happy here with me," he murmured, his voice low and full of feeling.

She kissed him to avoid answering, but it only distracted him briefly. "Are you sure you can leave Hope House?" he asked, his voice tinged with concern.

Lauren's breath caught in her throat. She could feel the sweat trickling down her back as nerves overtook her. This was her chance to say what had been on her mind for so long, but suddenly, she wasn't sure how he would react.

She watched his expression shift from one of pure love to a slight furrow of his brow, questioning, searching her face for the truth. "What is it?" he asked, his voice dropping to a whisper. "You don't want to leave? You've changed your mind about us?"

Her heart pounded, but she forced herself to speak, to be honest with him. "No of course not. I love you. You're my future." Despite the storm of emotions inside her, her voice sounded steady.

"But?"

Maybe she could compromise on Hope House. "I want to adopt Ruthie." The words tumbled out before she could stop them, and she instantly regretted how abrupt it sounded. All the time she had spent thinking about how to bring this up, how to explain her feelings, and she had just blurted it out like that. She could have bitten her own tongue, but there was no taking it back now. Her heart raced as she watched his reaction, fearing that she might have ruined the perfect moment.

Edward's eyes widened slightly, his expression unreadable for a moment. The silence that followed felt like an eternity, each second ticking by with the weight of uncertainty.

A wave of unease washed over her as she waited for him to respond. To say something, anything, that would tell her how he felt about her sudden confession. Then, to her surprise, he looked at her with a mixture of shock and admiration, as if seeing her in a new light.

"You want to adopt?"

Lauren nodded, feeling her throat tighten with emotion. "She's been through so much, and she needs a home, a real home. I can't imagine leaving her behind, Edward. I love her like she's already mine."

Edward's eyes glistened with understanding. "I know how much she means to you. And I know how much you mean to her. Ever since you endangered yourself to rescue her when Justin kidnapped her. There's a bond between the two of you: nobody should break that."

Tears welled up in Lauren's eyes as she listened to his words, the relief washing over her in waves. "So, you're not upset?"

Edward shook his head, a small, tender smile playing on his lips. "No, Lauren. I'm not upset. How could I be? You have the biggest heart of anyone I've ever known. Ruthie's lucky to have you. We're lucky to have her, if she'll have us."

Lauren's tears spilled over. She threw her arms around Edward, holding him tightly as she whispered, "Thank you. Thank you for understanding."

He wrapped his arms around her, pulling her close, his

voice soft in her ear. "We'll build our home here, Lauren. A home for us, Ruthie, and if we are blessed with more children, them too."

They walked hand in hand across the field. "I was thinking ..." Edward squeezed her hand. "That we could build a two-story house right over there, with a deep front porch where we could sit in the evening and watch the sunset on the mountain. And a stone chimney, of course, for a big fireplace in the living room, perfect for the colder months."

Lauren listened as he continued. "We'd have a large kitchen at the back, with plenty of space for visitors to sit when they come over. I thought we'd hire a cook and a maid."

"Edward. I'm not looking to replace the life I had in Rosehall."

"I know that but according to the children, your cooking skills are somewhat lacking and your talents lie in other directions." His eyes danced as he teased her. "Let's face it, darling. I will be traveling as a reporter, and you will be at Hope House most days. If you aren't, you will be somewhere rescuing children or fighting someone on their behalf."

"You make me sound lovely."

He pulled her in for a kiss. "You are perfect in my eyes."

He kissed her again deeply. When they broke apart, they were both breathing a little heavily.

"Upstairs we should discuss another day, definitely not now. I'm a gentleman but there is such a thing as too much temptation." He grinned at her before pointing to another area. "I thought we should build a small cottage there for Sam, near the stables. Prince would fret if anyone but Sam looks after him. Hopefully he will agree to move out here."

Sam loved the horses more than anything, especially Prince, the spirited stallion that had once been her pride and joy. The idea of giving Sam a place of his own, where he could continue to care for the animals he loved, filled her with a deep sense of gratitude.

"A small, comfortable cottage for Sam, with a garden where he can grow his herbs and vegetables. He'll be happy here, I know it. But we have to ask him and not make him feel obliged."

As they walked through the field, they began to discuss the details—the type of wood they'd use, the color of the walls, the layout of the rooms. As they reached the far end of the field, Edward stopped and turned to her, pulling her close. He looked into her eyes, his expression serious but full of hope. "Lauren, are you sure about this? About us? This place … it's our future, but I want to be certain it's what you want."

A surge of emotion so strong it nearly took her breath away flowed through her. She placed her hand on his cheek, feeling the warmth of his skin beneath her fingers. "Edward," she whispered, "there is nothing I want more in this world than to build a life with you."

He smiled then, a smile so full of love that it made her heart ache with happiness.

"Then let's do it," he said, leaning in to kiss her. "Let's build our home, together. We'll head into Richmond, finalize the purchase. I can't wait to get started. The sooner the house is built, the sooner we can get married and set up home together."

"First can we go back and tell the others we want to adopt Ruthie? We need to speak to Becky and Nanny."

Together, they walked back to the car, their fingers intertwined. Before getting into the driver's seat, she paused, looking back at the field, the place that could soon become their home. Could she really leave Hope House? She still wasn't sure, but one thing was certain: She couldn't imagine a future without Edward.

CHAPTER 22

Lauren drove Edward up the lane to Hope House, knowing they had an hour before the children returned from school. A perfect chance to talk in private. As the gravel crunched under the tires, she stopped the car and placed a hand on Edward's arm.

Edward glanced over, his brown eyes warm with concern. The engine idled quietly as Lauren turned to face him. "We didn't set a date. When do you want to get married?"

Edward's lips curled into a smile, his eyes twinkling with that familiar mischief that always made her heart skip. "Yesterday?"

She rolled her eyes but couldn't suppress a smile. "I'm serious."

"So am I." He took her hand, lifting it to his lips in a tender kiss. "I'd marry you today if I thought you'd run away to Richmond with me. But I'm guessing you want a big wedding, a church one?"

Lauren's gaze drifted to Hope House. Memories of her past engagement flooded her mind: the endless preparations, her father's demands, the feeling of being swept into something that wasn't truly hers. When she looked back at Edward, his steady, patient gaze grounded her.

"No, not necessarily a church wedding," she said softly. "But I want my friends and the children there. They're such a big part of my—our lives. It wouldn't feel right without them."

Edward sighed, leaning back with a playful groan. "I don't mind, as long as you're not inviting them on our honeymoon."

Heat rose to Lauren's cheeks at his teasing, an unfamiliar thrill coursing through her. Edward reached out, tracing a soft line across her lips with his fingertip, sending shivers down her spine.

"It will be wonderful," he murmured. "Real love between two adults isn't something to fear."

She nodded, her resolve strengthening. Leaning in, she pressed her lips to his, trying to show him the depth of her trust. And she did trust him, more than anyone in a long time. But as she pulled away, the shadow of her past tugged at her thoughts.

Edward cupped her cheek, his thumb brushing away the tiny worry lines. "Lauren," he said gently, his eyes searching hers, "don't go gathering trouble. It's you and me now. Forget him."

She opened her mouth to protest, but his knowing look silenced her. This incredible, compassionate man knew her inside and out, and loved her anyway. A wave of emotion swept through her, and she wrapped her arms around his neck, pulling him into a deep, lingering kiss.

When she finally pulled back, breathless and smiling, she whispered, "Maybe Richmond might not be too bad."

Before Edward could respond, a voice called from the porch. "Nanny Kat wants to know if you're comin' inside or if she needs to fetch you herself!"

Lauren blushed fiercely as Becky's voice echoed through the still air. She glanced at Edward, who was struggling but failing to hold back a laugh.

"We best go in before she comes out waving a shotgun or something," he said, grinning.

Still giggling, they stepped out of the car, hands entwined. As they reached the porch, the door creaked open, and Becky appeared, hands on her hips and a knowing smile on her face.

"Well, it's about time," she teased. "I thought you two were gettin' married out there in the car."

Lauren's cheeks burned, but she couldn't help but laugh, shaking her head at Becky's playful banter.

"Come on in," Becky added with a wink. "Sam's out in the barn with Terry, and I'm sure they'll want to hear any big news too."

Inside, Nanny Kat sat on the sofa, her needle moving deftly through the fabric in her lap. She glanced up, her eyes twinkling behind her glasses. She didn't speak, but the small smile on her lips spoke volumes.

Lauren took a breath. "I'm glad it's just us." She glanced at Edward, who nodded in support. "Edward and I have something to ask you both."

Nanny Kat set aside her sewing and leaned forward. "You can't ask for her hand in marriage again."

Becky appeared, handing Lauren a glass of water. "You both look a bit flushed. Must be from bein' out in the heat so long."

Lauren's hands trembled slightly as she set the glass down. Taking a steadying breath, she said, "Edward and I … we want to adopt Ruthie. What do you think?"

Silence settled over the room. Nanny Kat's smile faded, and Becky's usual lively expression grew still.

"Adopt Ruthie?" Nanny Kat echoed. "Lauren, have you thought about how that would affect the other children?"

Lauren blinked, caught off guard. "I thought they'd understand."

Nanny Kat's gaze remained kind. "The children look up to you, Lauren. If you adopt Ruthie, what message does that send to the rest of them?"

Becky nodded. "Lottie's still so young. She won't understand why you chose Ruthie and not her. Even the older ones might feel left behind."

A pang shot through Lauren's heart. "I love all of them."

"We know you do," Nanny Kat said gently. "But children don't always see things the way we do."

Tears welled in Lauren's eyes. She had been so focused on giving Ruthie security that she hadn't thought of the others.

Edward squeezed her hand. "We can still give Ruthie love and security without formal adoption."

Becky offered a reassuring smile. "She already knows she's part of your family. And so do the others."

Lauren wiped away a tear. "I just wanted her to feel safe."

"You're already doing that," Edward said. "That's what really matters."

Lauren sighed, accepting the truth. "Thank you for helping me see this."

Edward stood, brushing his hand gently over her shoulder. "I need to head to Richmond. Want to come with me?"

Lauren shook her head. "I'd rather be here when the children get home."

He gave her a look she couldn't quite read, and for a moment, she thought he might press the issue. But instead, he simply nodded.

As he said goodbye to Becky and Nanny Kat, Lauren remained rooted in place, the weight of their conversation settling heavily on her shoulders. She didn't want to go anywhere. She just wanted to go up to her room. Alone.

Thoughts tumbled through her mind like falling dominoes. She had believed that having Ruthie live with her and Edward would make leaving Hope House easier, a way to bridge the gap between the life she had and the one she was building. But now that plan was off the table.

Could she really live somewhere else?

The thought unsettled her, stirring doubts she wasn't ready to face.

"Lauren?" Edward's voice broke through her thoughts, the gentle concern in his tone suggesting he'd called her more than once.

"Sorry, I was woolgathering," she said, forcing a small smile. "I'll walk you out."

He kissed her cheek, lingering for just a moment. "No need. I'll head out to the barn to collect Sam and say goodbye to Terry. I'll see you soon?"

Lauren nodded but instead of a genuine smile, she had to force one. "Yes, darling, of course."

She caught Becky's quizzical glance, but as soon as Edward left through the back door, Lauren muttered an excuse and fled to her room.

Throwing herself on her bed, she let the tears flow. This was supposed to be a happy day, yet why did she feel her heart was breaking?

CHAPTER 23

JUNE 1936

May passed and June rolled around bringing with it extreme heat. Everyone was exhausted, the heat causing tempers to flare easily. Grateful for Chana's calming presence, Lauren took her seat at the supper table.

After a noisy meal, Chana announced she had a surprise. The warm, homely smell of milk pudding filled the kitchen, and for a moment, it seemed to push the worries of the world aside. Lauren watched as Cal eagerly spooned the pudding into his mouth, his freckled face lit with delight.

"Nanny Chana, I'm so glad you came to live with us," he said, muffled by another bite. "You cook real good."

Nanny Chana chuckled as she wiped her hands on her apron. "It's not so hard, child. You just have to let the milk sit in the cooker all day, slow and steady. The natural sugars will come through on their own, like a little gift from patience. Then, a sprinkle of cinnamon or lemon zest, and it's done."

"It's real tasty," Cal said, rubbing his stomach with a satisfied grin. "I don't even miss sugar."

Lauren couldn't help but smile despite her worries. "It's only for a while. We have to economize, just like everyone else in the country."

"What's 'economize' mean?" Ruthie asked.

"Eating more beans." Shelley stirred Joey's bowl, blowing on the contents so he wouldn't burn himself. The room erupted in laughter, and for a moment, the weight on Lauren's shoulders eased.

She glanced out the window, toward the parched garden. The cracked soil and drooping leaves were a constant reminder of how hard things had become.

Ruthie slipped her hand into Lauren's, her small fingers warm and trusting. "We'll be okay, won't we, Miss Lauren? We've got each other, and that's what matters."

Lauren kneeled to meet her gaze. "Yes, Ruthie. We've got each other. And as long as we do, we'll find a way."

"But love doesn't grow vegetables," Cal held out his bowl. "Can I have some more, please?"

Fred's voice broke through the chatter. "Miss Lauren, I've got an idea! I was reading about this man who made a pump out of an old bicycle. He used it to bring water to his crops. We could try it for the garden."

"Do you think it would work?"

Fred nodded eagerly. "If we use the lake water and the old bike in the shed, it might save us from carrying all those pails."

"Show me that book later and we will see can we make that work." Terry turned to Lauren. "Can't hurt to give it a try."

Lauren nodded. "What will we do without you when you go to college in the fall?"

Terry's head dropped, his voice low. "I'm not goin'."

The room fell silent. Lauren's chest tightened. "Terry, you said that last year."

"I've made up my mind," he said. "Not this year. Maybe next year. You need me here now."

Lauren straightened, her tone firmer now. "You earned that scholarship, Terry. You've got a gift. You can't just throw it away because times are tough."

"What kind of man would I be if I walked away?" His sharp tone highlighted his frustration. "You told me I was the man of the house."

"Terry!"

Chana touched Lauren's arm. "He's right, Lauren. He's old enough to make his own choices."

Lauren's breath caught, but she swallowed her frustration. "All right. But don't let your talent go to waste. Study when you can. Be ready when the time comes."

Terry muttered. "I will."

The scrape of chairs and the clatter of dishes broke the tension as the younger children hurried to their chores. Fred and Cal headed outside to milk the cows, and Ruthie began clearing the table. Lauren stood in the quiet kitchen, the weight of the day settling back onto her shoulders.

She heard a car. "That will be Ian and Nanny Kat back from their trip. Nanny Kat won't be happy with Terry."

Chana brushed the final crumbs from the table. "I don't think Kathryn will be surprised. It would be out of character for Terry to just leave. He feels responsible, not just for Carly but for everyone here. You taught him how to be a man, Lauren. You should be proud." Chana climbed the stairs to go to her room.

* * *

A MOMENT LATER, the kitchen door opened, and Ian held it wide as Nanny Kat stepped inside. Her sharp but kind eyes scanned the room, as she set her handbag down on the table.

"Evening, Lauren," Ian said, tipping his hat before hanging it on the hook by the door. "Hope the day treated you all right."

Lauren folded the dishcloth in her hands, returning his smile. "It wasn't bad. Did you manage to get everything you needed?"

"We picked up flour, some dried beans, and ..." Ian hesitated, glancing at Nanny Kat.

"And a bag of coffee," Nanny Kat finished for him, though her tone was light. "You'll have to make it last, Lauren. Coffee doesn't grow on trees around here, and it won't for some time."

Lauren raised her eyebrows. "Coffee? Real coffee?"

Ian chuckled. "We figured you deserved at least one small indulgence. But Kathryn's right. It'll need to stretch."

"Where are the children?" Nanny Kat asked, shifting her gaze toward the hallway.

Lauren put the water on to boil. "They're finishing their chores. Fred and Cal are out with the cows, and the girls are upstairs."

"And the adults?" Nanny Kat's tone was calm, but there was no mistaking the note of concern beneath it.

Lauren hesitated, glancing at Ian. "Chana and Victor are up in their room, Victor had a headache. Becky went for a walk. Terry…"

Before she could elaborate, Terry appeared in the doorway. His tall frame filled the room, but his posture was tense, his hands shoved deep into his pockets. He looked at Ian, then at Nanny Kat, then finally at Lauren.

"Did you tell them?"

Lauren shook her head. "I thought you should."

Terry exhaled sharply and squared his shoulders. "I'm not goin' to college this year."

The words hung in the air for a moment before Ian stepped forward, his expression steady but curious. "You mean you're delaying?"

Terry nodded. "I can't leave. Not with the drought this bad and the garden failin'. Lauren needs help, and so does everyone else. I can't just walk away."

Nanny Kat folded her hands in front of her, studying him closely. "And you think staying is the best way to help?"

"It's the only way," Terry said. "I don't see how goin' to college helps anyone here."

Nanny Kat nodded slowly, her gaze thoughtful. "I understand why you feel that way, Terry. It's not easy to leave when you think people need you. But are you sure staying is what's best for this family?"

Terry frowned, shifting his weight. "If I don't stay, who's goin' to fix the fences? Or haul water for the garden? Or help Lauren with the harvest? If I leave, it's just one more pair of hands gone."

Lauren opened her mouth to speak, but Nanny Kat raised a hand gently, stepping closer to Terry. "Terry, you've been a part of this family long enough to know one thing: we manage. We always have, and we always will. But what you have this chance to go to college. It's not something we can fix for you later if you walk away from it now."

Terry's jaw tightened. "I just don't see how it's fair. Everyone else is here, doin' their part, and I'd be off in some classroom."

"There's more than one way to 'do your part,'" Nanny Kat said. "You're not running away, Terry. You're preparing for a future where you can help this family, and others, in ways you can't even imagine yet. Think about what you could bring back with you. Skills. Knowledge. A way out of this cycle. For you, Carly and the others."

Ian stepped forward, resting a hand on Terry's shoulder. "It's not about leaving, son. It's about growing. You've worked hard for this scholarship, and you've earned the right to take it. None of us would ever think less of you for chasing something bigger."

Terry glanced between them, his defenses cracking slightly. "And if things fall apart here while I'm gone?"

"Then we'll handle it." Lauren stepped closer, her voice

steady despite the tightness in her chest. "We've gotten through worse. And we'll get through this, too. You have a chance to do something great. Don't let guilt hold you back. That's not what family is for."

"Lauren's right. No one here will resent you for going, Terry. In fact, I think you'll find that all of us, Lauren, Becky and the children, will be prouder of you than you'll ever know." Nanny Kat put a finger under his chin, forcing him to look at her. "Have you thought about Carly? Your plans for the future. This decision affects her too. Most of all."

Terry colored. "I'll talk to her. I'll think about it."

"That's all we ask." Ian clapped him on the back.

Terry nodded stiffly, then turned and walked out the back door. The screen banged shut behind him, and the room was quiet again.

Lauren sighed, leaning against the counter. "You think he'll change his mind?"

"He's got a good head on his shoulders," Ian said. "He just needs time."

Nanny Kat pulled out a chair and sat down, smoothing her skirt. "He'll think it through. Terry's always been a thoughtful boy. But don't rush him, Lauren. Big decisions take courage, and courage doesn't come overnight."

Glancing toward the door where Terry had disappeared, Lauren said, "I just hope he sees how much we believe in him."

"He will," Nanny Kat said. "Because he knows we care. That's what matters."

CHAPTER 24

*L*auren was sick of the sun, beautiful though it was. It had not rained in weeks, and the drought had choked the land dry. Fields that were once green now lay flat, the crops curled up and lifeless, as if they had given up waiting for salvation.

She stood at the edge of the yard, her bare toes digging into the cracked, sunbaked earth. Even under the oak tree's shade, the air pressed down like a smothering blanket. Sweat trickled down her neck, the salt of it sharp on her lips.

The fields in the distance were eerily silent. Even the chickens nearby scratched listlessly, their feathers limp. Lauren nudged the dirt with her toe, sending up a small puff of dust that quickly settled. She felt parched to her core, and every sip of the muddy-tasting well water left her more frustrated. The well was running low, but with Will and Earl tied up at the lumberyard and store, digging it deeper would have to wait.

Her gaze fell on the vegetable garden, looking worse by the day. Fred's bicycle water pump had been a bright spot of hope, one of those wild ideas she wanted to believe in, but the drought had won. Still, she had been proud of Fred for trying. That kind of determination would carry him far.

Across the yard, the children trudged toward her, the heat dragging at their steps.

"Miss Lauren, can we go to the lake? I'm too hot."

She turned to see Cal wiping his forehead dramatically, sweat streaking the dust on his face.

Before she could answer, Terry spoke up. "I'll take care of them. We'll try to catch some fish, though they are probably hidin' from this heat too."

Lauren saw the same worries she felt reflected in his eyes. The orphanage depended on their vegetable crops and fruit trees to make it through the year. The peaches and apples were holding on only because the children watered them faithfully.

She nodded at Terry. "Take them. A little time at the lake will do everyone good. Carly can go with you to help."

As the children eagerly rushed to grab baskets and fishing poles, Shelley corralled Joey. "Stay close to me, and do not go near the water without asking first, okay?"

Lauren smiled at her serious tone, watching as the group's energy returned just enough to chatter on their way down the dusty path.

Turning back to the house, she had barely stepped inside to wash her hands when she heard the low hum of a car pulling into the drive. Peeking out the window, she saw

Ian's Model A Ford pulling up, sunlight glinting off the windshield.

"Good afternoon, Ian," Lauren greeted as he stepped inside. Becky was already setting the kettle on the stove. "What brought you out in this heat?"

Ian removed his hat and wiped his brow. "I got fed up sitting in the office. All anyone can talk about is the Olympics, and I have never been much of a sports fan. Thought I would come out and see how my favorite people are getting on."

Ian hesitated, turning his hat in his hands. "I hope I'm not overstepping, but I have an idea. It's something I'd like to offer."

"For goodness' sake, Ian, spit it out," Nanny Kat said, though her tone was more tired than sharp.

Ian pulled an envelope from his coat and slid it across the table toward Lauren. "I want to help Terry get to college."

Lauren opened the envelope, her breath catching. Thirty dollars.

"Ian, we can't," Lauren began, but he cut her off.

"Please let me help. Barnardos gave me a lifeline. I would not be here but for them. Terry has a scholarship, but scholarships do not cover everything. Travel, books, clothes. There are always little expenses. This way, he will not have to feel guilty about leaving, and he can focus on building a future for himself and Carly."

Becky's cheeks flushed, but before she could protest, Ian added, "Hope House is the best place any orphan could hope for, but we all know every cent is stretched thin."

Lauren looked at the envelope again, her throat tight. Despite her instinct to refuse, she knew Ian was right. She glanced at Becky, who gave her a small nod. Turning to Ian, Lauren said, "We will talk to him."

THE RIGHT MOMENT didn't come for a few days. The oppressive heat had everyone on edge, tempers flaring over the smallest things. But tonight, the mood had lightened. A bowl of popped corn and the comedy show on the radio had brought a rare moment of laughter.

With the younger children asleep, Lauren called out to Terry, who was seated near Carly with a book in his lap.

"Terry, could you come here for a moment?"

He approached cautiously, his eyes wary. "Did I do somethin' wrong?"

"No, of course not. We just want to talk to you." She handed him the envelope Ian had left, watching his expression shift from confusion to shock as he opened it.

"Lauren, I…" he began, but she cut him off gently.

"I know what you're thinking," she said. "But Ian wants you to have this. He wants to help you get to college so you can focus on your studies and not worry about what's happening here."

Terry's hands tightened around the envelope. "I can't take this. This money could help with food or clothes, or …"

"It's for you," Lauren interrupted. "We'll manage, Terry.

We always do. But this is your chance to build a future for yourself, and for Carly too."

At her words, Terry glanced at Carly, who had quietly come to stand beside him. She slipped her hand into his.

Becky reassured him. "We all want this for you, Terry. Even Carly, and she will miss you most of all, won't you, love?"

Carly's cheeks flushed, but her tone was firm. "I want this for you. And you'll come back better than ever. For all of us."

Lauren saw the struggle in his eyes, the way his shoulders tensed as he wrestled with his doubts. Finally, he exhaled and nodded slowly. "I best say yes."

A wave of relief washed over the room as everyone moved to congratulate him. Lauren stepped closer, lowering her voice as she whispered, "We'll look after Carly for you. The time will pass so fast, you'll be back before you know it."

CHAPTER 25

JULY 4TH

*L*auren fanned herself with a folded newspaper as she stepped onto the porch of Hope House. The heat was already oppressive despite the early hour. This was a funny year, floods in March and now blistering heat with no rain for weeks. Her newspaper fan provided little relief. Where was everyone? Catching the low murmur of voices from the side yard, she walked closer.

Edward and Victor were seated in the shade of the large oak tree, their faces solemn as they spoke in low tones. Victor's coat was draped across the back of the chair, his shirt sleeves rolled up to the elbows, but even the relative coolness of the shade didn't ease the furrow in his brow. Edward leaned forward, his hat resting on one knee, his eyes steady and thoughtful.

"It's inevitable," Victor was saying, his voice clipped with frustration. "Franco has all the support he needs from the fascists. Mussolini. Hitler. And the League of Nations will do nothing, just as they did nothing for Ethiopia."

Edward nodded slowly, wiping his brow with a handkerchief. "If Spain falls, it's only a matter of time before the whole of Europe is caught in it. And the rest of us won't be far behind."

Lauren's heart thudded. These two were so similar, always talking about what was happening overseas. Well not today. The children deserved a day of fun and so did she.

Victor exhaled sharply, leaning back in his chair. "And meanwhile, people like Harlan in this town, they act as though it's all so far away. As if it can't touch them."

Lauren stepped forward, clearing her throat softly. Both men looked up, their conversation halting.

"Enough, you two," she said lightly, though her tone carried a quiet authority. "I won't have you souring the mood before the children get to enjoy a proper 4th of July celebration. This is a holiday, remember? And I expect both of you to play along."

Victor raised an eyebrow, but the corner of his mouth twitched in a faint smile. "I suppose some of the fascists can wait until tomorrow."

She caught the wink he sent in Edward's direction and, turning to her fiancé, had to hide her amusement as he struggled to keep a straight face.

Lauren placed a hand on Victor's shoulder. "Today is for the children and for us, too. Come on. We have pies to carry and a talent contest to win."

Edward stood, adjusting his suspenders, and Victor rose a moment later, shaking off the heaviness of the conversation. Lauren took a deep breath, her eyes drifting toward the sky, the relentless sun already pushing the temperature higher.

Becky walked towards them, the children following her.

"Lauren, are you ready to go? These children will mutiny if they have to wait much longer." Becky wiped a hand over her forehead, her hair covered in a bright scarf. Lauren wished she'd thought of doing the same, it might help reduce the feeling of the suns rays burning her scalp.

Hans darted out from behind Becky's back. "Miss Lauren, Cal said you shot a gun at the last July 4th party. Did you really?"

"I told you she did. She won a prize too. Old Foxy Flannery wasn't pleased." Cal kicked the dirt. "But he shouldn't have underestimated a woman."

Lauren and Becky exchanged a glance at Cal's comment, this coming from a boy who constantly complained some things were women's work. Hans's eyes were out on stalks as he glanced from Lauren to Cal and back.

"She did indeed Hans. You don't want to cross Miss Lauren. Now are we going to town or not?" Edward asked.

The children cheered as they clambered into the back of Will's truck, passing picnic baskets and lemonade bottles to store at the front. Lauren would drive the Meyers in her truck, with Sam driving Edward and Nanny Kat.

***

By the time they arrived at the town square, the heat was stifling, the kind that made the air shimmer over the pavement and left everyone sticky and irritable. The brass band near the gazebo did their best to sound cheerful, but even their rendition of Yankee Doodle seemed sluggish under the oppressive sun. The square was already bustling with activity. Children ran barefoot across the dusty ground, their cheeks flushed red from the heat and excitement, while parents fanned themselves with folded newspapers or paper fans from the general store.

The smell of fried chicken and fresh pies wafted through the summer air as Lauren led the Hope House children into the town square. Around her, the small town seemed transformed, alive with the colors of the 4th of July. Streamers rippled from lampposts, bunting hung across shop windows.

"I'm starving. I'm going to get me some of that fried chicken." Cal tugged on Fred's arm. "Race ya."

Hans ran after them, "Wait for me."

"Boys be careful and respectful." Becky shouted after them but it was doubtful they heard over the din. Wide-eyed, the girls scattered too, pointing out the sack races, the pie stands, and the dizzying assortment of games. Shelley walked with Joey, holding his hand, leaving Lauren with Maisie.

Edward walked beside her, quiet but watchful, his presence as solid and steady as always. He surveyed the bustling square with the sharp eye of a man who trusted few. "Bigger turnout than I expected," he observed, adjusting the brim of his hat.

"People need this," Lauren said. "Maybe not because of what you and Victor were discussing this morning. I think most Americans believe what happens in Europe has nothing to do with them. But with the floods and now the drought, never mind the lasting effects of the Depression, people are clinging to anything that feels normal."

She glanced around, her gaze catching Chana and Victor Meyer lingering at the edge of the square, hesitant. They stood in the shadow of a lamppost, Victor gripping Chana's hand protectively. The flags seemed to loom over them, stark reminders of how easily patriotism could be wielded as a weapon. Lauren could see it in their postures, the stiff tension in Chana's shoulders as her eyes darted across the crowd.

Adjusting her wide-brimmed hat, Chana whispered something to Victor, her voice too soft to hear, but Lauren didn't need words to know what she was feeling. She followed Chana's gaze toward a knot of townsfolk near the pie tables, their sideways glances unmistakable.

Lauren slowed her steps and turned toward them, offering a warm, reassuring smile. "You'll enjoy this, I promise," she said gently. "And everyone here could use a taste of your cooking, Chana. You'll have them singing your praises before the night is over."

Chana's lips twitched into a faint, reluctant smile, but her eyes betrayed her uncertainty. "If they're willing to try," she murmured.

"They will," Lauren said, hoping she sounded more confident than she felt.

Within minutes, Chana and Victor had set up their small table, carefully arranging trays of pastries. Chana's hands worked with practiced precision, setting out rugelach, apple strudel, and honey cake. The desserts glistened in the sunlight, little beacons of home and heartache. Lauren watched as the first curious townsfolk approached, coins clinking onto the table in exchange for sweets.

A little girl with blonde pigtails bit into a piece of strudel and froze, her eyes widening. "This is the best pie I've ever had!" she exclaimed, her voice cutting through the crowd.

Lauren chuckled softly as Chana's face lit up. "It's not pie, it's strudel," Chana corrected with a laugh, her accent lilting slightly. "It's from Germany."

The girl shrugged, still chewing. "Well, it's real good, lady."

Victor, standing beside Chana with his arms crossed, allowed himself a small smile. Lauren felt a quiet wave of relief at the scene. Their table had drawn attention for the right reasons.

"SIGN-UPS for the Great Independence Day Talent Contest close in five minutes!" a young man called from the makeshift stage, his voice echoing through the square. "Don't miss your chance to win a ribbon and a whole dollar!"

Cal's ears perked up, and he grabbed Hans by the arm, his enthusiasm brimming over. "Hans, we have to do this! Imagine how much chocolate and peppermint a whole dollar could buy!"

Hans blinked, his face turning pale. "No. No, I can't. Everyone will laugh at me."

"Of course they'll laugh!" Cal said, grinning. "That's the whole point!"

Shelley, standing nearby, smirked. "Bet you're scared, Hans. You can't dance in front of all these people."

Hans frowned, bristling. "I can dance just fine."

"Then prove it!" Cal clapped him on the back. "We'll do that German folk thing you showed Rachel. I'll add some funny bits, and we'll bring the house down."

Hans hesitated, his eyes darting to the stage, then to the crowd. Chana appeared at his side, her hand resting gently on his shoulder. "Go on, darling. You will do great," she said softly.

Hans looked at her, then back at Cal. "Fine," he muttered. "But only if you promise not to fall on your face."

Cal beamed. "Of course I will! Otherwise, it won't be funny."

Lauren smiled, lifting Maisie into her arms. "Come on, darling. Let's go laugh at Cal and Hans in the talent contest."

The contest had already started when they took their seats near the stage. Lauren gently rocked Maisie, who was already starting to doze, as a girl with long blonde braids took the stage to sing "You Are My Sunshine". Her voice cracked on the high notes, and Lauren winced sympathetically.

"Cal and Hans will easily beat her. She couldn't sing if she had a gun to her head," Shelley exclaimed.

"Shelley," Lauren frowned. "That's not kind. At least she entered. Think about the example you're setting for Joey."

Shelley glanced at the younger boy beside her, who was watching the stage with wide eyes. She sighed, folding her arms. "Fine."

Next up, two boys attempted a juggling act with lemons, dropping most of them to the crowd's laughter. They bowed graciously, their embarrassment giving way to sheepish smiles. A farmer's son followed with a patriotic poem about George Washington, earning polite applause.

Finally, it was Cal and Hans's turn. Chana leaned forward in her seat, her hands clasped as she whispered, "Please let them do well."

The boys stepped onto the stage, Cal in suspenders several sizes too big and Hans in his everyday shirt and pants, looking sheepish.

The crowd quieted, unsure of what to expect. Hans began with a simple Bavarian folk dance: rhythmic stomping, clapping, and precise arm movements. His confidence grew with each step, and the clarity of his movements drew curious murmurs from the crowd.

Cal followed along, deliberately exaggerating the moves for comic effect. He pretended to trip or miss a step, earning giggles from the children in the audience. At one point, Cal bowed so deeply that his hat fell off, prompting a burst of laughter.

Hans scowled, wagging his finger in mock seriousness. "You are ruining the dance!"

Cal responded in a hammy imitation of Hans's accent, "I am trying, Herr Hans! You're a tough teacher!"

The audience erupted into laughter and applause. Even Lauren found herself wiping tears of laughter from her eyes, the cheekiness of Cal contrasting perfectly with Hans's earnestness.

But as the boys took their bows, the laughter was interrupted by a sharp voice from the sidelines.

"What's so funny about teaching our kids foreign dances? German dances, no less!" Mr. Harlan stood near the stage, his face twisted with disdain. "I lost five friends over in the trenches. Their names are on that memorial over there. You should be ashamed of yourselves."

The crowd quieted, murmurs rippling uneasily.

Mrs. Simmons stood as well, pointing a finger at Hans. "He's one of those Jewish boys from Hope House, isn't he? We've got enough of our own problems without bringing their kind here."

Hans froze on stage, his face pale, while Cal's confusion turned to anger.

From nearby, Rachel's hands curled into fists, her voice trembling with fury. "You don't know anything! Hans is smarter and braver than all of you!"

Victor stood up, his voice low and cutting. "They are children. And they've done nothing to deserve your hatred."

Lauren quickly passed the now-sleeping Maisie to Edward before stepping forward, her voice calm but firm.

"This is a celebration of freedom, Mr. Harlan. Freedom for everyone, not just the people you approve of. If you can't see that, perhaps you've misunderstood the point of the day."

Mr. Harlan's eyes narrowed. "You're filling this town with outsiders, Miss Greenwood. It's not right."

Edward stood and took his place beside Lauren. "They're children," he said simply, his voice quiet but powerful. "And this is their home now. Leave them alone."

The tension built as Mr. Harlan glared at Edward, muttered something under his breath, and finally turned to walk away. Mrs. Simmons huffed and followed, dragging her son behind her.

The crowd began to disperse, some murmuring in agreement with Lauren and Edward, others looking uneasy.

Lauren glanced at Victor and Chana. Chana was trembling, and Victor's jaw was so tight a muscle flickered in his cheek. But when Lauren looked at Hans, she saw the boy standing tall, his shoulders back. She almost burst with pride as Cal, Fred, and the other children moved to be at his side. Even Shelley.

LAUREN LEANED against the side of her truck, fanning herself half-heartedly with her hands. It didn't do much good, but it gave her hands something to do. Around her, the remnants of the celebration were winding down. The steady hum of crickets, their rhythmic chirping rose and fell in waves, blending with the soft murmur of voices as families packed up their pies, folded their chairs, and began trickling out of the square.

Lauren ran a hand through her hair, her scalp still burning from hours spent under the sun. She tilted her head back and looked up at the night sky. It stretched clear and vast, the stars sharp and bright, as if the heat had scoured the heavens clean. The moon hung low on the horizon, swollen and yellow like an overripe fruit, casting a soft glow over the square.

The children had finally slowed, their energy worn thin after hours of running, laughing, and chasing sparklers. She watched Rachel coax a half-asleep Ruthie into Will's truck, the little girl's legs dragging against the dusty ground. In the distance, the boys' laughter carried softly on the breeze, their sparklers trailing lazy loops of orange light through the darkness. Beyond the square, fireflies blinked in the shadows, their quiet glow weaving through the trees like scattered stars fallen to earth.

She glanced at the few townsfolk who remained, mostly adults now. Their faces shone with sweat in the moonlight as they fanned themselves with whatever they could find: hats, folded newspapers, church bulletins. Their movements were slow and tired, like the heat had hollowed them out. She didn't blame them. This wasn't just the kind of heat that made you sweat; it was the kind that settled deep in your bones, wearing you down from the inside out.

Even Edward had taken off his hat, holding it in one hand as he leaned against the oak tree nearby. He'd been quiet since the fireworks ended, his sharp eyes scanning the square as if he were still watching for trouble. Lauren's gaze drifted to Victor and Chana, who stood a little apart from the crowd. Chana's hand rested on Victor's arm, her other hand carried the empty basket from her stall. It had been a wonderful success despite Mr. Harlan. Or maybe because of his behavior. Either way, the residents of Delgany had purchased every piece of baked goods.

Lauren sighed softly, turning her attention back to the square. It had been a good day, she reminded herself. Despite everything, the heat, the judgmental whispers, Mr. Harlan's disgusting remarks. The children had laughed. Hans had danced. Even Becky had managed to smile and let herself be pulled into a clumsy waltz near the bandstand, her worries about Luke set aside for a couple of hours.

"Miss Lauren, this is for you."

The sound of Hans's voice startled her. She looked down to see him standing in front of her, holding the crumpled dollar he and Cal had won in the talent contest. Cal stood beside him, his expression unusually solemn.

Lauren raised an eyebrow, taking in their earnest faces. "Thank you, boys, but you won that money fair and square. I thought you wanted to buy Clark bars and peppermint sticks."

Cal sighed, shuffling his feet in the dirt. He glanced at Hans, who gave him a subtle nudge. Cal shook his head and mumbled, "We want you to have it. It's our way to say thank you for everything you do. Maybe you could buy some ribbons or something with it."

Lauren bit back a laugh, pressing her lips together to

keep her composure. Ribbons? Since when did she have money for such frivolous things? But looking at the boys' earnest faces, she couldn't bring herself to dismiss their gesture.

She crouched down slightly, her tone soft. "I tell you what," she said, leaning in conspiratorially. "Why don't we find the man with the cotton candy stand and see if he has any left? Then we'll take it home and share it with everyone."

Hans's eyes lit up, and Cal grinned wide. "I love cotton candy!" Cal shouted, already tugging Hans toward the direction of the stand. "Come on, Hans!"

Lauren straightened, shaking her head as she watched them go.

"That was a clever trade," Edward's voice rumbled softly behind her. She turned to see him standing close, his hat dangling from his fingers.

Lauren shrugged. "It was their money. I wasn't about to take it."

Edward smiled, his eyes catching hers in the soft glow of the moonlight. "You don't give yourself enough credit, Lauren Greenwood. Those boys adore you."

Lauren was about to brush off the compliment, but before she could, Edward slid his arm around her waist and pulled her close. His voice was low as he leaned in. "I'll buy you some ribbons," he murmured, his lips brushing her ear. "And anything else that makes you happy."

Lauren opened her mouth to respond, but he stole a quick kiss before she could say a word. She blinked up at him, her cheeks burning hotter than the day's sun.

Edward stepped back with a teasing grin and tipped his hat. "I'll go wrangle the others so we are ready to go when the boys get back."

Lauren stood there for a moment, her breath catching in her chest. Then, shaking her head with a quiet laugh, she followed him back toward the dwindling crowd.

CHAPTER 26

The Meyers had gone into Charlottesville with Nanny Kat and Ian to the cinema. Becky and Will were off somewhere, leaving Lauren and Edward alone to enjoy a rare moment of quiet—well, as alone as anyone could be in a house full of orphans.

Lauren sat curled up on the couch, a book resting lightly on her lap, though she hadn't turned a page in quite some time. Across from her, Edward leaned back in the armchair, one leg crossed over the other, a notebook balanced on his knee. His pencil scratched softly against the paper, the only sound filling the otherwise still room. He was always writing something, even in moments like this.

"What's caught your attention tonight?" Lauren asked, tilting her head in quiet amusement.

Edward glanced up, a small smile tugging at the corners of his mouth. "Just mulling over an article I'm working on.

The papers are full of King Edward VIII these days—his ascension, his speeches, how the public is taking to him."

Lauren raised an eyebrow, rolling the name around on her tongue. "King Edward VIII," she echoed thoughtfully. "It sounds strange, doesn't it? After so many years of George V."

Edward tapped his pencil against the notebook, his eyes distant. "Odd, yes. But not surprising. He's a modern sort, charming, charismatic, a little too eager to shake up traditions." He paused, watching her closely. "A king like that will either captivate the world or make a few enemies along the way."

Lauren smirked and tucked her legs beneath her. "Is that your professional opinion, Mr. Belmont?"

Edward chuckled, closing the notebook and setting it aside. "Perhaps. I've always found it fascinating how the monarchy shapes the public's mood. England's grappling with enough troubles as it is. Unemployment, strikes, political unrest. But still, every move he makes dominates the headlines."

Lauren liked the way his thoughts always seemed to stretch beyond their small corner of the world. "And what do you think of him, really?"

Edward considered this for a moment, then said, "He's a complicated figure. Popular with the press, no doubt. But there's something restless about him, like he's chasing something just out of reach." He leaned forward, resting an elbow on his knee. "If I had to guess, I'd say his reign won't be as steady as his father's."

"That's a bold prediction," Lauren teased. "We'll have to wait and see."

Edward's gaze softened as he held hers. "History has a way of surprising us. Just like people do."

Lauren's breath caught in her throat. The weight of his words settled between them, unspoken but undeniable. She watched as he stood and crossed the room, lowering himself onto the couch beside her.

He reached out, brushing his fingers against hers before leaning in to press a gentle kiss to her lips. "Want to tell me why you've been avoiding me?"

Lauren swallowed hard. "I ... the children. Becky." She trailed off under his steady gaze.

"Lauren, talk to me. If I don't know what's wrong, I can't fix it."

Her throat felt tight, and for a moment, words failed her. She reached for the water glass beside her, taking a slow sip.

"Don't you want to get married?" His voice was quieter now, edged with something that sounded like hurt.

The floodgates broke. "I love you, Edward. I want to marry you more than anything."

"But?"

Lauren stared down at her hands, tracing the rim of the glass with her finger. "I don't want to leave Hope House."

There. She'd said it. The words hung heavy in the air, irreversible now.

Silence stretched between them, pressing in like a physical weight. Even the house, usually filled with the distant laughter and footsteps of children, seemed unnaturally quiet.

Edward leaned back, running a hand through his hair. "You want to start married life in a house full to bursting?"

Lauren's lips twitched despite the ache in her chest. "When you put it like that ..." But what was the alternative?

She exhaled slowly, steeling herself. "I know it's not ideal, but I can't bear to leave the children. Not even to move into a house across the fields. This place—" she swallowed hard, her voice trembling "—this is my home. The first place I've ever felt safe. Felt ... loved. I can't leave it. Not even for you."

Edward's expression shifted—half incredulous, half something else she couldn't quite place. He studied her for a long moment, then sighed.

And Lauren held her breath, waiting.

Finally, Edward spoke, his voice quieter than before. "I suppose now's as good a time as any to tell you." He leaned forward, resting his elbows on his knees, his hands clasped together tightly. "I have to leave for a while."

Lauren's heart gave an uneasy lurch. "Leave?"

He nodded, staring down at the floor. "France."

A hollow feeling settled in her gut. "France?"

Edward offered a half-smile, but it didn't reach his eyes. "It was your suggestion, remember? I've meetings set up with some of Victor's friends, those helping people in danger escape Germany." He let out a breath.

Lauren's fingers curled into the fabric of her skirt. "You were planning to tell me this when, exactly?"

He winced. "I was building up to it."

She laughed, but there was no humor in it. "Building up to it." The words tasted bitter. "And when do you leave?"

His hesitation was answer enough.

"Edward." Her voice was barely a whisper.

"There's a ship sailing tomorrow night."

Lauren pressed a hand to her forehead, feeling suddenly lightheaded. Tomorrow. Tomorrow he would leave, and they hadn't even figured out where they stood.

"I wanted to talk to you about it sooner," Edward said, reaching for her hand, but she pulled away instinctively.

Lauren stared at him, searching his face for something. An explanation, a reassurance, anything that would make this feel less like the ground crumbling beneath her feet.

Edward sighed, raking his fingers through his hair again. "I'm not walking away from you, Lauren. This is something I have to do. It's the compromise we agreed upon."

Lauren swallowed past the lump in her throat. "What happens to us?"

Edward's jaw tightened. "I don't know." He chewed the inside of his gum before facing her. "I love the children, I do. But I don't know if I'm cut out for moving in here."

The confession landed between them, heavier than anything either of them had said before.

Lauren let out a shaky breath and forced a nod, as if accepting it, but inside, everything felt like it was unraveling. "I suppose... we'll have to wait and see."

Edward's lips parted, as if he wanted to say something, but instead, he leaned in and pressed a lingering kiss to her forehead. It was tender and bittersweet, like a promise he couldn't quite keep.

"I'll write," he said.

Lauren shut her eyes, nodding against him.

And then he stood, collecting his notebook and tucking it under his arm. For a moment, he lingered, like he wanted to stay, but then he turned toward the door.

Lauren watched him go, feeling the quiet settle back in around her, heavier than it had ever been before.

Somewhere upstairs, a floorboard creaked under the soft steps of a child, and the house came back to life.

But she sat there, staring into the empty space where he had been, unsure of how to fill it.

CHAPTER 27

*L*auren knew something was wrong the moment the boys came through the door.

Cal stomped in first, his face dark with anger, his hands balled into fists at his sides. Hans followed a step behind, moving stiffly, like it hurt to walk. A bruise was already blooming on his cheekbone, and there was a cut on his lip that hadn't been there when they left.

She set down the dish towel and crossed her arms. "What happened?"

"Nothing," Hans muttered, eyes on the floor.

"Wasn't nothing," Cal snapped. "Tommy Rawlins and his gang jumped him."

Lauren's stomach tightened. "They what?"

"They were waiting for us outside the store," Cal said. "Started in on Hans, calling him a Nazi, saying he don't belong here. Punched him before he even saw 'em coming."

Lauren's eyes flicked to Hans. His shoulders were

hunched, his hands tucked into his pockets like he wanted to disappear inside himself. The sight of him like that, small and wounded, made something fierce rise up inside her.

"You should've come straight home," she said, her voice tight.

Hans shrugged one shoulder. "Cal took care of it."

"I would've taken care of them if they hadn't run off," Cal muttered.

Lauren exhaled sharply, running a hand through her hair. "Go wash up, Hans. I'll bring you some ice for that cheek."

Hans nodded and slipped away without another word. Cal hesitated, shifting from foot to foot, watching the spot where his friend had just been.

Lauren praised him. "You did good, standing up for Hans."

Cal's lips pressed into a thin line. "They don't even know him," he muttered. "He ain't like them."

Lauren reached out, squeezing his shoulder. "I know."

THAT NIGHT, Lauren was clearing the supper dishes when she heard voices outside the open window.

She paused, listening.

Down by the creek, Cal and Hans sat side by side, their feet skimming the surface of the water. The night air carried their words to her, soft but clear.

"So," Cal asked, "who you gonna root for in the Olympics?"

A long silence.

"I don't know."

Lauren set the dish towel aside, moving closer to the window. There was something in Hans' voice she hadn't heard before. Not just uncertainty. Hurt.

"You mean America, right?" Cal pressed.

Hans didn't answer right away. "I don't know," he said again, quieter this time.

The cicadas hummed, filling the space between them.

"I should say America," Hans said. "But I grew up with the German team. I know their names, their best records. I used to be proud of them." Hans paused. "But that Germany isn't mine anymore."

Lauren felt her throat tighten.

"My father used to take me to races. He was proud, too." Hans' voice cracked, just a little. "But they took him. And my mother—she's still there. I don't even know if she's safe. So how can I ...?"

He trailed off.

Cal didn't say anything for a while. Then she heard a soft plop as he threw a stone into the creek.

"You don't have to pick," Cal said. "You don't gotta choose."

Hans let out a short laugh, sharp and bitter. "Feels like I already have."

Lauren closed her eyes.

She wanted to go outside, to tell Hans he didn't have to choose, that he had a home here, with them. But she knew it wasn't that simple. She couldn't promise that the town would stop whispering about him, or that people wouldn't see him as an outsider, or that he would ever stop feeling caught between two countries, two selves.

All she could do was make sure he had one place in this world where he was safe.

Tomorrow, she'd make his favorite breakfast. She'd drive them to school and have Terry pick them up. She'd write another letter to the immigration office about his mother, even if she never got a reply.

It wasn't enough. But it was something.

She was still thinking about Hans when Becky finally returned, her boots kicking up dirt as she strode across the yard, face set in determination. The girl was ignoring all advice and searching for Luke every chance she got.

Lauren crossed her arms, her voice sharper than she intended. "Could have done with your help here today."

"What happened?"

Lauren filled her in, watching as Becky's temper fired.

"That little rat Rawlins. I swear, if I get my hands on him, he'll wish he wasn't born."

"An adult picking on a child is a great example to the children, isn't it?"

"What's rattled your cage? You not heard from Edward or something?"

"It's you, Becky. You are putting yourself and Hope House in danger by going looking for Luke. The sheriff told you, Will told you and I asked you not to. We're worried about you.

"He's my brother Lauren. He's out there somewhere and I ain't going to stop 'til I find him."

Becky stormed off indoors, letting the door bang behind her. Lauren rubbed her forehead, exhaustion creeping in. The world outside was burning with anger, and now it was creeping through Hope House's doors, tainting everything it touched.

CHAPTER 28

Lauren's fingers brushed the rough edge of the quilt as she tucked it around Luke, her stomach knotting at the sight of his pale, sweat-drenched face. His chest rose and fell in uneven jerks, each labored breath loud in the stillness of the room. The flickering light from the oil lamp threw shadows across the walls. She knew Becky wouldn't mind her putting Luke in her room. They had to keep him away from the children, fever could spread.

She glanced at Tom, who stood near the door, his hat clutched in his hands. Mud streaked his boots, and exhaustion etched deep lines into his face.

"Where did you find him?" Lauren's voice came out sharper than she intended.

Tom shifted his weight, avoiding her eyes. "Down near the old mill, in the woods by the creek. He wasn't hidin'. He was lyin' there, like he'd given up. Fever's bad, Miss Lauren. I couldn't just leave him."

Lauren sighed, her gaze drifting back to the boy in the bed. Luke Tennant. Becky's brother.

"You did the right thing," she murmured, though the knot in her chest didn't loosen. "Go wash up. I'll see to him."

Tom hesitated, his brow furrowed. "He's been mutterin' … sayin' things. Don't make much sense, but he mentioned Matt."

Lauren's breath caught as she watched Tom slip out of the room. The moment the door clicked shut, she sank into the chair beside the bed, brushing damp hair from Luke's flushed forehead. His skin burned under her touch.

"Becky's been waiting for you," she said, though she knew he couldn't hear her. "You've got a lot to answer for, Luke."

The door creaked open, and Becky stepped in, her coat dripping water onto the floor and her boots leaving muddy tracks behind. Her face was pale, her lips set in a tight line.

"I was at the sheriff's office," Becky said, her voice low, as she yanked her coat off and slung it over a chair. She ran a hand through her damp hair, her fingers trembling slightly. "Sheriff said he'd heard talk of some new folks movin' through the mountains—folks who don't belong. I thought maybe they'd know somethin' about Luke, but all I got was more questions."

Her eyes fell on Luke, and she froze. For a moment, all the fire drained from her, leaving only raw emotion behind. "And then I get back to find him here." Her voice cracked, and she pressed a hand to her mouth, taking a shaky breath.

Lauren stood, placing a hand on Becky's shoulder. "Tom brought him in just a little while ago. He found him near the old mill, barely conscious."

Becky's jaw tightened. "He's wanted, Lauren. The sheriff's gonna hear he's back, whether we tell him or not."

Lauren frowned, her voice calm but firm. "He's burning up, Becky. He's not going anywhere like this. We need to focus on getting him through the fever before we do anything else."

Becky rounded on her, her green eyes blazing. "And what happens if the sheriff finds out before we say somethin'? You think he'll care that he's half-dead? He'll drag him off in shackles, fever or not."

Lauren folded her arms, meeting Becky's gaze. "He's not like that. Not anymore. Look at the way he looks out for us. He'll understand why we waited. It's not like Luke is going anywhere now. Not in this state. I'll tell him in a couple of days when I head into town. You can stay here and mind Luke."

Lauren glanced at the boy on the bed. His face was flushed, his breathing uneven. His fevered words still echoed in her ears. "It was my fault. I didn't mean to leave him."

"I'm not saying we hide him forever," Lauren said gently. "Just long enough to figure out what happened and let him recover. If he can tell us the truth, maybe we can help him. Maybe the sheriff doesn't have to treat him like a criminal."

Becky looked away, her fists clenching and unclenching

at her sides. "And what if he is a criminal, Lauren? What if he's done things we can't fix?"

Lauren stepped closer, her tone soft but firm. "Then we still stand by him. He's your brother, Becky. And he's just a boy. Whatever he's done, he deserves a chance to make it right."

For a moment, the only sound in the room was the faint rasp of Luke's breathing. Becky's shoulders sagged, and she nodded reluctantly. "Alright. We wait. But the minute his fever breaks, we figure out what we're gonna do."

Becky exhaled slowly, pulling up a chair beside the bed. She reached out, brushing a damp strand of hair from Luke's forehead. "I just got him back, Lauren," she whispered, her tears spilling over. "I can't lose him now."

"You won't," Lauren assured her, though the weight of the situation pressed heavily on her chest. "We'll figure this out."

As Becky settled into the chair, Lauren turned to fetch more cool water for the compress. Her mind churned with questions. What kind of trouble was waiting for them once the fever broke and the truth came out?

CHAPTER 29

The room was stifling. Heat clinging to the walls and thickening the air. Lauren sat beside Luke, wringing out the cloth she'd been using to cool his forehead. His fever still burned as hot as when Tom had found him, and nothing they tried seemed to help.

Across the room, Becky stood by the window, arms wrapped around herself. Her green eyes flicked between Luke's restless form and Lauren. "Shouldn't the fever have broken by now?"

"If it doesn't, we'll have to get the doctor," Lauren replied. "But you should sleep, Becky. You can't fall sick too —you've been up all night nursing him."

Becky didn't reply. Her teeth worried at the inside of her cheek, and her arms tightened around her middle like she was holding herself together. A faint, broken sound escaped Luke's lips, drawing their attention. Lauren leaned in, brushing his damp hair back as his mouth moved, his voice barely audible.

"Ma ..." The word cracked, hoarse and raw. "Ma ... Donnie ... Don't let 'em take her ..."

Becky's hand flew to her mouth, her body going rigid. "He's torturin' himself. The memories."

Luke's face twisted, his muttering growing more frantic. "Matt ..." His voice broke. "Don't leave. I didn't mean to —" His body jerked, as though caught in a nightmare, before falling limp again.

Becky was at his side in an instant, gripping his hand with both of hers. "Luke. Luke, it's me. Becky. I'm here." Her trembling fingers brushed his fevered cheek. "Please ..."

There was no response. Becky sank into the chair beside him, still clutching his hand as though sheer will could tether him to her. Lauren dipped the cloth into the basin again, her movements deliberate, her mind racing. She laid the damp cloth back on Luke's forehead, watching Becky's hands linger on her brother's.

"What did he mean about Matt?"

Lauren hesitated. "I don't know," she admitted carefully. "But whatever it is, it's haunting him."

Becky exhaled a shaky breath, her gaze fixed on Luke's pale, sweat-soaked face. "They took everythin' from us, Lauren. How could there be anythin' worse?"

Lauren didn't answer. She couldn't. But the way Luke's fevered mind clung to Matt's name made a chill settle deep in her bones.

A low hum broke the tense silence, growing louder by the second. Becky froze, her hand still gripping Luke's, as

Lauren pulled back the curtain. The sight of the sheriff's truck sent a jolt through her chest. "It's the sheriff."

Becky's voice wavered. "What's he doin' here?"

"Probably just checking on folks with the drought and all." Lauren dried her hands on her apron, already moving toward the doorway. "We keep him downstairs, no matter what. No questions, no suspicions."

Becky hovered behind Lauren as they moved toward the doorway. Her breath was shallow, her steps uneven.

Lauren hoped her friend could act natural; they couldn't afford to give Dillon any reason to suspect something was wrong.

"Miss Lauren!" Cal's voice rang out, eager and bright. "Sheriff Dillon's here!"

Lauren straightened her shoulders as they stepped into the living room. Dillon was already there, leaning casually in the doorway, his broad frame casting a shadow across the children playing on the floor.

"Anybody home?" Dillon called, his tone cheerful, though his sharp eyes flicked across the room, scanning the dusty boots by the door and the faint streaks of grime on the floor.

"Sheriff Dillon!" Fred piped up, bouncing to his feet. "Did you bring your fishing gear?"

"Not today, Fred," Dillon said with a chuckle, ruffling the boy's hair. "Thought I'd stop by and check on how everyone's doing in this heat." He took a hanky from his pocket and wiped his face.

Lauren forced a warm smile as she stepped forward, wiping her hands on her apron. "Morning, Sheriff. We're managing, thanks to the kids pitching in. Can we get you a cup of coffee?" Lauren led the way into the kitchen.

Becky stayed a few steps behind. Dillon tipped his hat toward Lauren. "Wouldn't say no to that. Smells like you've been busy cleaning up in here." His gaze swept the room again, lingering on Becky for just a moment too long.

"We're lucky the house got repaired after the storm," Becky said quickly, stepping toward the stove. "It's easier to keep the dust out, some of it anyway. Dusty floors are nothin' compared to what some folks are dealin' with." Her voice was steady, but her hands shook as she reached for the coffee pot.

"True enough."

Sheriff Dillon accepted the steaming cup of coffee and leaned against the doorframe. He took a slow sip, his eyes sharp despite his relaxed posture. "I've been making my rounds. Some parts are in bad shape, they barely got a chance to recover from the flooding and now this drought. The weather folk says it's likely to last a while but folks are pulling together to get through."

"That's a blessin'," Becky said, her voice tight.

Dillon nodded, taking another sip of coffee. Then, almost casually, he added, "Course, there's been talk. You know how folks get when they get to talking. Said they saw someone coming down from the mountains the other night. Looked like trouble."

Lauren kept her expression calm, though her stomach churned. "We've been too busy cleaning up to pay attention to gossip," she said lightly, folding the dishrag in her hands.

"Funny thing about gossip," Dillon's gaze drifted lazily

toward the staircase. "It usually starts with a kernel of truth."

A faint thud echoed from upstairs. Becky froze midstep, the coffee pot trembling in her hands. Dillon's head snapped up, his eyes narrowing as he glanced toward the ceiling. "What was that?" he asked, his tone still casual, but there was an edge to it now, a faint hint of suspicion.

Lauren forced a laugh, stepping in front of him as though blocking his view of the stairs. "Hans and Cal. They were told to make the beds but you know kids and chores." Lauren hated lying, but she had no option.

Becky nodded quickly, her voice rising too fast. "I'll check on them."

"No need," Lauren said smoothly, giving Becky a pointed look. "I'll handle it."

The sheriff didn't respond right away. Instead, he set his cup down on the counter and straightened, his gaze flicking to Becky again. "You're looking a little pale yourself, Becky. Everything alright?"

"I'm fine, just a bit worried about how we'll manage. You know we depend on the vegetables and orchard a lot."

"Understandable." His casual tone didn't give Lauren any relief.

Fred tugged on Dillon's sleeve, breaking the tension. "Sheriff, when are we gonna go fishing again? You promised to teach me a new knot!"

The sheriff chuckled, the hard edge in his eyes softening as he glanced down at the boy. "The fish will be hiding in this heat. Soon as the weather cools down and the water settles, Fred. We'll catch the biggest fish in the county."

Lauren seized the moment to step toward the stairs. "I'll just check on the boys and make sure they're all set. Becky, can you see if we've got some cookies left for the sheriff?"

Lauren moved up the stairs as quietly as she could, her heart pounding in her chest. Every creak of the floorboards sounded deafening, like a drumbeat announcing her ascent. When she reached the door to Becky's room, she paused, listening. The muffled sounds of Luke's shallow, uneven breathing reached her ears, along with the faint rasp of his fevered whispers. She slipped inside, closing the door behind her.

Luke lay tangled in the quilt, his face pale and glistening with sweat. His head rolled weakly on the pillow, his lips moving in fractured murmurs. "Matt..." His voice cracked, barely more than a whisper. "Didn't mean to, don't let them take her."

Lauren sat beside him, brushing his damp hair back with a trembling hand. "It's alright," she murmured. "You're safe. You're safe here." But even as she said the words, she knew they weren't entirely true. Luke wasn't safe. Not while his fever raged, not while the sheriff lingered downstairs, and certainly not while whatever haunted him continued to claw its way to the surface. She stayed with him for another moment, watching as his muttering quieted, his body settling back into fitful stillness. Then she slipped out of the room and back down the stairs.

When Lauren returned to the kitchen, Sheriff Dillon was finishing his coffee, laughing at something Fred had said. Becky stood by the counter, pale but composed, her hands gripping the edge of the sink. The sheriff glanced up as Lauren entered. "Everything alright?"

"Just restless kids," Lauren replied smoothly.

He set his empty cup down and adjusted his hat. "Well, I'd better get back to it. Still got a few folks to check on before sundown."

Lauren forced another smile. "If you hear of anyone needing help, let us know."

Dillon nodded, tipping his hat again as he moved toward the door. "And let me know if you hear anything, anything at all." His gaze lingered for a moment, as though daring them to contradict him.

Lauren's mouth dried, as she tried to find her voice. "Of course."

The sound of the truck engine rumbling to life didn't ease the tension in the room. Lauren watched through the window as it disappeared down the road, the weight in her chest growing heavier.

Becky exhaled sharply, leaning against the counter as though her legs might give out. "He knows somethin.'"

Lauren didn't answer right away. She glanced toward the staircase, her mind racing. "If he does, he doesn't know enough. Not yet." She wondered who she was trying harder to convince, her or Becky.

CHAPTER 30

The faint creak of floorboards broke the quiet, but it wasn't from upstairs. Both women turned sharply toward the doorway leading to the front of the house.

Nanny Kat stood there, framed in the doorway of her small room—the office Lauren had converted for her years ago. Though her face carried a hint of fatigue, her gaze was as piercing as ever.

She fanned herself with a little paper fan. "Are you going to tell me why the sheriff has you two looking like Cal caught with his hand in the cookie jar?"

Lauren stiffened, her hand still clutching the edge of the counter. Becky froze mid-step, her face draining of color.

"I may be old but my hearing is just fine." Nanny Kat continued, planting her hands on her hips, "I heard him fishing for information and now the two of you acting as jumpy as rabbits. I want the truth. Who's upstairs, and why are you hiding him?"

Lauren opened her mouth to respond, but Becky beat her to it. "Nanny Kat, we didn't want to worry you."

"You thought I'd what?" Nanny Kat interrupted, narrowing her eyes. "Collapse into a heap because of a little trouble? Now, out with it."

Lauren whispered, "It's Luke."

"Luke?" Nanny Kat frowned, her sharp gaze shifting to Lauren.

"Tom found him near the woods last night. Fever, exhaustion, hunger. We've done what we can, but if the sheriff knew ..."

"If the sheriff knew, he'd have questions none of us are ready to answer," Nanny Kat finished, her lips pressing into a thin line.

Becky looked down, guilt flickering across her face. "We didn't want to worry you. And we didn't know how bad it would get."

Nanny Kat's expression softened, but only slightly. "You should've told me. There's no sense running yourselves ragged when I'm right here. Now, where is he?"

"In Becky's room."

"Well, don't just stand there gawking. Show me," Nanny Kat ordered, waving them aside. "If he's as bad off as you say, then he needs someone who knows what they're doing."

Nanny Kat climbed the stairs with surprising speed, her skirt swishing as she reached the landing. Lauren and Becky followed close behind.

When Nanny Kat opened the door to Becky's room and stepped inside, her expression shifted from sharp to focused. Luke lay tangled in the quilt, his face pale and glistening with sweat. His hair clung to his forehead, damp and matted, and his breathing was shallow and uneven.

"Oh, you poor boy," Nanny Kat murmured as she approached the bed. She brushed his damp hair back with a practiced hand, her lips tightening as she took in his condition. "He's burning up."

"We've been using cool cloths," Lauren said quickly. "And trying to keep him hydrated, but—"

"But the fever's not breaking," Nanny Kat finished for her. She turned toward Becky, her voice brisk again. "Get me fresh linens and a basin of water. Boiling this time. And where's that peppermint oil? I know we've got some left."

Becky blinked, startled. "I—yes, of course." She hurried out of the room, her footsteps echoing down the hall.

Nanny Kat turned to Lauren, her hands already working to pull the quilt off Luke. "Strip the bed. This thing's soaked through. And we'll leave the quilt off for now. Too much heat."

Lauren nodded, quickly pulling the damp quilt off the bed.

"What else has he been saying?" Nanny Kat asked, holding Luke while Lauren worked.

"Ma. Donnie. And…"

"And Matthew," Nanny Kat's gaze flicked to Luke's flushed face.

"Yes," Lauren said.

"I've a bad feeling about Matthew, but Becky doesn't need more to worry about. Let's keep it between us for now."

Becky returned with clean linens, the steaming basin, and peppermint oil. Together, they worked swiftly, changing the sheets and tending to Luke. When they finished, the faint smell of peppermint filled the room, and Luke lay tucked into fresh sheets, his breathing still shallow but slightly steadier.

Nanny Kat sat in the chair beside the bed, wiping her hands on her apron. "Becky," she said, her tone firm but kind. "I know Matthew is never far from your mind. And I'm not saying you shouldn't hope. But don't let yourself get lost in what-ifs. Right now, this boy needs you."

"I can't lose another brother, Nanny Kat."

"You haven't lost him. As long as there's breath in his body, you hold onto that hope."

Becky nodded, her tears brimming, then allowed Lauren to lead her out of the room. As they moved down the hall, Lauren glanced back. Nanny Kat sat by the bed, her lips moving in silent prayer, her steady gaze fixed on Luke's pale face.

IN THE DIMLY LIT KITCHEN, the air hung heavy with the scent of peppermint. Nanny Kat sat at the head of the table, her hands held together as if in prayer. Across from her, Victor leaned against the wall, his arms crossed, a thoughtful frown etched into his face. Chana perched on the edge of her chair, her fingers nervously twisting the hem of her apron, while Terry sat hunched over with his elbows on the table, tapping his fingers in a restless rhythm.

Lauren shifted uneasily on her seat, taking another long gulp of cold water. The heat was unbearable, the tension in the room making it worse. She glanced at Becky but her friend was lost in thought.

"We couldn't just leave him out there to fend for himself," she said, breaking the tense silence. "Tom was right to bring Luke here. He wouldn't have made it through the night."

"No one's saying you should have," Victor replied, his voice calm but firm. His dark eyes flicked to Nanny Kat. "But hiding him? That's another matter. We don't know who's looking for him."

Chana spoke up, her voice hesitant. "If the sheriff finds out we've been keeping him here, he'll have questions."

"Which is why he mustn't," Nanny Kat cut in, her tone brooking no argument. "Not until Luke is strong enough to tell us the whole story himself." She cast a sharp glance around the room. "I trust Sheriff Dillion, but I have no time for the government men. Those Feds have their own rules and they'd haul that boy off without a second thought, sick or not."

Victor rubbed the back of his neck, his brow creased with worry. "But what if he's dangerous, Kathryn?"

"My little brother ain't dangerous. He's barely out of short trousers."

Lauren couldn't look at Becky. Did she really believe that? The Luke she'd known all those years ago wasn't the same boy as the one who lay upstairs.

Nanny Kat folded her arms. "He's as weak as a newborn kitten. For now, he's just a sick boy who needs help."

Terry, who had been quiet until now, finally spoke, his voice low and measured. "We're not just hidin' a stray dog, Nanny Kat. If the wrong people find out we've been keepin' him here, we could all be in trouble." He looked over at Becky. "And you, more than any of us, need to be careful."

Becky lifted her chin again, though her voice was quieter this time. "I know the risks. But I won't let him die."

Chana let out a long sigh, nodding reluctantly. "It's settled. We care for him, and no one breathes a word." She glanced around the room, her gaze landing on each of them in turn. "Not to the children. Not to anyone."

Lauren met Becky's gaze, seeing the flicker of determination behind the fear. "We'll make it work," Lauren said, trying to sound more confident than she felt.

Victor lingered a moment longer, his gaze flicking toward the ceiling as though he could hear the faint wheezing breaths of the boy above. "I'll fetch some more supplies tomorrow. We'll need willow bark for the fever."

"Good," Nanny Kat said. In a softer tone, she added "Thank you, Victor."

CHAPTER 31

*L*auren stood in the doorway of Becky's bedroom, her nails pressing into the doorframe as her gaze swept the scene inside.

Nanny Kat sat in the chair by the bed, her head bowed, her hands folded in her lap. Though her eyes were closed, her presence radiated steadfast vigilance, as though even in sleep she refused to let her guard down.

Lauren stepped inside, her footsteps soft on the wooden floor. "Nanny Kat," she whispered, placing a gentle hand on the old woman's shoulder.

Nanny Kat stirred, blinking awake, and straightened immediately. "I'm not sleeping," she said briskly, though her voice carried a hint of weariness. Her gaze shifted to Luke, her sharp eyes assessing him. "His fever's broken."

Lauren let out a quiet breath of relief and moved to the bedside. Luke's face was no longer flushed with heat, his pale skin glistening with sweat. His breathing, while shallow, was steady. He looked younger now.

"How long has he been like this?"

"Since just before dawn," Nanny Kat rose slowly to her feet. "His color started coming back. He's out cold now, but it's a good rest. Body's doing what it needs to."

"I'll take over. You go rest."

"Thank you, Lauren. Wake me if there's a change, but I think we're over the worst."

Of the illness, maybe, Lauren thought, but what trouble was Luke in?

She took a seat by the bed, watching him sleep. The faint rise and fall of his chest soothed her nerves, though the knot in her stomach refused to loosen. Behind her, the door creaked open. Lauren turned to see Becky, her face ghostly with worry and sleeplessness, clutching a shawl around her shoulders.

"Luke?" Becky whispered, her voice wavering as she approached the bed.

At the sound, Luke's eyelids fluttered. A low, hoarse sound escaped his lips, and he stirred, his head rolling weakly against the pillow.

"Becky ..." His voice was a rasp, his eyes struggling to focus on her.

Becky sank to her knees beside him, her trembling hands gripping his. "I'm here," she said, her voice trembling. "You're safe now, Luke. You're home."

His lips moved, as if forming words he was too weak to say. Then he blinked hard, tears pooling in his eyes. "They ... they took him," he choked out. "Matt."

Becky froze. "Took him? Luke, who? Who took Matt?"

His breathing quickened, his fingers clawing feebly at

the sheets. "I couldn't stop them ..." His voice cracked. "They're comin'."

Lauren's stomach twisted. She crouched by his side, her tone urgent but calm. "Luke. Who's comin'? What did you see?"

Before he could answer, the sound of heavy footsteps on the porch made them both jump. Lauren stood, her pulse quickening, and moved to the window. A shadow moved across the porch. "It's Will," she said, her voice tight. I'll go let him in before he wakes everyone."

Lauren ran down the stairs, her bare feet cold against the wood. Becky followed, clutching her shawl around her. When Lauren opened the door, Will was there, his face pale and drawn. His shirt clung to his chest, damp with sweat despite the cool air. He looked like he hadn't stopped moving for hours.

"Where is he?" he said, his voice low, almost harsh, cutting through the quiet.

Lauren opened her mouth to answer, but Becky stepped past her, her voice tight. "Keep it down," she whispered. "He's here, Will. He's alive."

Will stared at her, his expression shifting from relief to something harder. "And Matt?"

Becky faltered, her hand gripping the frame. "He said they took him."

Lauren placed a hand on Will's arm before he could push past them. "He's not strong enough for this," she said. "You can't press him right now."

His eyes snapped to hers, dark with frustration. "Lauren, if Matt's alive, we don't have time for this."

"And if you push Luke too hard, we might never know where Matt is," she said, her voice cold steel. "You'll lose him. Do you want that?"

Will hesitated, tension rippling through his frame. Then he took a breath, glancing toward the bedroom. "Can I see him? Just for a minute."

Lauren studied his face. The sharp edges of his expression had softened, just enough to reveal the worry beneath. The desperation. "If you promise to keep it brief," she said. "And gentle."

Inside, Luke looked even smaller than Lauren had realized, his frame swallowed by the blankets. Sweat plastered his hair to his forehead, and the faint rise and fall of his chest seemed impossibly fragile.

Will crouched by the bed, his hand gripping the edge as he leaned in. "Luke," he murmured. "It's me. Will."

Luke stirred, his eyelids fluttering open. For a moment, his gaze darted unfocused around the room before landing on Will. A spark of recognition flared in his eyes.

"Will..." His voice was hoarse, his lips barely moving. "I ...I didn't..."

"You don't have to explain," Will said quickly. His voice was low, steady. "You're safe now. We've got you."

Luke swallowed hard, his breath catching. "They took him," he whispered. "I couldn't stop them. They were ... too strong."

"I know," Will said. He reached out, his hand brushing Luke's wrist lightly, careful not to startle him. "You did what you could. Now, you need to rest."

Luke blinked at him, tears glistening in his eyes. "They'll come back. For me. For all of us."

Will's jaw tightened, but his voice didn't waver. "Let them try. They'll have to get through me first."

Lauren cleared her throat, breaking the moment. Will glanced up at her, a question in his eyes. "He needs to be cleaned up," she said. "We didn't want to compromise his modesty. But it's overdue."

Will hesitated, glancing back at Luke. "I'll do it," he said, standing. "Just tell me what he needs."

Lauren handed him the basin of warm water and fresh underclothes, keeping her voice low. "Be careful not to push. If he talks, let him. Otherwise, just keep him calm."

Will called when he was finished. Becky and Lauren stepped back into the room. Luke looked calmer now, his breathing deep and even. Becky took a seat by his bedside, taking his hand in hers.

Lauren caught Will's gaze and saw the shadow in his eyes. He wanted to speak. She led the way into the hall, taking the dirty linen from him.

Will's eyes lingered on the door to Luke's room. "I think whoever is after him will be here shortly."

Lauren swallowed hard, her arms tightening across her chest. "Do you really think they'd come here? Risk it?"

"They already took Matt," Will said, his voice sharp. "If they think Luke knows somethin', why wouldn't they?"

CHAPTER 32

*L*uke stirred beneath the light sheet, his face pale and slick with sweat. His eyes fluttered open, unfocused at first, then locking onto Becky sitting beside him. Uncertainty flickered across his face, his voice hoarse and weak. "Did you really come lookin' for us?"

Becky let out a shaky breath, relief and frustration warring in her chest. She leaned over and wrapped her arms around him, holding him tight. "Of course I did. You're my baby brother."

Then, just as suddenly, she pulled back and swatted his arm. It wasn't too hard, but enough to make her point. "And that's for bein' stupid enough to get mixed up with that old goat."

Luke winced, offering a lopsided, sheepish smile. "I'm sorry. I thought Foxy and Matt were tellin' the truth. That you found a new family. They said you had a passel of kids."

Becky sighed, brushing damp hair from his forehead. "I do. But they ain't mine, not in the way you're thinkin'. They're all orphans, just like Terry." Her voice softened as she added, "And you and me."

Luke's face fell, his expression crumbling. "I'm in a huge lot of trouble, ain't I?"

Becky smoothed the edge of the blanket over him, her touch gentle. "Don't worry about that right now."

Luke swallowed hard, his voice barely above a whisper. "I was scared, Becky. I didn't want to be part of this. Not from the beginnin'. But they gave me a choice—work with them or ..." He trailed off, his gaze dropping to his hands, twisting the blanket between his fingers.

Lauren, standing quietly by the door, felt anger coil tight in her chest. If Foxy had been here now, she wouldn't have hesitated to make him pay for what he'd done. Forcing a scared child into a life of crime and hiding him away from Becky. Foxy had known how desperate she'd been to find her brothers, and he'd used that against them.

Lauren stepped forward. "You don't have to worry anymore. You're safe now."

Luke's eyes flicked up, searching hers for reassurance. "What about the sheriff?" he asked, his voice small. "He's gonna lock me up."

Becky squeezed his hand. "He'll want to talk to you, sure, but let's not borrow trouble." She smiled gently. "Right now, we just need to get you downstairs to meet everyone. Nanny Kat's waitin' on us."

Luke groaned, sinking deeper into the pillow. "I think I'd rather go see the sheriff. Nanny Kat's gonna kill me."

Becky laughed softly, ruffling his hair. "Yeah, well, you deserve it."

Lauren hovered near the staircase, watching as Luke carefully descended, his hand gripping the banister like he wasn't entirely sure his legs would hold him. He looked pale and a little unsteady, but determination set his jaw tight. The fever had drained the worst of his strength. He kept his eyes on the floor. She wished she could remove the shame and guilt he carried.

In the warm glow of the sitting room, Victor and Chana Meyers sat at the dining table, Chana sorting through a pile of clothes, selecting potential pieces for the wedding quilt. She glanced up first, her sharp eyes softening when she saw Luke. "Look who's up and walking," she said, setting aside a garment. "We were starting to think Becky had tied you to the bed."

Victor stood up. "My name's Victor Meyer, and that lovely lady over there sorting through clothes is my wife Chana. Still look like you could use another day of rest, son."

Lauren watched Luke shift awkwardly under their attention, rubbing the back of his neck. "I feel fine," he mumbled, though the way he lowered himself onto the couch with a slow wince said otherwise.

Before anyone could respond, Nanny Kat strode in from the kitchen, wiping her hands on her apron. The second she laid eyes on Luke, she let out a short huff and marched right over, standing in front of him with hands on her hips. "About time you showed your face."

Luke barely had a second to brace himself before she

bent down and wrapped him in a fierce hug, pressing his head to her shoulder like she was reassuring herself he was really there. "Scared us half to death, you did."

Lauren saw Luke hesitate for just a beat, then sink into the embrace. His voice was muffled. "Sorry, Nanny Kat."

She pulled back and gave him a once-over, lips pursing. "Sorry don't fill an empty stomach." She straightened, wiping at her eyes quickly. "I got cornbread and beans in the pot. You'll eat, and you'll eat *all* of it."

Luke offered a tired, boyish grin. "Yes, ma'am."

Lauren smiled to herself, leaning against the doorframe. It was a strange thing, seeing Luke like this. It reminded her of the day she'd first arrived in the Tennant house with the children starving and Nanny Kat taking charge.

Terry stepped forward, crossing his arms over his chest. "I'm Terry. You gave us a hell of a scare, kid." His voice was gruff, but there was a trace of amusement in it. "Becky told me what Foxy put you through. I, uh … I'm glad you're okay."

Luke looked up, guilt flickering across his face. "Thanks," he muttered, then added, "for lookin' after Becky. I know she can be a handful."

Terry snorted. "Yeah, well, I'd say you both got that trait."

Before Luke could respond, the front door creaked open, and Will stepped inside, brushing the cold from his coat. He paused in the doorway, his eyes immediately finding Becky across the room. The corner of his mouth tugged up in that quiet way of his, the kind that said everything without him needing to speak.

Lauren watched as Becky stood, brushing invisible lint from her skirt before crossing the room to him. Becky reached up and kissed him lightly. For Becky to show this affection in a room full of people was a major breakthrough.

Luke, however, wasn't so impressed. His eyes narrowed at their clasped hands. "Wait a second." His gaze darted between them, and Lauren saw the exact moment realization struck. His brows shot up. "You two—you're together?"

Becky met his wide-eyed stare, her chin lifting in that stubborn way she always did when she was bracing for a fight. "Yeah. We're gettin' married."

Luke gaped at her for a moment, then groaned, sinking further into the couch. "Great. First Nanny Kat's gonna kill me, and now I gotta deal with *him* too?"

Will smirked, stepping fully inside and closing the door behind him. "Looks that way."

Chana laughed softly from the table. "Poor boy. Just too many people who care about you."

Lauren watched Luke glance around the room taking in the familiar faces, the warmth of the fire, the comfort of knowing he wasn't alone anymore. He let out a slow breath, and for the first time in what felt like forever, the tension in his shoulders eased just a little.

Nanny Kat clapped her hands together, jolting Lauren from her thoughts. "Enough chatter. Come in and eat."

Luke sighed dramatically but took the helping hand

Will offered him and allowed him to escort him into the kitchen. Maisie banged her rattle on her table, Lottie sat with her hands clasped under her chin, and Joey stood staring at him. Luke glanced nervously in their direction taking a seat at the end of the table farthest from the children.

"Eat up. There's plenty of food to be eaten, and I won't have you wasting away in my house."

He reached for the bowl Nanny Kat handed him, offering Becky a small, lopsided smile. "Guess some things don't change, huh?"

Becky sat beside him, nudging his shoulder lightly. "Nope. And that's how it should be." Then Becky looked around the table. "Better eat up, the children will be home shortly and we can only guess what questions Cal will have for my brother."

Everyone laughed although Luke looked up, his fork mid way to his mouth. "You mean there's more people livin' here?"

Lauren nodded. "This is only about half of the residents. You won't be able to hear yourself think when the rest of them get here."

The meal continued with introductions made. Luke had never met the Meyers and they hadn't known Becky's family. Will filled him in on John Thatcher and his adoption of Cassie, Gene and Vivian Hillman's move to live with their daughter and the fact that Earl now ran the store.

Lauren watched as Luke finished the last bite of his cornbread and beans, wiping his mouth with the back of his hand before glancing nervously at the others around the table. Becky had mostly picked at her food, stealing glances at Luke when she thought he wasn't looking.

Now, with their plates pushed aside, Nanny Kat bustled around collecting dishes, muttering under her breath about growing boys who needed more food in their bellies.

Luke shifted in his seat, clearly uncomfortable. "Thanks for the meal," he mumbled, eyes darting toward Becky before settling on the worn wood of the table.

Lauren leaned back in her chair, watching Luke closely. He looked different sitting here. His sharp edges dulled just a little, but there was still a wary tightness around his eyes, the look of a boy who'd spent too long looking over his shoulder. She could see the questions piling up behind his gaze, but before he could say anything, the front door creaked open.

The children's voices drifted in first, high-pitched and lively, shoes clattering against the floorboards as they rushed inside.

"Slow down!" came Cal's voice, loud and authoritative as usual. "You'll knock something over, Shelley."

"I'm not gonna knock anything over, I have to check on Joey. He's been missing me." Shelley huffed, pausing when she saw Luke sitting at the table. Her bright blue eyes widened, and she immediately moved to Joey's side as if he needed protecting. Ruthie followed her in but turned on her heel and scampered back toward the front hall, yelling, "Rachel! There's a *boy* in here!"

Luke blinked, startled, and Lauren had to bite back a smile.

"Cal," Lottie pointed at Luke, "his name is Luke and he's Becky's brother."

Fred, trailing in behind Cal, shoved his hands into his pockets and regarded Luke with a mixture of curiosity and suspicion. "So you're Luke," he said after a beat, glancing toward Becky. "The one she's been going on about."

"Yeah," Luke muttered, straightening in his seat.

Cal crossed his arms, sizing him up like a foreman inspecting a new worker before saying bluntly. "You look older than fourteen."

Luke rolled his eyes. "That's what happens when you live like I did."

Lauren watched the way Cal's sharp gaze didn't waver, his expression turning serious. "You ran away from Becky."

Luke stiffened. "I thought she didn't want me no more," he muttered. "Thought she found herself a new family."

Cal let out a scoff and plopped down onto the bench beside him. "That's the dumbest thing I ever heard."

Ruthie, emboldened by the others, crept closer, peering at Luke with wide eyes. "Did you live in the woods? Did you have to eat possum?" Her voice rose dramatically. "Or your own shoes?"

Cal turned on her. "Don't be stupid. Who eat's shoes?"

"Apologize, Cal." Nanny Kat intervened. "Don't call Ruthie stupid. She's right you know. Some people do end up boiling shoes to make a sort of soup. You will eat anything when you're hungry."

Luke scratched at the back of his neck, looking vaguely embarrassed. "Sometimes."

Fred's eyes widened. "For real?"

Lauren saw the hesitation in Luke's expression, as if admitting it out loud made it all too real. "Yeah. For real."

Cal leaned forward, resting his elbows on the table. "Listen," he said, his voice quieter now, more thoughtful. "We all got stories, okay? Me, Lauren saved me from a fate worse than death." He tapped a finger on his chest. "I was in the cells. Like a real criminal. They were shipping me back to the orphanage I ran away from where children were killed."

Catching the look of horror on the younger childrens' faces, Lauren put her hand on Cal's shoulder. "Enough of that now. You're scaring the little ones."

Cal folded his arms, protesting, "But you did save me."

Lottie spoke up. "You and Becky saved all of us." She turned to Luke, her small face serious. "They hugged us real tight and said we were safe."

Cal smirked. "They make us clean up and stop smelling like barn animals."

Luke let out a soft chuckle, but it didn't quite reach his eyes. "Sounds like her."

Fred nudged his shoulder. "You're lucky, y'know? Being Becky's real family."

Luke's jaw tightened, his voice rough. "I didn't feel so lucky." He glanced at Becky, who had gone quiet, standing by the stove with her arms crossed tight over her chest. "Not for a long time."

Lauren saw the flicker of pain cross Becky's face, but she didn't step in. She knew Becky wouldn't want her to. This was between Luke and the kids now.

Cal let out a long breath, shaking his head. "You're an

idiot. Becky's the best thing that ever happened to us." He paused before adding, "With Miss Lauren of course and Nanny Kat, Nanny Chana and Mr. Victor, although he isn't as strict as the women. Becky, she don't give up on people, even when they don't deserve it."

Luke looked at him, something raw and uncertain in his expression. "Yeah. I'm startin' to figure that out."

Sophie and Clarissa appeared in the doorway then, their school bags slung over their shoulders. Clarissa gave Luke a once-over before nodding politely. Sophie, on the other hand, marched right up to him and plopped into the chair across from him, fixing him with a curious stare. "Are you gonna stay?"

Luke blinked, looking a little overwhelmed by the attention. "I dunno."

Becky finally spoke, her voice quiet but steady. "You've got a place here, Luke. If you want it."

Lauren watched him carefully, noting the way his fingers fidgeted against the table, how his eyes darted around the room, taking in the faces watching him. She could see the battle happening inside him. The instinct to run warring with the deep, aching need to belong.

After a long moment, Luke let out a breath and nodded. "Yeah," he said, his voice barely above a whisper. "I think I do. But I got to have a word with some people first. Mainly the sheriff."

"He takes us fishing. He ain't half as scary as he tries to be." Fred added before snaking a hand to the cookies in the middle of the table.

Becky spoke up. "Go wash up before you touch those, young man."

Fred flashed a grin at Luke. "See what I mean!"

A grin split across Lottie's face. "Does that mean you'll help us with our chores?"

Luke groaned, but there was a trace of a smile on his lips. "I just got here, and you're already puttin' me to work?"

Cal laughed and nudged his shoulder. "Welcome to the family."

CHAPTER 33

*L*auren wiped her hands on her apron and sighed, picking up the newspaper Victor had left on the kitchen table that morning. The front page was crinkled from where the children had used it to press wildflowers, and she almost tossed it aside until a bold headline caught her eye.

"QUAKERS MOBILIZE TO AID REFUGEES FLEEING EUROPE"

Her pulse quickened. She sank into a chair, smoothing the paper against the worn tabletop, eyes scanning the text hungrily. Her breath caught when she saw a familiar name nestled within the article.

"Edward Belmont, an American journalist, recently assisted in transporting several refugees to safety under the coordination of the Quaker-led relief efforts. His work with the Society of Friends has provided critical aid to those seeking asylum from persecution. Belmont, who has been working with networks across France, believes that with proper funding and political support, many more lives can be saved."

Lauren's fingers traced his name, the ink smudging slightly beneath her touch. Edward. He was really out there, doing it. Helping people. Making a difference.

But where did that leave them?

She leaned back in her chair, staring out the window at the familiar bustle of Hope House. The younger children were playing tag near the barn, Becky was hanging laundry on the line, and Victor was stacking firewood by the porch. Everything here was steady, constant. But Edward's world was anything but.

The front door creaked, and Nanny Kat's voice cut through Lauren's thoughts. "You're staring at that paper like it's about to sprout wings and fly."

Lauren startled slightly but forced a smile as Nanny Kat walked in, wiping her hands on her apron and peering over Lauren's shoulder. "What's got you so deep in thought, child?"

Lauren hesitated, then tapped the article. "It's Edward. He's been working with the Quakers, helping refugees."

Nanny Kat squinted at the paper, then huffed. "That boy always had a way of landing himself smack in the middle of trouble." She pulled out a chair and sat down with a grunt, shaking her head. "I suppose next he'll be trying to save the whole world."

Lauren gave a weak laugh. "Seems like he's already started."

Nanny Kat studied her for a long moment, then patted her hand. "So, what's really got you all twisted up, hmm? You proud of him? Or mad at him for leaving?"

Lauren sighed, folding the paper and setting it aside. "I don't know, Nanny Kat. I'm proud of him, of course I am. But he's off chasing big things, and I'm here. How do two people with such different lives even make it work?"

Nanny Kat pursed her lips thoughtfully, then reached for the teapot, pouring them both a cup. "You ever tried planting two different flowers in the same pot?"

Lauren blinked at the sudden shift in conversation. "No."

Nanny Kat stirred a spoonful of honey into her tea. "Some flowers, they do just fine together. Like Lavender and Roses. Grow side by side, nice and easy. Others ... well, they got different needs, different ways of growing. You put them in the same pot, and one of them is bound to wilt."

Lauren frowned. "So what are you saying?"

"I'm saying you got to figure out if you and Edward are the kind that can grow together, or if you need your own space to bloom."

Lauren stared into her cup, the steam curling up between them. "But what if I love him?"

Nanny Kat smiled gently. "Love's a mighty fine thing, child. But it isn't always enough by itself. You got to want the same things, fight for the same dreams." She squeezed Lauren's hand. "The question is, do you?"

Lauren swallowed hard "I don't know."

Nanny Kat leaned back. "Well, you got time to figure it out. He'll be back soon enough, won't he?"

Lauren glanced at the newspaper again, Edward's name standing out among the sea of print. "I hope so."

Nanny Kat gave her a knowing look. "Don't you go sitting around worrying too much. That boy's got his hands full. And so do you."

Lauren nodded, forcing a smile. "You're right."

Nanny Kat stood and patted her on the shoulder. "Of course I am. Now, get on with you. That floor isn't going to clean itself."

As Lauren rose and went back to scrubbing the floor, she couldn't shake the thought that maybe, just maybe, Nanny Kat was right. Some flowers needed different soil to thrive, but she wasn't ready to believe that yet.

CHAPTER 34

The bell above the door jingled as Lauren stepped into Hillman's store, the familiar scent of cedar and flour greeting her. Behind her, Chana carried a carefully wrapped basket of baked goods, while Victor followed with steady, measured steps.

Behind the counter, Jimmy Simmons glanced up from stacking jars, his face a mix of nervousness and bravado. He wiped his hands on his apron, straightening awkwardly.

"Earl had to step out. Said I could watch the store."

Lauren forced herself to be polite, it wasn't the boy's fault who his mother was. "We're just dropping these off for Earl and picking up a few things. Won't take long."

Chana placed the basket on the counter with practiced care, her expression reserved but kind. She reached in and selected two taster pieces offering them to Jimmy.

"Cal and Fred love Babka. I make it with chocolate although some use cinnamon. If you prefer honey-based cakes, this is my husband's favorite, Lekach. It never lasts long. I also put in some cinnamon rolls, and two apple pies. Mr. Hillman said last week they were selling well."

Jimmy glanced at the basket as if it might bite him. "Yeah ... sure. I'll, uh, put it back for him."

As the Meyers quietly browsed the shelves, Jimmy's gaze lingered on them. He fidgeted with the basket on the counter before blurting out, "Didn't know Earl let just anyone sell stuff here now."

The words dropped like a stone in the stillness of the store. Chana froze mid-reach for a jar of honey, her face carefully blank. Victor's hand rested briefly on her shoulder, a steadying gesture.

Lauren's tone remained calm but firm as she turned toward Jimmy. "Hillman's is open to everyone. And I don't think Earl minds when 'just anyone' brings in baked goods that help his business."

Jimmy shrugged, his face flushing. "Guess it's none of my business. But my ma says folks should stick to their own kind. Like Father Coughlin says, you let outsiders in, and next thing you know, they're takin' over."

Chana's fingers brushed the edge of her coat, a subtle grounding gesture, before she replied, "Hate always finds a way to sound righteous."

The doorbell jingled, and Earl strode in, his cheerful expression darkening as he took in the scene. His sharp eyes moved from Jimmy's flushed face to the tension radiating from Chana and Victor. His voice, usually warm, carried a steely edge.

"What's goin' on here?"

Jimmy stammered, "N-nothin'. Just ... keepin' an eye on things."

Earl crossed the room in three brisk strides, placing a firm hand on Jimmy's shoulder. "If you were keepin' an eye on things, you'd see good people dropping off baked goods and buyin' groceries. Not findin' excuses to spout nonsense. This ain't your ma's parlor, boy. It's my store."

Jimmy flushed a deeper red, his gaze dropping. "I didn't mean anythin' by it ..."

Earl's tone stayed firm. "Meanin's in how you make folks feel. You want to work here, you treat everyone with the respect they're owed. You understand?"

Jimmy nodded mutely, his voice barely a whisper. "Yes, sir."

Earl gave his shoulder a final pat before motioning toward the back. "Go check the shelves. And next time, think before you speak."

Jimmy shuffled off. He hesitated at the storeroom door, his gaze flicking briefly toward Earl and the Meyers before he disappeared into the back.

Earl turned to Chana and Victor. "I'm sorry about that. Jimmy's young and full of foolishness. But I won't have that in my store."

Chana offered a faint smile, her voice steady. "Thank you, Mr. Hillman. It means a lot."

Earl waved her gratitude off with a kind grin. "Those apple pies smell like a piece of heaven. They're a hit with everyone who tries them. They'll sell out by tomorrow, I'm sure." He lifted the lid of the basket, his eyes widening. "I thought I could smell chocolate. I know what I'm havin' for supper this evenin.'" He touched his stomach. "It's a good thing I can't afford to eat every cake you bake, Mrs. Meyer."

"Chana please. If Babka is your favorite, I will make you a special one for next time." She set the goods on the counter. "How much do we owe you?"

"You're square as usual, in fact with this next lot, you will be in credit. We're lucky to have your goods here."

Lauren placed a hand on Chana's shoulder. "See? We're not just welcome; we're needed."

Chana chuckled, though the tension in her posture hadn't entirely eased. "Let's finish up and head home."

LAUREN GUIDED the car along the winding mountain road, her shoulders tense as the earlier confrontation at Hillman's store replayed in her mind. The silence inside the car was heavy, and she wished she could find the right words to dispel it. But the road demanded her full attention, the debris and water-filled sinkholes from recent rains turning every turn into a hazard.

A sharp curve loomed ahead, and Lauren's pulse quickened as her headlights illuminated a massive tree lying across the road. She slammed on the brakes, the car skidding to a halt. Chana screamed, clutching the basket of supplies on her lap.

Lauren scanned the roadside, her breath catching as the shadows shifted unnaturally. Figures emerged from the trees. Four men with bandanas obscuring their faces. One held a crowbar, swinging it lazily, while another had a shotgun slung over his shoulder. They spread out, blocking any retreat.

"Stay in the car." Lauren pushed open her door and stepped out, hands visible. "We don't want any trouble." Her stomach churned with regret. She should have brought her gun. But even with it, four against one were bad odds.

The leader stepped forward, his crowbar gleaming in the fading light. His voice was smooth, almost casual. "Trouble finds you anyway, lady." He motioned toward the car. "Out. All of you."

Victor opened his door slowly, helping Chana out. She clung to the basket with trembling hands, her face pale but composed. Victor placed a steadying hand on her arm as they stood beside the car.

"Got a little far from Germany, didn't you?" one sneered, his voice thick with mockery. "Maybe we should find you a way home."

Chana straightened, a defiant look on her face. "We have done nothing to you."

Lauren stepped forward, her stance protective as she addressed the men. "Leave them alone. Move out of our way and let us go home. We have nothing for you."

The leader chuckled, his grip tightening on the crowbar. "Oh, I think you do. You've got a message to deliver."

The man with the shotgun stepped closer, his voice low and deliberate. "Tell your young friend to return to the mill and end this like a man. Otherwise, next time, it won't just be a warning."

Lauren's stomach twisted. Luke. It was about Luke.

"We don't want trouble," she said, her voice unyielding. "But if you come near my home, you'll regret it."

The man laughed, hollow and cruel. "Feisty. I like that." He tipped his hat mockingly and gestured to the others. "Let's go."

They retreated into the woods, their shadows vanishing into the trees. The silence they left behind was deafening.

Lauren exhaled sharply, her hands trembling as she gripped the car door. "Get back in the car."

Victor hesitated, his jaw tight. "What did they mean about the mill? Is Luke in more trouble than just running away?"

Lauren's gaze flicked toward the woods, then back to Victor. "Not here. Not now."

The car rumbled back to life, and she navigated carefully around the fallen tree. Chana sobbed quietly on Victor's shoulder, the sound cutting through the hum of the engine.

As they drove, Lauren's grip on the wheel tightened until her knuckles turned white. Her breath came in shallow bursts, but she forced herself to focus. Luke's past had finally caught up to him, and now it threatened everyone under her roof. Her hands stiffened on the wheel, motionless except for the faint tremor in her fingers.

Lauren brought the truck to a stop outside Hope House. She took a deep breath, steadying herself before speaking. "We need to tell the others, but not in front of the children. Agreed?"

Victor and Chana exchanged a look. Chana's hand

trembled as she rested it on the dashboard. "I'm not good at pretending," she admitted. "Perhaps you can make our excuses, and we'll go to our room. I don't think I can pretend, even for the children's sake, that everything is okay. Today in the store was bad enough, but those men ..." She lifted a shaking hand to her mouth. "They reminded me of things I'd rather forget."

A pang of worry hit her. She'd invited this lovely couple to live at Hope House, promising them safety, but now she'd caused them more pain. Her throat tightened, and she couldn't meet their eyes. Words of apology circled her mind, but none of them felt enough.

Victor helped Chana from the truck and lifted the shopping basket. He paused. "Lauren, this is not your fault."

His words were kind, but they didn't touch the heaviness pressing down on her chest. She nodded mutely and followed them inside, taking the basket so they could retreat upstairs. When she entered the kitchen, she was met by the curious gazes of those she loved.

Becky reached for the basket, a curious look on her face. "Somethin' happen?"

"Jimmy Simmons," Lauren set the basket down harder than she intended. "He was horrible to Chana. I could swing for him, and his mother." She leaned back against the closed door, trying to steady her breath. "Something else happened, but I need you to wait until the children are asleep before I explain. I don't want to worry them."

Becky opened her mouth, but Nanny Kat's sharp look silenced her. "Let's get on with our chores." Nanny Kat turned to Lauren. "You look done in. Do you want to go upstairs and lie down?"

Lauren shook her head. Being alone with her thoughts was the last thing she wanted. "No, but thank you. I'll head out to the barn. I need to put this anger somewhere, and hard work usually helps."

CHAPTER 35

*L*auren stood on the front steps of Hope House, twisting her hands in her apron as the distant hum of a dark blue Ford made her heart jump. She swallowed hard, steeling herself.

He was back.

The vehicle rumbled to a stop in the yard, and before the dust had even settled, Edward stepped out, looking sharper and more energized than she'd remembered. His hair was slightly longer, his suit more worn, but there was something in his eyes, something determined, almost feverish.

"Lauren." He smiled as he strode up the steps, but before she could answer, he swept her into a tight embrace. She stiffened for a moment, then relaxed against him, breathing in the scent of him: leather, ink, and the faintest trace of tobacco.

"You're back," she whispered.

"For now" he said, pulling away, his eyes searching hers.

"I've got so much to tell you, but you look worried. What's wrong?"

She couldn't help it, the tears starting falling. He pulled her to him and she soaked his shoulder, telling him between sobs about Luke and how they were pushed off the road.

"I can't believe, today of all days, you just turned up."

"I wish I could say I planned it that way, but I didn't know you were in trouble. If I had, I would have dropped everything and come here."

Her lip trembled, but she couldn't stop the hope blossoming in her chest. "You would?"

"Of course. I love you."

He took her hand and led her inside, straight to the sitting room, where he sank into the armchair with a sigh of exhaustion and excitement.

Lauren sat opposite, her hands clenched in her lap. "I told Chana and Victor we would tell the others about what happened today, after supper. Can you stay?"

"Yes."

"You're driving. Your leg is much better and your hand too? I'm so pleased for you." She listened to herself talking and couldn't believe what she was saying. It sounded so mundane. "Tell me everything about your trip. I saw the newspaper article."

"I met with the Quakers in Paris. They're doing incredible work. Helping families escape the worst of it, getting them out of Germany before things get worse." His voice was filled with a passionate urgency. "They have safe houses in France, and I've already helped bring a few men back, people who barely made it out of Dachau alive."

"You helped bring them here? To America?"

Edward nodded eagerly. "Yes. They were in terrible shape, but they're safe now. The Quakers have a network in Philadelphia, and they're working with churches and local communities to find places for them." He paused, running a hand through his hair. "And I think they might be able to help Aunt Rae."

Lauren reached for his hand, her fingers trembling slightly. "Edward, that's incredible. But it's dangerous."

He smiled, squeezing her hand. "I know. But it's worth it."

She studied him, the spark in his eyes that hadn't been there when he left, and for a fleeting moment, she let herself believe that maybe he could do it.

Then reality sank in. "And where does that leave us?"

Edward's expression sobered, and he leaned back in his chair, his excitement giving way to something more uncertain. "Lauren, I want to marry you. I still do. But living here …" He glanced around the cozy sitting room, the faint sound of children's laughter drifting in from upstairs. "This place. It's not me. I can't see myself settling down in one place while there's so much to do."

Lauren's heart twisted. She'd known it deep down, but hearing him say it still stung. "But you expect me to leave?"

"I'm not asking that," he said quickly, too quickly. "I know Hope House means everything to you. I just—" He let out a breath. "I need to be able to do my work. These people need help."

Lauren looked down, tracing the edge of her nail with her fingertip. "I understand. I just don't know if love is enough, Edward."

He leaned forward again, his voice quieter now. "It has to be."

She lifted her eyes to meet his, searching for answers in the face she loved so much. "How long will you be here?"

"Not long," he admitted. "I'm heading to New York in a few days. The Quakers are organizing a meeting there. Leaders from different relief efforts, people working on resettlement and aid programs. I need to be there."

Lauren forced a smile. "Always off somewhere."

Edward reached out and cupped her cheek gently. "Come with me, Lauren."

She shook her head, stepping back. "Hope House needs me."

He looked away, drumming his fingers on his knee. She saw the hesitation in his eyes, the flicker of frustration he tried to hide. A long silence stretched between them before Edward spoke. "Then I guess we'll just have to find a way to make this work."

Lauren watched him, feeling the weight of the impossible between them. "I hope so."

She wanted to believe they could find a way, wanted to believe love could stretch across continents and causes. But deep down, she feared it wouldn't be enough.

Cal and Fred came running in. "Mr. Edward, you're back. We missed you. Did you find the bad guys?"

Lauren excused herself. "I'll go make you a coffee. Boys,

give Edward time to respond to your questions. God gave you two ears and one mouth for a reason."

"Gee Miss Lauren, you sound an awful lot like Nanny Kat." Cal rolled his eyes.

* * *

AFTER SUPPER, in the sitting room, Lauren sat stiffly on the edge of the couch, Edward sitting to her side, while Will leaned against the mantle, his arms crossed. Becky, Nanny Kat, Victor, Chana, Carly, and Terry were gathered as well, their faces etched with concern.

Lauren began recounting the ambush, her voice calm but taut with suppressed anger. She described the men, the tree blocking the road, and the moment they emerged from the shadows. Her hands tightened in her lap when she got to the warning.

"They said to tell Luke to return to the mill and end this like a man. Otherwise, next time, it wouldn't just be a warning."

Victor leaned forward, resting his forearms on his knees. His face was grim, his mouth set in a thin line. "Their intent was clear. They wanted to send a message and they wanted to frighten us."

Will's jaw tightened, his knuckles flexing where they gripped the mantle. "They're testin' you. They want to see if you'll back down."

"We can't back down. We're not handing Luke over to those animals," Lauren said. "But we also can't risk the children."

Will straightened, his presence commanding the room. "First thing we do is set up watches. Nobody goes anywhere alone, and we keep the property covered day and night. I'll take the night shifts."

Becky frowned, crossing her arms. "And what do you plan to tell the children when they see us patrollin' with shotguns? We can't turn Hope House into a military camp, Will."

Lauren agreed with Becky, and judging by the expression on the faces of the others they weren't keen on Will's approach either.

"We need to tell Sheriff Dillon." Nanny Kat held up her hand as Becky opened her mouth. "Becky, it's the safest choice, for Luke and for Hope House. You know that."

Becky's shoulders slumped. "I do but I don't want to lose Luke."

"You won't."

The quiet words drew every eye to the doorway. Luke stood there, pale and thin, one hand gripping the stair post for support. His gaze swept the room, guilt and determination etched into his young face.

"I won't bring trouble to Hope House," he said, shifting his weight as if bracing himself for an argument. "Not more than I already have. I'll go into Delgany tomorrow and hand myself in to the sheriff. That way, Boone won't have anythin' to gain by threatenin' you." His gaze landed on Lauren, and his voice caught slightly. "I'm sorry, Miss Lauren. I shouldn't have stayed here so long."

"Nonsense. You were recovering from your illness.

Where else would you have gone?" Nanny Kat's tone didn't invite arguments.

"Did you say Boone?" Edward leaned forward, his eyes locked on Luke.

Luke nodded. "Boone Mullins."

Edward leaned forward slightly, his expression sharpening. "Boone Mullins," he repeated slowly. "That's a name I haven't heard in years."

Luke's eyes widened with surprise and not a little fear, "You know him?"

"I know of him," Edward took Lauren's hand in his and squeezed. "When I started investigating William Greenwood and Justin Prendergast, I came across his name more than once. Boone kept to the shadows, but there were whispers about him. A man who used people like Lauren's father and Justin to get what he wanted. He let them take the risks while he reaped the rewards."

Luke nodded, his jaw tightening. "That's exactly what he did. Justin and Mr. Greenwood were his 'respectable' men. The ones who could move in fancy circles and make deals Boone couldn't. Boone's the kind of man who makes people nervous just by walkin' into a room. He couldn't pass himself off as polished or charmin', so he stayed hidden and let Mr. Prendergast and Mr. Greenwood do the dirty work he couldn't afford to show his face for. Mind you, Boone didn't have to force Prendergast. That man was just about as nasty as they came."

Her breath caught in her throat, her chest tightening as the name landed like a blow. For a moment, she couldn't move, couldn't speak, the memory of his cold eyes pinning her in place. Heat rose to her cheeks as her fingers twisted the fabric of her dress. She hated how easily the memory of him could unravel her, even now, when she thought she'd left it all behind. She let Edward's hand fall, but he put his arm around her shoulders and held her.

Luke's shoulders sagged slightly, but his hands remained clenched. He glanced at Lauren. "I'm sorry, Miss Lauren. I didn't know how to tell you."

Lauren's heart twisted at his words. She drew in a steadying breath, her mind racing with the implications of what Luke had said. "I thought it had ended when Father and that man died. Boone Mullins." The name tasted bitter on her tongue. "I never heard of him before." She turned to Edward. "Why didn't you say anything?"

"There was no point. I didn't think he would have any interest in staying around these parts. Not when Rosehall and all your Father's other assets were appropriated by the government." Edward looked back at Luke. "I'm surprised he returned to this area."

"He never left. He just moved higher up into the mountains where nobody, not even the government men can find him." Luke sighed. "Your father was good at makin' deals. People trusted him because he was rich, respectable. They didn't see what was happenin' behind closed doors. Boone needed him to open doors, to smooth things over when deals went south. But Mr. Greenwood wasn't runnin' the show. Boone was always the one in charge."

Lauren's pulse raced, anger and shame warring within her. "And Boone? What kind of man is he?"

Luke hesitated, his gaze flicking toward Edward as if

looking for permission to speak. When Edward gave a small nod, Luke took a deep breath. "He's the kind of man you don't want to cross," he said. "I only saw him once, but that was enough. He came to a cabin one night, meetin' with some of the men. I wasn't supposed to be there, but I saw him through the window. He's ... rough. Mean. The kind of man who doesn't have to say much to make you feel afraid."

He took a deep breath, his voice lowering as if the walls themselves might be listening. "Boone Mullins was the man behind everythin' your father and Justin were involved in. The smugglin', the thefts, the violence, it all led back to Boone. But he was smart, ruthless. He knew how to stay hidden, how to make sure other people took the risks for him. Men like your father and Justin. And good men like my brother."

Becky's head jerked up. "You're sayin' this Boone did something to Matt?"

"He had Matt workin' for him. He made him do some stuff, things Matt didn't want to do. Said he would kill me if he didn't. Matt tried his best to get away but someone always snitched. Boone knew everythin' we did, almost before we did it. One night, some of the men ...they ...they took Matt away. Never saw him again." Luke choked back a cough, impatiently brushing the tears from his face with his arm.

Becky turned, sobbing into Will's arms. Luke stared at her, his pale face stricken with guilt and grief.

"Why didn't anyone stop him?" Lauren asked finally, her voice barely above a whisper.

Edward's expression darkened. "Because Boone is a predator, Lauren. He's ruthless in a way few men are. He doesn't just silence his enemies. He erases them. Anyone who tried to stand in his way disappeared, or worse. He made sure no one could tie anything back to him." Edward looked back to Luke who stared at Becky, his eyes wide with pain. "Which begs the question. Why now? Why expose himself by threatening Hope House. Just what do you know, Luke?"

Luke shrugged his shoulders. "Everythin', nothin'."

Nanny Kat pushed herself up from her chair, her stern gaze locking on Luke. "Get yourself back upstairs to bed, young man. You're in no fit state to go anywhere. You need your rest if you're to face tomorrow." She motioned toward Terry. "Terry, go with him. Make sure he gets there in one piece."

Terry rose immediately. "Yes, Nanny Kat."

Luke opened his mouth as if to argue, but the warning in her raised eyebrow made him think better of it. With a weary sigh, he turned toward the stairs, his shoulders sagging. Each step he climbed seemed to age him, his body moving as though he carried the weight of the world on his back.

Nanny Kat waited until Luke disappeared around the corner, his slow footsteps fading. Then, with a heavy sigh, she lowered herself back into her chair, her sharp gaze sweeping the room. "Nothing will happen tonight," she said, her tone leaving no room for doubt. "This Boone Mullins will wait to see what Lauren does with his warning. He's playing a long game, and men like that don't act in haste."

Her eyes moved to Will. "In the morning, you and Terry will take Luke to see the sheriff. At the very least, Luke can explain to him what's been happening right under his nose. Maybe it'll be enough for Dillon to act."

"But ..." Becky's voice wavered, her face tight with worry.

"But nothing, Becky." Nanny Kat's tone softened but didn't lose its edge. "I won't stand by and let that monster anywhere near Hope House. We have to trust the law to protect us, even if it's not perfect. Will and Edward can't be here all the time, and we can't do this alone. Whether we like it or not, it's our best chance."

Becky looked like she wanted to argue further, but Will placed a steadying hand on her shoulder, and she stayed silent, though her lips pressed into a thin line.

Across the room, Chana and Victor exchanged a glance before rising to their feet. Victor spoke first, his deep voice carrying a quiet resolve. "It's time we went to bed. But tomorrow ..." He paused, glancing down at Chana, who nodded. "Tomorrow, I'll ask Terry to teach me how to shoot. I won't be defenseless again."

Chana placed a comforting hand on his arm, her head held high. "We won't let fear rule us."

Will turned to Becky, his expression gentle but serious. "We should go and let you get some sleep. Unless you want us to stay?"

Nanny Kat answered for her, her tone firm but kind.

"No, it's best for everyone to get an early night. Tomorrow will be here soon enough."

The room fell silent as the others left, their footsteps fading up the stairs and into the quiet of the night.

Lauren remained frozen on the couch, her hands resting limply in her lap as the firelight cast faint shadows across the walls. She barely registered the soft press of Edward's lips against her forehead. He put his arm around her shoulders but stayed silent letting her mull over what she'd learned.

Her mind spun in a hundred directions at once. Boone Mullins. Her father. Justin. The smuggling. Matthew. The connections tangled together like a suffocating web, tightening with every thought. She closed her eyes and pressed her fingers against her temples, as though she could push the memories away. When would it end?

Her father and Justin had been dead for years. She'd thought their crimes, their sins, had been buried with them. But their legacy of pain lingered like a specter, clawing at her even now. It wouldn't let her go.

Nanny Kat's voice interrupted her thoughts. "Edward, you should go now. I'll look after her."

Beside her, she felt his nod of agreement before he asked, "Lauren, will you walk me to the car?"

She nodded, stood up and grabbed a cardigan from the hanger by the door. They walked in silence to his car.

"I'm sorry all that came out about your father and Boone. I hope you are not too upset?"

"I'll live."

Edward sighed. "I can come back in the morning. I don't have to leave..."

She waited for him to say he'd put her first this time but instead the silence became oppressive.

"You have to do what you think best." Despite her words, she wanted to beg him to stay.

Instead he kissed her softly on the forehead.

She whispered, "Stay safe, Edward."

He paused, flashing her one last crooked smile. "I'll try."

And then he was gone.

Lauren stood there for a long moment, the faint smell of leather and ink lingering in the air.

She whispered to herself, "I hope love is enough."

She watched as his tail lights disappeared before heading back into the house, taking a seat on the couch. She didn't bother lighting the lamp.

The scrape of Nanny Kat's chair startled Lauren slightly, and she looked up as the older woman crossed the room. Nanny Kat placed a hand on Lauren's shoulder, firm but gentle, and leaned down slightly so their eyes met.

"We'll face it," she said quietly, her voice steady with the kind of reassurance only Nanny Kat could give. "But for now, you need rest. Go on. Tomorrow will come soon enough."

Lauren hesitated, her heart still heavy, but the warmth of Nanny Kat's touch grounded her. She nodded slowly and rose to her feet, her legs stiff and unsteady. She turned toward the stairs, her movements sluggish, as though the weight of everything she'd learned tonight was holding her down.

Nanny Kat's voice followed her as she climbed. "You're not alone in this, Lauren. Remember that."

Was Nanny Kat talking about the run in with Boone, or Edward? Lauren wasn't quite sure.

CHAPTER 36

The sound of Becky's voice carried down the hallway. "Luke! You're goin' to miss breakfast!"

Lauren paused mid-sip, the warm mug of coffee resting against her lips. Becky's tone was light at first, but when no answer came, her voice grew sharper, tinged with irritation. "Luke?"

Lauren set her cup down, the unease that had been quietly gnawing at her all morning now flaring into something stronger. She followed Becky out of the kitchen and up the stairs, the wooden floor creaking under her boots. She reached the landing just as Becky pushed open the door to Luke's small room.

"Becky? What's going …" Lauren's voice trailed off as she looked inside.

The bed was neatly made, the room tidier than usual, but it was empty. Too empty. Luke's boots, which usually sat near the door, were gone, along with the small bundle of belongings he kept in the corner.

Becky stood frozen in the middle of the room, her fingers clutching the edge of the bedframe as though it might steady her. Her eyes were wide and glassy, fixed on the folded piece of paper resting on the pillow. Lauren's heart sank as she followed Becky's gaze, the scrawled name on the front of the note sending a chill down her spine: *Becky*.

Becky reached for the note, her hand trembling. For a moment, she just stared at it, her breath hitching in her throat. Lauren stepped closer, her pulse quickening.

"What does it say?" Lauren asked, her voice barely above a whisper.

Becky didn't answer immediately. She unfolded the note slowly, her eyes darting across the page. With each line she read, her face crumpled further, her lips parting in a silent gasp. Finally, her voice broke, shaky and thick with emotion, as she began to read aloud:

Becky,

I can't stay. It's too dangerous for me to be here. Lauren being run off the road yesterday proved that. I can't risk the people I care about gettin' hurt because of me. And I can't go to the sheriff. Not yet. Boone's men might be watchin', and if they see me with him, everythin' could fall apart.

I have to deal with this alone.

I promise I'll be back when it's safe, but please don't come lookin' for me. If you try to find me, it'll only make things worse. Please trust me on this.

Tell Miss Lauren and Nanny Kat I'm sorry for runnin' out like this. Tell them thank you for everythin'.

Luke

BECKY'S HANDS trembled as she lowered the note, her face pale and stricken. "He's gone," she whispered, her voice cracking. "He left because of us, because he thinks it's safer to deal with this alone." She lifted her gaze to Lauren, her eyes brimming with tears. "Nanny Kat was wrong. She shouldn't have told him Will and Terry would take him to the sheriff."

Lauren's stomach churned as the weight of Luke's words hit her like a blow. She took the note from Becky, her hands tightening around the paper as her eyes scanned it quickly. Her pulse hammered in her ears when she read the line about Boone: Boone's men might be watching…

The thought of Luke out there alone, slipping into danger, made her chest tighten painfully. She lowered the note, exhaling slowly. "He thinks this is the only way to protect us."

Becky let out a choked sob, pressing her hands to her

face. "Why didn't he just trust us? We could've helped him. We could've kept him safe!"

Lauren stepped closer, her hand resting gently on Becky's shoulder. "He didn't want us caught in the middle. He's trying to protect us, Becky. He thinks he has to do this on his own."

"But he doesn't!" Becky pulled away, pacing to the window, her movements frantic. She stared out at the mountains, her shoulders heaving. "We're his family, Lauren. Families don't just let each other walk away into danger!"

Lauren wanted to argue, to say something to ease Becky's pain, but she couldn't find the words. Her own heart ached, torn between frustration and fear. She knew how deeply Luke's guilt had burrowed into him, twisting his sense of what was right. She could understand why he felt he had to do this, but it didn't make it any easier to accept.

The quiet creak of the floorboards made them both turn. Nanny Kat stood in the doorway, her gaze sharp and knowing, but tinged with the weight of concern. "Enough, Becky," she said gently but firmly.

Becky blinked, her lips trembling, but she stayed silent as Nanny Kat stepped into the room.

"Let me see that," Nanny Kat said, holding out her hand for the note. Lauren handed it to her without a word, watching as the older woman read it with a practiced eye. When she finished, she folded the paper carefully and handed it back to Becky.

"That boy's got a lot of fight in him," Nanny Kat said

quietly, her voice steady. "He's made up his mind, and nothing we do will change that. But chasing after him won't help anyone. Not him, not us. We have to trust that he knows what he's doing."

Becky shook her head, tears streaming down her face. "But what if he doesn't? What if he gets hurt, or worse?"

Nanny Kat crossed the room and placed her hands on Becky's shoulders, her touch firm but comforting. "I won't pretend this isn't dangerous. But Luke's not some helpless child. He's smarter and stronger than you give him credit for. He'll come back when he's ready."

Becky sagged under Nanny Kat's grip, her tears soaking into her apron. Lauren stepped forward, placing a comforting hand on Becky's back. "He'll come back," Lauren said, her voice steady but tinged with emotion. "We have to believe that."

The three of them stood there in silence for a long moment, the weight of Luke's absence pressing down on them like a storm cloud.

Finally, Nanny Kat straightened, brushing her hands on her apron. "There's no use fretting ourselves into a state. We've got work to do, and so does he. Let's trust that boy to keep his word."

Lauren nodded, but her heart still ached as she glanced toward the mountains, their peaks bathed in the soft glow of morning light. She couldn't shake the feeling that Luke was walking straight into danger, and the thought of Boone Mullins waiting in the shadows sent a chill down her spine.

Wherever you are, Luke, please be safe.

CHAPTER 37

*L*auren stepped out of the general store, balancing a small parcel of supplies in her hands, when she spotted Sheriff Dillon standing outside his office. His hat was tipped low against the sun, and his stance was stiff, shoulders set with the kind of tension that told Lauren trouble wasn't far off.

She hesitated, adjusting the parcel under her arm. She couldn't ignore him. She drew in a breath and crossed the street, her boots scuffing against the dirt road.

"Afternoon, Sheriff."

Dillon turned at the sound of her voice. He was unshaven and the weariness in his eyes didn't lift despite his attempt at a smile. "Afternoon, Miss Lauren. Didn't expect to see you in town today. It's mighty hot."

"Wedding errands," she said, holding up the parcel. "Becky's got us all running about. Figured I'd handle a few things before she roped me into the next list of chores."

A faint smile tugged at Dillon's lips, but it faded almost

as quickly as it appeared. He glanced over his shoulder at the open door of the sheriff's office, then back at Lauren. "You got a minute?"

Lauren tilted her head, curiosity prickling at the back of her neck. "Of course."

Dillon motioned toward the bench outside his office. "Sit a spell. There's something I need to talk to you about."

She followed him to the bench, setting her parcel beside her as she sat. Dillon leaned forward, resting his elbows on his knees, his hands clasped together. For a moment, he stared at the dirt road in silence, as though searching for the right words.

"Luke left Hope House, didn't he?" he asked.

Lauren stiffened slightly, surprised by the question. She'd assumed Edward or Will had told him. "He did. Left us a note, said he'd be back. What do you know about it?"

Dillon sighed, his jaw tightening. "He came to see me."

Lauren made no attempt to hide her surprise. "What? When? Will and Terry were supposed to drive him in to see you. The next day he was gone."

The sheriff scratched his chin. "I went fishing. He must have followed me as he came right up to me out there at the lake. Said he couldn't come into town in case someone saw him. Said he wanted to help me catch Boone Mullins and his crew." Dillon's gaze raked the street as he spoke, keeping his voice low. "Said he knew things. Routes they use, hideouts, people they work with."

Lauren's heart sank, a wave of dread washing over her. "He's working with you?"

"In a manner of speaking," Dillon replied. "He's feeding

me information, pointing me in the right direction. But he's doing it on his terms, Miss Lauren. Slipping into places I can't send my deputies without blowing the whole thing wide open."

She couldn't believe her ears. "You're letting him walk into danger?"

Dillon met her gaze, his expression grim. "I didn't let him do anything. He came to me, determined to make this right. Said he owed it to you and Becky and to himself."

Lauren shook her head, her hands knotting in her lap. "He's just a boy, Sheriff. He's already been through enough."

"You think I don't know that?" He retorted and stood up. He paced a little bit before sitting again. "But he's not the kind of boy to sit still when he thinks he can make a difference. And he's got good instincts, Lauren. Knows how to stay out of sight, how to listen without being seen. I'd rather know what he's doing than have him out there alone, running blind."

Lauren exhaled slowly, trying to process what she was hearing. Luke had carried guilt like a stone in his chest, but this? This was more than she'd expected.

She forced the words past the lump in her throat. "He said Boone's the one who worked with my father and Justin."

Dillon's expression darkened. "That's right. Boone Mullins is dangerous, Miss Lauren. Your father and Justin were part of it, but Boone was the one pulling the strings. He's smart, ruthless, and he's got a long reach. If Luke's trying to get close to him…"

He trailed off, but Lauren didn't need him to finish. She could feel the weight of what he wasn't saying.

He held her gaze, "I'll keep Luke as safe as I can, but if we're going to put an end to Boone's operation, I need every piece of information Luke can give me."

Lauren looked down at her hands, her mind spinning. She wanted to march out of town, find Luke, and drag him back to Hope House where he'd be safe. But she knew Luke wouldn't come willingly. He was determined to prove he wasn't the boy who'd got his brother killed.

She swallowed hard, "You think this is the only way?"

Dillon nodded. "It's a risk, no question about it. But if Luke's right, if he really knows what he says he does, we might finally have a shot at takin' Boone down for good."

Lauren sat back slightly, the heat of the sun on her head, the sweat trickling down her spine. The thought of Luke walking into danger, of him crossing paths with Boone Mullins, made her stomach churn.

"What do I tell Becky?"

Dillon locked eyes on hers. "Nothing. She will go chasing up those mountains like a hound after a coon. That will only bring trouble down on everyone."

Her chest tightened, making it difficult to breathe. She didn't like keeping secrets from her best friend.

"Does Will know?"

The sheriff gazed up at the mountain.

"Sheriff?"

"Will's my deputy. All the men in town are, at least those I trust. They don't know my source but when word comes to take Mullins down, I need all the guns I can get."

Lauren opened her mouth, but he got there before her. "Men, Miss Lauren."

They both knew she could out shoot most of the men in town, but it was pointless her saying anything. "You'll let me know if anything happens to Luke?"

"You have my word."

Lauren stood, picking up her parcel. She wanted to say more, to argue, to demand that Dillon send someone else into the lion's den. But she knew it wouldn't change anything. Luke had made his choice.

As she turned to leave, he spoke again, his voice softer this time. "Lauren, he's doing this for Becky. For all of you. Don't forget that."

She swallowed hard, nodding once before walking away.

CHAPTER 38

A few days after her unexpected encounter with the sheriff, Will arrived at Hope House just after midday, the strong sun beating down on the dried earth. Lauren spotted him from the front window, his boots sending up dust from the ground as he walked from his truck.

She ran into the kitchen just as he stepped inside with a sharp nod to Victor, who sat at the table sorting through a pile of letters.

Chana glanced up from the dough she was kneading, wiping flour-dusted hands on her apron. "Will," she greeted, arching a brow. "You're early."

"Not early enough," Will said, his tone serious as his eyes landed on Terry, finishing his lunch at the kitchen table. "Sheriff's deputized you. Come on."

Terry wiped his mouth with the back of his hand, already pushing back his chair. "Right." He grabbed his coat off the hook. "What's the situation?"

Will cast a glance around the room before answering. "Don't know all the details yet, but it's big enough to need more hands." He hesitated, then added, "And we're keepin' it quiet." His gaze settled on Victor. "That means Becky don't find out."

Victor leaned back in his chair, arms crossing. "She's visiting Miss Chaney with Carly. Won't be back till late afternoon."

Will's eyebrows lifted. "Miss Chaney's?"

Chana nodded. "Carly's been working hard on some dresses. They've gone to see if they're good enough to sell in Hillman's." She looked at him anxiously. "Becky needed the distraction. Is this about Luke?"

Will didn't answer her question. "When she comes back, keep her in your line of vision. The last thing we need is her riskin' everythin' to try to get near Luke."

Lauren folded her arms, leaning against the wall. "She's going to find out eventually, Will. And when she does—"

Will's jaw tightened. "Let's just hope it's not *today*."

Before they could head out, Nanny Kat appeared in the hallway, her sharp eyes flicking between Will and Terry. "And where exactly do you boys think you're off to in such a hurry?" She gave Terry a pointed look. "Your lunch isn't even settled yet."

Terry winced. "Nanny Kat."

She cut him off with a raised hand. "Don't 'Nanny Kat' me, boy. You're going off to do something dangerous, aren't you?"

Terry looked torn between pride the sheriff had included him and worry he'd upset Nanny Kat.

Will's tone smoothed. "Sheriff just needs a hand, that's all."

Nanny Kat pursed her lips. "Hmph. Well, don't bring back any trouble." She wagged a wooden spoon in Will's direction. "And you best not let Becky get wind of this. You know how she worries."

Will shrugged. "We'll handle it."

Satisfied, Nanny Kat turned to Lauren, her sharp eyes narrowing. "And you, don't go getting any ideas."

Lauren put on her most innocent expression. "Me? Never."

Nanny Kat muttered something about "girls with more curiosity than sense" and disappeared back toward her room.

Will gave Lauren a long look. "That means you stay put."

Lauren shrugged, too casually. "Of course."

Will didn't look convinced, but he didn't argue. He stepped outside with Terry, and Lauren waited until their footsteps faded down the path before turning to Victor.

Already calculating how long it would take to slip out unnoticed, Lauren said, "I'm just going to take advantage of the children being occupied and grab a few minutes to myself. I have letters to write."

Victor didn't look up. "You're planning something, aren't you?"

Lauren smiled sweetly. "Who, me?"

Victor sighed. "Just don't do anything *too* stupid."

* * *

LAUREN STOOD IN HER BEDROOM, pulling on the faded work trousers she'd borrowed from the donation pile. They hung loose, cinched tight with a belt. The shirt was equally ill-fitting, but with an old jacket and a flat cap pulled low, the disguise would do. She wouldn't pass as a man up close, but from a distance, it might buy her time.

The floorboards creaked behind her, and she turned to see Nanny Kat leaning against the doorframe, arms crossed, eyes brimming with concern.

"You think you're clever, don't you?" Nanny said flatly. "This is foolhardy, Lauren."

Lauren tucked her hair beneath the cap, stealing a last glance in the mirror. "I can't sit here and do nothing. My father and Justin started this smuggling ring. It's my responsibility to end it."

Nanny Kat sank into the chair by the door. "Your responsibility is here. To this house, to these children. What happens to them if you get yourself killed?"

Lauren's hands stilled for a moment. Then, quietly, "Becky's strong. Stronger than she knows. She'll carry on."

"I know you can shoot, but can you take a life?" Nanny Kat tried again.

Lauren stayed silent.

"Your father forced you to hunt, and you retaliated by becoming a crack shot so you wouldn't have to kill an animal. But now, you think you can shoot a man?"

Lauren turned sharply. "I don't intend to kill anyone, but you and I both know those men don't value human life. We know what they did to Matthew."

"All we know is that they roughed him up, took him

away and no one has seen him since. Don't mean they murdered him." Nanny Kat's voice wobbled, her eyes filling with sorrow, no doubt remembering the boy who she'd once known so well. "That's for Sheriff Dillon to worry about, not you."

Lauren's voice hardened. "You, who never backed down from a fight in your life."

"I never aimed a gun at anyone."

Lauren took a breath, arguing with her great aunt wasn't going to achieve anything. "You would if you had to." She glanced toward the window. "The sheriff doesn't have enough manpower. And if I were a man, you know Sheriff Dillon would've deputized me by now."

Nanny Kat sighed, defeated. "Stubborn as your father." She caught Lauren's arm as she passed. "Just ... don't do anything reckless, you hear me?"

Lauren nodded, her throat tight. "I promise." She hugged her great-aunt. "Make sure Becky stays here."

LAUREN PARKED her truck behind a copse of trees on the outskirts of town. She had waited until she saw Dillon and his deputies leave the sheriff's office, then trailed them from a safe distance. Now, with the truck hidden, she pulled the cap lower on her head and jogged to catch up.

The group moved on foot, their boots scuffing against the dry gravel road that led to the old mill. She kept to the shadows, close enough to hear their low murmurs. Dillon was at the head, his hand resting on the revolver at his hip.

Will, Earl, Terry, and the young Simmons boy followed behind the other deputies. Two men she didn't recognize walked just ahead of them, their postures stiff with authority.

At the tree line, Dillon raised a hand. "Mill's just ahead," he whispered. "We go quiet from here. Fan out and stay alert."

Lauren followed, stepping carefully through the underbrush the way her father had taught her. She took position behind a thick oak, scanning the mill. Lantern light flickered behind its warped wooden slats, throwing restless shadows. Inside, dark figures moved. Some were slow and deliberate, others nervous, shifting from foot to foot. Rifles gleamed in the dim light, their barrels catching the glow.

Then, a voice rang out, mocking and loud enough to carry across the clearing.

"Sheriff Dillon! Thought you'd come pokin' around sooner or later. Brought the whole cavalry too. Brave, but foolish."

Dillon stepped forward, his voice steady. "Boone Mullins. It's over. Your operation's finished. Come out with your hands up, and maybe the judge will go easy on you."

A tall, wiry figure stepped into the lantern glow. Boone Mullins. His grin was sharp and wolfish, his revolver hanging loose at his side, barrel down but ready.

"You think you've got the upper hand, Sheriff?" Boone scoffed. "You're outnumbered, and you don't know what you're dealin' with."

One of the strangers, a broad-shouldered man with a

hard jaw, spoke up. "You're sitting on a pile of illegal liquor, Boone. The Bureau doesn't take kindly to tax dodgers."

Lauren stiffened. Federal men. That explained the stiff postures, the unfamiliar faces.

Boone let out a slow chuckle. "Tax dodgers? That what we are?" He glanced back toward the mill. "I prefer to think of us as businessmen."

Dillon wasn't in the mood to argue. "Surrender now, or we come in after you."

Boone laughed. A cold, hollow sound. "Suit yourself."

The first shot shattered the night.

Lauren flinched, ducking lower as chaos erupted. The forest came alive with gunfire. Muzzle flashes lit the darkness like bursts of lightning. Rifles barked back and forth, bullets slamming into the mill's brittle walls. Splinters flew, dust and smoke thickening the air. Shouts rang out, some angry, others panicked, mixing with the thudding of boots and the sharp metallic clatter of fallen weapons.

Lauren pressed herself against the rough bark of the tree, gripping her rifle. The cold metal felt slick under her trembling hands, but she forced herself to breathe.

Her father's voice echoed in her mind. *Breathe steady. Keep your head. Look for your opening.*

A flicker of movement caught her eye. Jimmy Simmons had strayed too far from cover, crouched near a support beam with his back to the mill. His hands fumbled with his rifle, struggling to reload. Above him, on the second floor, a shadow moved. A smuggler stepped into view, shotgun poised.

Lauren raised her rifle, braced against the tree, and

squeezed the trigger. The shot rang out, sharp and deafening. The smuggler's arm jerked back, his shotgun spinning from his hands as he let out a pained cry. The weapon clattered to the floor below, lost in the shadows.

Jimmy whipped his head toward the trees. For a split second, his wide eyes met Lauren's shadowed form. Then, with a quick, shaky nod, he scrambled behind a pile of crates.

The fight raged on. Deputies and the federal men moved up carefully, using what little cover they had. The smugglers fought hard, but some were faltering, their gunfire turning sporadic.

Lauren's eyes flicked toward the mill. She had to do something to tip the balance. Then she saw it, a lantern swinging from a ceiling beam inside, swaying wildly from the vibrations of the gunfire.

An idea struck. A dangerous one. She lined up the shot slowly, this had to work.

Once more, she heard her father's voice. *A clean shot is a merciful one.*

She squeezed the trigger. The bullet hit dead center, shattering the glass. Fire bloomed instantly. Oil splashed across the wooden floor, catching on dry planks and feeding the hungry flames. With the recent drought, the fire spread within seconds, licking up the walls and along the rafters.

Shouts of alarm rang out from inside. Boone's men broke rank. Some bolted for the back exit, choosing flight over fight. Others hesitated, torn between self-preservation and their leader's orders.

Boone's sharp voice cut through the smoke. "Hold your ground!"

But it was too late. The fire crackled hungrily, smoke billowing through the gaps in the mill's walls. Deputies and federal agents surged forward, pressing the advantage as the remaining smugglers panicked.

Boone stumbled back, his revolver jerking upward. His eyes darted between the fire and the lawmen closing in.

Dillon's voice rang out, steady and final. "It's over, Boone. Drop the weapon."

For the first time, Boone hesitated. Sweat dripped down his temple. The fire was closing in fast, eating through the dry wood above him. His men were either down, captured, or running.

Lauren shifted her aim. One more shot, one well-placed bullet to the beam behind Boone, and he'd be trapped. She exhaled, braced, and fired.

The wooden beam splintered. A section of the ceiling groaned, weakened by fire and impact. Boone flinched as burning embers rained down, the sudden collapse cutting off his path to escape.

His jaw clenched. He looked from Dillon to the flames, to his dwindling options. And then, finally, his shoulders sagged. His revolver slipped from his grip, clattering onto the mill floor.

One by one, the remaining smugglers followed his lead, tossing their weapons aside. Deputies and federal agents moved in, cuffing them swiftly before the fire could swallow the rest of the building.

Lauren exhaled, her body sagging against the tree.

Smoke drifted into the night sky, curling upward as the last echoes of gunfire faded into silence.

* * *

THE FIGHT WAS OVER, but tension still crackled in the air. Smoke curled from the mill, glowing orange at its edges where the fire still smoldered. The acrid scent of gunpowder lingered, sharp and bitter.

Lauren stepped from the shadows, her rifle slung over her shoulder. She had barely taken three steps when Dillon spotted her. His face darkened, and he strode toward her, his boots grinding against the dirt.

"You have a death wish, Lauren Greenwood." His voice was low but filled with frustration. "What were you thinking?"

She squared her shoulders, refusing to back down, even as her heart pounded. "I was thinking our town was in danger, never mind what that man already did to Becky's family. You didn't have enough deputies." Her voice was steady, but she clenched her fists to keep them from shaking. "You said yourself you would deputize me if I were a man."

Dillon halted, his hand hovering near the revolver at his hip. For a moment, she thought he might keep arguing, but instead, he exhaled sharply and rubbed a hand over his face. His jaw tightened like he was chewing on words before speaking.

"You shouldn't have been out here." His voice was quieter now but still rough. He glanced toward the trees before shaking his head. "People died tonight, Lauren. That could have been you." Dillon sighed and adjusted his hat. "You're a Greenwood, all right. Stubborn, reckless, and too brave for your own good."

He turned, taking a few steps before pausing. "Your father would have been proud of you tonight. But I bet he'd be telling you not to push your luck."

Lauren swallowed, her grip tightening on the rifle. Her father had done unforgivable things, but in the end, he had tried to make it right. A quiet cough pulled her attention.

Jimmy Simmons stood a few feet away, twisting his hat in his hands. His face was flushed, his movements uncertain, like he wasn't sure he had the right to speak.

"Miss Greenwood," he said hesitantly, glancing toward the mill before looking back at her. "Back there, when that man had the shotgun on me. I don't ..." He swallowed, his throat bobbing. "I don't reckon I saw much, but that shot came from the trees." His gaze searched hers. "That was you, wasn't it?"

Lauren hesitated, then gave a small nod.

Jimmy exhaled sharply, his shoulders sagging like a weight had been lifted. "I ... I don't know how to thank you."

Lauren managed a small smile. "Thank me by growing up more like Earl than Mr. Harlan."

Jimmy turned scarlet, but after a moment, he straightened and gave a small, determined nod.

* * *

THERE WAS no sign of Luke at the mill. Sheriff Dillon was too busy to ask, and Lauren couldn't just go asking anyone. Boone and his men, those that lived, could carry tales, and she wasn't about to jeopardize Luke's safety. She waited for Terry and Will to finish up and took advantage of a ride home.

Once they were out of earshot, she asked, "Where's Luke, Will?"

"Gone."

Lauren's stomach churned. "He's dead?"

Will shook his head. "No. Not at all. Sorry, wasn't thinkin'. He's gone. Sheriff struck a deal with the Alcohol Tax Unit. Luke gets a fresh start, but first, he's gotta spill everythin' to the authorities in Washington. They'll have him for a few weeks, then he can come back."

Lauren swallowed hard. "Does Becky know?"

Will took his hat off and wiped his brow with his sleeve. "Not yet. I still got a head on my shoulders, don't I?" He gave her a lopsided grin, but it didn't quite reach his eyes.

"Will they let her see him?"

"Nope," he said with a sigh. "Not allowed visitors 'til everythin's signed, sealed, and delivered. They can't risk him runnin'."

Or getting killed. Lauren left those words unspoken.

She hesitated, then asked, "Do you want me to be there when you tell Becky?"

Will shook his head. "Thanks, but I gotta do it. We get wed in less than a month. She may have calmed down by then."

Lauren managed a small smile. "Maybe."

Will smiled. "Yeah, well, a fella can hope."

The truck rumbled down the road, dust kicking up behind them, but Lauren's thoughts were far away. A fresh start. That's what they said. But nothing about Luke's life had ever been easy, and she couldn't help but wonder. Would he ever really come back?

CHAPTER 39

Weeks passed with no news from Edward or Luke. Becky had just about forgiven them for not telling her about Luke's plans with the sheriff. The letter she'd received from Luke helped. He'd promised he was being looked after and would be back as soon as possible.

"What's that man of mine up to now?" Becky asked, watching Will approach with a stranger in tow. "Do you recognize him?"

Lauren shook her head, eyeing the roughly dressed man carrying a small satchel and walking barefoot. "Maybe he's looking for work. Will knows we'll need help with the harvest."

Will waved, grinning wide, and as soon as he was close enough, he scooped Becky up and spun her around. "I found us a preacher."

Becky's mouth dropped open, her eyes darting between

Will and the man beside him. She opened her mouth once, then twice, but no words came out.

Lauren stepped forward, offering her hand with an amused smile. "Welcome to Hope House, Reverend."

The man took her hand with a firm shake. "Gabe. Though some are more comfortable with Reverend Dobbs." He turned to Becky, his smile warm. "And you must be the blushing bride."

Becky still hadn't found her voice, but Will pulled her close with a chuckle. "I need you to call around here more often, Reverend. Usually, she can't stop talkin'."

"Will!" Becky turned on him, face flushed.

Lauren seized the moment, stepping in smoothly. "Perhaps you'd like to come in and have some coffee, Gabe, while the happy couple sorts themselves out?"

Gabe laughed, a deep, belly-rumbling sound. "Sounds good to me. I hear you've got a passel of kids living here. I can't wait to get acquainted."

REVEREND DOBBS SAT COMFORTABLY on the front porch of Hope House, a chipped coffee cup cradled in his hands. The evening air was thick with the scent of honeysuckle, and the distant sound of crickets played in the background. A few of the children lingered on the steps, drawn in by the easy rhythm of his voice. He wasn't telling stories, just talking, as if he'd known them all his life.

Will sat nearby, his arm draped over the back of Becky's chair. Lauren leaned against the railing, sipping her own coffee while Chana, Victor, and Nanny Kat watched from their usual seats around the porch.

"I guess you're not what we expected, Reverend," Nanny Kat said, her eyes crinkling at the corners. "We're used to the likes of Reverend Curtis."

Gabe chuckled, his eyes twinkling with good humor. "Ah, Brother Curtis. Fire and brimstone, all stiff collars and stern faces, I reckon?"

Terry grunted. "That's him, alright."

Gabe took a slow sip of his coffee before setting the cup down on his knee. "I don't have much use for fear, friends. There's enough of it in the world already. God's not in the business of scaring folks straight. He's in the business of loving them right. And I reckon we find Him in a lot more places than just four walls and a pulpit."

Lauren tilted her head. "So where do you preach, Reverend?"

He smiled, his eyes drifting toward the children playing on the lawn. "Anywhere He's willing to listen. Out in the fields, under the trees, beside a river, or sitting on a porch just like this one. God's in the sunshine that wakes you up, in the dirt under your nails, in the laughter of children." He looked at Becky then. "And most of all, He's in the hearts of those who love."

Becky blinked, and Will gave her hand a squeeze.

Reverend Dobbs turned to Nanny Kat, "Ma'am, if you've ever seen a field of wheat swaying under a blue sky, tell me it didn't feel like a church all on its own."

Victor let out a small chuckle at that. "You're not

wrong, Reverend. I'm not of your faith, but I feel closer to God living out here."

Gabe nodded. "Exactly. Folks think God's too high up to notice the likes of us, but I think He's right here, down in the mud and the mess of life with us." He held out his hand to Victor who shook it. "We might not be of the same faith but I believe we worship the same God."

Lauren watched Nanny Kat, Chana, and Victor exchange glances. Even they, who had heard every kind of preacher pass through town, seemed taken with Dobbs' gentle wisdom.

Will cleared his throat, drawing everyone's attention. "That's why I want Reverend Dobbs to marry us," he said, looking at Becky. "I've been thinkin' about it ever since I met him. I don't want a man standin' up there scowling at us, talkin' about sin and duty. I want someone who understands us, what we've been through. Someone who knows what love really is."

Becky's eyes filled with something soft and unspoken, and for once, she didn't have a quick remark.

Chana smiled warmly. "That's a beautiful reason, Will."

Becky finally found her voice, her fingers lacing through Will's. "Alright, Reverend. You've got yourself a weddin' to do."

Gabe smiled wide. "It's an honor, Miss Becky."

Lauren leaned against the railing, watching the fireflies flicker in the dusky sky. Somehow, having Reverend Dobbs around made everything feel a little lighter, a little brighter.

CHAPTER 40

The kitchen at Hope House was warm and bustling, the smell of fresh coffee mingling with the faint scent of cinnamon from the cookies Chana had left on the counter that morning. Terry had taken her and Carly down to Delgany to buy more material for Carly to fashion into dresses.

Lauren sat at the table with Ian, Becky, and Nanny Kat, the air heavy with anticipation at Ian's announcement he had news.

Ian took a measured sip of coffee, his expression thoughtful. "I stopped by on my way back from Blue Ridge. The doctors are pleased with Bart's progress, so much so that they've cleared him to leave."

Lauren's heart leaped. "That's wonderful news!" But the cautious look on Ian's face stopped her short. "You're worried about him coming back here, aren't you?"

Ian hesitated. "Not worried, exactly. It's just Hope

House is lively, and that's not ideal for someone who needs peace to heal."

"I agree," Nanny Kat said gently, patting Lauren's hand. "We need to think about what's best for Bart. He's been through so much already."

Ian glanced at Nanny Kat. "I've offered to take him in for a while. My house is quieter, and my housekeeper can help keep an eye on him. Clarissa and Sophie could come too, if they want, but it would mean leaving school here in Delgany."

Lauren's chest tightened. She looked down at the table, her fingers tracing the grain of the wood. "The girls love it here," she said. "This is their home. Losing their mother was hard enough ... I hate the thought of them having to leave."

"I know," Ian said. "It's not an easy decision."

Becky, who had been quiet until now, spoke up. "We'll have to explain everythin' to the girls carefully," she said. "They've been through enough. They need to know they're not bein' forced to choose between their father and their home."

Nanny Kat nodded in agreement. "Clarissa's a smart girl. She'll understand. And Sophie ... well, she'll follow her sister's lead."

Lauren took a deep breath. "Let's call them in. It's their decision to make."

CLARISSA AND SOPHIE entered the kitchen hesitantly, their small hands clasped together. Lauren immediately noticed the tension in Clarissa's jaw and the way Sophie stuck close to her sister's side. Clarissa's face was carefully guarded, her shoulders squared like she was bracing for a fight, but Lauren caught the way her fingers tugged at the hem of her sweater—a small, almost imperceptible crack in her armor. Sophie's eyes darted nervously between the adults, her lips pressed into a thin line, like she was waiting for bad news.

"What's wrong?" Clarissa's eyes flicked warily toward the table. "Why do you need to talk to us?"

"There's nothing wrong." Standing and taking a small step closer, Lauren said, "Actually, we have some good news. Your dad is doing so much better, so much so that the doctors say he can leave the hospital."

Sophie's face lit up. "He's coming home?"

Lauren's heart clenched. "Not right away. The doctors think it would be better for him to go somewhere quieter for a little while, where he can rest and get stronger before coming back here."

"Where?" Clarissa held Sophie's hand even tighter.

"Mr. Ian has offered to let your dad stay at his house for a while. It's peaceful there, and your dad will have everything he needs to recover. You'd still get to visit him, of course. And if you want, you could go live there too, just for a little while. But that would mean leaving Hope House and switching schools for a bit."

Sophie's smile disappeared as she turned to her sister.

"Leave Hope House?" she whispered. "But this is our home."

Lauren kneeled, reaching for Sophie's free hand and giving it a comforting squeeze. "It is your home. It always will be, no matter what. This is your safe place, and it's not going anywhere."

Clarissa looked down, her expression tight with concentration. Lauren could almost see the thoughts racing behind her eyes, the weight of the decision pressing on her small shoulders. Finally, she looked up. "What about Daddy? If we stay here, won't he think we don't want to be with him?"

Lauren placed her hand on Clarissa's arm. "Your dad loves you both more than anything in the world. He knows how much you miss him, and he'd never think that. If you want to stay here, that's okay. If you want to go live with him, that's okay too. Whatever you decide, he'll understand, and so will we."

Sophie's lip trembled. "But why can't he just come here? We can be really quiet. I promise. He can have my bed and I can sleep on the floor."

Lauren pulled Sophie onto her lap, brushing a strand of hair out of her face. "Oh, sweetheart. I know you would. But your daddy needs a lot of rest right now, and this place is so full of life. He'll come back, though. He just needs a little more time."

"Will we still get to see him?" Sophie's voice was small.

Lauren brushed a tear from her eye. "You can visit him as much as you want, and he'll want to see you too. This is just about making sure he has the best chance to get better."

Clarissa looked up again, her chin trembling for a moment before she squared her shoulders and took a deep breath. "Can we talk about it? Just the two of us?"

"Of course. Take all the time you need. Whatever you decide, we'll support you."

Clarissa nodded, squeezing Sophie's hand as she led her out of the room. Lauren watched them climb the stairs, their footsteps soft against the creaking wood. Her heart ached as Sophie glanced up at her sister with wide, trusting eyes, waiting for her to make the decision.

* * *

WHEN THE GIRLS RETURNED, Clarissa's face was calm, though her cheeks were flushed, and she wouldn't quite meet Lauren's gaze. Sophie stayed close, her fingers gripping the sleeve of Clarissa's sweater.

"We talked about it," Clarissa said, stopping in the middle of the kitchen. "And we've decided to stay here. This is our home." She hesitated, glancing down at Sophie, then back at Lauren. "But we want to visit Daddy as much as we can."

Sophie nodded, her small voice resolute. "We'll stay, Miss Lauren. But only if we can see Daddy a lot."

Tears pricked at Lauren's eyes, but she blinked them back and opened her arms. The girls rushed into her embrace, holding on tightly. "Of course you can," she whispered. "You'll see him as often as you want. And he'll be so proud of you both."

Becky, standing in the doorway, smiled. "They made the right choice," she murmured to Nanny Kat.

THAT NIGHT, after the girls had gone to bed, Lauren stood at the kitchen sink, scrubbing the last of the day's dishes. Becky leaned against the counter beside her, drying the plates without a word.

"You handled the Leroy girls beautifully," Becky whispered. "Norma would be proud."

Lauren shook her head, her voice tight. "I just hope they feel safe. I don't ever want them to feel like they're losing another piece of their family."

"They know they're loved," Becky said, placing a hand on Lauren's shoulder. "And that's what matters. You've given them somethin' solid to hold on to. That's no small thing."

Lauren managed a faint smile but couldn't ignore the tension twisting in her chest. She glanced toward the ceiling, where the girls were sound asleep. "We've given it to them, but ... I just hope it's enough."

"It will be." Becky left the kitchen, her footsteps fading into the quiet.

Lauren lingered by the sink, staring out the window into the dark yard. The house was silent now, but her thoughts wouldn't settle.

Everything seemed to be falling into place. Bart was

coming home, well not to Hope House but out of the sanitorium. He would return when he was ready. Becky was all set to get married. Nanny Kat and Ian were getting on like a house on fire. Leaving her and Edward. Were they ever going to find an answer?

CHAPTER 41

Lauren cleared the last of the dishes and wiped her hands on her apron, the scent of cornbread and butter thick in the warm evening air. Outside, cicadas droned, their steady hum filling the silence that had settled in the kitchen. The open windows brought no relief; the outside air was just as thick and warm.

Becky and Carly sat in the kitchen quilting. The wedding quilt was almost finished now and they needed a large space to work. She walked into the living room, watching as Victor unfolded the newspaper. The children were gathered around him. Cal, sitting up straight, his elbows resting on his knees; Ruthie, curled up in a chair with her knees pulled to her chest; and Hans, perched stiffly on the edge of his seat, his hands folded so tightly his knuckles had gone white.

Lauren noticed how he always sat like that as if he were ready to run, or defend himself. He'd been that way since being set upon by boys from the town. If she could get her hands on the Rawlins boy, she might have to be restrained.

Victor adjusted his glasses and cleared his throat. "Alright," he said, tapping the paper. "This one's from your Uncle Edward. Straight from Paris."

Cal perked up. Hans barely moved.

"Why Paris? The Olympics are in Berlin," Cal asked, his eyes wide.

Hans ran his fingers through his hair in a gesture like Victor. "Uncle Edward isn't safe in Berlin."

"Why? Who would want to hurt Mr. Edward?" Ruthie's innocence made Lauren want to hug her.

"He stood up to the Nazis and they don't like it when you do that." Hans looked to Victor. "What does it say?"

Victor began to read.

A Victory With Missing Runners
By Edward Belmont, Special Correspondent Paris

The world watched today as America's men's relay team sped to gold. The baton passed cleanly, the runners flew, and the final time set a new Olympic record. A moment of triumph. A moment of pride.

But not for everyone.

There were supposed to be different men on that track today. Sam Stoller and Marty Glickman, two of America's best sprinters, had trained for this race. They were ready. And yet, this morning, they were told they would not run. Their spots were given instead to Jesse Owens and Ralph Metcalfe. Two brilliant runners, yes, but ones who had not trained for this event.

The reason given? 'To give America the best chance of winning.' But Owens had already won three gold medals. He had offered to step aside, to let Stoller or Glickman take their rightful place. He was told, simply, to do as he was told.

It does not take much to read between the lines. Two Jewish athletes, removed from a race, on German soil, in a stadium where Nazi officials watched from the stands. America won gold today. But at what cost?

Sam Stoller and Marty Glickman came to Berlin to run. They left the stadium as spectators.

Victor's voice faded, leaving behind a silence so thick Lauren fancied she could hear the ice settling in the water pitcher on the table. The cicadas droned on outside, indifferent to the weight pressing down inside the room.

"That ain't fair," Cal muttered, his voice hot with frustration.

Lauren looked at Hans. He hadn't spoken. He hadn't moved. His eyes were locked on the wood grain of the coffee table, his expression carefully blank. But she could see the tension in his shoulders, the way his throat bobbed slightly as he swallowed.

"Did ... did Jesse Owens really ask to step aside?" Hans' voice was so quiet that Lauren almost missed it.

Victor nodded. "He did."

Hans inhaled sharply through his nose. His jaw tightened. "And they wouldn't let him."

"No."

Lauren searched for the right words. She wanted to ease the weight pressing down on Hans' narrow shoulders, to make things better. But there was nothing to say. Instead, she watched as Hans stared at the table, blinking rapidly, his breath coming just a little too fast.

Ruthie, still curled in her chair, spoke up hesitantly. "But... America still won, didn't they?"

Victor folded the paper. "They did."

Ruthie frowned, tilting her head. "Then why does it feel so bad?"

Lauren exhaled slowly. "Because it wasn't right."

Hans finally lifted his head, his blue eyes dark and unreadable. "Do you think anyone will care?" he asked, his voice flat.

Victor studied him for a long moment. Then he nodded. "The right people will."

Hans' fingers twitched slightly against the table, but he didn't look convinced. He turned away, staring out the window, toward the darkening sky.

"Your Uncle Edward had more to say. Do you want to hear it?" Victor asked.

Hans shrugged.

Victor cleared his throat and read:

> Jesse Owens has now won four gold medals for America. His performance in the 1936 Olympics set a record for the most gold medals won by a single athlete in the Olympics to date. A huge achievement, but will it be enough? Will it gain him access to awards celebration

dinners held back home in the USA? Will it make his fellow American citizens treat him as an equal? Here in Germany, Jesse is allowed to reside in the same hotel as his white teammates, use the same facilities, and eat in the same restaurants. Will that be the case when he returns stateside? Jesse Owens hopes so, but I, and many others, feel he may as well hope for a trip to the Moon.

Cal sat up straighter. "What does he mean he can stay in the same hotel in Germany? Why is that a big deal?"

Victor opened his mouth to respond, but Hans beat him to it. "Because it isn't just us Jews people hate. It's everyone who is different. Mr. Owens wouldn't be allowed into Hillman's or to come swimming with us in the creek. That's right, isn't it, Miss Lauren?"

Lauren hesitated. She wished she could tell them otherwise. "I'm sure Earl would have no problem serving Mr. Owens or anyone else, Hans. But yes, in many places, including Virginia, people like Mr. Owens aren't welcome in the same hotels, restaurants, or even train cars as white people."

Hans frowned. "Even after everything he's done?"

Lauren nodded. "Even then. In some cities, he wouldn't even be allowed to walk through the front door of a hotel where a white man could stay. He might have to eat outside or in a separate room, just because of the color of his skin."

"But that don't make any sense," Cal muttered. "He's a hero. He should be able to eat wherever he wants."

Lauren met his eyes. "So should everyone, Cal."

* * *

Later that evening, Lauren sat with Victor's newspaper in front of her. The words swam on the page as she blinked back tears.

"Would you like some company?" Victor asked from the doorway.

"Of course. Don't mind me. All this dust gets in my eyes." She forced a smile, babbling, but Victor wasn't fooled. She could see it in his eyes.

"You miss him," he said gently. "But he's doing important work. Without people like Edward, the world would remain blinkered. He's saving lives."

Anger bubbled up, and Lauren couldn't stop herself. "What about our life? We're supposed to be married, yet he can't get away fast enough. I needed him, Victor. I wanted him to stay when Luke was in trouble, when Hope House was in danger. But he left."

Victor studied her. "Did you ask him to stay?"

The quiet question made her pause. "No… but he should have known. I shouldn't have to beg."

"Begging doesn't come into it, Lauren. Edward loves you. But he sees you as an independent woman. Maybe he thought you could handle things. And you did."

She hesitated. "But …"

"From what Kathryn has told me, Edward has waited a long time to make you his wife. He's been patient, loving, and supportive. Perhaps …" He gave a small shrug.

Lauren stared at him, the truth settling heavily on her

chest. "It's my turn now. Or maybe... you think I should have married him the first time he asked."

Victor smiled slightly. "Only you can answer that, Lauren."

She let out a slow breath, staring at the paper without really seeing it. Maybe he was right.

CHAPTER 42

Lauren followed Becky along the narrow dirt path, her shoes tapping against the dry earth. Becky had been quiet since they'd left Hope House, but the quickening of her steps and the way her bright eyes darted toward the field ahead gave her away.

When the house came into view, Becky stopped so suddenly that Lauren nearly bumped into her.

The small wooden house sat at the edge of the field, bathed in the soft glow of the afternoon sun. Its wide porch stretched across the front, the green shutters catching the light just so. The front door stood open, as if inviting them in.

"It's really ours," Becky whispered.

Becky reached for Lauren's hand and tugged her forward. The porch creaked beneath their weight, sturdy and strong, just like everything Will made. She ran her fingers along the railing, her touch light, as if afraid the house might disappear.

"Will wanted the porch wide," she murmured, motioning to two handmade chairs. "Said we'd sit here in the evenin's, watchin' the sun set over the field."

She pushed the door open, stepping inside. "It still smells like fresh wood."

Lauren followed, her gaze sweeping the room. The smooth, paneled walls gleamed in the light, and the stone hearth stood proudly at the center. Handcrafted shelves lined the walls. The house wasn't fully furnished yet, but Becky was already there in small ways. A blanket draped over a chair, wildflowers on the windowsill, soft gingham curtains framing the kitchen window.

Becky ran her hand along the cool stone of the hearth. "Can you believe this?" she asked, looking back at Lauren, her eyes bright. "Will did it all. He'd never built a whole house before, but look at it." Her fingers skimmed the edge of the oak kitchen table. "He made this too. Said we'd eat every meal here, just the two of us." A small smile tugged at her lips. "For now."

Lauren squeezed her arm. "It's beautiful, Becky. You and Will deserve this."

Becky exhaled softly. "I never thought I'd have somethin' like this. Ma did her best, but you remember how we lived. The roof leaked every spring, and there was never enough wood for winter. Hope House was wonderful, but it wasn't mine." Her gaze drifted toward the kitchen before she whispered, "But now..."

They moved through the hallway, Becky opening each door like she was revealing a secret. The master bedroom was simple but cozy, a hand-stitched quilt draped over the bed. She ran her fingers over the fabric, her touch reverent. "I remember all the nights we spent sewin' this."

Lauren smiled. "And I remember Miss Chaney's face when I told her you were thinkin' of ordering bedding from Sears. She nearly had a conniption." Lauren mimicked Miss Chaney's stern tone. "It's tradition for mountain brides to have a weddin' quilt, child."

Becky laughed, shaking her head. "She was right, though. It's beautiful."

The second bedroom was for guests. The third, unfinished but full of possibility, made Becky pause in the doorway, her cheeks flushing. "Will says we'll fix it up when the time's right."

They stepped back onto the porch, Becky leaning against the railing as she gazed out over the field. Her chest rose and fell with slow, measured breaths.

Lauren stayed quiet, giving her the space she needed.

After a long silence, Becky spoke, her voice softer. "I keep thinkin' about Ma hummin' while she hemmed my Sunday dress. About Matt teasin' me, sayin' no man would ever have the nerve to marry me." She let out a shaky laugh, blinking quickly. "They'd be here if they could."

Lauren stepped closer. "I know."

Becky swallowed hard, her fingers tightening on the railing. "I miss them every day, but now ... I thought it'd get easier. And sometimes it does. But today ..." Her voice faltered. "It's hard knowin' they won't be here to see this."

Lauren's chest ached for her friend. She didn't hesitate. "They'd be proud of you. So proud. Your mam liked Will, and she'd be overjoyed to know he's looking after you so well."

Becky nodded, brushing at her eyes.

Lauren gave her a moment before nudging her gently. "Come on. We best get back before the others worry. And you need sleep. Nobody wants a washed-out bride on her wedding day."

Becky let out a soft laugh, casting one last look at the house before turning toward the path home. As they walked, they talked about the final wedding preparations.

"Becky, who's giving you away tomorrow? Have you asked Ian or John Thatcher?"

Becky grinned, her steps light and quick. "I asked Terry. I wanted someone from my family to do it."

CHAPTER 43

The stars twinkled in the inky dark sky as the children bustled about, whispering excitedly while trying to keep their voices down. Lauren smiled to herself as she arranged a bouquet of fresh daisies on the dining table, sneaking a glance outside where Will and Becky sat on the porch, lost in conversation.

Fred, his hands still dusted with wood shavings, peeked through the doorway. "Is it ready?" he asked in a hushed voice.

Victor stepped in from the workshop, carrying the hope chest, its surface smooth and polished, the initials B + W carved elegantly into the lid. "It's ready," he said with a proud grin. "You boys did a fine job."

The chest was simple but beautiful, made from reclaimed oak, sanded to a warm, honeyed hue. The carvings were modest yet filled with love featuring floral patterns along the edges and the words *"With Hope, Always"* etched delicately beneath their initials.

Nanny Kat, wiping her hands on her apron, leaned in to inspect it. "Fine work," she said with a nod. "This'll last them a lifetime."

Chana smiled as she helped Lauren place the small treasures inside. Each one a symbol of the life Becky had built at Hope House and the traditions of a proper wedding gift.

Lauren carefully arranged the items, ensuring everything fit neatly inside.

Becky's voice called from outside. "What's all the whisperin' about in there?"

The children giggled, and Nanny Kat quickly closed the lid, shooing them to the side. "Come on in, dear, we've got something for you."

Becky stepped inside, her eyes widening at the sight of the chest. "What's this?"

Victor placed a gentle hand on her shoulder. "A gift. From all of us."

Will nudged her gently. "Go on, open it."

Becky kneeled beside the chest, running her fingers over the smooth wood, her eyes misting over at the sight of their initials. She lifted the lid and let out a soft gasp, her fingers tracing each carefully placed item. "Oh ... this is ... I don't even know what to say."

Lauren smiled. "We wanted you to know how much you are loved."

Becky picked out the pressed wildflowers, tied with a ribbon, gathered by the younger children.

"For beauty and remembrance," Chana said softly.

Will stood by, watching with a quiet smile, his hand resting on Becky's shoulder as she examined each gift with care. Next was a tin of homemade preserves, wrapped in a square of gingham fabric.

"Something sweet, for the sweet times ahead," Lauren said with a smile. "You'll be relieved to know I didn't make them."

Everyone laughed again as Becky put her hands together. "Thank the Lord." But she kissed Lauren on the cheek just the same.

A hand-stitched tea towel came next.

"This is so beautiful, thank you."

Ruthie spoke up, "Nanny Chana embroidered it. It says 'A happy home is built with love.'"

Cal came forward and handed Becky a set of wooden spoons, lovingly carved by Fred and the boys.

"Every home needs a good set of spoons," Fred said proudly.

"Yeah, but you're not to hit us with them." Cal added, making Becky giggle as she pulled the squirming boy in for a hug.

Becky took out the other gifts. A small Bible, a candle, and a sketch of everyone at Hope House, courtesy of Clarissa.

Becky's lip trembled, and she looked around at the expectant faces, her voice thick with emotion. "But you're not gettin' rid of me. I'll be back here the day after the weddin'."

"Not if I can help it," Will teased. "I'm plannin' on a long honeymoon in our new house. Alone."

Everyone laughed, and Becky wiped a tear from her cheek before pulling Lauren and Chana into a tight hug.

"Thank you," she whispered.

Nanny Kat cleared her throat loudly, her hands landing on her hips. "Alright now, that's enough carrying on. Will, you need to get on home. It's bad luck to see the bride before the wedding."

Will grinned, tipping his hat. "Reckon I'll take my chances, Nanny Kat."

She fixed him with a stern look. "You reckon wrong. Now off with you."

Will laughed and kissed Becky's cheek. "See you tomorrow, darlin'." He hefted the hope chest into the back of his truck, patting the side before climbing in. The truck rumbled to life, and he drove off into the night, the tail lights flickering down the dusty road.

Nanny Kat turned to the children, narrowing her eyes. "And as for the rest of you, off to bed. It's late, and tomorrow's a big day."

A chorus of groans rose up.

"But Nanny Kat," Ruthie whined, "we're not even tired!"

Nanny Kat crossed her arms, arching a brow. "Not tired? Well then, I reckon you can help me scrub the kitchen floors."

A scuffle of feet and giggles erupted as the children scrambled toward the staircase, vanishing like mice before she could change her mind.

Lauren chuckled. "You've still got the magic touch."

Nanny Kat smirked. "Ain't nothing magic about it. Just a firm hand and years of practice."

Chana sighed, stretching. "We should all get some rest. Tomorrow's a day full of love and hard work."

Becky lingered by the doorway, watching the children disappear up the stairs. She turned to Lauren with a wistful smile. "I guess this is real, huh?"

Lauren squeezed her hand. "It's real. And it's wonderful."

Becky nodded, taking a deep breath. "Then I guess I'd better get some sleep, too."

As Becky turned to leave, she paused, giving Lauren a knowing look. "You've been awful quiet tonight."

Lauren forced a smile. "Just thinking about tomorrow."

Becky tilted her head. "Or about someone who might, or might not, show up tomorrow?"

Lauren's smile faltered, and she glanced out the window into the dark night beyond, where Will's truck had long since disappeared down the road. The stars twinkled overhead, but they gave her no answers.

"I haven't heard from him," she admitted. "Not in weeks. I'm still angry he left after the incident with …" Lauren stopped, not wanting to bring up unhappy times.

"Boone's men. You can say it. Edward must have good reason to leave when he did. He loves you." Becky reached out and squeezed her arm. "He'll come, Lauren. If he knows what's good for him."

Lauren let out a soft laugh, but it didn't quite reach her eyes. "Yeah. If."

Becky studied her for a moment, then gave her one last quick hug. "Night. Don't stay up worryin'."

Lauren watched as Becky disappeared upstairs, her footsteps light against the creaky old wood. Alone now, she stepped onto the porch, wrapping her arms around herself against the cool night air.

The stars stretched endlessly above. Lauren sighed, whispering into the quiet, "Where are you, Edward?"

The wind carried her words away, leaving only the rustling trees and the distant hoot of an owl in reply.

CHAPTER 44

The morning of the wedding dawned with clear blue skies. Lauren wiped her hands on her apron and stepped outside, the smell of borax still clinging to her. She shaded her eyes against the glare, squinting down the long dirt road that stretched toward town. Dust swirled in the distance, rising in a steady cloud, and her heart gave a hopeful lurch.

"Nanny Kat!" she called back into the house. "We've got company."

Becky appeared beside her, eyes wide with anticipation. "Is it the sheriff?"

Lauren nodded slowly. "Looks like it."

By now, the sound of tires rolling over the sunbaked gravel reached them, and moments later, Sheriff Dillon's car rolled to a stop in front of the house, its engine sputtering before cutting off. The door creaked open, and out stepped Reverend Dobbs, his ever-present satchel slung over his shoulder and his face split in an easy grin.

But it wasn't Gabe who held their attention.

Lauren's breath caught as Luke climbed out of the car, looking thinner than she remembered but stronger somehow. He stood uncertainly for a moment, running a hand through his hair, his gaze flickering between Becky and Nanny Kat.

Becky was already down the steps throwing her arms around him. "Luke!" she cried, squeezing him tight. "You're back!"

Luke hesitated, then hugged her back. "Hey, sis. Careful, you'll squeeze the life out of me."

Sheriff Dillon slammed the car door shut, dust billowing up around his boots. "Alright, alright," he said gruffly. "He's back where he belongs, but let's get one thing straight." He fixed Luke with a hard stare. "You so much as sneeze in the wrong direction, and I'll be back here faster than you can say 'Amen'. You hear me?"

Luke swallowed and nodded. "I hear you, Sheriff."

"Good." Adjusting his hat and turning to Reverend Dobbs, he said, "And you, make sure he keeps his nose clean. I went out on a limb vouching for him."

Reverend Dobbs smiled, tipping his hat. "I'll keep a good eye on him, Sheriff. Hope House is a fine place for a fresh start." He patted Luke on the back. "Ain't that right, son?"

Luke offered a half-smile, looking down at his worn boots. "Guess so."

The sheriff grunted. "We'll see." With that, he climbed back into his car.

"Wait a minute. Where are you going?" Nanny Kat called after him.

He grinned. "I got to go wash up and get my clean uniform on. Can't attend a wedding looking like a dusty coon hound."

He drove off in a swirl of dust, leaving silence in his wake.

Becky grabbed Luke's hand, her voice thick with emotion. "Come on, you must be starvin'. We just laid the table for breakfast. There's plenty of food."

Lauren watched as Luke allowed himself to be led toward the house, his posture stiff.

Reverend Dobbs lingered beside Lauren, watching the boy go. "That one's carrying a lot of weight on his shoulders. But I reckon he's in the right place to lighten the load."

Lauren nodded, relief washing over her. "We'll help him find his way. We always do."

Gabe grinned. "That's why I like this place." He glanced at her. "Mind if I grab some of that breakfast, too?"

Lauren laughed. "You'd better, or Becky will never let you hear the end of it."

CHAPTER 45

*L*auren was gathering the last of the wildflowers when she heard voices near the edge of the yard. A polished, familiar deep voice cut through the warm air.

She went still. It couldn't be. Her fingers tightened around the flowers, her breath suddenly shallow. Slowly, she turned.

Edward stood just beyond the gate, his clothes worn from travel. And just like that, a storm of emotion crashed into her. Her heart lurched, but anger was quicker.

Lauren let the flowers fall from her hands and strode toward him, her pulse pounding in her ears. Before he could speak, she shoved against his chest.

"You," Her voice trembled. "You left."

Edward flinched, not from the shove, but from the force of her words.

She laughed, bitter and breathless. "I'd just found out about my father's relationship to Boone. After his men stopped my car and threatened my loved ones, Edward." Her voice was rising now, sharp and raw. "They could have attacked Hope House. And where were you?"

Pain flickered across his face. "Lauren..."

"You knew things were dangerous here. You knew what I was facing." Her hands curled into fists at her sides. "And you still left."

Edward swallowed hard. "I wanted to write." His voice was rough. "I couldn't."

"You couldn't?" The words came out in a sharp whisper. "You mean you didn't."

His jaw tightened, but he didn't argue.

Lauren exhaled sharply, turning away for half a second because if she looked at him too long, she might start to cry. She forced herself to meet his gaze again.

"I woke up every day wondering if you were dead," she said, her voice shaking. "Or if you just forgot me."

"I never forgot you."

"Then why wasn't I first?" She hated how unsteady the words sounded, how vulnerable they made her. "Why didn't I matter enough for you to stay? I know people, strangers, need you, but I needed you."

Edward hesitated, and in that hesitation, she had her answer.

Her breath caught. She pressed a hand to her stomach, trying to steady the ache inside her.

Edward swallowed hard, his gaze dropping for the first time. "I came back," he said quietly. "Just like I said I would."

Lauren let out a hollow laugh. "And now you think everything will go back to the way it was?"

Edward didn't speak.

Her chest tightened. "You're leaving again." It wasn't a question.

His silence was all the confirmation she needed.

Something inside her cracked, but she refused to let it show. She turned away before he could see the tears burning in her eyes.

"Becky's wedding is starting," she murmured. "I don't have time for this."

Edward took a step forward. "We're not finished, Lauren."

She stiffened. "Yes, we are."

Then, without another word, she stepped past him, her shoulder barely brushing his as she walked toward the house. She didn't look back.

* * *

LAUREN STOOD at the edge of the gathering, hands clasped, forcing herself to stay present. The late afternoon light filtered through the oak branches, dappling the grass in golden patterns. Becky stood beneath the tree, wildflower bouquet in hand, her red hair catching the glow.

She looked radiant, not just because of the dress they had spent days sewing, or Chana's delicate veil, but because of something deeper. A certainty in her eyes, as if she knew she was marrying the love of her life.

Lauren swallowed hard.

As Luke walked Becky down the aisle, Lauren noticed the way Becky's hands trembled slightly. Despite her steady calm that morning, the nerves had caught up with her at last. But when she reached Will, and his fingers closed around hers, a breath of relief passed over her features.

Lauren's chest ached. Becky would never have to wonder if Will was coming back. She would never have to doubt. Lauren wasn't sure she'd ever know what that felt like.

Reverend Dobbs spoke, his voice a low, familiar comfort, but Lauren barely heard the words. She watched Becky, the way her shoulders relaxed as she said her vows, how her voice didn't waver. And Will, who had never been one for grand declarations, spoke with a quiet certainty that left no room for hesitation.

Lauren exhaled slowly, willing herself to be happy for them. And she was happy for them. But deep down, beneath the warmth of the moment, something in her splintered.

Her gaze flickered across the yard. Edward stood near the back, half in shadow, watching just as she was. Their eyes met. Something tightened in her throat. But before she could even think about what to do, the moment was gone.

"You may kiss the bride."

Will lifted Becky's veil, his hands gentle, reverent. Becky's breath caught, and for a single heartbeat, the whole world seemed to still. Then, softly, simply, he kissed her.

No sweeping passion, no grand display, just the kind of love that was sure and unwavering.

The kind of love that stayed.

Cheers erupted around them. Cal, Fred, and Hans set off firecrackers near the tree line, sending the children squealing with delight. Baby Maisie clapped her hands, giggling at the sparks.

Lauren stayed where she was, watching as Becky leaned into Will, fitting against him like she'd always belonged there.

Becky caught her gaze from across the yard, her expression wide and bright, filled with joy. Lauren smiled back, swallowing the lump in her throat.

Becky turned back to Will, whispering something that made him laugh. He reached up and tucked a loose strand of hair behind her ear, his touch full of tenderness.

Lauren dropped her gaze, her fingers curling against her skirt. She had wanted this moment to be nothing but happiness. For Becky. For Will. But no matter how hard she tried, the ache was still there. And for the first time, she let herself wonder: *What if Edward was never meant to be her Will?*

* * *

LAUREN WALKED over to Nanny and Chana, who stood at the edge of the gathering, taking in the sight of the long wooden tables spread beneath the oak trees. The air was warm, the sun dipping lower, casting a golden hue over the celebration.

Nanny Kat smiled at Lauren. "It all looks beautiful, Chana. People were very generous, don't you think?"

"Yes, they were, but you two ladies made it look incredible." Chana gestured toward the arrangements. "I love how you used mason jars for the wildflowers: daisies, goldenrod, and Queen Anne's lace."

Lauren gave credit where it was due. "The girls wanted to help, so they picked them fresh this morning."

"My stomach's growling something fierce, Miss Lauren," Cal declared, clutching his middle dramatically.

Lauren chuckled, ruffling his hair as he eyed the tables longingly. The scent of roasted chicken, seasoned with whatever herbs people could spare, filled the air. Her own stomach tightened in response, but she ignored it.

"Soon, Cal. Becky and Will need to take their places first."

"Can I tell them to hurry up?"

She smirked. "Why not? Everything will get cold."

The table was a feast, with pitchers of thick, rich gravy standing beside steaming bowls of collard greens, the buttery scent of biscuits mingling with the smoky aroma of ham hock.

"This is more than enough," Chana murmured beside her.

Lauren glanced at her. "You've outdone yourself again. I don't know what we did without you."

Chana's gaze drifted toward her husband, her lips curving into a wistful smile. She blinked quickly, pushing back tears, and turned back to Lauren. "You gave us more than a home," she said softly. "You gave us hope." Her fingers lingered on a wildflower in the nearest jar. "We feel younger than we have in years, like we've been given a second chance."

Across the yard, Chana's husband caught her eye and raised his glass in a silent toast, his face alight with gratitude.

Before Lauren could respond, children barreled past, shrieking with laughter as they wove between the tables.

"You'd better sit down before they knock you over."

"I see Edward is waiting for you, Lauren. Go. I'll be fine."

Her spine stiffened slightly, but she gave a nod before moving toward her seat.

As she approached the table, she caught sight of Becky and Will at the head, their hands entwined, smiles exchanged between them.

Lauren sat beside Edward, careful to keep a polite distance. It was a small space, but she made sure not to brush against him.

Baskets of cornbread passed from guest to guest, alongside bowls of sliced tomatoes and cucumbers fresh from the garden. The tangy scent of potato salad stirred memories of Mary, now all the way in California.

The orphanage children darted between guests, refilling cups of strong, sweet tea and pouring homemade lemonade into glass jars, condensation dripping down the sides. Their laughter floated on the warm evening air, light and infectious.

Cal dragged Hans over to Lauren.

"Hans thinks it's time for dessert, Miss Lauren. They eat it first in Germany."

Lauren pressed her lips together, fighting a laugh just as Edward leaned in.

"I don't know about that," he said, amused, "but I did hear that whoever finishes all their dinner gets first pick of the pies."

Lauren expected warmth to spread through her at the sound of his voice. It always had before. But now, something inside her stayed cold.

The boys ran off, eager to test the theory, and Edward turned to her.

"Ian thinks Cal will be a reporter like me one day. Says he's got the imagination for it."

Lauren nodded, keeping her gaze on the table. "He's bright. I just hope we can keep him on the right path."

Edward hesitated, as if expecting her to say more. Their conversations were usually easy, flowing. But tonight, her words felt clipped, measured.

His brow lifted slightly as his gaze drifted down the table. Following it, Lauren spotted the reason for his concern, a small hand reaching from beneath the table toward the dessert platters.

She giggled as Carly caught the culprit by the collar, sending him scurrying away with a sheepish grin.

"With a family like ours," Edward mused, "he'll turn out just fine."

Lauren's fingers tightened around her napkin. She kept her voice even, but there was no warmth in it. "A family like mine, you mean."

Edward blinked, as if the words had knocked the wind out of him. His mouth parted slightly, like he wanted to say something, needed to, but no words came.

Instead, his gaze flickered downward. His fingers trailed the rim of his glass, but this time, the motion wasn't absentminded. It was careful, measured. His jaw tensed for just a second before he exhaled slowly.

For a brief moment, Lauren thought he might actually respond.

Before he could, someone called out, "Hurry up with the cake!" The sudden noise jolted her, snapping the moment in half. Laughter rippled through the gathering like wind through the oak leaves. A man leaned back in his chair, patting his stomach with satisfaction, while a woman dabbed at her mouth, whispering something that made her neighbor chuckle.

Lauren let the shift in attention carry her away from Edward.

The children performed their party pieces, and when Shelley put on a dramatic reenactment of Becky and Will's courtship, dragging a reluctant Fred into the role of Will, the guests roared with laughter.

Then came time for the wedding cake, a modest, three-layer confection with vanilla frosting, adorned with wildflowers Becky had chosen herself.

Lauren reached for Edward's hand beneath the tablecloth, then stopped.

For a second, her fingers hovered, heart lurching toward old habits. The instinct was still there, the part of her that wanted to reach for his steadiness, his warmth.

But what good was reaching for something that had never really been hers?

She hesitated. Then, instead, she clasped her hands in her lap.

Edward didn't say anything, but she felt the shift between them like a thread pulled too tight.

At the head of the table, Becky and Will stood to make the first cut. Will leaned in slightly, his fingers grazing Becky's wrist in a reassuring touch as she hesitated, the knife trembling faintly in her grasp.

"I've got it," he murmured, steadying her hand with his.

Together, they cut the first slice, and the guests erupted into cheers.

Lauren spotted Miss Chaney dabbing at her eyes with a hanky. Lauren couldn't do the same. If she let the tears fall, she wasn't sure she'd be able to stop. She took a slow breath, steadying herself.

Across the yard, Ian leaned down to press a kiss to Nanny's cheek, her laughter soft and full of warmth. Perhaps Nanny would make it to the altar before she ever did.

CHAPTER 46

*L*auren sighed, relieved the wedding had gone to plan but hoping it would end soon. Keeping up the pretense of being happy when her heart had shattered was tiring. She was happy for Becky, truly, but it made the knife to her heart that much sharper.

Get a hold of yourself, Lauren. This is Becky's special day.

The moon hung high in the clear night as she leaned against the porch railing, watching the lively shivaree unfold.

Becky's laughter rang through the air as the crowd marched up the hill, lanterns swaying, pots clanging. Earl's booming voice, Terry's racket, and John Thatcher's fiddle filled the night with joyful chaos.

"Reckon that's the fellas comin' to give us a proper shivaree," Will had said, grinning. And now, here they were, sweeping him onto a barrel, hoots and cheers all around.

Lauren chuckled, shaking her head. Becky, who had

always resisted the spotlight, was right in the thick of it, looking like she belonged.

"They make quite the pair," Nanny Kat murmured beside her. "Like another couple I could mention." With a knowing smile, she slipped into the crowd before Lauren could respond.

A voice beside her made her tense. Lauren's fingers curled around the porch railing.

"They've really outdone themselves tonight."

Edward.

She didn't turn right away. She focused on Becky, who deserved nothing but joy tonight.

Finally, she forced a small nod. "They did."

Edward exhaled, but he didn't move away. "You should be proud. You helped make this happen."

Lauren's smile felt tight. "It was Becky's dream. She made it happen."

The words landed heavier than she meant them to.

Edward shifted, and for a moment, it seemed like he might say something.

Lauren didn't give him the chance. She stepped away from the railing. "I should go help with the cider."

Before he could respond, she slipped into the crowd.

Lauren busied herself among the guests, passing pitchers of cider, laughing in the right places, nodding along to stories, letting the warmth of the night mask the weight in her chest. Edward didn't follow.

She stared at Becky and Will. Will spinning Becky so clumsily that she tripped right into his arms, both of them breathless with laughter.

Lauren's throat tightened. This was what Becky deserved. Lauren wrapped her arms around herself, trying to push the thoughts out of her mind. *Didn't she deserve it too?* She glanced at her engagement ring? *What had happened to their dream of happiness?*

As the last notes of "Shady Grove" echoed into the night, the cheer that went up could have knocked the stars from the sky.

"That's how it's done," John called. "Reckon y'all passed the test."

Lauren's gaze lingered on Becky, flushed and breathless, leaning into Will.

"Well," Will said, his voice soft in the cooling air, "that wasn't so bad."

Becky laughed again, resting her head on his shoulder. "Might even say it was fun," she said, grinning. "Maybe we'll have to throw one for Lauren next."

Lauren forced a chuckle. "I think one w—" she caught herself in time, "shivaree is plenty for this year."

As the crowd began to drift away, Lauren pulled her friend into a tight hug.

"Enjoy your honeymoon, Mrs. Big Will."

Becky gave her a playful slap. "You know it's Mrs. Strauss. Thank you, Lauren. I don't think this could have happened without you." She kissed Lauren's cheek before whispering, "Next weddin' night will be yours."

Lauren's breath caught. She stepped back quickly, offering Becky one last smile before turning toward the darkened edge of the yard.

She needed air. She needed space.

Lauren walked in silence, the sounds of the wedding fading behind her. The weight of the night pressed down on her chest.

The first tear rolled down her cheek before she angrily rubbed it off.

She couldn't fall apart now. Hope House depended on her.

Will and Becky were only a short walk away, but their absence had unsettled everything. The children complained the house would feel different now. They were right, it would be lonelier. She bit back a sob.

A voice behind her cut through the quiet.

"Dance with me."

Lauren closed her eyes. *Edward.* She shook her head, her back still to him. "No."

"Lauren."

She swallowed hard, her pulse quickening. She turned to face him. "You don't get to hold me just because you're leaving again."

A heavy silence stretched between them as he moved closer, his nose almost touching hers.

Then, barely above a whisper, he said, "I might not come back. Not because of danger, but because this fight ... it doesn't end. Every time I think I'll be able to leave, something else keeps me there. And one day, I might not be able to walk away at all."

Her breath caught. She had braced for danger, for the possibility of losing him to something bigger than them.

But not this. Not the idea that he wouldn't come back because he wouldn't let himself.

Her fingers curled into the fabric of his jacket, like holding on could make him stay.

"Then why did you come back at all?" she whispered.

Edward's breath hitched but he didn't answer.

And somehow, that silence hurt more than anything he could have said. She turned, picking up her dress and ran towards home. She hoped he wouldn't follow her.

He didn't.

CHAPTER 47

Lauren woke the next morning with a thundering headache, her stomach swirling.

The night had been endless. Every time she closed her eyes, Edward was there. His voice low, his gaze steady, his words stealing the air from her lungs. *I might not come back.* She had braced for losing him to the Nazis, to a bad crossing, to fate. But not to this. Not to his own choice.

A sharp pain pressed behind her eyes. Lying in bed wasn't an option; the children needed her. Hope House still needed her. Pushing the blankets back, she forced herself to get up, wash, and dress before heading downstairs.

The scent of cookies baking filled the kitchen, mingling with the warmth of the morning sun streaming through the window. The familiar hum of life carried on.

Lauren hesitated in the doorway, then pasted on a smile and stepped inside. Chana stood at the kitchen counter, kneading dough with steady, practiced movements. Terry leaned against the doorframe, sipping coffee. Nanny Kat was seated by the window, peeling apples with slow, careful strokes.

"Miss Lauren, are Will and Becky coming to breakfast?" Ruthie's hopeful voice broke into her thoughts.

Lauren avoided the adults' gazes, walking to the stove to pour herself a cup of coffee. "Not this morning," she said lightly. "Remember what we talked about? Will and Becky are staying at their cottage now."

"But the cottage is right there," Ruthie piped up, nudging a chair closer to the table. "Why can't we go visit?"

At the back door, Terry made a choking sound, quickly disguising it as a cough.

Lauren exchanged a glance with Nanny Kat, who didn't look at Ruthie as she said, "Married folks need time to settle into their new home. That's just the way of things."

Ruthie frowned, crossing her arms. "Well, I think it's silly. I miss them."

A few of the other children murmured in agreement. Lauren walked over, crouching beside Ruthie's chair. "You only saw them yesterday, darling. Becky will be back to work in a few days' time. She doesn't love you any less now that she has her own house. Will'll still visit. And I'm sure if you write Becky a letter, she'd love that."

Ruthie sighed. "I guess." Then her gaze drifted down to Lauren's hand. "Miss Lauren, where's your ring?"

Lauren's breath caught, but she forced her expression to remain neutral. "I took it off."

Ruthie tilted her head. "Did you lose it?"

Lauren's fingers twitched around her coffee cup. The room had gone still. Nanny Kat's paring knife paused mid-slice, her gaze flicking up, sharp and knowing. Lauren swallowed. "No, Ruthie." She glanced toward the window, where sunlight caught on the wildflowers just beyond the porch. "Some flowers just weren't meant to grow in the same pot."

Ruthie wrinkled her nose. "That don't make much sense."

Nanny Kat gave Lauren a sympathetic look before answering. "You'll understand when you're older, darling."

Ruthie huffed but let the matter drop, turning her attention back to her cookie.

Lauren picked up her coffee. "Please excuse me." Without waiting for a reply, she fled back to her room.

* * *

CHANA BROUGHT lunch on a tray a few hours later. "We told the children you were feeling a little under the weather." Her voice was gentle. "You take some time, Lauren. Nanny Kat and I can manage for now."

Lauren nodded, grateful Chana didn't press for more. After the door closed, she pushed the tray aside. Her stomach wasn't ready for food. She lay back on the bed, listening to the sounds of the world moving on without her.

Laughter floated through the window, the children playing their favorite games.

Downstairs, she heard the murmur of adult voices. The steady, grounding presence of Nanny Kat and Chana.

Terry's deep chuckle. Reverend Dobbs' voice. He must have called in to say goodbye.

Lauren rolled onto her side, curling up. She pressed her fingers against the bare skin where her ring had once sat. She had loved Edward. Who was she kidding? She still did.

She turned her face into the pillow, squeezing her eyes shut. But the tears slipped through anyway, silent and hot. They came slow at first. Then all at once.

She must have fallen asleep as it was dark when she woke up. She sat up slowly, blinking in the darkness. Her head felt clearer, though her eyes ached.

She could stay here. Just for tonight. No one would blame her. But no. Hiding wouldn't change anything. She swung her legs over the edge of the bed, straightened her shoulders, and left the room.

Downstairs in the living room, she found Terry reading, Carly curled beside him on the couch. Chana and Nanny Kat sat nearby, busy with embroidery and knitting. Victor had the newspaper spread over his lap, though he wasn't reading it.

The house felt still, the air thick with the lingering heat of the day. The faintest breeze drifted in through the open window, but it carried no relief, only dust and the dry scent of earth.

The moment Lauren stepped inside, all eyes turned to her. She swallowed, pressing her nails into her palm. *Just say it. Get it over with.*

"Thank you for covering for me today." Her voice was steady, but too quiet. She cleared her throat and tried again. "Edward and I have called off our engagement."

Carly hesitated, then stood. "I thought you loved him. And I know he loves you, Miss Lauren."

Lauren brushed a tear from her cheek. "Sometimes love isn't enough, Carly."

Carly stepped forward, wrapping her arms around Lauren. Lauren hugged the girl back, holding on for a moment longer than necessary. Nanny Kat set her knitting aside, rising with a slow, careful movement. She walked over, cupping Lauren's face in her warm, wrinkled hands.

"You're stronger than you think, child."

Lauren closed her eyes briefly, letting the comfort of those words settle deep. When she opened them again, she didn't look at the others. Instead, she crossed the room to the small wooden drawer near the bookshelf. She pulled open the drawer and took the ring from her pocket. Cool metal against warm skin. A small thing, really. And yet, it had carried so much. She turned it once. Twice. Then, finally, she let it go. The drawer closed with a soft snick.

She exhaled. "I don't want to talk about this again. It's over. That's final." She hesitated. Just for a second. "I'll see you all first thing in the morning."

EPILOGUE

The early evening light filtered through the windows of Hope House. Nanny Kat sat at the head of the kitchen table, her reading glasses perched on her nose, slowly turning the pages of an old newspaper someone had used to wrap a bundle of fresh peaches.

Lauren was busy doing the accounts when she heard a sharp intake of breath.

"Well, I'll be," Nanny Kat muttered.

Lauren turned, frowning. "What is it?"

Nanny Kat didn't answer right away. She just kept staring at the paper, then glanced over her glasses. "Lauren, come here a minute."

Lauren put down her pencil and crossed the room. The newspaper was spread out in front of Nanny Kat, the bold headline blaring:

Labor Strike Turns Violent – Army Called to Control Unrest in Ohio Steel Mills.

Beneath it, a grainy black-and-white photograph captured the chaos, smoke billowing from factory windows, angry workers, and soldiers standing guard.

Lauren's gaze swept over the image ... and then her breath caught.

In the middle of the frame, partially obscured by another man, was a familiar face. Leaner, older, but unmistakable. He could have been a twin for Luke.

"Matthew."

Her fingers trembled as she traced the blurry figure.

Nanny Kat nodded. "Looks like the boy's been keeping himself busy."

Lauren swallowed hard. "But why didn't he ever ...?" She shook her head, unable to finish the sentence.

"Don't matter why right now," Nanny Kat said, tapping the page. "The question is, what are we gonna do about it? You have to write to Edward."

Lauren stiffened.

"Don't look like a rabbit staring down a shotgun. He's got the newspaper contacts to find out more. Put aside your pride and do this for Becky."

Stung, Lauren retorted, "Yes, ma'am."

* * *

THAT NIGHT, after the children had gone to bed, Lauren sat at the writing desk, pen in hand. She hesitated only a moment before pressing the nib to paper.

Dear Edward,

What should she say? She scrunched up the piece of paper and started again. Keep it casual.

Dear Edward,
I need a favor. I don't know how well you can investigate something from New York, but I think we've found Matthew. His picture was in a newspaper covering the steel mill strikes. He's in an army uniform. I have attached the copy.
I don't know if he's in trouble, if he's safe, or even if he'd want to be found. But Becky needs to know. Can you help?
Lauren.

Before she could change her mind, she put it in an envelope, put a stamp on, and addressed it to his New York contact address.

JUST AS LAUREN was beginning to lose hope of hearing back, Sheriff Dillon's car pulled into the yard.

He climbed out, the familiar creak of his leather belt cutting through the quiet afternoon air. He had a folded telegram in one hand.

Lauren met him halfway down the steps, heart hammering. "Did you find something?"

Dillon exhaled and handed her the slip of paper. "Came through this morning. From New York."

Lauren unfolded it, scanning the brief message.

> Confirmed – Matthew Tennant enlisted under false name. Last stationed in Ohio. Paperwork sent. He's coming home. – E.

Lauren pressed a hand to her mouth. "He's really alive."

Dillon gave her a steady look. "And he's got some explaining to do."

* * *

DAYS LATER, the sheriff's car pulled into the yard. This time, with Sheriff Dillon driving and a worn, tired soldier sitting beside him.

Lauren stood frozen on the porch as the man in uniform climbed out slowly, his boots hitting the dirt with quiet finality. He wasn't the boy she remembered. He was leaner, his face lined with something older than time. A scar marked his temple. His hair was cut short, military style. His uniform was dusty and wrinkled. Beside her, Becky gripped her hand so tight it hurt.

Luke stepped out from the barn, his expression unreadable. The soldier took off his hat and looked at them, his throat working as if trying to form words. He glanced from one to the other before saying, "Becky, Luke."

Becky let out a sob. "Matt?"

He swallowed hard. "Yeah."

Becky darted forward first, crashing into him with a choked cry. "I thought you were dead." Her arms clung around him, as if afraid he might disappear again.

Matthew tensed for half a second before wrapping his arms around her. "I know," he murmured. "I know."

Lauren blinked back tears. She glanced at Luke, but his stance was rigid, his fists clenched at his sides. He wasn't moving.

Finally, Becky pulled away, tears streaking her cheeks. She laughed shakily, swiping at her face. "Look at you. You're so thin. Are they even feedin' you in the army?"

Matthew almost smiled. Almost.

Then his gaze shifted to Luke. The air between them turned heavier, thick with years of absence, of questions left unanswered.

Luke's voice was tight. "Where have you been?"

Matthew exhaled sharply, gripping his hat between his fingers. "I was arrested," he admitted. "After what happened with Boone's men, they left me for dead. I got picked up for vagrancy. The judge gave me a choice: prison, or the army."

Luke let out a slow breath. "And that was it? You just disappeared?"

Matthew hesitated, then nodded. "I didn't have much of a choice."

Luke clenched his jaw. "Neither did I."

Another silence.

Lauren swallowed. She had spent so many years imagining this moment. Matthew home with Becky's arms around him and Luke standing beside him. But it wasn't that simple. Too much time had passed. Too many choices had been made. She glanced at Matthew, then at Becky. At the way Becky held onto him, like she could keep him here if she just held tight enough.

Another silence stretched.

Lauren stepped forward then, clearing her throat. "Are you staying?"

Matthew turned to Sheriff Dillon, then back to her. His fingers curled around his hat. "No."

Becky put her hands on her hips, one eyebrow raised, "What do you mean, no?"

Dillon sighed, crossing his arms. "Army don't just let a man walk away. He enlisted under a false name, but that doesn't erase his service contract. They're insisting he finish his term." He glanced at the dirt. "It's that or prison."

Becky gasped. "Will they put you in prison?"

Matthew looked into the distance. "Probably, if I don't go back into service."

Becky's voice wavered. "For how long?"

Dillon hesitated. "Could be months. Could be years."

Matthew ran a hand over his face, exhaling hard. "I tried to argue. Told them I wasn't the same man who enlisted. That I had no choice, it was either enlist under a false name or die by Boone's hand. Didn't matter." He let out a bitter laugh. "The Army owns my time … they own me."

Becky's voice rose. "But, that can't be right? There must be somethin' we can do? Sheriff?" Becky turned to Lauren, her voice barely above a whisper. "Lauren?"

Nanny Kat stepped forward. "Maybe Matt could stay for a couple of days. Give us time to wash his uniform and feed him a little. What do you say, Sheriff?"

Sheriff Dillon groaned. "I knew bringing him out here was going to cause trouble."

The group crowded around leading a bewildered Matt into the house. Sheriff Dillon hung back, motioning to Lauren.

"Miss Chaney gave me this. Said I should give it to you in private." Handing over the letter, he hitched up his trousers, clearly uncomfortable. "I … I guess I'll go in and get me some of that food Nanny Kat is so eager to share."

Lauren barely noticed him going, her heart racing so fast, it was hard to breathe. She walked over to the porch swing, sat and stared at the letter. Edward's handwriting. What would he say? Was he coming back? Did she want him to?

Staring at the letter wouldn't tell her the contents. She tore it open, the envelope fluttering to the ground as she scanned the contents. She sat back, wishing her stomach would settle. She read through the letter again, slowly this time.

My darling Lauren,
I wanted to write sooner, but I couldn't

find the right words. That's rather ironic, given what I do for a living, but it's the truth.

I love you, Lauren. My actions may not have proven that, but I do with every fiber of my being.

If love were enough, if this world were different, I would spend the rest of my days proving to you that you were always my first choice. That you always have been.

But just as you could never turn your back on the children, I cannot turn my back on my people. Our people. Ordinary, innocent victims of a horrific regime. I have to get Aunt Rae out not just for Hans and Rachel, but for myself. I can't bear to lose her.

I bought the field we looked at. The one where we dreamed of building our home. But dreams don't always fit reality, and one thing I've finally accepted is that I can never ask you to leave Hope House. It is your home. It always will be.

So, I've asked my attorney to sign over the field and some money to you, Lauren. Please use it to build a house, maybe several small houses, not for us, my darling, but for the

Meyers, and perhaps in time, Carly and Terry. The Meyers deserve more than one room in a house full of laughter and children. And someday, Carly and Terry will want a home of their own, though I suspect they'll never want to stray too far from their family.

When my work is done, when Aunt Rae is safe, I will come back. If, by then, you have found someone who loves you the way you deserve, I will walk away.

But if Hope House still fills your days, and your heart remains unclaimed, then perhaps we might still find our way back to each other.

At Becky's wedding, when you told me the children were your family, not ours, that cut deep. It made me see what I was about to lose. I can't walk away from my work just yet. But I want that family, Lauren. With you.

Yours,
Edward

LAUREN SAT VERY STILL, the letter trembling in her hands. The words blurred together as she stared at them, her breath coming unevenly.

"Lauren, you comin' in to join us?" Becky's voice rang from the doorway, full of warmth. "My family is your family too, you know. No way I'm lettin' you out of moldin' them into upright, law-abidin'—" She paused, eyes dropping to the letter in Lauren's lap. Her hands went straight to her hips. "What has he gone and done now?"

Lauren let out a breath, something close to a laugh, something close to a sigh. Slowly, she folded the letter and pressed it to her chest, fingers curling around the paper for just a moment longer.

"Nothing, Becky." She slipped the letter into her pocket. "It's all good."

Becky didn't look convinced, but she let it go.

"What were you saying about your brothers?"

"They need the Hope House touch," Becky said, shaking her head. "Heck, they need more than a touch."

Lauren smiled as Becky laughed at her own joke before grabbing her hand and pulling her inside.

"Come on," Becky said, tugging her forward. "Before my brothers corrupt the whole house."

LETTER TO READERS

Dear Reader,

Thank you so much for reading Echoes of Yesterday! I hope you enjoyed following Lauren, Becky, and the children of Hope House on their journey. Writing historical fiction is both a challenge and a joy, as it requires weaving real events and period details into a compelling story that feels authentic. I can't tell you how many times I've gone searching for one small fact in an old newspaper from the 1930s, only to look up hours later wondering why I now know the price of canned peaches in Virginia that year!

I have always loved both reading and history, and now I have the incredible opportu-

LETTER TO READERS

nity to combine those passions into a career. I am so grateful to you, my readers, for making that possible. Your support allows me to continue bringing these stories to life, and I can't thank you enough for being part of this journey with me.

If you enjoyed this book, I would truly appreciate it if you could take a moment to leave a review. Reviews help other readers discover the series and allow me to continue sharing these stories with you.

I'm excited to share that the next book in The Orphanage Chronicles, The Orphan's Choice, is coming soon. The story continues as Hope House faces a new challenge that threatens its future, while some of the children take matters into their own hands in ways that could change everything. Old loyalties will be tested, new choices must be made, and the Hope House family will have to stand together once again.

Thank you for being a part of this journey. Your support means the world to me, and I can't wait to share the next chapter with you.

Best wishes,
Rach x

ACKNOWLEDGMENTS

Writing a book may be a solitary act, but bringing it to life is anything but. I am deeply grateful to the incredible team of people who supported me on this journey.

To my editing team, whose keen eyes and sharp insights helped shape this book into its best form. Thank you. A special thanks to my proofreader, Sherry Parks, for her meticulous attention to detail and unwavering dedication. Your expertise has made all the difference.

To my wonderful beta readers, Meisje, Theresa, Valerie, Jean, Maureen, Rita, Sue, Grace, Deb, and Laurie, your thoughtful feedback, encouragement, and honest critique were invaluable. You each helped me see my work through fresh eyes, and I am so appreciative of the time and care you put into reading my words.

To my husband and children, thank you for your patience, love, and support through the late nights and endless rewrites. Your belief in me kept me going, even when I doubted myself. And to Gracie, my ever-faithful companion, who kept me company through long writing sessions. Your presence was a comfort more than you'll ever know.

This book would not exist without each of you. From the bottom of my heart, thank you.

ABOUT THE AUTHOR

Rachel Wesson is a USA Today Bestseller and author of several series, including a number set against the backdrop of World War II. Having always been a fan of history, Rachel tries to combine her love of history with a good story.

Rachel Wesson was born in Kilkenny, Ireland but considers herself to be from the capital, Dublin, as that's where she spent most of her life. Her dad brought Rachel and her two sisters out every Saturday to give their mother a break. He took them to the library and for ice-cream after. It took a long time for her sisters to forgive her for the hours she spent choosing her books!

She grew up driving everyone nuts asking them questions about what they did during the War or what side they were on in the 1916 rising, etc. Finally, her granny told her to write her stories down so people would get the pleasure of reading them. In fact, what Granny meant was everyone would get some peace while Rachel was busy writing!

When not writing, or annoying relatives, Rachel was reading. Her report cards from school commented on her love of reading, especially when she should have been learning. Seems you can't read Great Expectations in Maths.

After a doomed love affair and an unpleasant bank raid during which she defended herself with a tea tray, she headed to London for a couple of years. (There is a reason she doesn't write romance!). She never intended staying, but a chance meeting with the man of her dreams put paid to any return to Ireland. Having spent most of her career in the city, she decided something was missing. Working in the city is great, but it's a young person's dream. Having three children you never see isn't good for anyone. So, she packed in the job and started writing. Thanks to her amazing readers, that writing turned into a career far more exciting and rewarding than any other.

Rachel lives in Surrey with her husband and three children, two boys and a girl. When not reading, writing or watching films for "research" purposes, Rachel likes to hang out with her family. She also travels regularly back home—in fact, she should have shares in BA and Aer Lingus.

ALSO BY RACHEL WESSON

The Orphanage Chronicles

Echoes of Yesterday (The Orphanage Chronicles 1)

The Orphan's Choice (The Orphanage Chronicles 2)

Orphans of Hope House

Home for Unloved Orphans (Orphans of Hope House 1)

Baby on the Doorstep (Orphans of Hope House 2)

The Resistance Sisters

Darkness Falls

Light Rises

Hearts at War

When's Mummy Coming

A Mother's Promise

WWII Stand Alone

Stolen from her Mother

Song of Courage

Women and War

Gracie Under Fire

Penny's Secret Mission

Molly's Flight

Hearts on the Rails
Orphan Train Escape
Orphan Train Trials
Orphan Train Christmas
Orphan Train Tragedy
Orphan Train Strike
Orphan Train Disaster
Orphan Train Memories

Trail of Hearts - Oregon Trail Series
Oregon Bound (book 1)
Oregon Dreams (book 2)
Oregon Destiny (book 3)
Oregon Discovery (book 4)
Oregon Disaster (book 5)

12 Days of Christmas - co-authored series.
The Maid - book 8

Clover Springs Mail Order Brides
Katie (Book 1)
Mary (Book 2)
Sorcha (Book 3)
Emer (Book 4)
Laura (Book 5)

Ellen (Book 6)

Thanksgiving in Clover Springs (book 7)

Christmas in Clover Springs (book8)

Erin (Book 9)

Eleanor (book 10)

Cathy (book 11)

Mrs. Grey

Clover Springs East

New York Bound (book 1)

New York Storm (book 2)

New York Hope (book 3)

Printed in Great Britain
by Amazon